THE ETERNAL SONG

THE ETERNAL SONG

SUE FARWICK

TRIBUS PRESS | CEDARBURG, WISCONSIN USA

Published by Tribus Press LLC
Cedarburg, Wisconsin USA
www.tribuspress.com

Cover illustration by Madeline Friend

ISBN 979-8-9884459-2-0

LCCN 9798988445920

For discounts for schools, bookstores, libraries, and nonprofit groups, bulk sales, media inquiries, or questions please contact:

Email: tribuspress@tribuspress.com
Phone: 262-421-5158

FOR MAC AND ELSIE

I would like to thank my family for all their help and encouragement, especially Chris, without whose inestimable assistance I would never have made it this far. I would also like to thank Madeline Friend, who did such a wonderful job with the cover illustration.

1
WHAT DID IT MATTER

THE GIRL WAS ALONE. The dark clouds, low and ominous, ushered in by the blustery west wind, had chased the other children away. But she did not mind—they were not her friends. She never spoke to them or joined them in their games.

She sat on the swing, idly kicking her thin, bare legs backwards and forwards as the rusty chains squeaked and rasped in protest against the metal supports.

The park was deserted now, but solitude was not something that the girl found disconcerting. Her parents, who struggled to make ends meet in the uncertain economic climate of post-war England, were seldom at home during the daytime, working all possible hours to pay the rent on their three-bedroom row house in Birchford.

As an only child, she quickly learned a self-sufficiency common to youngsters left to their own devices. By the time she was eight years old, she was quite capable of taking care of herself, especially during the lengthy summer holidays; getting herself up in the mornings long after her parents had left for work; preparing make-shift meals; and helping with the household chores.

She only had one fear—one might almost call it a phobia. Although she did not understand it, she had quickly learned to avoid the thing that caused her such irrational dread; as a result, the problem seldom affected her young life.

The wind skittered about the playground, blowing crisp autumn leaves underneath the roundabout and around the steps of the slide. She watched as a piece of paper, caught up in a miniature whirlwind, flapped against the wooden seesaw. Seeing it catch for an instant, she jumped down from the swing and ran over to arrest its progress across the playground. The distant hum of traffic from a nearby road was audible for that brief moment, as the wind paused in its gusty journey just long enough for the girl to grasp the paper and clutch it in her hand. Then, resuming its way across the playing field, the squall caught at her hair, blowing the long, tawny-colored strands wildly about her head.

She looked down at the note and saw that it was a discarded shopping list: oranges, butter, steak, asparagus—the words spoke of a bill of fare far more extravagant than her family's table was used to seeing. A secure roof over one's head had taken precedence over such luxuries.

As she read this catalogue of unfamiliar delicacies, a large drop of rain splashed down on the ink, instantly smearing the letters. She crumpled up the list and threw it down.

Should she run home? The rain was becoming more insistent now, but she was in no hurry. What did it matter if she got wet?

The ragged, black clouds racing overhead fascinated her as she stood heedless of everything about her, gazing up at the ever-changing patterns in the sky.

She did not see the person approaching from the east end of the park—a distant figure at first, growing larger as he neared the playground, his silent tread going unnoticed on the damp grass. He was not alone.

A Borzoi dog, tall and lean with long silky hair, walked at his side, looking up occasionally at its master, obediently matching his stride as it padded noiselessly across the field. The dog seemed out of place, built more for running and hunting then a leisurely stroll through the park.

The rain was falling harder with every passing minute, but neither child, man, nor dog seemed to notice.

Still, she had not turned around, but the animal, its small ears pressed back against its head, quickened its pace, pulling gently on the sturdy leash that kept it tethered to its master's hand.

Closer now, the dog began to pant, its lips pulled back from long teeth that appeared poised to kill at its master's command.

But it only wanted to play.

And then, as though sensing an approaching threat, the girl whirled around, a look of sheer terror in her eyes as she saw the dog. Her mouth opened to scream, but no sound emerged. She did not faint, but her legs gave out from under her and she crumpled to the ground, unable to move or escape.

The man, who was hardly yet a man, youthful yet old for his years, his face gaunt, his long dark hair streaming with rain, and his eyes as cold and grey as the weather, stopped abruptly. But the dog, intent upon reaching its goal, strained on, and the leash slipped from his grasp—whether deliberately or by accident, it would have been difficult to say. The animal, now joyfully unrestricted, bounded forward, coming to a halt over the body of the child.

The stranger, whose rough, country clothes had become darkened by the steady downpour, did not speak but stood gazing down at the girl. The dog, standing close by his side, its long, feathered tail tucked between its back legs, looked down curiously, sniffed at the inert figure, and began to whine.

Several minutes passed, then the man strode away. Suddenly, a shrill whistle cut through the wind and rain, and the dog turned, running back to its master, who bent down to retrieve the leash. Taking one last look at the recumbent figure, the two resumed their trek across the field, leaving the child—her pleated, plaid skirt hitched indecorously to her hip—lying sprawled on the gravel, her rain-soaked hair plastered against her face, hiding her staring eyes.

2

BREAKING POINT

GORDON STREET SCHOOL HAD A REPUTATION. If you failed your 'eleven-plus' exams and ended up there, you were in for a rough time, not from the teachers but from the fourth-year students, reputedly a crowd of juvenile delinquents who, it was rumored, spent their time when not actually in class, fighting, smoking, and snogging behind the trees at the back of the playing fields and tormenting first-year students with seeming impunity.

When Lucy Rowe's parents were informed that their daughter had earned the dubious distinction of securing a place at Gordon Street Secondary School due to unexpectedly poor test results, they were naturally disappointed, but only that.

They hadn't heard the disquieting speculation that had run rampant among the impressionable young school leavers at Greenfields Elementary, but Lucy had, and she was terrified.

Of her small coterie of friends, only she had been unsuccessful in her efforts to gain a position at Birchford Grammar School, which would have all but guaranteed her a first-class education with a chance to go on to college or university. Her so-called mates, with all the fickleness of youth, had dropped her like a brick—a social pariah at twelve years of age who had failed to make the grade.

But, as is so often the case, when truth is separated from the world of myth and make-believe, things turned out to be not as bad as Lucy had initially feared. At least, the transition from Greenfields had not proved fatal. She had survived the rigors of three years at Gordon Street, and even if many of the rumors had proved to be true, Lucy had avoided trouble for the most part by maintaining a healthy distance between herself and the more prevalent troublemakers in the school.

Academically, she had outstripped her classmates by a wide margin and had been placed at the top of her class two years in succession. This automatically made her unpopular; no one liked a swot or a teacher's pet.

The majority of students at the school, many of whom were from families who had migrated north from the East End of London, were for the most part well-adjusted and reasonably well-behaved, but a few of the children—for that is all they were, after all, despite the things they got up to when not attending classes—seemed to go out of their way to exhibit a lack of intelligence and common courtesy. Lucy, who had been strictly brought up, found this attitude puzzling. *Why would anyone deliberately strive to be thought ignorant and rude?* She could not understand it.

For Lucy, introverted and painfully self-conscious, the excruciating minutes spent in the school playground during break times were sheer hell. Nearly always by herself, she wandered about the playing fields or sat on the grass, reading or watching the others as they stood about in groups, laughing and joking.

Occasionally they would look at her and lower their voices, and she knew instinctively that they were talking about her, making fun of her unfashionable clothes, outdated hairstyle, and chronic shyness.

Not only had she been abandoned by her childhood chums, but it also had not taken long for Lucy to realize that she did not belong at Gordon Street either. No, she definitely did not belong there.

With no intimate friend in whom to confide, and unwilling to discuss her problems with her parents—who, despite their overprotective care of her, had no real understanding of her complex nature—Lucy passed from one day to the next, miserable and alone.

There was, however, unknown to Lucy, one person who had seen her through the window of his classroom at break-times. As she passed by, looking solemnly down at the ground, counting the minutes till she could escape the freedom so highly prized by the others, he thought he recognized the telltale signs of Lucy's isolation.

Jonathan Amor, the only son of an Indian mother and English father, was Lucy's music teacher and, as such, knew her to be a good student, willing and eager to learn.

Being of a somewhat quiet and unprepossessing disposition himself, he felt a certain empathy for Lucy. He had spent much of his early life in India, but despite having lived and taught in Birchford for many years, he sensed that he did not really belong there. Nor did he feel comfortable on the rare occasions when he visited his mother's family in India.

It was around the time when Lucy had almost completed her third year at Gordon Street that he caught her in a fight with another girl in one of the cloakrooms.

Although she seldom got involved with the others, there were times when confrontation was unavoidable, and Lucy was quite capable of holding her own in a verbal argument. This time, however, the situation had escalated into something more physical when the other girl, exasperated by Lucy's unwillingness to prolong a minor altercation, pushed her, forcing Lucy to stagger backwards and hit her head painfully against the white-washed cinder-block wall.

For an instant she remained there dazed. Then, something seemed to snap inside her. Propelled by an all-consuming urge to strike back, she lunged toward her antagonist's retreating figure and delivered a stinging blow to the girl's back with her elbow.

Normally, such matters were settled outside in the schoolyard, far from the watchful eye of the teacher on duty that day, but on this occasion, the affray rapidly got out of hand. The crowd that had inevitably gathered immediately took sides, cheering loudly as, momentarily stunned by this unexpected retaliation, Lucy's adversary recovered her wits and threw herself back into the struggle, carrying Lucy to the ground, scratching and swearing.

The tussle had not lasted long, for Jonathan Amor, hearing the commotion from his classroom, had come running out to investigate the hubbub, and the onlookers parted to reveal the two girls disheveled and red in the face.

Lucy, who was not physically strong, had never before allowed herself to be drawn into such a situation—she burned with embarrassment. What on earth had compelled her to hit back like that? She was bewildered by her own uncharacteristic behavior, but Amor could have told her that even the most mild-mannered person had their breaking point.

Fights such as these were not uncommon at Gordon Street, even amongst the girls, and given the headmaster's well-known aversion to dealing with irritating and time-wasting matters of this sort, it was seldom thought necessary to bring the miscreants to his attention unless some serious injury resulted. Accordingly, the combatants were summarily dealt with by the teacher first on the scene.

In this case, the other girl had been given lines, but Amor had opted to mete out a more stringent sentence on Lucy, who remained winded and on her knees, her long hair pulled awry in the scuffle, escaping untidily from its habitual ponytail.

"You'll give up your mid-day breaks for the rest of the month, young lady. Report to my room after you've eaten lunch," Amor told Lucy, dragging her unceremoniously to her feet, his eyebrows drawn in a look of severity and displeasure.

Even her adversary had thought the punishment excessively severe, but Lucy, much to everyone's surprise, was delighted. This unexpected reprieve from the daily torture of recess seemed heaven-sent.

The following day, she arrived at the door of 4b as its inmates streamed noisily out of the classroom, jostling against her as they made their way to lunch break. When the last of them had gone, the room was silent, and she stepped inside.

Amor was sitting at his desk, leafing through some papers, and when he looked up, he was surprised to see her standing there in front of him.

"I said you could eat lunch first," he told her in a soft voice, his dark-brown eyes with their long, black lashes looking at her with something like amusement.

"Oh, that's alright," Lucy assured him brightly. "I bring sandwiches." That had always been preferable to sitting down to the disgusting and oftentimes inedible muck that they dished up in the school cafeteria.

"I'll eat them now," she told him.

He smiled, sensing, as he had suspected all along, that Lucy was not inclined to look on this enforced detention as a punishment.

"Alright. Why don't you sit there?" He pointed to a place in the front row by the window near his desk."Don't you go for lunch?" she asked him inquisitively as she settled into her seat. Some of the more gastronomically fearless teachers at the lower end of the income scale ate in the cafeteria. The others sought refuge at nearby cafes or restaurants.

"No. I bring sandwiches also." He opened a drawer and extricated a brown paper bag, placing it on the table in front of him.

"My wife, as you see, takes good care of me." He smiled and nodded as he thought momentarily of Mrs. Amor, but almost immediately his thoughts changed direction. "What was the fight about?"

"I've forgotten. Something stupid, I expect." Lucy dismissed the question, looking out of the window.

He accepted the answer without further comment, but after unwrapping his lunch, he asked, "Do you mind if we listen to some music while we eat?"

Lucy shook her head. What else would one expect from a music teacher?

Amor went over to the record player that he sometimes used during his classes. Music was a mandatory part of the curriculum at Gordon Street, and although some of the younger girls did not mind singing, many of the students, especially the older boys, were decidedly unwilling participants. This period of the week, however, was the only time that Lucy had felt at one with the others—their young, tuneless voices, if not harmoniously, at least noisily combined to produce such songs as *Jerusalem* and *The Minstrel Boy*. She enjoyed Amor's method of teaching, which was interesting and even entertaining to those who wanted to learn.

He carefully placed a record on the turntable and the needle swung into position. After a second's silence, the music started up and the words played out.

If you want to know who we are,

We are gentlemen of Japan.
On many a vase and jar.
On many a screen and fan.

Amor looked at her occasionally as they sat eating their sandwiches, listening to Gilbert and Sullivan's famous operetta. Lucy continued to gaze out of the window, and he noticed, with an unaccountable feeling of satisfaction, what appeared to be a brief smile tilt the corners of her mouth upward.

He finished the contents of the brown paper bag and crumpled it into a ball, throwing it deftly into the waste bin beside his desk, then resumed his examination of the papers in front of him.

When the music concluded, he asked, "Did you like it? The Mikado?"

"Yes." She sounded surprised.

"I have the libretto here somewhere, if you'd like to borrow it—take it home with you."

He saw her doubtful expression. "Oh, don't worry," he laughed. "It's not homework. You don't have to memorize it or anything like that. Just…you know…if you're interested, I thought you might want to look at it."

"Yes. Thanks." She watched as he searched for the libretto amongst a pile of books on the shelf, and, having found it, he came back to Lucy and handed it to her.

"There's no hurry to return it," he told her as he turned back to clean the chalkboard in preparation for the next class.

Soon the bell rang, signaling the end of recess, and she stood up to leave.

"Thank you," she said simply, holding up the libretto, but Amor guessed she was thanking him for much more than that.

"I'll see you tomorrow. Bring a book to read if you like," he told her.

She made towards the door, but just then the noise of approaching voices reverberated in the hallway outside and several burly and boisterous boys came bursting into the room. Amor saw Lucy hesitate and step back, and he instantly rounded on the incoming group with an uncharacteristic display of anger.

"Out! Get out! You'll wait outside until I tell you to come in in the future!"

They turned around and went out grumbling, pushing back the latecomers who were pressing in behind them.

"Hooligans," Amor muttered. He looked at Lucy. "Tomorrow then."

She nodded and went out past the waiting class, and as she walked by them, she heard a mocking voice calling after her, "Ooh! Someone's in trouble," and a girl replying facetiously, "Na. He fancies 'er." A chorus of laughter followed Lucy down the hallway.

* * *

When she arrived at his room on the third day, another girl was already sitting in her seat. "Rose will be joining us today," Amor informed her.

Lucy recognized the tall, dark-haired girl, a fourth-year student who was constantly getting into trouble. She was reputed to be one of a large family of travelers who had come into town the previous year. There was talk that her father, who had been involved in a scuffle with the local police, had stabbed a constable to death and was sent to jail to await trial.

These itinerant peddlers had come to the Rowe house occasionally to sell ribbons and clothes pegs, and Lucy's mother would buy one or two trinkets from the tray that hung around the Romani woman's neck or have her fortune told. It was always considered good luck to cross a gypsy's palm with silver, she told her daughter; but Lucy wondered if she had done it more out of fear than a desire to know her fortune.

Once when Lucy had been alone in the house on Dover Street, an elderly, weather-beaten woman dressed in a shabby jacket and voluminous skirts had knocked at the door. Lucy peeped from behind the lace curtains of the room overlooking the street and saw her standing there on the doorstep, her tray at the ready, but the child had been warned by her parents never to open the door to strangers when she was by herself, so she remained concealed behind the drapes.

The sharp-eyed old woman with the large gold-hooped earrings had seen her, however, and, infuriated at being shunned by the occupants of the house, shouted invectives through the letterbox in a tongue that Lucy couldn't understand. She left, banging the garden gate shut and shaking her fist in Lucy's direction.

The incident had left Lucy extremely wary of these fiery characters, and seeing the young girl there in the classroom, she automatically slid into a seat on the opposite side of the room.

Amor, laughing, chided her: "I don't think Rose has anything catching. Why don't you sit together? It would make things a lot easier." Lucy, shamefaced, got up and moved next to where Rose was sitting. The swarthy and sullen-faced child did not look up.

Lucy noticed that the other girl had not brought a lunch, and thinking that this detention—if that was what it was—had caught her unprepared, she held out half of the sandwich that she'd taken from her school bag. The girl regarded her suspiciously. An ingrained mistrust of any such gestures proffered by these people with whom she was reluctantly forced to spend her days, prevented the young girl from accepting this well-intentioned offering immediately, but the innocent friendliness with which it had been tendered and the humiliating betrayal of an empty, rumbling stomach finally persuaded her. She reached out a rather grubby hand towards Lucy.

There was no music that day. Instead, Amor took a book from the drawer of his desk and held it up.

"Shakespeare. Have you ever read any of his works?"

Lucy shook her head. Rose ignored him.

"You probably think he's too dry and boring, but that's only because you don't understand what he's saying. He can be very funny, very sad. This is *The Merchant of Venice*. I thought you might like to take a look at it."

He stood up and walked over to where the two girls were sitting, opening the book and setting it down between them, pointing to a particular passage.

Rose glanced down at the page and turned to Lucy, rolling her large, expressive eyes and putting her finger to her open mouth, making a gagging gesture. Lucy guessed, however, that Amor was trying to make a point, and she looked more closely at the lines he'd indicated.

As she read them silently, he spoke the words aloud with such feeling and expression, giving them life and meaning, that he seemed to transform before their eyes into the sly and formidable moneylender.

"I am a Jew! Hath not a Jew eyes?" Amor began the speech from act three.

He knew it all by heart and rendered it without fault from start to finish in such a manner that Lucy sat staring at him awe-struck, and even Rose managed to look suitably impressed.

"Do you see?" he asked when he'd given them a couple of minutes to digest the words. "We're all the same, under the skin."

The girls remained silent, and he wondered if they'd understood.

* * *

On the last day of her detention, two younger boys were there, tidying cupboards as a punishment for some infringement of classroom etiquette. *The Honfleur Suite*, music composed by Neville Wyndham, was coming from the record player, and occasionally she would see the two lads make obscene gestures at Amor behind his back. When the bell rang to summon the crowd back to class, the boys made their escape, but Lucy lingered, unwilling to end these sessions.

Amor knew what was in her mind, and he was prepared. "Would you like to come in next week to help me with some marking?" he asked.

"Alright," she replied diffidently, but inside she was experiencing an immense feeling of pleasure and relief.

The weeks went by. Amor always managed to think of a reason for her to come in, always found some little chore that she could perform. For him, it was a minor victory of sorts—a reaffirmation that what he was doing there at Gordon Street was to some extent worthwhile.

For Lucy, it was an oasis of interesting conversation and music in a desert of comparatively dull and uninteresting schoolwork.

There was nearly always someone else present in Amor's room during these sessions, and Lucy sometimes resented having to share those precious moments with him, but he had deliberately seen to it that they were seldom alone.

It was not unheard of for a teacher to have the occasional fling with one of the older pupils at Gordon Street. Lucy had heard several of the girls boasting of their sexual exploits involving some of the younger and more easily led student teachers; even one or two of the more mature schoolmasters were known to enjoy the odd grope with a willing female pupil in the dark and airless classroom supply cupboards. Already tongues were beginning to wag regarding her friendship with Amor.

But she was only fifteen, and he was not about to jeopardize his teaching career because of any misconstrued interest that he had in her. After all, he was only concerned with developing her mind. He wanted to open her horizons to include an appreciation of music, literature, and art, instilling in her an awareness of everything beautiful and worthwhile in life. It was, he felt, the least he could do.

3

THREE LITTLE MAIDS FROM SCHOOL

ANOTHER YEAR PASSED, and Lucy's parents noticed a subtle change in her behavior—they assumed she was just at that awkward age. Every child went through it, yet knowing this did nothing to allay their fears for the future. They dreaded the time when she would insist on more independence. It wouldn't be long now before she would want to go out on dates and stay out late, and they were terrified at the prospect. She was beginning to shed her ugly duckling appearance, and there was no denying that she was starting to blossom into quite an attractive girl. A few more weeks at Gordon Street and they would have to see about getting her into some kind of job.

Lucy didn't want to think that far ahead. She lived for the moments she shared with Jonathan Amor.

It wasn't that she had a crush on him or anything like that. She saw him strictly as a mentor, someone who understood her. But she realized that once she left Gordon Street, their friendship would most likely come to an end, and it saddened her.

It was hardly surprising that ever since the day of the fight, Lucy had risen in the estimation of some of her schoolfellows, at least to the extent that they were willing to include her in their conversations. Although now they tended to look on her more with a scornful pity that was almost as unpalatable to Lucy as the merciless taunting she suffered during her earlier years at Gordon Street.

"We're going to France as soon as they let us out of this dump," one of her newly acquired friends informed her as they walked home from school one afternoon a few weeks before the end of term.

"Lucky you." Lucy tried not to be envious, but it wasn't easy.

"You goin' anywhere?" The girl examined her fingernails, showing little interest in Lucy's response.

"I don't think we're doing anything." Lucy would rather say that than admit to a rainy week at a run-down boarding house in Margate.

A third girl, the one with whom Lucy had fought in the cloakroom, who could only boast of a fortnight's visit to her grandparents in Skegness, shifted the conversation to other matters and asked the others if they had seen a particularly gruesome film that was showing at the local cinema.

"Yeah!" the first girl, Bunny, replied enthusiastically, turning briefly to make an obscene gesture at a truck that had sounded its horn as it rattled by, the workmen inside whistling and shouting out something that Lucy couldn't quite catch.

"Cheeky buggers!" Bunny called after them with little conviction, quite pleased with the effect that her new skirt was creating.

"Did you see it?" the other girl, Jennifer, asked Lucy.

"No."

What a drag. It was hard for them to find anything in common with this shy, unadventurous girl. They didn't know that Lucy had almost died of pneumonia some years earlier. Her mother had quit her job in order to care for her, leaving Lucy's father to shoulder the family's financial burden on an income that was barely adequate to cover the rent on their house. There was little left over for such luxuries as entertainment or extravagant holidays.

"You never do anything, do you?" Jennifer persisted.

Lucy did not; it was true. Apart from the money aspect, her parents had kept her figuratively wrapped in cotton wool ever since her illness. For eight years, she had been cosseted and guarded from every conceivable ailment or accident.

The three girls parted at the corner of Dover Street.

"I'll see you later at The Bolero," Jennifer called after Bunny as they said their goodbyes.

"Do you want to come?" she asked Lucy as an afterthought, already knowing the answer.

Lucy shook her head.

"Her mother won't let her out after five," Bunny quipped over her shoulder.

The two girls laughed derisively and walked away in different directions as Lucy continued along Dover Street towards home, burning with humiliation.

Damn them anyway! She didn't need to hang out with a bunch of giggling ninnies, guzzling soda and furtively smoking cigarettes that made your breath and clothes reek. She had tried it once, just to show she was one of the gang. It made her sick, right there on the pavement outside The Bolero café. She had coughed for a week, prompting her mother to march her down to Dr. Evan's office to find out what was wrong.

When the reason for the cough became known, she was forbidden to go to The Bolero again, and although they could not stop her from associating with those 'damned delinquents' during school time, she was ordered not to see them outside of school. Even walking home with them was frowned upon, but, as Lucy explained to her mother, as they all lived in the same neighborhood, she could hardly do otherwise.

"You don't need them! You don't need any of them!" her mother had told her over and over again.

Despite the strict constraints placed on her social life, there was one person whose friendship was encouraged by her parents. Jaqueline Ward, the same age as Lucy, moved into a house several doors away just after Lucy started at Gordon Street. Although she attended a private school in a neighboring town, she was considered suitable company for Lucy and was invited over on several occasions for Sunday tea.

At first, Lucy resented having her friends picked out for her and treated the girl with a coolness that others might have found off-putting. But Jaqueline, or Jackie, as she preferred to be called, did not seem to notice, and she and Lucy continued to hang out together until, almost as suddenly as they had arrived, Jackie's family packed up and moved away, deserting Birchford for better prospects in London.

Much to Lucy's amazement, she found that she missed Jackie and was quite overjoyed when she received a letter from the girl some months later giving a description of her new home and inviting Lucy to come and stay with the family for the weekend sometime.

Somewhat surprisingly, she was allowed to go, her parents seeing her off on the train with the understanding that Jackie's mother would be there at the other end of the journey to meet her. Lucy, enjoying the freedom that time away from the house on Dover Street afforded her, had found herself taking a secret, if guilty, delight in the unsuspected latitude that the Wards allowed their daughter.

These visits were, perhaps fortunately, few and far between. But in the meantime, there was always Jonathan Amor and, of course, Philippe. She would be seeing him again today.

* * *

Lucy reached home just as the hands of the clock on the mantlepiece in their living room reached four o'clock. On the dot, it seldom varied; her mother would be there in the kitchen preparing the evening meal. Her father would be home from work just after six—the same routine, day in and day out. The monotony of this staid and uneventful existence made her want to scream sometimes.

"Hello dear. How was school?" Her mother could see her from the kitchen as Lucy hung her coat on the stand in the hallway.

"Okay. School is school." What else could she say? She bent down to retrieve the heavy satchel.

"Have you got much homework, dear?"

"Just the usual stuff. It won't take long." Lucy went into the kitchen and sat down at the table, where biscuits and a glass of milk were laid out as they always were, a snack to keep her going till dinner. When she had finished them, Lucy looked at her mother, who was washing dishes in the sink.

"Could you let me have some money, Mum? I've just remembered I need a new notebook for school. I'll run down to the shop now and get it. Do you need anything while I'm there?"

Her mother dried her hands and went to fetch her handbag. She came back, counting the money in her purse, calculating how to make it stretch to the end of the week.

"Here you are, dear." She handed Lucy a pound note. "Pick up some more toothpaste, will you?"

Lucy took the money, feeling a momentary pang of guilt as she put her coat back on and went out.

Once outside, she ran along Dover Street, turning left down Winslow Road until she got to Carstairs' shop. It was only a small place, but it somehow gave the impression that you could find anything you wanted there. As quickly as she could, Lucy looked along the shelves and selected the cheapest notebook she could find, then went in search of toothpaste.

Good Lord! However did the man keep track of his stock? she wondered, as she rummaged through boxes of detergent, packs of nylons, and bottles of aspirin in the dim light until she found what she was looking for.

Lucy took her purchases to the counter, where Mr. Carstairs, a burly north-countryman with a friendly face and ruddy complexion, stood waiting to ring the items up on his till.

"Hello Lucy, luv. How's things? How's your mum?" He smiled at the girl who was fumbling in her pockets for the money to pay him.

He saw her more and more often these days. She was always popping in for something or other, and, as he had said to her mother just the other day, she was getting to be quite the young lady.

"Alright, thanks, Mister Carstairs." Lucy was impatient to get going and hoped that the normally garrulous shopkeeper would not keep her standing there talking.

"Nearly finished with school, then?"

"Yes, sir."

"Ahh. Right. Summer'll soon be here. What're you going to do, when you leave?"

"Don't know yet, Mister Carstairs. Something in an office perhaps, or maybe I'll come and work for you, eh?" she laughed.

"Well, best think on it, lass. Time'll soon go round."

"Yes, I will." Lucy, anxious to leave, wished the man would hurry up.

"There you are then, lass." He handed over a brown paper bag containing her purchases.

Lucy was about to make her escape when he called her back. She immediately felt guilty.

"Don't forget your change." He grinned at her, holding out the coins. She returned, smiling sheepishly, and thanked him, thrusting the coins into her pocket.

Jack Carstairs watched as she turned away and went quickly out through the door that banged shut after her, past the shop window, and out of sight.

Instead of returning back the way she had come, Lucy continued on down Winslow Road until she crossed the street and, looking briefly around to see if anyone was about, started off down Morgan Avenue towards the park.

Iron railings separated the pavement from a narrow creek that ran along the back of a row of terraced houses, and the way was lined with chestnut trees. She and Jackie had collected conkers there a couple of years ago. She still had some of them in a box in a drawer in her room, a souvenir of more innocent days.

She turned in at the gates of the park and followed the path, past the public toilets and under the beech trees, towards the playground.

Several small children were running back and forth between the swings, and she watched for a moment as she recalled the times when she had played there as a youngster not so very long ago.

* * *

Among these recollections, however, she had no memory of the events of that day, eight years earlier, when her Uncle George, who was the park warden at that time and a frequent visitor to the house on Dover Street, had made his rounds after the rain ended and found her soaked and shivering, huddled up under the slide in the playground, speechless with fear.

All Lucy knew was that something had happened to her here in the park—she had a vague recollection of a man walking a dog—but she had a nagging suspicion that there was something more.

After that day in the park, she became very ill. She remembered little about the time she spent in the hospital. "Double pneumonia," they had said, and some other words that she did not understand.

"She was lucky to have survived," Lucy had heard her mother telling friends and neighbors.

* * *

She walked on now, leaving the laughing children behind, and struck out across the playing fields towards the lake. She and Jackie had sometimes come here on weekends to feed the ducks, and Lucy kept up the practice if for no other reason than to escape the tedium of the house on Dover Street.

It was here, twelve months ago, that she first met Philippe, the middle-aged son of a French whore from Paris and an English soldier, employed as one of the groundskeepers in the park. If asked, Lucy would have been hard-pressed to explain what it was that had drawn her to this man. He was old enough to be her father, and it was not as though he was good-looking. His hairline was rapidly receding, and his once healthy complexion had turned sallow in the dreary English climate. But his romantic speech, delivered so winningly in that sexy continental accent, more pronounced when occasion demanded, had fascinated her.

She found it flattering that he would show any interest in her, a plain and, to her mind, unattractive schoolgirl. It never once occurred to Lucy that his amorous advances were wrong. And this forty-year-old predator evidently felt no qualms about pressing his attentions and a seemingly constant erection on a fifteen-year-old innocent. It hadn't taken long for him to persuade Lucy that what she really needed was the love and sexual gratification that he could so ably and willingly give her.

That first sexual encounter with Phil had been awkward and far from satisfying, at least from her point of view, and the disappointment that she felt afterwards was rather akin to that of a child who has been promised a treat that turns out to be not quite what they had anticipated.

It happened last summer. Philippe had drawn her into the dark, musty-smelling recesses of the boathouse by the lake, filling her head with whispered endearments and promises that became more urgent as his need for her increased.

Dave, the acne-scarred youth who was in charge of the rowing boats that were hired out by the hour during the summer months, was well aware of the fact that the boathouse was used for such purposes by his lecherous friend; he was not averse to using the facilities himself on the rare occasions when he got lucky. But more often than not, he would watch furtively from behind the stacks of un-used or damaged boats whenever his pal Phil brought girls in for a quick bang.

And this one had been special—very young, the youngest yet—couldn't have been more than fourteen or fifteen. *How on earth did he manage to pull in these birds?* It was beyond Dave's comprehension. *But good luck to him*, he thought with grudging admiration.

And Phil was not the only one interested in her, apparently. A skinny, long-haired bloke had recently asked him who she was; Dave said he didn't know, and the chap had walked away. But Dave had seen him hanging about the park on several occasions since, usually accompanied by a large dog.

He watched now, trembling and open-mouthed, as the Frenchman, grunting with raw animal lust, took the girl, thrusting his body against her over and over again until he and Dave had simultaneously exploded in a stupendously sweaty climax.

"Phew! That was really something!" Old Phil had given it to her good and no mistake. But the girl had not responded much—not like some of the tarts that his friend had brought in there—hot bits of stuff who could not wait to get it. She had just laid back, letting Phil do his thing without a murmur.

Lucy hadn't really known what to expect, despite all the talk she had heard at Gordon Street and the books that she and Jackie had read surreptitiously beneath the covers when they stayed overnight at each other's houses. Lucy had always been rather relieved that her mother never actually got around to giving her that talk about the birds and bees.

She had always imagined that the first time would be more romantic somehow—more tender and less hurried. This was real life, not some sentimental novel. But in that brief and frantic moment, her back pressed painfully up against the wooden rowing boats, she experienced a chilling sensation that something like this had happened before—an unpleasant and oppressive thought. The feeling was momentary, however, and she quickly brushed it aside.

There were no encouraging words afterwards. His passion spent, Phil quickly rearranged his clothes, pulled down her skirt, and led her back outside before the park warden, thankfully not her Uncle George, was due to make his mid-day rounds. He winked at Dave, who had scurried back to his place by the water's edge.

"Will you come back tomorrow?' Philippe asked her hopefully.

"Perhaps. I'm not sure." Lucy, who was still feeling dazed, just wanted to get away.

"I'll be waiting for you. Don't disappoint me." Philippe watched her walk away across the bridge, confident that she would come back for more. They always did.

But she did not go back—not the next day or the day after.

She could not say exactly what her feelings were. The experience had left her emotionally numb. When she eventually returned to the park, it was not because she missed or wanted him. It just seemed like it was the only thing to do, something over which she had no control. And when he playfully scolded her for staying away so long, then gripped her arm— almost lifting her off her feet—to hurry her to the same dark corner of the boathouse, she felt neither joy nor fear. There was only acceptance, a resigned belief that this was how things were meant to be.

That she had not become pregnant as a result of these furtive episodes was something of a miracle, but that thought hadn't occurred to her.

She did not tell anyone about Phil—not Amor, or Jackie, or even the girls in school—not even when they laughed and bragged about their conquests. It wasn't anybody's business. It was her life, not theirs.

Shaking off the tug of her memories, she returned to the present. She always went across the bridge rather than walk the path around the water's edge to reach the boathouse on the other side of the lake. As she gazed across, everything was still.

No one was about, not even Philippe, who could usually be seen at this time of day returning a lawn mower or some piece of equipment to the shed next to the boathouse. The boats remained stored away. Dave hadn't returned from college yet; the summer season was still some weeks away.

When Lucy reached the middle of the bridge, she stopped and, leaning over the parapet, looked down at the ducks that had come swimming towards the bridge as soon as they had spotted her. She laughed as they circled beneath her, their paddling feet agitating the water.

"Sorry—I haven't got anything for you today," she told them. But they continued milling about, quacking as though they suspected her of lying, especially since she was carrying a paper bag.

She smiled, shaking her head. As she did so, Lucy heard the sound of a metal latch lifting and, looking toward the red brick boathouse, saw the wooden door swing open.

A young woman stepped out. Lucy watched as Philippe followed her out of the boathouse. The woman turned and put her arms around his neck, and Phil, with his hands all over her, kissed her passionately on the mouth. She playfully pushed him away and walked off towards the distant end of the lake. As she moved, her hips swayed provocatively, her hands smoothing the material of her tight skirt. Philippe looked around, doubtless checking to see if the warden was about, but he didn't notice Lucy standing on the bridge and, reaching down, tugged at the zip on his trousers and went back into the boathouse.

Lucy watched this scene play out and, with something of a sense of relief, turned around and walked back across the bridge and out of the park.

It was over—finished. She had been replaced.

She quickened her pace and almost ran the length of Winslow Road until she turned into Dover Street. Then, with a more measured tread, she made her way back home, hugging the brown paper bag and singing, *Three*

FARWICK

Little Maids from School.

4

THE END OF THE ROAD

"ARE YOU GOING up to the Civic tonight?"

Lucy paused, her fingers hovering over the keys of the typewriter as she considered the question.

"Probably. Are you?"

"Yeah. Not much else to do on a Monday night, is there?" the other girl answered unenthusiastically. "Who's playing, do you know?"

"No idea. Not the Rolling Stones anyway," Lucy quipped regretfully

They laughed. Monday night at The Civic Center meant a few drinks and the chance to dance to some no-name band who played for next-to-nothing and were grateful for the opportunity. The usual crowd would be there: Trevor and Dave, who worked in the offices at Bradstone's, the factory up the road; Jen and Bunny, two girls Lucy had known from her days at Gordon Street; Maggie Anderson, who now sat at her desk on the other side of the office that they shared with their boss, Mr. Papadopoulos at Vanguard Industries; and the boys from the garage across the street.

It was always the same crowd, going through the same weekly ritual: drinking, dancing, retelling the same stale stories, and forcing herself to laugh at often-repeated bad jokes. Although there had been that time when someone had sent her a note via Trevor, asking her to meet him in the bar—but when she arrived, no one had come forward to speak to her. She guessed the message was probably a hoax, sent by Jennifer or Bunny.

Trevor couldn't remember, or hadn't noticed, what the man looked like. Maybe he was in on the joke.

Lucy didn't have a steady boyfriend. She had never been short of dates, but she either grew tired of them or they of her. Besides, she was only twenty-one. There was no need to tie herself down just yet—or, at least, she thought sometimes ruefully, not more than she already was. She still lived at the house on Dover Street, a situation that had been dictated more by necessity, or, more accurately, by a sense of duty rather than choice.

* * *

Lucy had been on the verge of moving out. She had planned to share a flat with Maggie and was nearly euphoric at the thought of finally breaking free from the suffocating routine of the Rowe household. Had she known what was to come, she sometimes reflected guiltily, she might not have wished so ardently for her liberation.

It seemed like a lifetime ago, but in fact, it had happened a little less than a year before. One week before she was due to leave Dover Street, Lucy's father was killed in a car accident.

Ironically, they had never owned a vehicle of their own. One cold and rainy evening, as Tom Rowe returned home from work, a neighbor pulled up at the bus stop where he had been standing for what seemed like an eternity and told him to hop in. Tom was grateful to accept.

As Lucy later learned from an eyewitness account, the two men had been traveling down an unusually open stretch of the busy motorway at quite a high speed when a tire blew. The car spun out of control, smashing into a concrete barrier and turning end over end before landing upside down in a ditch. Her father died before the paramedics could extricate him from the wreck. The neighbor died later that night.

Lucy and her mother, who had been in the process of shaking out dripping umbrellas and divesting themselves of raincoats and hats, had only just arrived home from work when the doorbell rang. An icy chill of foreboding washed over Lucy as she approached the door. They listened incredulously as the policeman stammered and looked helplessly down at the floor. He was a young, sandy-haired chap with pale blue eyes, new to the force and clearly unaccustomed to dealing with anything like this before.

"I'm sorry," he told them over and over, as though he were somehow responsible for the tragedy. The WPC (woman police constable) who accompanied him was evidently more experienced in these matters. She took charge, ushering the two women into the kitchen, where they sat in stunned silence at the table as she bustled about, putting the kettle to boil on the stove and finding tea and mugs in one of the cupboards. All the while, the young constable stood uncomfortably in the doorway, watching them as they came to grips with their loss.

After that, of course, Lucy abandoned all thoughts of moving. How could she leave now and let her mother cope alone? Naturally Maggie understood: Lucy was needed at home.

There was some insurance money, but not much. Her mother, who had returned to work part-time after Lucy left school, was obliged to seek full-time employment in a neighboring town. Their combined income was now stretched to the absolute limit. The idea of giving up something for which her husband had worked so hard all his life was a possibility that Doris Rowe refused to contemplate. Mother and daughter, despite their difficulties, remained in the home on Dover Street.

* * *

Lucy, who had worked in the customer service department at Vanguard Industries ever since leaving school, was reasonably happy there, but though the job paid a decent wage, she sometimes found herself wondering if she couldn't do better elsewhere. Despite these murmurings of discontent, however, she always managed to talk herself out of making any kind of move. After all, Vanguard's was within easy walking distance of home, and she wasn't qualified to do anything beyond typing letters and occasionally answering the phone. These flimsy excuses may have served to keep her from improving her lot, but the truth was that Lucy lacked the self-confidence to try anything new.

"You should go to night school," Maggie had told her once when they were discussing the possibility of new jobs after a particularly frustrating day with Mr. Papadopoulos. "Maybe take a shorthand class; learn another language: French perhaps, or Italian."

Italian might be helpful. Lucy already knew some French words—coarse and filthy, remnants of her days with Phillipe—but she doubted if these would be of any use.

"No," she had replied resignedly. "I'll make do with this for now. Something else will come along eventually," she added with Micawber-like optimism.

But here she was, still typing letters for Mr. Papadopoulos at Vanguard's.

The hands of the oversized clock on the office wall jerked spasmodically towards five, and Maggie, a short, plump brunette with an easy-going manner and infectious laugh, pulled the cover over her typewriter and pushed her chair away from the desk.

"That's it!" she exclaimed. "Time to go! I've had enough for one day. These damn papers for the Baines account are taking forever! Come on." She looked at Lucy who was still typing.

"Go ahead, Mags. I just want to finish this. It won't take long, but you go or you'll miss your bus. I'll see you later at the Civic."

"Well, if you're sure," her friend answered doubtfully.

"Yes, go!" Lucy insisted.

Maggie pulled on her coat and hat and, picking up her purse, walked slowly to the door.

"Watch out for Arnie," she warned half-jokingly as she turned to look back over her shoulder at Lucy.

"Oh, he won't give me any trouble."

Arnold Joyce, the janitor who began his work when everyone else was leaving, was a notorious skirt chaser: a sixty-year-old man who saw his vitality and virility rapidly ebbing with the years but who gamely continued to make his bid for any 'piece of crumpet' who was willing to take him on.

"Just don't let him get you in a corner."

They giggled, and Maggie went out, closing the door behind her. Lucy could hear the chatter of the other women in the adjoining offices as they streamed into the corridor, but gradually the sound died down. Silence descended like a blanket over the empty building.

She went back to her work, carefully copying the hastily written notes that Mr. Papadopoulos had left, trying to decipher the scrawl that passed for handwriting and struggling to make sense of the atrocious spelling that, more often than not, defied understanding.

She heard the door of the adjoining office open and close and the sound of chairs being pushed about the floor—Arnie was on his nightly rounds.

Although she had dismissed Maggie's warning lightly, she was nevertheless uneasy when she heard him moving about in the room next door. He was harmless enough but persistent, and she did not feel like fending off his unwelcome advances just now. She quickened her pace, her fingers hitting the keys of the typewriter rapidly as she watched the words accumulate on the page.

Yours Respectfully and done! She pulled the sheet from the machine, took it over to her boss's desk, and left it there for him to sign in the morning.

Everything was quiet now. Lucy quickly put the cover on her typewriter and went to the closet to retrieve her things as silently as possible so as not to telegraph her presence to the man who was lurking on the other side of the thin partition. Pulling on her coat, she tiptoed to the door. Gently turning the handle, she opened it—finding herself face-to-face with a man of medium height and a slight paunch, whose bare arms sported several faded tattoos.

"Ah, Arnie. How are you this evening?" She took a step backwards—a mistake because he moved forward, effectively blocking her means of escape.

"All the better for seeing you, duck." He leered at her through yellowing teeth, his greasy, grey hair flopping over his forehead. "Working late are you, dearie?"

"I was but I've finished now. Just off home."

"How about nipping round the corner to The Dog and Duck for a quick drink, eh?"

"Not right now Arnie. Anyway, you're working."

"No one's going to know. I'm my own boss, see? I do what I like."

"Well, thanks anyway, but no. I've got to get home. If you'll excuse me." She went to edge past him, but he put rough, nicotine-stained fingers up against the door jamb, preventing her from leaving.

This was not the first time he had tried his luck with her. Once, he even followed her home one evening and called to her from the pavement as she entered her house on Dover Street. But he was temporarily distracted by an approaching pedestrian walking a large, rather vicious-looking dog. By the time he turned his attention back to the house, the door had closed, leaving the aging Lothario disappointed but still hopeful. 'Never say die,' was always his motto.

"What's your hurry, darlin'?" he asked, continuing to block the doorway. "You got someone waiting for you?"

"Yes, my mother, actually. It's my turn to cook dinner."

"Oh, she can take care of herself," he casually dismissed the objection. "She's a big girl now. And so are you, dearie." He gave Lucy a suggestive wink and grinned hopefully, but the smile faded when he received no encouragement.

"Why don't you come back home with me?" he persisted, desperation creeping into the rasping voice that had been so confident just moments before. "You wouldn't be sorry, honest. I'll give you anything you want. I've got money."

Lucy didn't doubt it. Some said that he even had more money than the owner of Vanguard Industries. They had seen him with wads of the stuff sometimes, down at the pub. It was a well-known fact that he liked to bet on the dogs, and he had in the past been linked to some shady deals involving goods that had occasionally 'fallen off the back of a lorry.'

"No thanks, Arnie. I'm sorry. Maybe another time." She hated to say it and risk raising his hopes, but it seemed like the only way to shake him off.

He sighed as he ogled her breasts under the tight cream-colored sweater through watery, blue eyes. "Ah, Lucy love, you wouldn't regret it if only you'd just give me a chance. I could do you like no one else has." He reached his trembling hand out towards her.

That is it! That is enough! She reached out and pushed his arm aside.

"Goodnight, Arnie." She squeezed quickly past him. He watched as she strode down the corridor, the silk lining of her short skirt swishing as her legs moved rapidly and the stiletto heels of her shoes tapping on the tiled floor. He sighed again as she turned the corner and was gone from sight.

"Never say die," he called after her. He would have another go in a day or two. Meanwhile, there was always that young Irish girl down in accounts—the one with the enormous tits and nice smile. Perhaps he would try his luck there. He went back to his mop and bucket, and his fantasies.

Lucy was glad to get out in the cold, fresh air. She took it in in deep gulps and looked back at the door to make sure Arnie hadn't followed her. He disgusted her, and yet she couldn't help feeling a bit sorry for him. *He was pathetic! But there was no way in hell that he was going to lay a finger on her.*

Pulling her hat down firmly on her head and her coat collar up around her ears, she turned towards home. It was just a twenty-minute walk. She banished thoughts of Arnie for those of the evening ahead. It wouldn't take long to prepare dinner; she always got something easy for Monday nights. Her mother would be getting home from her job at Fisher's at six. That was if she could get on the crowded bus that served the area between Swannington and Birchford. If not, she would be sure to be in by six thirty—plenty of time for Lucy to take a bath and eat before she met Mags at the Civic Center.

Lucy usually left the house before her mother in the mornings, and that grey winter day had been no different. However, she detected with some apprehension the telltale signs of depression that surfaced now and then on her mother's pinched and somber face as they sat across from one another at the breakfast table. She had said goodbye with some misgivings, reluctantly pulling the door closed behind her.

Well, things would get better, she supposed. But just how long did it take to get over the passing of someone you loved? She was sad about what had happened to her father and missed him, naturally, but her mother had obviously felt the loss much more intensely. Lucy was always uneasy whenever her mood appeared melancholy, as it had that morning, something that was occurring more and more often of late.

She walked briskly down Winslow Road, turning into Dover Street just as the number 46 bus lurched around the corner and stopped with an ear-piercing squeal to let several passengers off. It was already quite dark and Lucy hurried on with an eerie sense that someone was following her—maybe someone who had gotten off the bus. It might be one of their neighbors, but when she turned to look back and greet them, there was nobody there.

Her mittened fingers fumbled with the key as she struggled to fit it into the latch and, thrusting open the door, quickly stepped inside to escape the biting wind. As Lucy crossed the threshold, she saw several envelopes, pushed through the letterbox by the mailman, lying scattered on the carpet. She bent down and picked them up—a couple of bills, never welcome, and a letter from Jackie that was. They seldom got together these days. Jackie had gone on to college, and Lucy often wondered whether they would ever have anything in common to talk about in the future. She was rather surprised that their friendship had lasted as long as it had.

She dropped the letters onto the little table in the hallway and noticed her mother's brown, woolen coat already hanging there.

"Strange," she said aloud as she hung her own coat up next to it. There were no lights on in the house.

"Hello! Mum? You home already?" Lucy called out. But there was no reply. She walked through to the kitchen and turned on the light to reveal the dirty breakfast dishes still littering the table. Her mother always washed them before she left for work.

Lucy felt a prickling of uneasiness as she went back into the hallway.

"Mum? Is everything alright?" she called out again, listening intently for any hint of sound.

But the house was silent.

She must not have been feeling well that morning, evidently. She hadn't said anything, but then she wouldn't, of course. She wouldn't want to worry Lucy. Maybe she went back to bed.

Lucy dropped her purse at the foot of the stairs and, kicking off her shoes, ran silently up, not wanting to wake her mother if she was sleeping. The door of the bedroom that overlooked the garden at the back of the house was shut, and Lucy, carefully turning the handle, pushed it open just a little, enough to peek in and make sure that everything was alright.

The room was in darkness—Lucy could barely make out the form lying on the bed. She reached to turn on the light and saw her mother, stretched out as if asleep, an empty pill bottle beside her. With this final, irrevocable act of despondency, both Lucy and her mother, each in their own way, had gained their freedom.

5

THE PATH TO HAPPINESS

SHORTLY BEFORE HIS DEATH, Lucy's father had purchased the lease on the house on Dover Street. With both she and her mother working full-time, they were able to make the mortgage payments, but after the death of her mother, things were difficult for Lucy financially. After much consideration and some misgivings, she reluctantly came to the conclusion that the only answer to her difficulties would be to take in a lodger.

She knew her mother would have hated having a stranger living in the house, and Lucy too would have much preferred not to compromise her independence. But there seemed to be no alternative. She was more than relieved when the first person to answer her advertisement in the local newspaper turned out to be a personable young woman named Marianne Clay. Lucy took an instant liking to Marianne, and the two quickly settled into a comfortable routine in the Dover Street house.

Despite this additional income, however, Lucy realized that she was going to have to improve her position at Vanguard's in order to meet the seemingly endless stream of bills that were coming in every month. Having taken a couple of courses at the night school in Birchford, when the chance of promotion within the company came along, she grabbed the opportunity with both hands.

This new position brought her into contact with a different stratum of management at Vanguard's. It wasn't long before she became acquainted with a brash and successful young salesman named Lawrence Welbourne, who, it was rumored, was destined for great things.

Their involvement began almost immediately. Lucy fancied herself in love. Lawrence merely regarded her as an additional reward for all his efforts. Unfortunately, Lucy, rather a romantic at heart and caught up in the emotional entanglement of her first real love affair, was too blind to realize it.

They had been discreet. Welbourne was only too aware that any hanky-panky between them would be frowned-upon by his bosses and, not wanting to make waves yet still determined to take a dip in the water, had insisted that Lucy keep their affair to herself. Naturally, she agreed but saw no harm in telling Maggie who was, next to Jackie, her closest friend.

She had anticipated enjoying a certain amount of confidential complicity with the other girl but was disappointed when Maggie, being rather worldlier, felt obliged to warn her not only of the dangers of dating a fellow employee but also of the reputation for a certain mercenary ruthlessness that Lawrence Welbourne had earned in pursuit of his advancement.

Lucy ignored these warnings, however, and eventually, despite taking what she considered to be adequate precautions, found herself pregnant.

To say that Lawrence Welbourne was unhappy about this unwelcome turn of events would be a gross understatement. But recognizing that even this setback could be turned to his advantage, he bore the burden of his responsibilities and, with forced cheerfulness, made a proposal of marriage, which Lucy readily accepted. By this means, Welbourne calculated, he would acquire not only a wife and family but also, he considered with some satisfaction, the house on Dover Street.

Of course, everyone at Vanguard's, excepting Maggie, had been surprised when Lucy and Lawrence calmly announced their intended nuptials, and there were more than a few raised eyebrows when it became apparent that a certain amount of expediency was called for. But apart from a little harmless gossip, which was only to be expected, nothing occurred to mar Lucy's happiness, and her wedding day went without a hitch.

The only thing that had given Lucy cause for concern was Lawrence's attitude towards Marianne's continued presence at the house on Dover Street. He obviously wanted her out, but Lucy wasn't even sure if they could legally ask her to vacate her room. She didn't see the need for it anyway.

Why should Marianne have to leave her home? Although they hadn't exactly become close friends, she and Marianne understood each other very well. Lucy felt a certain responsibility for the young woman, despite knowing very little about her. She was aware that Marianne had a younger brother and an older, married sister living in London, and a father of whom she rarely spoke, and that she worked in Swannington as a professional photographer.

Marianne had only ever received one visitor at the house, and that just recently: a man closer to Lucy's age, she guessed, who had been introduced as Vincent, a university professor. Lucy had no idea what their relationship might be, and Marianne hadn't volunteered any further information.

It was only a matter of weeks after Lucy's marriage that Lawrence Welbourne began pressuring her to ask Marianne to leave. Because Lucy really wanted to please him and couldn't face another argument, she gave in to what had become an almost daily demand, explaining to Marianne that they would need the extra room once the baby arrived.

"And I'm sure you won't want to be kept awake half the night by a screaming infant. You know what they're like," Lucy gabbled, expecting Marianne to dig in her heels. But to her surprise, her young tenant offered no argument.

"Of course! I understand, Lucy. Don't worry about it. In fact, I was going to tell you, I'd been thinking about moving out anyway."

Lucy felt unaccountably hurt, and her face must have shown it.

"Oh, you've been very kind to me," Marianne reassured her. "Don't think I'm ungrateful, but to tell you the truth, Vincent...you remember Vincent?" Lucy nodded, and Marianne continued bashfully, "Well, he's asked me to move in with him."

Lucy felt relief flood over her. There would be no unpleasant arguments with Marianne or Lawrence and no guilty feeling about having to let the former go.

Lawrence Welbourne was rather surprised by his easy victory but looked on it as a good sign. Life on Dover Street settled into a reasonably happy routine.

~

Twenty-five years had passed since Lucy's marriage to Lawrence Welbourne. How long ago it all was, and yet sometimes it seemed like only yesterday.

Lucy sighed and stepped back with her head tilted slightly to one side, surveying with a critical eye the canvas in front of her. Had she managed to capture the colors of the sky? She was never wholly satisfied with her work, even when a picture was completed, and always found it difficult to resist the temptation to make that one last finishing touch.

Light streamed in through the windows of the bedroom at the back of the house, which she had converted into a studio of sorts. The room had been cleared of its original furniture. The bed, chests, and dresser were all gone and were replaced by a stool, small table, and storage cabinet, and it was devoid of any decoration. Lucy even removed the rose-patterned paper that had begun to peel away from the walls, tearing at the pieces as if she were stripping away the last remnants of an unpleasant memory that no longer had a place in her life.

Although Lucy had found plenty to keep her busy and had become accustomed to living alone, there were times when the house seemed unnervingly deserted and quiet.

Her daughter, Robin, just turned twenty-two, left home some time ago, and was now living in Cheltenham.

David, her eldest, had always been a difficult child. Lucy had never seen eye to eye with her son, who had inexplicably blamed her for the breakup of his parents' marriage. His fiery temper had landed him in trouble both at school and with the police—though thankfully the latter had been resolved with a *caution*. Their constant arguments had left Lucy exhausted.

David had long held the view that Lucy much preferred his sister to himself, a misconception that had been fueled by his father, who, despite having remarried, continued to refer to his ex-wife in the most vituperative of terms. So, it came as no surprise when David announced his intention to go and live with Lawrence Welbourne and his family. Although she could have contested it, Lucy had viewed this move with equanimity and a profound sense of relief.

She put the brush back into the blue paint on her palette and dabbed absent-mindedly at the scene that had taken shape on the canvas.

"Twenty-five years," she repeated to herself; so much of her life used up already, and yet she was still waiting. *Waiting for what?* Lucy didn't know. She was happy enough—but something had happened nine years ago that had changed the direction of her life. The event stood out as clearly in her mind now as it had on that fateful day. She stepped back from the easel once more and, staring blindly at the canvas, recalled a sunny spring morning that had begun like so many other mornings at the house on Dover Street.

* * *

It was a Saturday, and Lucy was using the time off work to clean the house in between dashing to the store for groceries and pulling a few weeds in the garden. Lawrence, a nit-picking perfectionist, expected everything to be kept just so, although he did very little to help around the house, even though Lucy worked as many hours as he now that she was secretary to the Director of Vanguard's. She had just finished vacuuming the carpet in the hallway and was about to move on to the more arduous job of scrubbing out the bathtub and cleaning toilets when the doorbell rang. Caught off guard, she unthinkingly opened the door without first looking to see who was there, finding herself face-to-face with a woman of roughly her own age and height, dressed in jeans and a brightly colored blouse, with a large basket on her arm.

"'Ello love." The woman, speaking with the strange and somewhat abrasive accent that Lucy associated with the travelers who occasionally passed through Birchford and who sometimes camped in the fields on the outskirts of town, wasted no time in introductions—"Like to buy a bracelet or how about a nice necklace?"

She pushed the wicker basket forward, lifting the cover to reveal an assortment of cheap home-made jewelry, and Lucy, remembering her previous encounter with the irate traveler as a child on Dover Street, instinctively backed away. Despite her apprehension, Lucy seldom turned one of these itinerants away without making a token purchase, for fear of triggering another such angry outburst. Reaching out to finger the trinkets, she picked up a gaudy bangle to examine the color and workmanship.

"How much?" she asked.

The woman named a modest price, and Lucy told her to wait while she went to fetch her purse, prudently closing the door in the meantime. When she returned, the unexpected caller was still waiting patiently on the doorstep. Lucy handed her the money, and she reached out to take the proffered note. Something in the movement stirred in Lucy's memory the picture of a young girl reaching out to accept the offer of a shared lunch, and she gasped involuntarily.

"Rose? Rose Cooper?"

The woman smiled, her shining white teeth contrasting starkly with the prematurely lined and weather-beaten face. Nodding her head, she looked at Lucy with amused satisfaction, as though she had been testing her and had received the desired result.

"Yes. That's right. Well…Rose Arnold now."

"You probably don't remember me," Lucy said. "I'm Lucy Rowe. We were at Gordon Street together."

"Yes, I remember you," the other woman replied, rubbing a finger against the side of her nose. "I recognized you as soon as you opened the door."

"How are you?" Lucy asked, feeling awkward. Being confronted by someone she'd known from school who was selling cheap jewelry from a basket on her doorstep wasn't something that happened every day.

Rose was unabashed, however. "I'm doing alright. You've got a nice place here," she remarked chirpily, looking past Lucy into the hallway, as though seeking an invitation to enter.

Lucy took the hint rather reluctantly. "Would you like to come in for a minute?"

"Thanks." Rose swiftly moved forward past Lucy and directly into the living room without waiting for any further bidding.

Lucy hurried after her with some misgivings.

"Not married then?" the woman asked with uninhibited curiosity as they sat down.

"Yes," Lucy replied quickly, as if making it clear that she wasn't alone in the house even though the others were out pursuing various activities. She then added, "And we have two children: A girl, Robin, who's twelve, and a boy, David. He's sixteen. And you?"

"Yeah. I got married soon after I left Gordon Street," Rose said, setting her basket down on the carpet as if she were planning on staying for a while.

Lucy made a rapid calculation. The girl must have only been about seventeen years old, if that!

"I couldn't wait to leave there, but I promised Auntie Sarah I'd stick it out till the end of term. Then, when Marshall's Fair came into town, I got a job on one of the stalls and met a bloke who worked on the dodgems."

"We got married after Dad...died. No kids though. Maybe it's just as well." She added philosophically: "This kind of life's alright for me, but I don't know as I'd want a sprog of mine to be brought up that way. Sometimes I think I wouldn't mind living in town, but Cliff couldn't never settle down in one place. It'd drive him crazy." She shrugged and changed the subject abruptly. "Would you like me to tell your fortune? No charge."

Lucy had never really believed in such mumbo jumbo, but she didn't want to risk giving offence to her one-time schoolfriend. All the same, she couldn't allow the woman to think that she gave these mystic readings any credence. She said doubtfully, "Well, okay, but between you and me, it's just for fun, all that stuff, right? Those things are not for real, are they?"

Rose looked aggrieved. "I wouldn't lie to you, Lucy. You did me a good turn. I don't forget it. Sure, I tell people what they want to hear, mostly a lot of junk about good health and tall, dark, handsome strangers. But I do have the sight, and for a friend like you, I speak the truth—no bullshit."

Lucy was somewhat taken aback by Rose's honesty and felt

unaccountably afraid. Did she really want to know what the future had in store for her? Did she want to be warned of some impending upheaval in her life or, worse yet, be told that there was nothing awaiting her—that her existence would go plodding on as it had for the past sixteen years?

"Alright," she relented, slowly extending her hand. The other woman took it in her own roughened ones, turning the palm upwards, and traced her fingers along the lines that she could normally read as easily as one reads a newspaper or book.

At first, Rose seemed puzzled by what she saw there and continued to scrutinize the hand that Lucy held out to her. Then she looked up and smiled.

"Things haven't been easy for you. I can see that, dearie, but it will all change soon. A big shift coming. Someone will leave your life, and someone else will come in—someone important. You will know great love and travel far. When the time comes to leave, you mustn't be afraid. You will gain much and be very happy. But…"

Rose hesitated and seemed unwilling to continue.

"Go on. You can tell me," Lucy assured her, forgetting for the moment that she didn't really believe in such things. "I want to know everything."

"There is danger," the woman went on. "Someone wishes you ill, but he is far away, and he may never reach you. If he does, though, beware, because he will harm you if he can."

Lucy pulled back her hand. "Thanks for the warning."

Rose, fearing that she'd upset her hostess, retrieved her basket. "I'd better get going. We're leaving tomorrow. We're off to Appleby Horse Fair, and…well, you know how it is."

"Yes. Well, it was nice to see you again, Rose, and please take something for the reading." Lucy reached for her purse.

"No, Lucy! Take the reading as a gift. Wear the bracelet and remember your old friend Rose."

"I hope everything goes alright for you," Lucy told her sincerely. "Come back and visit if you're ever in town, won't you? I'll tell you then if your predictions were right."

"Oh, I'm never wrong," the woman told her confidently. Turning, she walked down the path. But when she got to the gate, she looked back over her shoulder and called out, "Just remember, when the time comes, don't be afraid. Don't turn away from the path to happiness. It will lead you to everything you've ever desired."

Lucy waved her hand and watched as Rose made her way down Dover Street and out of sight.

* * *

At least part of Rose's prediction came true. Almost one month to the day after Rose's visit, Lawrence left her. Of course, she had always known that there must be another woman or women—all the times when he had come home so very late at night, the constant business trips. He'd found it all so easy. Lucy didn't look for proof, didn't want to find it, and although she was desperately unhappy, she allowed him to come and go as he pleased. Was it because deep down she didn't really love him? *Did she ever? Possibly.* She thought she had, at first, but it quickly turned to a comfortable indifference. She guessed it must have been the same for him.

Then one day she found a letter—a letter that she was certain Lawrence intended her to see because he left it lying open on the dressing table in their bedroom. She picked it up and calmly sat on the bed as she studied the unfamiliar handwriting. It was from someone called Eileen. She was asking Lawrence when he was planning on telling Lucy that he was leaving her and how wonderful it would be when they could all be together—her, Lawrence, and their baby. Lucy found it odd, reading about herself in this context, and put the letter back where she found it. *Poor Lawrence!* Despite all his bravado, he was such a coward. This was his way of telling her, so he wouldn't have to say the words to her face.

When Lawrence Welbourne arrived home that night, he assumed it would be to a tearful wife who had learned the truth and been forced to accept the reality of his infidelity. But things didn't go quite as he had planned.   He guessed immediately that she had read the letter. Robin and David were already in bed; their schoolbooks and papers were left scattered on the table in the dining room. Lucy hadn't bothered to tidy them away as she usually did before he came home, and there was no appetizing smell of cooking coming from the kitchen. She was sitting, her eyes closed, in the armchair by the fireplace, her favorite music playing on the stereo.

"Lucy?" There was no reply, no sign of any movement—and for one horrible moment, he thought she had taken an overdose of sleeping pills, just as her mother had done. He repeated her name and moved closer, his heart beginning to pound, when she suddenly opened her eyes and looked at him in stony silence.

"You know then?" He couldn't think what else to say.

"Yes." She seemed unusually calm. Lawrence was apprehensive. He had expected acrimony, hysteria, tears, or even blows, but not this unnerving composure.

There was no reason to deny anything. He wanted her to find out, after all, so he merely shrugged his shoulders and said, "Right then. Well, that's it. I'll pack my things and leave in the morning."

"Now." The monosyllabic response stopped him in his tracks like a bullet.

"What?"

"Now. I think it would be best, Lawrence, if you left now." She stood up. "In fact, I've already packed for you. One last little task that I was quite happy to perform. Your suitcases are up in the bedroom. Whatever I couldn't fit in, I'll send on if you leave an address. I don't want you coming back here again. Ever."

"Damn it, Lucy!" He had secretly and sadistically hoped she would beg him to stay; he had pictured the scene, he crushing her heart and hopes with some cruel rebuff, she pleading with him. But, just like that, he was robbed of the moment and could only add, "Is that all you've got to say?"

Lucy looked surprised. "All? What did you expect me to say? Were you hoping I'd beg you to stay?" It was as though she had read his mind.

"I…I…I don't know. I thought…well, honestly Lucy, I thought you'd be more upset."

Lucy gave a cynical laugh. "Really? You don't know me very well, even after all these years, do you?"

He glanced up at her, but he could tell nothing from her expression. It was a cold, inscrutable look that offered no hint of what his wife was really feeling, and for the first time in their married life, he no longer felt confident, so cocksure of himself.

"What will you tell the children?"

"They're not babies anymore, Lawrence. I know you haven't spent much time at home lately, but even you must have noticed that. I'll tell them the truth, that you left. That you've gone to live with someone else. I see no reason to sugarcoat the facts only to have them find out the real story later on. I'm not being hard, Lawrence, just realistic. Please leave."

It wounded his ego terribly to think that she was so willing to let him go without a fight, but he was also shrewd enough to realize that he was being handed his freedom on the proverbial platter. Turning on his heel, he left the room, running quickly upstairs to collect his things. Lucy followed him out into the hallway and waited at the foot of the stairs until he appeared a few minutes later on the landing, wearing a heavy grey overcoat and carrying a large suitcase in each hand. She watched him as he descended and walked ahead of him to the front door, opening it for him and standing aside to let him pass through. When he reached the doorstep, he turned to look at her as she stood there, illuminated by the light above the door.

"Say goodbye to the kids for me? I'll send you my address." He sounded rather pathetic now, but Lucy was unconcerned. She neither knew nor cared where he would be—a week, a month, a year from now, or even that night.

* * *

"Someone will leave your life," Rose had told her, and she'd been right. The divorce had seen to that. Lucy had received a sizeable settlement and custody of their children, with visitation rights awarded to Lawrence despite Lucy's objections. Not long after the divorce, Welbourne was fired from his job at Vanguard's because of some inconsistencies in his expense claims. Rightly or wrongly, he suspected that Lucy had used her position to engineer his dismissal, which only added fuel to his already smoldering fire of resentment.

But as to the rest of it, there had been no one else, no great love. Did she really think there would be? No, those kinds of things seldom happen in real life. The overwhelming passion that one saw on the screen or read about in books was the stuff of which dreams were made and was rarely experienced first-hand. And there was little chance now, Lucy thought, at fifty-three, of ever meeting her soulmate. Besides, was she really even looking for him now? She didn't think so. She was reasonably confident that, barring some kind of miracle, that part of Rose's prediction would never come true, nor, for that matter, the part about traveling. She was content to stay close to home.

Over the years, Lucy maintained her friendship with Jackie. The pair continued to visit one another occasionally, with Lucy staying with Jackie and her husband Lionel in Chelsea and Jackie coming up to Birchford for long weekends. During these visits, Jackie left Lionel to take care of their book shop, The Turning Page. But that was about the extent of Lucy's travels, apart from the occasional coach ride to Folkestone or Brighton.

Although Lucy learned to drive, she never bought a car and instead occasionally rented one for vacations and rare work trips. She always felt that public transportation was good enough and could not see the point in adding the unnecessary expenses of car insurance, licensing, and maintenance to her annual budget. There was no need. Everything that she required was close at hand. She was happiest taking care of her garden or painting, a hobby she adopted soon after Lawrence's departure.

And there was always work. Still at Vanguard's, she was rewarded over the years for her hard work and loyalty by a series of promotions. These culminated in her position as secretary to the Managing Director. Lucy regarded all this with a somewhat bemused acceptance.

The last part of Rose's prediction had caused Lucy more concern than she cared to admit. The thought that someone might wish her harm was unthinkable. She had never made many friends, especially since her marriage to Lawrence, but by the same token, she had made few, if any, enemies—except perhaps for Lawrence himself. And yet, despite her skepticism over much of what Rose had told her, Lucy had to admit that she had been right about Lawrence's defection.

Lucy put down the brush and wiped her fingers on a rag. Almost finished—maybe tomorrow it would be done.

She walked—or more accurately, was pulled by some unseen force—closer to David's old boombox. It was playing a familiar tune: *The Honfleur Suite*, a romantic piece written in the 1920s by a composer named Neville Wyndham. There was an inexplicable magic woven into the notes—like a siren's call drawing her to a realm of endless summer days, the warm smell of hay, and the bright red splash of poppies in sun-kissed fields. Each note caressed her soul, wrapping her in a blanket of serene, almost sensual languor. Yet, beneath the surface of this tranquil reverie, a restless undercurrent tugged at her soul, leaving a void of emptiness and unfulfillment.

Lucy couldn't shake the feeling that there was something profound about this enigmatic melody, something that transcended the confines of her studio and even her own life. It was as if the melody was whispering hidden truths—a forgotten tale pulling her to unravel its mystery.

6

DÉJÀ-VU

LUCY HESITATED BEFORE DIALING the number to Jackie's shop. She rarely got in touch with her friend there these days, usually confining casual conversations to the evening hours when she knew Jackie would be at home with Lionel in Chelsea. Now, finding herself on the verge of breaking this self-imposed rule, she felt her resolve to call rapidly evaporating. She fought down the urge to abandon the idea, however, knowing full well that if she didn't act now, she would probably talk herself out of it by evening. Her finger went through the motions of tapping out the digits for The Turning Page. She waited while the phone rang repeatedly at the other end without response and was about to hang up, almost with a sense of relief, when she heard a click. A woman's voice said brightly, "Good morning! The Turning Page. This is Jackie. How can I help you?"

Lucy, suddenly pulled back from the act of replacing the receiver, was momentarily caught off guard. She remained silent, holding the instrument at arm's length as though it were an unexploded bomb, until the woman reiterated her greeting and Lucy slowly raised the phone back to her ear.

"Hello. Jackie?"

"Yes." There was a pause, and then the person at the other end said uncertainly, "Lucy? Is that you?"

"Yes."

"Lucy! It's wonderful to hear from you. How are you? It's been an age.

You never answered my last letter, so I thought you must be really busy."

Apart from the occasional phone call and sporadic visits, the two women had maintained their life-long friendship largely by means of the rather old-fashioned custom of letter-writing, the form of correspondence they had first adopted when Jackie had moved with her family to London back in the 60's. They shared a mutual pleasure in expressing their thoughts and observations, committing hopes and fears to paper, and, in turn, reading about each other's day-to-day activities. They enjoyed the ability to put their hands on the tangible proof of their continued relationship.

"I'm fine," Lucy told her, trying to sound convincing but not succeeding. "Things *have* been pretty hectic here. You know how it is: work, work, work. How are you? How's Lionel?"

"We're fine. Disgustingly healthy," Jackie told her heartily.

"And the shop?"

"Business is booming. In fact," Jackie lowered her voice confidentially, "I've got quite a crowd in here now."

"I'm sorry," Lucy, mentally kicking herself for calling, apologized hastily. "I really didn't mean to bother you there. So stupid. I wasn't thinking…I'll—"

"No, no," Jackie quickly reassured her. "That's alright. They're all just browsing at the moment." She had sensed that something was wrong. Just the fact that Lucy had called her at the shop was unusual. And during the day? From the office?

"Is everything alright, Luce? You sound—well—not quite like your old self."

"No," Lucy admitted reluctantly. Then, making up her mind, she added, "Actually…I know this is a bit sudden, and just say if it's not convenient, but could I come down and see you?"

"Of course!" Jackie exclaimed wholeheartedly. "You know you're welcome any time. Can you hop on a train this afternoon? We could make it a nice, long weekend. Lionel can come and pick you up at the station. I should be finished here by about seven thirty. I'm coping on my own today. I gave Theresa the day off to go to a friend's wedding, and Mark doesn't come in on Fridays."

"No, no. That's alright." Lucy abhorred fuss and couldn't bear to be the cause of any inconvenience. "I'll get a taxi from the station. Don't bother Lionel, please," she begged.

"Oh, it's no bother, really," Jackie insisted. "It'll give him something to do. He's getting rather lazy."

"But he's working on his book, surely?"

"Yes, when the mood's on him, which isn't very often just lately."

"Still, I'll be fine. I'd much rather just get a taxi, really." Lucy was adamant.

"Alright, stubborn!" Jackie gave in, realizing from long experience that it was useless to argue. "Give us a call when you get into town and we'll put the kettle on. You will be able to stay at least until Sunday evening, won't you?"

"Yes. In fact, I was due for some time off. I don't need to go into work at all next week. I was thinking of putting up at a hotel for a few days."

That was definitely out of character. Lucy hadn't taken a vacation in years. Her old schoolfriend had often teased her that she was as obsessed with her job as Jackie was with the book shop. Even Lucy's daughter Robin's constant entreaties for her to take a break once in a while had largely gone unheeded.

"Wonderful! Then stay the whole week. And none of this nonsense about staying at a hotel!" Jackie told her with evident pleasure. "We can take in a show, do some shopping, collect conkers in the park." She laughed. "Well, maybe not. Wrong time of the year. But we'll have fun."

"That'll be lovely. I really appreciate this, Jackie." Lucy sounded relieved.

"Looking forward to it," Jackie said, her delight obvious. "We'll see you later, then. Don't forget, call when you get to the station at this end. I should be home around eight, but Lionel will be there if I'm not back by then. I'll give him a jingle now; let him know you're coming."

"Right. Thanks. See you later, then. Bye." Lucy replaced the receiver cautiously, as though the call had been made, in some way, surreptitiously, and went back through the silent house to the studio. There, the unfinished painting of a large house surrounded by a field of poppies, for so many weeks abandoned, lay propped up on an old wooden easel, awaiting her attention.

"Did I do the right thing?" she asked vaguely, looking across the room as she tightened the cap on a tube of vermillion paint, setting it back down on the table. A bird twittered testily somewhere outside the open window as Lucy waited expectantly for a reassuring answer, but there was no reply.

* * *

It was already late into the evening by the time the train pulled into the London station. Lucy stepped down onto the platform, suitcase in hand.

The journey itself didn't take long—just over two hours with all the stops. She had traveled the same route many times over the years, so even in the dark, she could visualize the rapidly passing scene. More lights were visible now than there had been when she took her first trip to the city as a child—taller buildings, blocks of flats where there had once been open land. Urban sprawl had finally merged with suburban encroachment until it seemed to become one big conglomeration of homes, factories, shops, and offices.

It was a singular and inexplicable fact, however, that although Lucy had never lived in London or cared much for the hectic pace of the city life into which she was inevitably drawn when she was there, she nevertheless always felt a sense of returning home whenever she came back to the bustling and noisy metropolis. It was as if she belonged there somehow.

Striding quickly past her fellow travelers, Lucy emerged from the dust and diesel fumes of the station and took the first available taxi waiting at the rank. She adroitly stepped ahead of an indecisive couple with a mountain of luggage who evidently weren't sure where they were going and gave the driver Jackie's address in Chelsea.

When she was settled in her seat and the cab had pulled out into traffic, Lucy rummaged in her purse. She extracted the phone that Robin had insisted she carry with her in case of emergencies—one she seldom used— and called Jackie's home number.

A mild-mannered voice came over the line. "Hello. Lionel Shellaby speaking."

"Hello Lionel. It's Lucy."

"Hello, Luce!" His exuberant expression of pleasure on hearing her voice was genuine. She smiled as she pictured him standing by the phone, tall and gangly, his brown wavy hair beginning to turn just the tiniest bit grey, the hawk-like nose, the wide mouth, and gentle yet perceptive eyes.

"I'm on my way from the station. I shouldn't be long. Is Jackie home?"

"Yes, shall I put her on?"

"No, it's alright. I'll be there in a bit."

"Okay, I'll tell her you're on your way. Bye."

Lucy put the phone back in her bag and looked out absentmindedly at the bustling nightlife of the city—people going about their busy lives, coming and going in an unending procession, like a colony of ants, each with their own appointed purpose.

Lucy wondered whether she was doing the right thing, burdening her friends with her troubles. She had put off going to the station in Swannington for as long as she could, waiting until the last train was scheduled to depart, and had almost changed her mind even then about coming down. But she felt she *had* to tell someone. And if she must entrust her secret to someone, it seemed only natural to confide in the two people who had for so many years shared the triumphs and tragedies of her life.

After all, it was so much easier to talk to Jackie and Lionel. It wasn't that Robin didn't care, but she was busy with her own life. Robin had such a firm and realistic grip on life that Lucy was certain she would never in a million years understand the situation in which she now so bewilderingly found herself.

* * *

Jackie, watching from the first-floor window of the Shellaby's elegant eighteenth-century terraced house, saw the taxi pull up outside. The front door was already open as Lucy emerged onto the quiet residential street just off Sloane Square.

The two friends hadn't seen each other for several months, and Jackie was startled to observe Lucy's appearance, which was rather pale and drawn. She had lost some weight too, which wasn't a bad thing in itself, but still—

"Darling! How are you?" Jackie welcomed her friend with open arms, instinctively sensing the other woman's hesitancy and feeling an unfamiliar fragility as they hugged each other. The two went inside, arms linked, Jackie solicitously taking Lucy's suitcase and putting it down for later collection in the hallway.

The long-time companions went into the drawing room, and as promised, the tea tray was ready on the low glass table in front of the sofa.

This familiar scene had been the precursor to so many shared confidences between the two women over the years: Jackie's dream of opening the book shop soon after she and Lionel had moved into the house in Chelsea; the announcement of Lucy's first pregnancy five months before her marriage to Lawrence; and the eventual breakdown of the troubled relationship that, doomed from the very start, had ended in divorce. Jackie and Lionel's decision not to raise a family had been discussed there too, and that rough patch when the couple faced financial ruin following a disastrously bad year at the shop and an equally unproductive year from Lionel's normally fertile pen. That had all been many years ago.

Recently, their conversations had taken a more optimistic turn: Robin's new job, Lucy's latest pay raise, Lionel's string of best-sellers, and Jackie's entrepreneurial success now that The Turning Page had become well-established. These were all things that were cause for rejoicing, and the three friends naturally looked to each other to share in their happiness and good fortune.

Now, however, Jackie sensed that the reason for Lucy's visit would offer little justification for celebration. She suddenly felt a strange reluctance to hear Lucy's news, a disinclination that she could never remember experiencing before, given their history of confiding in one another since childhood.

"It was good of you to take me in on the spur of the moment like this," Lucy began, but Jackie dismissed the idea.

"Rubbish!" she scolded her. "You know you're welcome anytime. How's Robin?"

"Fine. This new venture really seems to suit her," Lucy replied, helping herself to one of the deliciously decadent pastries that her friend had thoughtfully provided along with the usual pot of Earl Grey tea. "She sounds so much happier, and the flat she's sharing with Dianne is very nice, much better than that horrid bedsitter she was renting in Alston Street. I went over there for a visit a few weeks ago, and I must admit I'm relieved to see her settled there. I know she managed alright on her own before, but it's so much easier with two of them sharing the expenses and just the fact that there's someone else around, you know, in case of an emergency." Lucy had long ago come to accept her daughter's lesbian relationships, and she like Dianne.

"And what about you, Luce?" Jackie asked, visualizing her friend alone at the house in Birchford.

"Oh, everything's fine," Lucy assured her rather unconvincingly.

"Come on," Jackie admonished her gently. "This is me you're talking to."

Lucy adopted a puzzled expression, professing not to understand, but Jackie stuck to her guns. "What's wrong, Luce?" Anyone who knows you as well as I do can tell with half an eye that something's up. You more or less admitted as much on the phone this morning."

Lucy, studiously pretending to examine the cover of a glossy magazine that she had picked up from the table, remained for a moment in obdurate denial, then, relenting, looked up with a wry smile and confessed, "Yes, you're right."

"What is it, Luce?" Jackie put her hand tentatively on Lucy's arm.

"Oh, this is all going to sound very silly." Lucy sighed heavily. "It's as though I've never been involved in my own life. I've just been watching myself, ever since I was a child, from the outside, you know, like a play, as though nothing that's happened has really happened to me. It's all just been part of the show." She stopped and looked at Jackie, half expecting to see an expression of amusement on her face, but her friend continued to gaze back at her with concerned interest.

Lucy ran her fingers through shoulder-length hair that had been carefully colored to conceal the streaks of grey that were becoming more prominent now, pushing it back from her brow as though trying to clear the way for her thoughts.

"I know I'm not making much sense. Nothing seems to matter much anymore; gardening, painting, even my job, which incidentally I came very close to losing this week."

Jackie looked aghast, thinking of all the hard work her friend had put into the garden on Dover Street, finding it difficult to imagine the tidy flower beds and perfectly manicured lawn in disarray. And losing her job? "Lucy! What on earth's wrong?"

Then, looking more closely at her friend's changed appearance, as if for the first time, she was struck by an unsettling thought.

"Oh my God, Luce! You're ill, aren't you?"

Jackie, never one to do anything by halves, jumped to the obvious conclusion, and once given voice, the hypothesis took root and quickly grew out of control, assuming dire proportions. "It's something serious, isn't it? You're not...?"

"Dying?" Lucy, unaware that the change in her appearance had been so noticeable, was alarmed by Jackie's misapprehension and hurried to reassure her. "No, no! Nothing that melodramatic; at least—" She stopped, her thoughts seeming to drift elsewhere.

"It's not one of the kids, is it?" Jackie knew that, despite her estrangement from David, Lucy still cared very much about her son.

"No. They're both fine, as far as I know."

Jackie continued to scrutinize her friend's face, her mind running speculatively over the various possibilities. All of a sudden, there came a burst of illumination, as though someone had flipped a switch and turned on a very bright light. *Of course!* If it wasn't illness or family problems, there was only one other thing, in Jackie's estimation, that could make a woman behave so irrationally.

"It's a man!" she exclaimed, certain that she had solved the puzzle. "You've met someone!"

Jackie, who had often tried unsuccessfully to persuade Lucy to get back into the dating scene, was thrilled with the idea, and when Lucy didn't deny it, she went on: "That's marvelous, Luce! I'm so happy for you. Who's the lucky guy?"

"It's not that simple," Lucy told her, immediately throwing cold water on her friend's enthusiasm.

"Oh no!" Jackie looked at her shrewdly. "He's married, isn't he?"

"Yes, but that's not the problem," Lucy admitted, further arousing Jackie's curiosity.

"Is he getting a divorce?" Jackie asked hopefully, feeling no hesitation in being forthright. They had never kept secrets from each other and had always been open and honest on any subject, no matter how personal.

"No, he never did," Lucy answered cryptically.

"Did? You make him sound like a bigamist. He isn't, is he?" Jackie asked, aghast.

"No. But let's not talk about him now."

Lucy suddenly dropped a tantalizing veil over what had become, for Jackie, a most intriguing subject. She made to pass the matter off with a shrug as if it were of no consequence and was unwittingly aided in her attempt by the sudden appearance of Lionel Shellaby.

"Talk about who?" Lionel asked, coming into the room.

"Lionel! How are you?" Lucy got up to greet him, and they embraced with all the warmth of long-time friends.

"Hello, Luce! I'm fine." He held her at arm's length and looked at her critically. "*You* look as though you could do with a vacation though."

"Lionel! What a thing to say!" Jackie declared reprovingly.

"Well, it's true. Lucy doesn't mind me saying so, do you, Luce?"

"No, Lionel. You're right. I could use a break."

"And that's exactly what she's going to get," Jackie added resolutely. "Rest and relaxation."

Lionel laughed. "If I know you two, you won't stop for breath all week. What's the betting she'll have you shopping from morning till night the whole time you're here?" he quipped.

"That's alright. I was rather looking forward to a shopping spree anyway."

"There are other things besides shopping," Jackie told her husband, who looked at her disbelievingly.

"Since when did you subscribe to that theory?" Lionel joked from the safety of the armchair furthest from his wife.

"Men!" Jackie playfully threw a cushion at him. "Take no notice. They think we're only good for two things, and one of them's shopping. Anyway, great news! When you told me you were coming down this morning, I called around and managed to finagle a couple of tickets for *Mefistofele* at the Garden."

"That's wonderful! But what's happening with the shop?" Lucy asked with a look of concern. "I don't want to disrupt your schedule or anything."

"Don't worry. I called Theresa, and she says she and Mark can hold the fort, and Lionel has gallantly offered to fill in when needed, so everything's taken care of. But Lucy…" Jackie grasped her friend's arm, as if to prevent her from escaping further interrogation, and adroitly steered the conversation back to Lucy's earlier disclosure. "You really have tweaked my curiosity about this man of yours."

"Man? Man?" Lionel jumped up with a look of mock horror. "What man? Lucy! Have you been deceiving me all these years?" He clutched melodramatically at his chest and fell to his knees.

"No. Don't worry, Lionel." Lucy laughed at his absurd antics. "There is no man."

"Well, what's this stupid woman talking about then?"

"I was just going to get it out of her when you came in," Jackie explained, silently cursing her husband for having made such an untimely entrance.

"Would you like me to leave?" Lionel inquired diffidently, getting to his feet and retreating a few steps.

"No, for goodness' sake, Lionel! Don't be silly." Lucy laughed, waving him back. "The whole thing is…well…just so…stupid. Very stupid! Let's forget about it, please. I'd much rather hear all about you two. How are you both? How's the writing going, Lionel?"

"Remarkably well, actually," Lionel replied, flinging himself back down into his chair. "*Rendezvous* should be on the shelves next month, and the latest one is almost finished. It's enough to keep the wolf from the door for a while anyway, and meanwhile, *Vespers* is keeping Jackie in shoes and earrings."

"Monster!" Jackie threw another cushion at him, laughing.

The two of them had remained remarkably young at heart, Lucy thought affectionately—very carefree, especially now that everything was going so well for them. How lucky her friend was to find someone with whom she was so obviously happy and contented. It was hard not to be envious sometimes, but Lucy didn't begrudge them their happiness. They had paid their dues, worked their way over the rough spots, and through it all, their love had endured.

They sat late into the night reminiscing. Lucy showed them photos taken at Robin's new home. Jackie shared news of the latest acquisitions at the book shop, while Lionel regaled the two with amusing anecdotes about several interesting people he had met at a literary party the week before.

No further mention was made of Lucy's mystery man. The Shellabys were keenly aware that this was more than just a trivial incident to be airily discussed over tea or cocktails. Lucy would open up all in good time, but until then, they would have to hold their burgeoning curiosity in check.

The next morning, as Lionel had predicted, Jackie suggested that they do a little shopping.

"Just a quick look. Nothing drastic," she assured her husband, who, from long experience, knew better.

The *quick look* developed into a three-hour reconnaissance of all the latest fashions. Exhausted and loaded down with shopping bags, the two women went to restore their flagging energy at a nearby coffee shop. Once seated at a table, Jackie, unable to contain her inquisitiveness any longer, took the opportunity to pose the question that had been on her mind ever since the previous evening.

"Alright Luce, what's the story about this mystery man of yours?"

Lucy didn't reply right away, seeming to search for the right words to explain an evidently difficult situation. She answered the question with a question of her own, catching Jackie off guard.

"Do you believe in reincarnation?"

"I don't know." Jackie gazed ruminatively at the contents of her coffee cup, appearing to give the matter some consideration. "I've never really thought about it, to be quite honest—except... sometimes...perhaps. You know what it's like when you get that feeling of déjà vu?"

"Exactly," Lucy agreed. "I've never given the whole idea much thought myself until now. But think about it: why is it that so many people have, right from early childhood, a favorite color, a natural talent for something, or an unexplained fear?"

The question immediately conjured a picture in Jackie's mind of Lucy hastily crossing a street to avoid walking directly past a dog. She had always been afraid of them, especially the large ones. They were often forced to abandon their outings in the park if any such dogs were running loose. Lucy had refused point blank to visit her daughter Robin when her former flatmate owned a rather high-spirited Doberman. Lucy herself had no idea why she was so afraid, and Jackie couldn't convince her to get help. The fear remained a lifelong problem.

Meanwhile, Lucy continued her train of thought. "Why do we prefer one kind of music over another and have such vivid, recurring, but inexplicable dreams? And you're right about the déjà vu thing too. That's why, when all this happened, I never questioned whether it was possible. I just knew it was real."

"Lucy, you've got me absolutely enthralled! When did all this start?" Jackie, caught up in the excitement of Lucy's mysterious romance, was eager to know all the details.

"Just a few months ago. Everything was going along pretty much as usual. Work was hectic, as always. I was spending most of my free time at home, either mucking about in the garden or painting, so everything was plain sailing. No stress, no problems—nothing to keep me awake at nights. And then it happened."

Jackie pulled her chair a little nearer. Propping her elbows on the table, she rested her chin on her upturned hands, listening with rapt attention.

"I was working on a picture—a scene that had just popped into my head for some reason. Anyway, you know how I like to listen to music while I'm painting; I'd gone to the library just to see what they'd got in the way of CDs. I picked up a couple of things: pieces by Rachmaninov, Wyndham, and some other stuff—I forget what. I was just about to leave when I saw this recording by someone called Nikolai Dvorkin. I'd never heard him sing before, but I seemed to recognize the name right away, so I scooped it up just out of curiosity and took it with the rest." Lucy stopped to take a sip of her rapidly-cooling coffee and went on.

"I didn't even bother to listen to it until a few days before it was due back, and I thought, 'Well, I'll give it a whirl.' I played the first few songs, but it wasn't my kind of thing at all; the language was totally incomprehensible, and the music very solemn and depressing. I turned it off and put the disc back in its case. There was an insert, a little booklet—you know the kind of thing. I thought I'd just take a look, because I couldn't for the life of me think how I'd come to recognize the name. There was a brief bio and some pictures of Dvorkin. Of course, they were pretty old; I could tell by the fashions. I remember thinking, 'Sorry, but you don't do anything for me,' and that was that. I put the disc back in the bag, ready to return to the library."

Jackie sipped at her coffee without taking her eyes off Lucy. Her friend continued, "The next day was Sunday, and I planned to spend the whole day on the painting. I wanted to get it finished, so I got everything set up and went to dig something out to listen to, and, God knows why, I took the Dvorkin disc out of the bag. It was like I felt some weird kind of compulsion to hear it again. 'Glutton for punishment,' I supposed. I played it while I was working, and this time, it didn't sound nearly so strange. When it was done, I played it again. I just sat and listened to it and…" Lucy shook her head.

"I can't begin to describe how I felt. It was as though…" She struggled to find the words. "I'd suddenly been brought back to life. I was filled with such a feeling of passion and excitement. Oh, Lord, this sounds so stupid." Lucy laughed at herself, biting her lip apprehensively. But when she saw that Jackie seemed to be taking the matter seriously, she went on.

"Even though I couldn't understand a word, it turned my whole world upside down. Naturally, I was curious to find out more about him. I searched and searched and finally located an ancient biography and read it from cover to cover. It was the strangest thing. Although I didn't know anything about him, when I came to certain parts, I found myself thinking, 'No, that's not how it happened,' or 'Yes, that's right, he did say that.' It was as though I should have been able to remember all those things but couldn't. And of course, I couldn't, because it had all happened so long ago, before I was even born. And yet, I knew I'd been there."

Lucy finished the last of her coffee and put the cup back on the table, dabbing at her lips with a paper napkin.

"The painting was forgotten. The garden looks like a jungle, and worst of all, I made several really bad mistakes at work, which got me into a huge row with the boss, hence the time off. He practically ordered me to take a break. I've spent every spare minute since looking for anything written about Dvorkin: newspaper and magazine articles, photos, portraits, anything. It's become an obsession, like a drug I can't live without. He's with me all the time. I wake up in the middle of the night thinking about him. There are moments when I feel he is so close that I could reach out and touch him, walk around any corner in the house and see him standing there. And there's one photo in particular. I brought it with me. Here." She reached into her purse, took out a much-thumbed picture, and slid it across the table to her friend.

"I found it quite by chance in an antiques shop in Swannington. Goodness knows how it came to be there, but when I saw it, I recognized the place immediately. I don't know who these people are, except Dvorkin of course, but I know this place,"—she tapped emphatically at the picture with her finger—"and I know this sounds crazy, but I'm certain I was there when this was taken."

Jackie studied the portrait, the sepia tones of which had faded over the years. It clearly showed a group of people posing happily together, with a large house covered in vines just visible in the background.

"That's Dvorkin in the middle alright," Jackie confirmed, nodding her head. "I have heard of him. I read an article in a music magazine once, and I remember there were a couple of pictures too. Wasn't he involved in some kind of scandal back in the late 1920s?"

"Yes, several, in fact, during the course of his lifetime," Lucy admitted.

Her friend looked more closely at the people in the picture. The central figure, a tall, fair-haired, middle-aged man with his head tilted back slightly as if he were laughing, had one arm around the shoulders of a much younger man and the other resting casually on those of a slim, bespectacled individual with a neatly trimmed beard. There were two women in the picture, both dressed in the fashion of the twenties.

"I'm not sure, but I think the older man next to him is the composer Neville Wyndham," Jackie said, pointing to the man with the beard.

"So that's him!" Lucy scrutinized the picture more closely. "I've often wondered what he looked like."

"Wyndham was a fairly prolific composer before Dvorkin's death, but afterwards he rather disappeared from sight. I don't think there was ever very much written about him, and not many pictures. He was, apparently, a very private person," Jackie remarked. "I don't recognize any of the others, except maybe…yes. The young one at the end. He looks a bit like the artist, Dimitri Gurvich. Whereabouts was this taken?" Jackie asked, turning the picture over but finding nothing to enlighten her.

"I'm not sure, but I do know that I've seen this house before. For years I've had dreams about the place. I've walked around it, inside and out. For instance, I know that just to the right there," Lucy indicated, "behind the house, through the trees in the distance, there's a stream, and just beyond it, a field. I've even painted a picture of it. And, of course, yes!" Lucy exclaimed animatedly. "It all makes sense. The idea came to me after I'd heard a piece of music written by this Neville Wyndham. We were all very happy. The weather was warm, and Nicky kept saying that he wished he could stay there forever." Lucy's expression was withdrawn now, as though she were miles away, recalling something that had happened in the past.

"You do remember it, then," Jackie said, becoming more and more intrigued by this bizarre story.

"No, that's the funny thing. It's a feeling more than a memory. It's like I'm living in a perpetual fog. I'm homesick for a place and time that, to all intents and purposes, I never knew.

Lucy unconsciously clenched her hands as though desperately trying to hold on to something or someone. "How can that be? How can you miss something or someone you've never known? The first time I read the account of his death in that old book, it hit me like a physical blow. I thought my heart would break I cried so much."

Jackie saw tears welling up in Lucy's eyes and reached across the table to clasp her hand. "Don't Luce. Don't upset yourself."

Lucy quickly rubbed her free hand across her face, brushing away the tears and recovering her composure.

"I know this must all sound absolutely idiotic to you. I sometimes think I'm losing my mind, but it's taken over my life so completely and has left me wanting so much more."

The sound of absolute defeat in the words spoken so dejectedly by her friend made Jackie wince involuntarily. The situation appeared so tragic in its impossibility. And yet Lucy seemed so convinced of its plausibility. Did she really believe that she had known this man in a former life? This was so unlike her friend's normally down-to-earth, practical self. Jackie desperately wanted to help but couldn't begin to imagine how she possibly could.

They ordered more coffee and sat for a while in silence, the noise of the traffic outside and the muted sounds of conversation from the people at the adjoining tables recalling them to the present. Then Jackie, who'd been cudgeling her brains to come up with a solution to the problem, suddenly had a flash of inspiration.

"I wonder…it's a wild idea, but…Jasper, Jasper Frakes."

"Who in the name of heaven is Jasper Frakes?" Lucy asked.

"Didn't I ever mention him to you? I took him on at the shop about six months ago," Jackie explained. "The sweetest little old man. I felt so sorry for him. He used to come in quite often to look at the books. Never bought anything, but I didn't mind. I thought he was on his beam ends, and it turned out I was right."

"He came in one day and asked me if I had any odd jobs he could do around the place, just to earn a bit of extra cash. I don't suppose the old age pension goes very far these days. Well, of course, normally Lionel would take care of any minor repairs at the shop, but at the time he was busy with the book, and I didn't want to bother him. As luck would have it there were a couple of shelves that needed putting up, and the tap in the back room was dripping like Niagara, so I told Jasper to come on in anytime and fix things up. We agreed on the payment, and he came back the next day."

Jackie stopped to take a sip of coffee. "He did such a good job, and then, to top it off, young Barry abandoned us to go back to school up in Manchester, which just left me with Theresa. So, I thought, why not give the old boy a permanent job if he wanted it? Nothing strenuous, of course—dusting and rearranging the books, sweeping the floor, helping out wherever needed. He was thrilled to bits with the idea, and for a while things worked out fine."

"He came in as regular as clockwork for a couple of months, but then he started missing odd days here and there. I did wonder if he had a bit of a drinking problem. He seemed a bit glassy-eyed sometimes when he came in, but he always had a reasonable excuse for the absences, and I didn't really have the heart to give him the boot. Then he didn't show up at all for a few days. Naturally, I called the number he'd given me. I was worried in case he was ill or had been in an accident. At that age, anything could happen. He didn't answer the phone; someone else did. I think he lives in a bed-sit, and they must have a pay phone there."

"Well, the man who answered the phone said that, as far as he knew, Jasper was alright. He'd seen him that morning. Of course, I was rather miffed that he hadn't got in touch with me, so I asked this man if he would give Jasper a message. I told him to say that if Jasper didn't want the job anymore to let me know and I'd get someone else to replace him. I didn't hear anything for a couple of days, and then, when my patience had just about run out, he called. He was very apologetic, said he was sorry that he'd let me down, was thankful for the opportunity but he just didn't think he could handle the responsibilities of the job anymore. Well, I didn't want to press him, poor old soul. He said if I ever needed any help fixing anything, I should give him a call; he'd be happy to come and help, but he just couldn't cope with coming into the shop on a regular basis anymore."

"And have you seen him since?" Lucy asked, wondering where all this was leading.

"Oh yes. He still comes in from time to time, just to look at the books, and I find something every once in a while for him to do. Anyway, getting back to the nub and crux of the matter, when Jasper first came to work at the shop, he and I were just sitting chit-chatting about this and that, and we got on to talking about the theater. He told me that many years ago he had actually 'trod the boards,' as he put it, in the old-time music halls, as a conjurer, of all things. He was absolutely fascinating. After that, we often talked about the old days, and once, he mentioned that as part of his act he had done some hypnotism. I've always been more than a bit skeptical about all that stuff, but he made it sound very convincing. He even offered to try it on me, and just for a laugh, I gave it a shot."

"Well, it wasn't a total success, but I think that was probably because I didn't really believe he could do it. Anyway, what I'm getting at is, why not let him try? It's a well-documented fact that these people can sometimes take you back into past-life experiences."

"Yes, qualified professionals maybe, but not some crackpot music-hall turn," Lucy said doubtfully.

"But it might work," Jackie persisted. "What have you got to lose? Look, I'll give you his phone number. Give him a call. He might tell you outright that he can't do it, but at least give him a chance."

"Well, I suppose it couldn't hurt to try." Lucy agreed rather dubiously. And with that, they gathered their shopping bags together and headed back to the Shellabys' house in Chelsea.

* * *

That night, when they were alone together in their bedroom, Lionel asked his wife if Lucy had told her anything further regarding the reason for her visit. Although Lucy was in a room further down the hallway, they spoke in lowered voices for fear of being overheard.

"Yes." Jackie confided to her husband. "It's quite a strange tale, actually, and coming from anyone else, I might be inclined to laugh or think they were deranged. But I know Lucy too well to suspect anything like that, and I'm sure there's something in it. But she does need help, Lionel."

"Is it a man?"

"How perceptive of you! Yes."

"Ah! And there's a problem?"

"Yes."

"Married?"

"Yes, but that's not the half of it."

"Oh dear. Well, naturally I'd like to help if I can, but you'll have to be a bit more specific. Could it possibly have something to do with age difference?" Lionel continued as if he were playing *Twenty Questions*.

"You could say that." Jackie caught his mood, kept the ball rolling, playing the game.

"No!" Lionel looked shocked. "A lot younger? Good Lord! Lucy's got a toy-boy stashed away." He burst out laughing, and Jackie reached across, clamping her hand over his mouth.

"Shh! For goodness' sake, idiot! This is serious. No, he's not younger; a good bit older in fact, but that isn't it either."

Lionel looked mystified. "You've lost me, dear girl. What on earth's the problem? Does his family object? Or is he in jail? My God! He's not a murderer, is he?" Lionel speculated, his guesses becoming wilder as Jackie shook her head, finally digging him in the ribs with her elbow to bring him to order.

"Help me out here," her husband capitulated. "I'm running out of options."

"He's dead."

Lionel looked at her in amazement.

"Dead? Jackie, dear, are you having me on? Are you telling me some kind of joke because, if so, I have to admit, I'm not getting it?"

"No Lionel. There's no joke; no funny punch line. It really is quite sad."

"I'm sorry." Lionel, seeing that his wife was taking this seriously, apologized. "I didn't mean to make light of it," he told her contritely. "Tell me all about it and I promise I'll listen. I'll be good as gold and not make any more silly comments."

"Well, alright. But remember to keep an open mind. This is Lucy's life we're talking about and I have the most awful feeling that if we don't help her, she may do something drastic."

Lionel was suitably chastened. As Jackie related Lucy's story, he listened in silence, shaking his head occasionally and frowning.

"Well, you're right, my love," he said when she finished. "Coming from anyone else, I would have said she was out of her mind. But Lucy is as sane as you or I, which isn't saying much, I agree, but there's definitely a ring of truth to it. I just don't really see what we can do to help."

"I did suggest something to her."

"And what was that, my little genius?"

"Jasper Frakes."

Lionel couldn't help laughing again.

"Jasper? I think you're losing it, old girl. What the devil has he got to do with it?"

"You can mock, but I happen to think it was a brilliant idea. You remember me telling you about his former career as a magician in the music halls and how he did hypnosis. Well, I suggested to Lucy that she try regression through hypnosis. Some people claim they can take you back to a previous life by that method."

"And you think a poor old soak like Jasper Frakes could pull it off? Really Jackie! That's asking a bit much."

"Oh, I know you think he's a joke, but there's a lot more to Jasper than meets the eye. He may only be an old music-hall has-been now, but he was—*is*—an intelligent man."

"If he was so intelligent, what was he doing wasting his time pulling rabbits out of hats and making people believe they were chickens? No, my dear girl. Face it, your protégée turned out to be nothing more than a *tuppenny-ha'penny* vaudeville turn with an alcohol problem; good at fixing shelves and sweeping the floor, granted, but as a solution to Lucy's problem, a dead duck, I'm afraid."

"I don't know. I have more faith in him than that. Anyway, I told her to think it over and give him a call. It's worth a try."

"I'm not so sure. It could do more harm than good."

"We'll see," Jackie said confidently as she turned off the bedside light.

But Lionel's skepticism had dampened her enthusiasm. By the morning, she began to wonder if she had done the right thing by suggesting it.

Whereas the night had only served to sow doubt in Jackie's mind, it had nourished the hope in Lucy's heart that this might be the solution to her problem.

The next morning, while Jackie was busy with some unavoidable household chores, Lucy called the number that her friend had given her.

7

A LEAP OF FAITH

THE OLD MAN HEARD THE PHONE RINGING out in the hallway and waited to see if the man from 1b would pick it up. It continued its strident jangling. Sighing, he grudgingly left the comfort and security of his armchair and went with unhurried steps to the door. He cautiously opened it and looked out to see if anyone was disposed to answer the summons. There seemed to be no one else available, however, so he shuffled out into the hallway and, reaching the pay phone on the wall, picked up the receiver and put it gingerly to his ear.

"Hello. Jasper Frakes here," he volunteered mildly at first, then, receiving no reply, raised his voice slightly. "Hello? Hello?" And finally, all attempts at politeness abandoned, he asked, "Is anyone there? Dammit!" His agitated query was met with silence, and yet he sensed that someone was there at the other end of the line.

He heard a small, nervous cough. "Yes…Yes, I'm sorry, Mr. Frakes. My name is Lucy. Lucy Welbourne. I'm a friend of Mrs. Shellaby. She gave me your number."

"Oh, yes?" There was a pause while he processed the information. "Well, what can I do for you, Ms. Welbourne?"

"Mrs. Shellaby happened to mention to me that you did hypnosis at one time."

"Mm…Yes." He seemed reluctant to make the admission. "I may have done, a long time ago. Not anymore."

"Oh." She sounded disappointed.

"Are you interested in the subject, Ms. Welbourne?" Frakes couldn't help asking, despite his habitual caution.

"I...I'm sorry. I think I've made a mistake. Sorry. Sorry."

She rang off, leaving Frakes still holding onto the receiver, annoyed that he had been disturbed for nothing. Yet, there was the tiniest seed of curiosity about the person who hadn't really made a mistake, he was quite certain, but had just lacked the courage to speak up.

* * *

Jasper Frakes was apparently ageless, a relic of a time long past when there had been no such thing as television, women's lib, or travel by jet plane. He could converse on any subject yet conveyed all the innocence of childhood. One-time music-hall act, part conjurer, part mind-reader, and, as some would say, mostly charlatan, he had been determined to make a name for himself. *Could have done, let's face it,* he told himself a million times, if he hadn't made that one little mistake.

But then, it wasn't really so little, was it, Jasper old boy? It cost someone their life. The bright promise of a glorious and rewarding future came crashing down in what seemed like the twinkling of an eye. And now, here he was, penny-pinching and cheese-paring to make ends meet, playing out the rest of his life in this tawdry little flat when things could have been so much different.

At least Mrs. Shellaby had given him a chance to recover some of his dignity, giving him a job at the bookshop dusting the shelves and helping out at the counter sometimes. *But what on earth was she thinking, giving his number out to people?* He told her about the old music-hall act in confidence. *Couldn't women ever use what little brains God had given them?*

He had just settled himself back into the armchair by the fire when the phone rang again. He was tempted to just ignore it, but his curiosity got the better of him. He shuffled out into the hallway once more, irritably picking up the receiver and clapping it to his ear.

"Hello. Jasper Frakes here."

"Hello, Mr. Frakes. This is Lucy Welbourne."

He felt his temper rising once more. "Now look, Ms. Welbourne, I don't know what it is you want, but—"

She cut him off abruptly, needing to get the words out before she lost her nerve again. "I want to come and see you." When he didn't reply, she persisted, "Did you hear me, Mr. Frakes?"

"Yes. I heard. What exactly is it that you want?"

"I can't talk about it on the phone. I need to come and see you."

Who on earth was this lunatic that Mrs. Shellaby was sending him? Frakes wondered. He wanted to just hang up the phone. Common sense warned him that this wasn't something with which he should get involved. *But...what the hell! When had common sense ever played a major role in his life?* Besides, he would never be able to sleep tonight, wondering what the blasted woman wanted.

"Alright. Can you get over here tonight?" He half hoped she would say no and was surprised by her prompt acquiescence.

"What time?"

"Oh, well..." He seemed to be giving the matter some consideration. "I've got some things to take care of," he lied, stalling for time. Even now, he was having second thoughts. "How about nine o'clock, or is that too late?"

"No, I'll be there. I know you live south of the river, but Mrs. Shellaby didn't give me your address."

Frakes gave her the address with a little sigh of resignation.

"Okay, got it. Thank you, Mr. Frakes. I'll see you at nine."

Lucy was determined to see things through, strictly on her own terms and with as little fuss as possible. After much discussion and argument, she declined Lionel's well-intentioned offer to drive her to Jasper Frakes's home that evening, electing instead to make the comparatively short journey by bus.

"How about I pick you up when you're finished then?" Lionel had persisted, unwilling to abandon Lucy entirely to public transportation.

But Lucy put her foot down, confidently insisting that she could very well take care of herself and manage the return trip to Chelsea with no problem. As usual, her obstinacy proved insurmountable.

* * *

Carmichael Street, unlike many of the surrounding thoroughfares that had benefited from urban renewal, was ill lit and run down. The rows of terraced houses on either side, shabby remnants of the late 1800s, had somehow been overlooked in the grand scheme of things, like rotten teeth in an otherwise healthy mouth. They were badly in need of restoration or, more realistically, extraction.

Lucy wondered how long the local residents could possibly cling to their present existence before they were compelled to leave. It was surely only a matter of time before these dilapidated homes were torn down to make way for more up-to-date and outrageously high-priced accommodations. The majority of lower-income tenants, many of whom had lived in the neighborhood most of their lives, would be forced to relocate. Progress was all very well, she thought bitterly, but it had little regard for the feelings of those who were displaced as a result.

The air was damp and insinuating. A thin, chilly mist had descended shortly after nightfall, blurring the rows of broken-down, banged-up cars that lined either side of the road—a sorry collection of dented and rusty vehicles that, like the buildings, had seen better days.

Somewhere nearby, a cat—disturbed in its nightly perusal of the contents of a partially covered garbage can—meowed fractiously. The metal lid of the can gave a discordant clang as it crashed to the ground. The sudden noise, piercing an otherwise unbroken silence, made Lucy jump skittishly as she slowly made her way along the deserted street, seeking the house number.

She found the address with some difficulty. The numbers on the houses were either missing or small and hard to read from her vantage point on the pavement. She stood, looking up at the grimy facade with its dirty windows and faded paintwork, wondering if she hadn't made the most horrible mistake in seeking out Jasper Frakes. She debated whether to go ahead with her plan or just return to Chelsea without troubling him, when the choice was abruptly taken out of her hands.

A gang of youths, making a rowdy exit from the pub on the corner, began heading in her direction. Instinct told Lucy that, given their obvious state of intoxication, it would probably be safer to walk up the steps and ring the doorbell than stay out there, alone and vulnerable, on the pavement. Consequently, a few seconds later, she found herself looking down at an elderly man with old-fashioned wire-rimmed spectacles perched precariously on the end of his nose. He opened the door almost immediately, as though he'd been waiting on the other side in eager anticipation of her summons.

"Mr. Frakes?" Lucy asked uncertainly.

He pushed the glasses closer to his clouded blue eyes and peered at her myopically.

"Yes." He gave a slight cough, discreetly clearing his throat. "Ms. Welbourne? Please, come in."

He stood to one side, allowing her to pass. She squeezed by him into the narrow, poorly lit hallway that smelled strongly of fried food and stale cigarette smoke.

"I thought you might not come," he confided softly, closing the door behind them and shutting out the sound of the passing revelers as they made their way singing and shouting along Carmichael Street.

"Oh? Why?" Lucy asked, feeling somewhat ill at ease in the cramped and unfamiliar surroundings.

"Well, you don't know me," Frakes offered candidly. "It's late. In a strange house...who knows? It puts you at rather a disadvantage, wouldn't you say?"

He looked back at her over his shoulder. "And you did sound rather hesitant on the phone," he added, leading her down the passageway. They edged past a pram and a bicycle propped precariously against the wall underneath a payphone.

Lucy tried to sound self-assured as she followed him. "I was willing to take a chance. And besides," she countered, wondering why she suddenly felt the need to bolster her drooping confidence in the presence of this seemingly innocuous senior citizen, "Mrs. Shellaby said you were a very nice man."

He laughed wheezily. "Mrs. Shellaby doesn't know me that well, but tell her I said, 'thank you' for the compliment."

He ushered her inside a small, one-room apartment, whose only light appeared to emanate from a lamp. He indicated an armchair drawn close to the meager warmth exuded by an ancient, hissing gas fire. Lucy sat down, not certain that what he had just said made her feel any more comfortable.

Frakes followed her, and taking up a position on the opposite side of the fireplace, stood pensively looking down at feet comfortably encased in well-worn carpet slippers. Lucy noted the old, grey cardigan he wore had holes at the elbows.

Neither spoke for a moment, then as if to break the ice, "Cigarette?" he asked. Reaching into his trouser pocket, he produced a crumpled packet and offered it to her.

Lucy shook her head. "No, thanks anyway."

"Do you mind if I...?" He fiddled with the wrapping and held a somewhat battered cigarette up to his lips.

"Go ahead." Although she didn't smoke herself, Lucy felt she was hardly in a position to dictate what the man did in his own home. All the same, she appreciated the old-fashioned and uncommon courtesy that he showed in asking her permission. How many men bothered with that, these days?

Taking her at her word, he retrieved a box of matches from the mantlepiece. He lit up, drawing the smoke deep into his lungs, coughing asthmatically as he moved away from his post by the fireside. He went over to a ramshackle kitchen table covered by a dirty, red and white checkered cloth littered with greasy plates and the remains of what looked like a Chinese take-away meal.

He stood with his back to her, fiddling with something on the table. Lucy could hear the clink of glasses as she looked inquisitively around. She noticed with something akin to embarrassment, in the darkest recesses of the farther side of the room, a narrow, unmade bed with what seemed to be an old overcoat thrown over the thin covers for extra warmth.

"Would you care for a drink?" he asked hospitably, in a voice that Lucy noticed for the first time was that of a man well-educated and articulate. She found herself wondering what strange twist of fate had led him to his present situation.

"I've only got a couple of bottles of brown ale, I'm afraid, but you're welcome to one if you'd like it." He turned and held the bottles up for her inspection.

"No, thanks anyway," Lucy politely declined.

"Just as you like."

He put down one of the bottles and opened the other, pouring its contents into a glass that still contained the remnants of an earlier drink. He returned to the fireside and sat down slowly, facing Lucy, perched on the edge of his chair, glass in one hand and a cigarette in the other.

"Not exactly Dom Pérignon," he said, looking ruefully at the glass, then added philosophically, "But beggars can't be choosers."

He swallowed a mouthful of the brew and drew on his cigarette once more before declaring, "So, Ms. Welbourne, let's get down to business. What is it that you want from me?"

Despite his gentle voice and apparently amiable disposition, Lucy found herself rather disconcerted by the old man's sudden forthrightness. He was wasting no time in getting down to brass tacks.

"I was hoping you could put me under hypnosis," she stated succinctly, feeling that the sooner she made her reason for being there clear, the better.

Frakes felt an unaccustomed tingle of excitement. *Well, it couldn't hurt, could it?* he asked himself guardedly. And he was getting desperate. Despite his meager pension and the extra money that he made at the book shop and other occasional odd jobs, he was in serious danger of not paying his rent again, and the landlord was not a patient man.

And there was his little addiction. If pressed to make a choice, he would willingly have sacrificed everything—beer, cigarettes, even this pathetic rat hole that he called home—before he gave up what had become an overwhelming necessity to him these past many years.

He put the glass down carefully on the floor beside him, sat further back until his head touched the old-fashioned antimacassar draped over the back of the chair, and slowly tapped his fingers on the threadbare upholstery of the arm.

"Are you trying to quit smoking or lose weight, perhaps?" He looked at her, considering the possibilities, and then answered his own question before she could speak. "No, obviously neither of those things."

"I need to find out something about my past," Lucy told him.

Frakes crushed the partially smoked cigarette into an ashtray already brimming with dogends.

"I see," he murmured, still tapping his fingers as though marking off the seconds with the pendulum of the clock that stood on the mantlepiece, the third hand ticking relentlessly past the numbers on the dial.

"You want to know something about your childhood?" he asked cautiously. *Oh Lord!* he thought with sinking spirits. Was she one of those people you read about so often in the newspapers these days who thought they'd been sexually abused by their parents, parish priest, or fourth-grade gym teacher? Looking for reasons and excuses—solutions to who knew what kind of problems.

"No, further back." She looked at him, hoping he would understand. "I want to know who I was."

A gratifying thrill of recognition seized him: a kindred spirit—more than that, his possible salvation. He could hardly bring himself to ask the question for fear he misunderstood.

"In a previous life, you mean?"

"Can you do it?"

He appeared to be thinking, carefully weighing the question before making his reply. "That's rather a tall order, Ms. Welbourne."

He looked more closely at the not unattractive middle-aged woman sitting across from him. She seemed a sensible enough person—not without a pound or two in the bank either, he thought speculatively. He was not, however, an imprudent man, and if nothing else, life had taught him to view such a gift horse with a certain amount of circumspection.

Steady now. Let's not rush into things, he cautioned himself. Did he really want to share this uncanny gift? He'd never done so before. For so many years, he had jealously guarded the entrance to that other world. He kept the secret locked safe within him, never disclosing to another living soul the method by which he slipped so often and so effortlessly from his dreary, pathetic existence in the present to the pleasurably exciting life of the past.

But then he'd never needed the money quite as badly as he did now.

"But you can do it?" she broke into his thoughts.

Frakes remained non-committal. "Is it really so important to you?"

"I've never been more serious about anything in my life."

"Can I ask what makes you feel so strongly about finding out?" he asked inquisitively.

Lucy didn't reply immediately, once again finding it hard to put her thoughts into words. Frakes sat waiting patiently.

"Something happened to me a few months ago. A voice...it's difficult to explain."

Frakes shook his head almost imperceptibly. "Oh dear." He sounded disappointed—let down. "Hearing voices." He sighed. "It sounds, if you'll forgive my saying so, my dear, as if you might be better off consulting...well...a psychiatrist." He looked at her, not totally without sympathy, and she took heart from this small sign of compassion.

"No. It's not what you think." She would have to tell him everything she supposed. Well, she was prepared to do that anyway, wasn't she?

"It's like this, Mr. Frakes." She leaned forward confidingly. "I recently came across a recording of a singer—someone I'd never heard before, although I'd heard *of* him. And the more I listened, the more certain I became that I'd known this man."

"Maybe you had heard him before," he suggested kindly, "but just didn't remember it."

"No, no. It was more than that, I'm sure."

"Start at the beginning," he encouraged her. "Tell me exactly what happened."

"At first, when I heard him, it didn't register. I didn't think to myself, 'I know this man!' I didn't even really enjoy listening to him that much, not at first. There was a picture of him, and even that didn't ring any bells. In fact, I thought he was rather—oh I don't know—not ugly exactly, but well, not my type, anyway. But I found myself playing the disc over and over, and the more I listened to it the more I began to realize just how beautiful it sounded. I listened to him, Mr. Frakes, and found myself experiencing emotions, longings that I haven't felt for quite some time."

She suddenly looked embarrassed, but Frakes urged her to continue.

"Go on, my dear." He smiled at her avuncularly. "Don't be afraid. You can tell me everything."

Unaccountably, Lucy felt, despite their short acquaintance, that she could trust him and went on with more confidence. "I can't actually remember anything that happened between us, but I'm as certain as I've ever been of anything in *this* life, that there is something there that I should remember."

Hallelujah! Saved by the bell! Frakes thought with overwhelming relief. But just to be sure, he prodded and probed further, shaking the idea like a terrier worrying a rat.

"Are you certain there isn't a possibility that you may have met him, maybe only for a moment, but long enough for it to have left a lasting impression?"

Lucy shook her head emphatically. "No. It's not possible. You see, this man died long before I was born."

The old man digested this piece of information for a moment, his interest now becoming evident in spite of his desire to be cautious.

"I see," he said, rubbing his fingers thoughtfully against his jaw. "Interesting. And you believe that you knew this man in a previous life, is that it?"

"Yes, but I need to be sure. I have to know that it's not just my imagination—that I'm not going mad."

"Quite."

Lucy watched anxiously as he appeared to wrestle inwardly with an almost insurmountable dilemma.

"It's an interesting proposition, but—"

"I'm willing to pay. I don't expect you to do it for nothing, of course."

And there it was, the deciding factor, but still he wasn't ready to commit to anything. He smiled and held up a cautionary hand. "I haven't said yet that I can do it."

"But you can, can't you, Mr. Frakes?" She was beginning to sound desperate, but he was not quite ready to land his fish just yet.

"It's possible." More thought. *Be careful now, Jasper old lad,* he told himself.

"Are you married?" he asked suddenly.

Lucy was surprised by the question and wondered apprehensively why he needed to know.

"No, divorced."

"Children?"

"Two," she told him, then thought with alarm, *Stop! Why are you telling him all this?* But she couldn't arrest the urge to speak. It was as though she'd started running down a steep slope and couldn't hold up.

"Live at home, do they?" he continued to question her.

"No. My son lives in Swannington. My daughter moved to Cheltenham. I'm quite alone, Mr. Frakes." And again, she silently berated herself, *FOOL! IDIOT!*

"Do they know about this—experience—shall we call it?"

"No."

"Does anyone know?"

"Only Mrs. Shellaby. She's my closest friend. I've known her since we were children. We don't see too much of each other these days, but we keep in touch. I'm staying with her this week; naturally, I told her all about it and she gave me your number. She said that you'd done some hypnotism in the past and might be able to help me."

"Yes," he mused. "Nice lady." Then suddenly he changed course and his next question startled her.

"Do you suffer from depression, Ms. Welbourne?"

It was as though he'd hit a button and detonated a bomb within her head. Long-suppressed images of her mother, lying lifeless on the bed, flashed before her, the well-remembered face peaceful in its final repose.

"No!"

She vehemently pushed the suggestion and the thoughts aside. Then, realizing with dismay that now that they'd been summoned up, these morbid recollections would refuse to remain concealed, she relented.

"At least, not depression, no. But just lately, an empty feeling; a sense of being left behind. It's hard to describe, but it's as though when this man died, he took away everything that meant anything to me and I'm only just now beginning to feel it. Can you understand that, Mr. Frakes?"

He didn't answer her immediately, and she wondered if she'd made a total fool of herself.

"I know I'm not making myself very clear," she apologized.

"No, no. I understand, absolutely," he assured her. *Oh, I know alright!* "Perhaps we could begin by talking a little bit about this man, this singer. Who was he?"

"His name was Nikolai Dvorkin."

Frakes appeared momentarily taken aback, as though the name held some special significance for him. Then he gave a chuckle and she suddenly felt extremely silly and adolescent.

He realized his mistake and hastened to reassure her. "Oh, I'm not laughing at you, Ms. Welbourne," he explained. "Or may I call you Lucy?" he asked, trying to recover lost ground, mend broken fences. She nodded but remained disconcerted by his amusement.

"It's just such an amazing coincidence." He almost couldn't believe it himself. *What a stroke of luck!* Maybe he was destined to help her after all.

He got somewhat unsteadily to his feet, shambled over to the bed, kneeling down beside it with considerable effort as though about to recite a litany of night-time prayers, and retrieved something from beneath the metal framework.

Lucy couldn't make out what he was doing, but when Frakes returned, she saw that he was carrying a stack of old records in dusty, yellowing paper sleeves.

He put them down on the little table that stood beside her chair, brushing away a stubbornly clinging dust bunny from his sleeve and picking up a disc from the top of the pile, holding it out for her inspection.

"Is this him?"

Her heart leapt as it always did, even at the sight of the name of the man who had taken over her life so completely. "Yes! Yes, that's him! How extraordinary!"

"Ha! Nicky Dvorkin!" the old man exclaimed reminiscently. "He's been a favorite of mine for a long, long time as you can see." He nodded towards the collection of recordings.

He was still thanking his lucky stars or his guardian angel or whatever else it was that had prompted him to obtain and listen to Dvorkin's recordings on an old wind-up gramophone that he had purchased with the proceeds from an unexpected windfall at the race track many years ago.

But now, he felt, was not the time to tell her that particular story. Nevertheless, he felt obliged to give her some explanation of his coincidental knowledge of the man.

"I remember my father talking about him once. I didn't become familiar with his work until I was in my forties, rather like yourself."

"Now you're flattering me, Mr. Frakes. I'm fifty-eight."

"Well, that's hard to believe." *A little flattery never hurt, and besides, it was true— she didn't look her age.*

"Thank you." Lucy found herself ridiculously pleased by this piece of badinage and felt as though she were blushing, but he quickly brought her down to earth.

"Not a bit of it." He dismissed her gratitude airily with a wave of the hand.

"Now, this impression you have of knowing him—you have no definite memory you say?"

"No, although I seem to feel that he was no longer a young man. Nothing that I read of his earlier life seemed familiar to me, but as I came to events that occurred when he was forty or so, that was when I had this feeling; such a strong sense that I'd been there, that we'd met."

"And much more, I'm guessing." the old man remarked intuitively.

"Yes." Once again, she felt her cheeks color and she looked down at her hands. "I have an overwhelming sensation of loving and being loved by this man," she admitted.

"Ah, love!" the old man ruminated. It was enough to cloud any person's thinking. Had she really known him, or had she merely become infatuated, as so many others had done before her, with that magical voice?

Lucy went on to explain about the dreams and the photo of the house and he let her go on without interruption, listening with rapt attention until she'd finished.

"So, will you help me Mr. Frakes?"

"I might be able to."

"Oh, thank you, thank you!"

"Wait a minute." *Now he wasn't so sure. Was it worth the risk?* "Don't jump the gun," he admonished her gently. "I haven't said yes, yet."

"Please! Please, Mr. Frakes! Won't you help me?"

She sounded desperate, poor woman, and he knew without a doubt that he could help her. Maybe he would chance it. *After all, it had worked for him, hadn't it?*

"Alright," he consented. "But I must ask you to accede to a few minor points first."

"Anything!" Lucy blurted out rashly, then thought with dismay, *Oh God! What have I let myself in for? Did he want sex? Or something more perverted? Did he want her to kill someone or rob a bank, she speculated wildly?*

"Well, to begin with, you mustn't tell anyone about coming here—for now anyway."

"But what about Mrs. Shellaby? She knows."

"That's alright, but you must tell her not to say anything about it to anyone else. It'll just be our little secret for a while, till we see how things go."

"Well…"

Was she going to be difficult? "We're not off to a very good start, Ms. Welbourne. If you can't agree to that, then I'm afraid it's not on."

"I'm sorry, yes, alright." Lucy relented, thinking, *anything, anything!*

"Good! Then there's the little matter of my fee." Here was the giant leap of faith. *Would she take it? Would she be willing to accept the risk?* He named a sum. "For the initial sitting, not quite so much for every sitting after that." Mentally he kept his fingers crossed. *Had he priced himself out of the market? Well, in for a penny, in for a pound, as the old saying went, or several hundred pounds, if he was lucky.*

"But what if it's unsuccessful?" Lucy was aghast at the sum and, moreover, suddenly dubious about Frakes's abilities. It seemed like an awful lot of money to squander on such an unpredictable venture.

The old man, feeling that his whole future—what was left of it—was hanging in the balance, took the bull by the horns. At least she hadn't rejected his terms outright. There was still hope.

"I'm afraid you'll have to take a chance on that, Ms. Welbourne. The money is non-refundable, of course." He lifted his shoulders, his hands held out before him in supplication. "After all, how do I know for sure if I've been successful? I will only have your word for what you see and hear. No," he was adamant, "those are my terms, take them or leave them as you please."

"Alright."

"Good. Now we're getting somewhere. There's just one other thing."

Here it comes. Here comes the bad part—the part I don't want to hear, Lucy thought, biting her lip anxiously, her fingers digging unconsciously into the arm of the chair.

"My methods are, I have to admit, somewhat unorthodox."

Her heart sank, but only momentarily, for Frakes, realizing that she was beginning to waver, went quickly on to explain. "Many years ago, I made a fortunate discovery—a formula that I believe aids my clients in their travels into the past."

He looked at her with what he hoped was an appearance of supreme confidence. Inwardly, however, he was experiencing more than a little twinge of guilt. *Frakes! You shocking old fraud! What clients? And a formula? Well, yes, but something that up until now he had mercifully tried on no one other than himself.*

"A small concoction, quite innocuous I assure you, prior to hypnosis seems to clarify the picture, so to speak."

"If all you're offering me are drug-induced hallucinations, Mr. Frakes, I'm afraid I'm not interested." Lucy made as if to get up, but he waved her back into her seat, putting his bony hand on her arm in an attempt to keep her there long enough to proffer an explanation.

"Look, I could tell you exactly what's in this harmless little potion of mine, but I doubt very much if you'd be any the wiser. And before you ask, yes, I do know what I'm doing."

Never before had he felt the need to reveal the well-kept secrets of his past, but now the situation demanded at least a partial admission of the truth.

"The fact is, Ms. Welbourne, I have had some previous experience as a medical man."

She looked surprised. "Mrs. Shellaby never mentioned—"

"No, well, she wouldn't have. I never told her and," he added as an afterthought, pointing a warning finger at her, "you're not to either." He looked at her, trying to gauge her reaction to this admonition as he recognized the familiar look of suspicion creep across her face. He'd seen it before in others, on the extremely rare occasions when, in the grip of drink and an unwholesome melancholy, he had partially betrayed his own confidences.

"I don't think I—" Lucy sounded apprehensive.

"It just wasn't what I really wanted to do with my life," he cut her off. "But people always seem to jump to the wrong conclusion; think you've been struck off for groping the patients or something equally offensive."

Lucy flushed. "I'm sorry," she said contritely. "I didn't mean to imply—"

But Frakes went on as though he hadn't heard her. "My family expected great things of me. My grandfather and father, both medical men, were highly regarded in their chosen fields, and naturally, it was assumed that I would follow in their footsteps. I tried not to disappoint them, but it was no good. You see, I had already lost my heart to another calling. I was in love with the theater, entertainment, and especially the world of magic. It was all I wanted to do, and after studying with some of the greatest names in the business, I realized my ambition and took my place on the stage. Naturally, my parents were appalled by my decision; my father disowned me. My mother never forgave me." That at least was true. "But I was determined to live my life the way I wanted. Made quite a name for myself too," he added with pride, starting to get into the spirit of the thing, almost believing the story that he was telling.

"Top billing." He looked with self-satisfaction at his visitor and then once more felt his conscience pricking.

Stretching the truth a bit there, aren't we? the little voice in his head reprimanded. *More than a little embroidery, Jasper, old boy.*

"But," he broke off, recalling himself from this masterly piece of fabrication, "Where was I? Oh yes. I think I can promise that you will be amazed by the results." He tried to ignore that little voice of conscience, successfully blocking it out, banishing it temporarily from his mind. "But you're going to have to trust me. If this means as much to you as you say, a little bit of trust is a small price to pay."

"And the fee," Lucy reminded him. *Yes, let's not forget the fee,* she thought cynically.

"Believe me, dear lady, you won't be sorry." Jasper's whole demeanor gave the impression of someone who considered the money aspect of little or no importance. "Look, I understand your hesitancy, naturally. If you want to go away and think about it, by all means do so. Let me know by tomorrow evening, shall we say? But remember, tell no one what you're contemplating or I will not be able to help you."

"Alright," Lucy agreed, standing up to take her leave. "Thank you, Mr. Frakes. I'll think about it." She held out her hand to him, and he took it in his own gnarled and slightly arthritic fingers.

"I appreciate you giving me your time," she told him.

"Time. Why, yes. Of course," Frakes muttered, thinking that he could give her all the time in the world, if she would only let him. "It was a pleasure, my dear. I don't get to enjoy too much company here these days."

He peered into her face and tried to read what was there, unable to tell whether she was merely humoring him. He'd been able to do it once, many years ago; tell just what people were thinking. It wasn't so easy nowadays.

He opened the door for her and led her back down the hallway to the front door.

"It's rather late. Will you be alright?" he asked, feeling guilty for making her come out at such an hour.

"I think so," Lucy reassured him, although she had been somewhat alarmed herself when, looking at the clock on the mantelpiece, she realized that she had stayed much longer than anticipated. "I'll get a taxi back to Chelsea."

"Well, if you're sure. Goodnight Ms. Welbourne."

She stepped out onto the path and turned to say goodnight, but he had already closed the door.

* * *

When Lucy returned to Chelsea, she found Jackie waiting up for her and guessed that her friend was anxious to hear what had happened.

"So how did it go?" Jackie asked as soon as they settled down in the living room with a welcome nightcap.

Lucy felt weary and perplexed. She would have liked nothing better than to go straight to bed to continue mulling over her strange conversation with Jasper Frakes. However, she felt that she owed Jackie some explanation of the evening's events.

"He thinks he can help. I just have to decide if I want to go ahead with it."

"Will you try it? What did he say?" Jackie fired at her, bursting with curiosity. Then, recalling her husband's pessimistic warnings, she added more cautiously, "Do be careful, Luce. I'm beginning to regret telling you about him."

"Don't worry," Lucy assured her, though she was far from convinced herself. "It's alright, honestly. I think he's quite genuine, though he *is* a strange little man, isn't he?"

"Yes, I thought so." Jackie agreed. "Something about him." She mused, tantalizingly torn between encouraging Lucy on the one hand and dissuading her from pursuing her proposed course of action on the other.

"I'm willing to give it a go, anyway." Lucy was resolved. "It's just that he's asked me not to tell anyone about what I'm doing."

"Mm, that sounds a bit shady, doesn't it? I mean, why the secrecy? I don't know about this, Lucy."

"He knows that you know about it. He didn't seem to mind that."

"Well, all the same. Do you want me to come with you?" Jackie asked.

"Heavens, no!" Lucy quickly dismissed the idea, but seeing her friend's disappointment, she added, "I really don't think that would be a good idea.

Jasper wouldn't like it, I'm sure. No, I'll be alright, honestly. At least you know where I am—who I'm with. I don't think he has anything sinister planned. So long as he doesn't have me believing I'm a chicken or something."

They both laughed, though Lucy suspected that her friend wasn't entirely convinced.

"Will you call him tomorrow?"

"Yes," Lucy answered firmly. For better or worse, she'd made up her mind to trust Jasper Frakes, and the sooner she began this bizarre experiment, the better.

8

CROSSING THE BRIDGE

EARLY THE NEXT MORNING, Lucy dialed the number she'd called before, but when someone finally answered, she didn't recognize the voice at the other end. It wasn't Frakes but a younger man, sounding rough and bleary.

"Yeah. 'old on a minute. I'll get 'im." She could clearly hear him hammering on Frakes's door and shouting, "Frakes! You miserable old bugger! PHONE!"

She waited a minute or so, then heard someone pick up the receiver.

"Hello, Mr. Frakes?"

"Yes. Lucy? Have you decided?"

"Yes."

"And?"

"I agree to everything."

"Excellent. I thought you would." Frakes sounded delighted and supremely self-confident.

"When should I come over there?"

"Well, we might as well get started as soon as possible. Um…do you have the money?" he asked, as if it were an afterthought.

"Yes."

"Then shall we say this afternoon? Will four o'clock be alright?"

"Fine."

"Good. I'll see you then, Lucy, and remember, mum's the word."

"Yes, of course."

When she hung up, Lucy realized with consternation that her palms were damp and her heart racing.

Lucy hadn't told the Shellabys about the money or the fact that she'd agreed unconditionally to Jasper Frakes's other more sinister stipulation, preferring to keep his use of a possibly dangerous drug to herself.

She was confident that when her friend had suggested consulting Frakes, Jackie had never envisioned so drastic a measure as he proposed, nor that he would charge Lucy so dearly for the benefit of his dubious talents. In fact, she was certain that Jackie would have vehemently opposed such a wild scheme and was afraid that, given her own reservations, she would find herself being talked out of going through with it. She wanted to avoid that at all costs.

At any other time, she would never have dreamed of taking such a risk, but rationality had, for once in her well-ordered existence, deserted her. It was all or nothing now. She had incontrovertibly made up her mind to cast her lot in with this strange little man.

She went out early in the morning on the pretext of having to pick up some items at the pharmacy and slipped into the nearest branch of her bank to withdraw the necessary cash.

If the truth be told, she would have willingly emptied out her entire account to bring about the desired results following her meeting with Jasper Frakes. She was quite prepared to do so if need be, so ardently did Lucy find herself pinning her hopes on his questionable assertions.

After all the years that she had scrimped and saved in order to raise her family, the careful financial planning, the final reward for all her labors was on the verge of being irrevocably wiped out. Only a fool would have dared to take the risk. But then, love makes fools of even the most sane and rational people—and Lucy was, for the first time in her life, head over heels in love.

That afternoon she boarded the bus that would carry her back across the Chelsea Bridge to Frakes's flat. It was crowded, and as she took her place, she was quickly joined by a large, leather-clad man who'd been standing behind her in the queue. He flopped down on the seat beside her. Lucy, looking up at a craggy, pock-marked face adorned with several grotesque piercings, then down to the tattooed wrists protruding from the sleeves of his leather jacket, took a firmer grip on her purse and edged closer to the window.

As she looked out, she could see the barges making their way up and down the sludgy, brown waters of the Thames, and a little further on, looming above the railway tracks that ran to and from Victoria Station, the abandoned towers of the old Battersea Power Station. She recalled the old Battersea Fun Fair that had closed down sometime in the '70s. She and Jackie had visited there a couple of times when Lucy first went to visit her friend in London. Happy days.

When the bus pulled up at the terminus, Lucy got to her feet and followed the leather-clad man, who, she had realized with some trepidation, shared the same destination. He jumped heavily to the pavement ahead of her and turned briefly to look up at Lucy as she prepared to step down from the platform. She breathed a sigh of relief, however, when, standing undecided for a moment as to which way to take, he crossed the street in the direction of the park. Lucy walked hurriedly, the money tucked safely in her purse, towards Jasper's flat.

In the cold light of day, Carmichael Street didn't seem nearly so threatening. There were more people about for one thing, and the sun, which had finally broken through the remnants of the mist from the night before, threw everything, even the darkest corners, open to public scrutiny.

Once again, Frakes greeted Lucy at the door and ushered her through to the room at the back of the house.

As she followed him, she could hear evidence of other tenants in the building: a TV playing a little too loudly, a child crying, a door closing, and the sound of someone running down the stairs from the floor above—commonplace noises but oddly reassuring.

Lucy lingered, looking back, hoping to catch a glimpse of Frakes's fellow boarders, but the old man called to her, and she turned back obediently.

Just as she was about to enter the flat, Lucy suddenly froze. Something had brushed surreptitiously against her legs, and looking down in alarm, she observed a sleek black cat that had taken advantage of the open door to dart silently past them into the room beyond. She wondered briefly if it was the same cat that had startled her the previous night.

Once inside, Lucy could see that the old man had made an effort to tidy the place. The bed had been made and the table cleared of the detritus from the previous night. Despite the early hour, heavy, dark blue drapes had already been pulled across the windows—the room illuminated only by the small lamp on the table by the armchair.

Frakes fussed around, solicitously patting a cushion on the chair and putting aside a book that he'd been reading. He motioned for Lucy to sit down.

He hovered over her, rubbing his hands together as if eager to begin. But if Lucy anticipated getting down to business right away, she was disappointed.

"Let's just relax for a while, shall we?" he suggested brightly. "Have a cup of tea, perhaps?"

"Alright," Lucy agreed, feeling that she had very little choice. *Besides, what did it matter? He'd probably been looking forward to a bit of company. Goodness knows, life must be pretty dull for the old boy in this dreary room with very few creature comforts, by the look of things,* Lucy reflected. Suddenly, the money nestling in her purse didn't seem like such a big deal anymore. *So what if he couldn't do the things he'd claimed?* She wouldn't quibble about paying him, she decided. It would be a gesture of kindness. If things didn't work out, she would just hand over the cash and leave it at that; go away and never see him again.

Meanwhile, Frakes busied himself, filling a small aluminum kettle at the barely adequate enamel sink by the window and setting it on the single gas ring that served as the only means of cooking his daily meals.

He felt sprightlier today, more alive somehow. Could it be the prospect of finally sharing his secret with someone that had made his aged heart flutter and jump so erratically? Or was it just that he had, ever since last night, been looking forward to entertaining this woman again in his home?

He had never married and had seldom in the past been able to sustain a lasting relationship with anyone, due in part, or more accurately, almost exclusively, to the secretive nature of his life. But his seemingly solitary existence never bothered him. As long as he could indulge in the one thing that made life bearable, he had been willing to forego the bonds of marriage, the pleasures of an intimate relationship, and the ties of close personal friendships.

"How was your journey here?" he asked as he assembled all the usual tea-making paraphernalia on the table. "Did you have to wait long for the bus?"

"No, only a few minutes," Lucy answered as she watched him carefully spoon tea leaves from a battered tin caddy into a blue China teapot.

"Good."

The cat, which had initially sought shelter behind the chair, emerged as the old man came and sat down, rubbing its side against Frakes's legs and purring loudly.

"Oh, my goodness! Well, well. Here again Mephistopheles?" Frakes observed, leaning down to scratch the cat's ear.

"Is he yours?" Lucy asked.

"No." Frakes gave a little laugh. "But he seems to have adopted me. I probably shouldn't encourage him. I'm sure the landlord wouldn't approve, but the little scamp always seems to find a way in here."

He ran his hand lovingly over the cat's arching back, and Lucy wondered why, if the cat was not his, he had given it such an unusual name. She was about to ask but Frakes had already turned his attention once more to Lucy.

"Are you alright, my dear? Is there anything I can get you? I want you to feel as comfortable as possible, you know."

He looked at her thoughtfully. She seemed to be calm and collected, but he wondered if he was feeling so comfortable.

"I am very nervous Mr. Frakes, now that the time has come," Lucy admitted self-consciously as she became aware of his close scrutiny.

"Naturally. That's to be expected, but believe me there's nothing to be afraid of—absolutely nothing." Did he really believe his own patter? Had he really convinced himself that nothing could possibly go wrong?

They continued to make small talk, observations on the weather and such, until the kettle began whistling shrilly. Frakes went back to his task, carefully pouring the bubbling water into the pot, stirring the scalding infusion, and replacing the lid. As a final touch, he pulled a knitted woolen cozy over the teapot and left the contents to brew, returning once more to Lucy's side.

"Um…Forgive my asking but…did you bring the money?" he asked her as though the subject was somehow indelicate.

"Yes. I have it here," Lucy said, reaching inside her purse. She produced the crisp new notes and handed them to Frakes, who transferred them to his trouser pocket without verifying the amount.

He offered no thanks, merely nodding his head in acknowledgment as Lucy closed her purse and put it back down by the side of her chair.

The cat, having taken the opportunity to appropriate Frakes's vacated chair, jumped down and, spurred by natural feline curiosity, cautiously approached the bag, tentatively sniffing at the leather straps. Lucy watched as it quickly lost interest and returned to look up at the old man expectantly.

"Alright. Don't worry, Mephisto. I'll take care of you too," he told the animal.

Frakes, returning to his tea-making duties, poured the steaming brown liquid into two mismatched cups, one of which was missing its handle.

"I'm afraid there's not much milk," he apologized, though whether to her or the cat, Lucy couldn't quite be sure. "Is that alright?"

"Yes, fine thanks," she responded, and watched as he poured a few drops sparingly into the cups, decanting what was left at the bottom of the bottle into a saucer that he placed on the floor. The cat, wasting no time in taking advantage of this offering, bounded across the intervening space and began quickly lapping up the milk.

"Sugar?" Frakes asked.

"Please. Just one spoon."

He scooped the granules from a plastic bowl into her cup and vigorously stirred the contents, the handle of the spoon chinking noisily against the China. He carried the tea carefully back across the room, slopping some of it over the rim of the cup onto the saucer, unnoticed, as he handed it to her.

"There you go," he said as he sat down. "And now, there are just one or two things you should know before we begin."

Lucy waited expectantly as he blew gently on his tea, making little waves across the surface of the cup.

"First of all, you must understand that there are three possible ways that this can go."

Lucy nodded to show that she understood and sipped the piping hot tea, listening carefully to Frakes as he explained.

"The best outcome we can hope for is that you will see yourself in your past life and merge with that person, become one with them—an occurrence that happens very rarely, I may say. In that case, you will have no memory of your present life, no control over that past entity, but will be guided by their actions. Although you will," Frakes added brightly, "remember everything that happened in the past clearly when you return to the present."

"More likely, however, you will find yourself watching from the sidelines, so to speak; observing everything that happens as though it were a play." His wintry smile faded, and he cautioned, "Or there may be absolutely nothing. I can't guarantee anything. As I told you before, it's a chance you'll have to take."

"Yes, I understand that," Lucy accepted meekly.

Frakes, fearing that he had struck too pessimistic a note, went on in more optimistic tones. "Well, we'll see, shall we?"

They sat for a while in silence then, putting down his empty cup, Frakes got up slowly, and taking a key from his pocket, carefully inserted it into the lock of a cupboard built into an alcove beside the fireplace. He opened it to reveal an odd assortment within.

Packets of tea and biscuits, several candles, and two boxes of matches stood next to cans of soup and baked beans. On another shelf, books were piled one on top of another, and what looked like sheaves of notepaper were stacked haphazardly beside them.

On the top shelf were several small, brown glass bottles. Frakes carefully took one down and carried it, along with a larger bottle, over to the kitchen table. Lucy watched as he pulled the cork from the neck of each with a barely distinguishable pop and poured a generous measure from the larger bottle into a glass tumbler. He then meticulously measured a lesser amount from the smaller bottle. Having mixed the concoction thoroughly with a spoon, the old man held the contents up for inspection and surveyed the results with evident satisfaction.

He came back to her, smiling in what he hoped was an encouraging fashion, but the result was more like an ingratiating grimace that merely served to put Lucy's nerves more on edge.

"Here you are, my dear," he told her, handing over the glass which Lucy saw with dismay contained a rather ominous-looking green fluid. "I want you to drink this down. It doesn't taste too bad," he assured her, seeing Lucy wrinkle her nose and tighten her lips.

She held the glass at arm's length and looked at it doubtfully. Her stomach was turning over. Just the idea of putting the rim of the tumbler to her mouth made her feel queasy, but then, inexplicably, a voice from the past came whispering through her apprehension: *Don't be afraid when the time comes. Don't turn aside from the path that will lead to great happiness.*

Strange how, after all these years, she suddenly remembered the Romani woman's exhortations echoing resolutely in her brain. Could it be that Rose foresaw just such an event? Did she know, even then, that she was destined to take this gigantic leap of faith, Lucy wondered.

It was as though Lucy received some fortifying, spiritual assurance and taking courage from her friend's words, she lifted the glass to her lips, tilted her head back, and emptied the contents into her mouth.

As the liquid trickled down her throat, she experienced, with sudden alarm, a sensation of having swallowed a burning flame and gasped involuntarily. But then, almost immediately, the effect changed to one of numbing cold which quickly passed, leaving her with a warm fuzzy sensation and a taste of anise mingled with herbs.

Lucy felt like Alice in Wonderland, waiting to see what effect the potion would produce. She was mildly disappointed and yet at the same time relieved when she experienced nothing more than an indefinable sense of well-being—a consequence, she thought with a degree of exasperation, that could just as easily have been accomplished with the aid of a decent glass of sherry.

While Frakes waited anxiously for the mixture to take effect—he knew it would not be long—he went back to the cupboard and took a candle from the shelf. He wedged it with some difficulty into an old-fashioned tin candlestick already copiously covered, as if from constant use, in melted wax. He placed it on the mantelpiece next to the clock, the pendulum of which continued to swing back and forth with monotonous regularity. Frakes felt for the box of matches in his trouser pocket. Finding it, he slid the cardboard tray open, taking one of the little wooden spills out with fumbling fingers and scraped it against the side of the box, his hand continuing to tremble ever so slightly. The end of the match flared instantly with a hiss, and the old man held it shakily to the wick of the candle, which in turn produced its own flickering flame, the warm glow reflecting back from the tarnished mirror hanging on the wall behind it.

Looking around as if to assure himself that everything was as it should be, Frakes went to the window, gave a final adjustment to the curtains, then shuffling back to where Lucy was sitting, turned off the lamp, leaving the light from the candle as the room's only source of illumination.

"Feeling alright?" he asked, though whether for his benefit or hers, he couldn't be sure.

"Yes, just…rather…lightheaded." Lucy told him, trying hard to suppress a giggle.

"Good. That's normal; nothing to worry about," Frakes reassured her as he pulled his chair nearer and sat down. Lucy could hear him breathing wheezily as he leaned towards her.

He raised his hand politely to his mouth and gave a little cough, ostensibly to clear his throat but also to banish the last vestiges of doubt that had plagued him so annoyingly ever since Lucy's first visit.

"I want you to relax now, Lucy. Empty your mind of everything and just concentrate on the light up there on the mantelpiece."

She obeyed him with just a moment's hesitation, still beset, despite the rapidly increasing sensation of tipsiness, by a nagging feeling of apprehension. *Had this been such a good idea after all? Was it too late to turn back?* And yet, supposing he was genuine, perhaps he could actually bring about the seemingly impossible.

Anxious to begin, Frakes, sensing that she was on the point of calling the whole thing off, leaned so close that she could smell the nicotine from the cheap cigarettes that hung on his breath and permeated his clothes.

At any other time, she would have been repulsed and drawn back instinctively, but by now the whole situation was somehow becoming easier to accept.

Yes, she thought hazily, everything will be alright. No need to worry. *Good old Jasper! Just follow his directions and everything will be quite alright; no problem…no problem at all.*

She smiled and the old man gave a little sigh of relief. Frakes could tell she was beginning to succumb to the effects of the drug.

"Excellent! Now my dear, I want you to imagine that you are as light as a feather, that you're drifting up, higher and higher until you are among the clouds." He watched as Lucy's eyes focused intently on the flame.

"Yes, that's right. You're floating high above the world, leaving everything and everyone behind you. You are escaping your earthly existence, passing back through the years, back to another time. It is a long journey, and you are weary. Your eyes are becoming heavy and you must rest. But even as you rest, you will travel on the ocean of the air, back to that earlier time."

Lucy felt her eyelids droop. A little voice, far off, seemed to be trying to tell her to keep them open, but it was no good. She was feeling very woozy—so very, very lightheaded. She had to close her eyes. "Just for a moment; just for a…" Her voice trailed away into silence.

Frakes, seeing her respond so gratifyingly to his suggestions, sidled crab-like, never taking his eyes off her, over to the old gramophone where he had already placed one of Dvorkin's recordings on the turntable. He cranked the handle of the machine, winding the mechanism up as far as he could, and with hands that had now recovered some of their nerve, carefully placed the needle on the outer groove of the disc.

The old man lingered as the first notes of the music crackled forth before returning to Lucy's side, having first extinguished the candle's wavering flame, leaving the room in darkness.

"Can you hear the music?" he asked cautiously.

"Yes," Lucy replied vaguely, as though speaking in a dream.

It was an old recording of a Russian folk song, scratchy but still audible, Dvorkin's voice rising clearly with bell-like resonance above the aberrations in the black disc as it spun on its green baize platform.

"Good," Frakes responded, removing his glasses and leaning even closer until his thin, bloodless lips were almost touching her ear, as though he were about to impart a secret message.

"I want you to concentrate on that sound," he whispered. He was unable to see her face clearly in the darkened room. He hoped that her mind would remain receptive to his suggestions—that she wasn't subconsciously doubting his abilities as so many of the others had done. Like the ones who, to humor him, had gone through the motions 'just for a laugh' when in the old days he had brought them up on stage as part of his act. But this was different. He'd never used the travel enhancer, as he called it, on them.

"The man you hear, Nikolai Dvorkin, you have never met him before," the old man continued in calm, even tones, gaining confidence as he spoke. "But tonight is a special occasion. You are going to see him for the first time."

"Listen to his voice now," the old man commanded. "Reach back into the past—back to the time when you first heard his voice."

His instructions were becoming more urgent and insistent, as though he were willing her, through the very force of his words, to summon up elusive visions of her former life.

"Where were you? Think and reach back. Listen to his voice," Frakes pressed her, repeating the same words over and over like a mantra.

"Where were you when you first heard that voice? You can hear it now, and you are there."

He paused expectantly, and then, as if tearing away some invisible veil, he demanded, "Where are you, Lucy?"

She could hear Frakes talking, but his voice was not so clear now, as if he'd moved away from her. And she was beginning to experience an unpleasant feeling of nausea which increased as the seconds on the clock ticked by.

"You can hear him. Where are you?" The old man persisted, afraid now that the experiment was beginning to fail. She was on the verge of returning prematurely to the present.

"You can hear his voice. He is there," he told her almost desperately.

She strained to catch some sound. The record had stopped playing, and now that the music was no longer filling the air, Lucy thought she could hear voices very far off, faint at first and then more clearly, like the echoes she had heard once in the Whispering Gallery in St Paul's Cathedral.

Then suddenly she gasped. "Yes! Yes, I...I can hear him!" she cried out, hardly daring to believe that she could recognize the voice that until now she had only heard through the benefit of old recordings.

Frakes felt a burst of elation, an exalted sense of triumph and vindication.

"You are there, there where he is. Open your eyes, Lucy! Tell me what you see," the old man exhorted, confident now that things were going just as he had planned.

Lucy could barely make out what Frakes was saying. The other sounds were beginning to drown him out—the voices, the ticking of the clock. It was as though he were drifting further and further away from her. A succession of different smells assailed her nostrils: tobacco, the cloying scent of lavender, other indefinable odors, and underneath it all, the faint but unmistakable reek of death.

* * *

She opened her eyes and was disconcerted to realize that the room was in complete darkness.

"See? I...I can't see anything. It's as black as ink in here!" she exclaimed in frustration, wondering if Frakes had totally lost his mind.

It was as though she had suddenly come to her senses. *This was ludicrous! What kind of trickery was he trying to pull anyway? Did he really think I was going to fall for all this nonsense?* She had desperately wanted to believe that he could do it, but now she was angered by her own blind credulity. *Enough! It was time to put a stop to this stupidity.*

All she could feel was a crushing sense of bitter disappointment that the experiment had failed; that Frakes was, after all, the charlatan that she'd been afraid he must inevitably turn out to be.

She was about to tell him that she'd had enough when, without any warning, like an electric shock, a tremendous jolt shook her whole body, almost lifting her out of the chair. The sound of a loud rushing wind filled her ears until she thought her brain would explode, and her heart began to beat so wildly that it seemed inevitable at that moment that death was only a hair's breadth away.

She wanted to scream out for help, but she couldn't make a sound or move a muscle. She was helpless, and at the height of this sensation, the Romani woman's voice resounded once more: *There is one who wishes you ill! He will harm you if he can!"*

So here he was! The man of whom she'd been warned—Jasper Frakes. And like the biggest bloody fool on earth, she had walked right into his trap.

Then miraculously, as quickly as they had come, the sensations that so terrified her ceased, and Lucy, dry-mouthed and trembling, drew a deep breath, releasing it in a heartfelt sigh of relief.

Thank God! She offered up a silent prayer. He hadn't managed to kill her yet, but who knew? He might try again, she thought, trying to quell the rising tide of alarm that threatened to sweep over her.

This is insane. This can't be happening, she reasoned with herself.

She must be mistaken. It really was too ridiculous to suspect Frakes of such sinister intentions. Her overactive imagination was obviously getting the better of her. But Rose's dire warnings, for so many years disregarded, had come forcing their way back into her mind. Now that they had resurfaced, Lucy had trouble pushing them aside.

Get a grip, for goodness' sake, she told herself crossly. He was probably nothing more than a harmless old man who was doing his best to help her. She had practically forced him into this situation, after all. How foolish she would appear if she made a fuss now, now that she'd come this far. The whole thing was bound to end in failure anyway, an embarrassment for both parties. *Why make matters worse by causing a scene?* She began to regret coming to see him.

Summoning up every ounce of her rapidly dwindling courage, she struggled to resist the urge to get up and run from the room, desperately fighting to regain her composure. But try as she might, she couldn't get it out of her head that there was an underlying threat of peril here in Frakes's flat.

And before too many more seconds had passed, this insidious feeling of menace—a mere trickle of suspicion at the outset—quickly gave way to an engulfing wave of panic.

An uncompromising fear of the unknown and an ingrained sense of self-preservation proved to be stronger motivators than curiosity. Yet even so, Lucy was unwilling to simply rush from the scene of this fiasco. She would politely excuse herself from what she had now come to think of as an impossibly crazy experiment and make her escape as soon as she decently could.

The room was still in darkness and an overwhelming silence enveloped her like a shroud. She could no longer hear the voices; even the monotonous ticking of the clock had ceased. The air around her had acquired the stale, musty smell of a room that had not been properly aired for some time. She stood up uncertainly, holding onto the arms of the chair for physical and moral support as she tried to adjust to her surroundings, her eyes gradually becoming accustomed to the dark.

She wasn't even sure if the old man was still in the room, it was so quiet; but it didn't matter. All she wanted to do was get out and escape from this absurd and self-imposed charade. As she peered about her, she began vaguely to perceive the outline of shapes and sensed rather than saw a slight movement on the further side of the room.

She dared not move, however, until she was certain of not bumping into or falling over some unseen obstacle in her path in these comparatively unfamiliar surroundings. She waited with bated breath, expecting at any moment to hear Frakes's wheezy voice asking her if she were alright.

Now, however, Lucy became aware that someone had turned on a very dim light. Perhaps Frakes had rekindled the candle on the mantelpiece. But as the feeble glow gradually began to strengthen, when she looked towards where the fireplace had been, she realized with stunned disbelief that the whole thing had inexplicably disappeared, and that she was no longer standing in Jasper Frakes's humble bedsitter but in an immense, high-ceilinged apartment.

* * *

How on earth did I get here?

Lucy, who had only moments before been virtually in a drunken daze, was now mercifully clear-headed but nevertheless felt completely baffled. She could have sworn she'd remained conscious the whole time, despite feeling sick, ever since Frakes had given her that awful drink, yet now she was in a totally different place with absolutely no idea how the mysterious transference had taken place.

Had he carried her there, wherever it was? No, surely not! Lucy shook off the suggestion as absurd. He could never have managed anything so physically demanding, she was certain.

Did he have an accomplice, though, and if so, what did they hope to achieve by bringing her here? She shuddered to think.

She looked around for the old man, but he was nowhere to be seen. Instead, the only other person in the room appeared to be a woman dozing in a large plush armchair. Lucy studied her with unabashed curiosity.

She must have been to a fancy-dress party, she conjectured, or perhaps she was one of Jasper's old theatrical cronies from the music hall days, dressed up for some part in a play. Lucy stared at her in amazement, taking in every detail of the other woman's appearance.

Her skirt of plain, dark blue broadcloth reached all the way to the floor. The little, stiffly frilled collar of her white linen blouse stood high around her thin neck. Her long, dark brown hair, greying slightly at the temples, had been dressed quite elaborately, but she wore no jewelry, and her unadorned, long-fingered hands rested quietly in her lap. Her face, though not old, was no longer that of a young woman and was beginning to show telltale signs of wrinkles at the corners of her heavy-lidded eyes. The cheeks, unrouged and high-boned, also bore testament to the passing years.

As Lucy watched her, she stirred slightly and moved one foot beneath the heavy folds of her skirt, her chin drooping further down towards her chest.

Lucy dared not move now for fear of waking her. She continued to look about at these strange, new surroundings, indignantly determined to demand an explanation from Jasper Frakes when, or even if, he ever returned.

In the center of the room stood a heavy, mahogany table, casually draped with a richly tasseled, red velvet cloth. Around this were drawn four high-backed chairs, while overhead hung a massive chandelier with ornately convoluted brass sconces. Several other pieces of furniture of equally impressive quality and size stood about the room, and thick oriental rugs were scattered about the polished wood floors.

The walls, covered in damask and embellished by cornices, pilasters, and pediments of intricately molded plaster, were decorated with what appeared to be original oil paintings in elaborate gilt frames. Lucy noticed with interest, too, several exquisite porcelain vases holding a profusion of gaudy blooms, and some apparently valuable pieces of *objets d'art* placed strategically about the apartment.

It was not yet dark outside, for the last of the dwindling daylight filtered coldly through two large windows covered with delicate lace curtains flanked by heavy red velvet hangings. In that dim twilight, Lucy thought she could glimpse the figure of a child partially concealed behind the sheer white cloth of the drapery.

A little girl of possibly six or seven years of age was standing with her back to the room, her hands pressed against the windowpane, looking down into the street below. Lucy could, now that her eyes were becoming accustomed to the light, see her clearly. Thinking that it would be advisable to say something to reveal her presence without startling the child too severely, she gave a discreet cough and offered a timid, "Hello there."

At least she tried to say it, but although she mouthed the words, no sound emanated. She tried again, but the words melted like spring snow into nothing as soon as they left her lips.

Lucy, although alarmed, put this momentary inability to communicate down to the attributes of the drug, confidently assuming that this disagreeable and inconvenient side effect would wear off before too long. Cursing Frakes for having left her so abruptly in the lurch, she took a step towards the sleeping figure of the woman, resolved now to rouse her and ask, once she had recovered her powers of speech, just where in the hell she was.

But unaccountably, as Lucy moved forward, it was as though she were walking in a dream, at an agonizingly slow snail's pace, pushing through air that was so close and heavy as to be almost suffocating. Not only that, but she was horrified to realize that she could no longer feel her feet touching the floor.

This was a dream! It had to be! She pinched herself and winced as she felt the pressure of her fingernails digging into the skin of her forearm. That was real, at least.

She concluded this was not a dream. She wondered what on earth had been in the drink he'd given her.

After what felt like an eternity, she found herself near enough to the woman to extend her hand in order to shake her from her slumber. But the figure and the chair in which she sat seemed to be merely a mirage. Lucy's fingers, as she grasped at the woman's arm, caught hold of nothing but air, although she could still see her quite clearly.

And all the while, the child, veiled behind the curtains, remained unaware of her presence.

It was only then that a frightening thought crept into Lucy's head. *Was the woman dead? Merely a spirit haunting the room?*

Or worse yet, am I dead? Had she actually expired there in Frakes's room, poisoned by the potion that he'd given her? Was she wandering, a ghostly presence, in some strange afterlife, robbed of all sensation but her sight?

Once more, she forced her legs to carry her through the oppressive atmosphere of the room, a growing tightness in her chest slowly squeezing the air from her lungs. She moved towards the table where she could see several children's books spread haphazardly on the plush cloth: Beatrix Potter's *Tale of Two Bad Mice* and *The Tale of Peter Rabbit*, the cover illustrated with Peter in his little blue jacket. Another somewhat larger publication, bound in red cloth with white lettering on the front cover, proved to be Rudyard Kipling's *Just So Stories*. Beside these, a sketchbook lay open, and Lucy, filled with curiosity, looked down at the artwork with growing interest. The picture, a carefully executed pencil drawing of a Pekingese dog, although done in a childish hand, was really quite good, and she reached out to turn back the pages in order to see what other work this accomplished young artist had achieved. But her hand merely passed wraithlike through the paper and on through the surface of the table.

It was true then! I am no longer alive! Couldn't be! How else could one explain this bizarre and alarming phenomenon?

Now she felt an almost overwhelming need to make contact with the child—one final chance to disprove an awful reality—and with one last desperate effort, Lucy succeeded in crossing the final few feet that separated her from the figure standing by the window.

It seemed strangely inevitable, however, that the child would remain oblivious to her presence. Lucy's worst fears seemed to materialize as the young girl, turning as though about to come back into the room and pushing aside the curtain, stood almost toe-to-toe with her, looking directly at her, yet showed not the slightest hint of alarm or recognition. Lucy fell back, afraid that they would collide, but just as the girl was about to step forward, she appeared to change her mind, for the girl turned away once more, compelled to gaze through the window for just a moment longer.

With a surge of panic, Lucy reached out and grasped, like one who is drowning, at the back of the child's dress and was startled yet relieved to find that, unlike everything else in the room, the material was tangible and oddly reassuring.

This welcome sense of relief was fleeting, though, for almost immediately Lucy experienced the most peculiar feeling of being sucked into a vacuum. It was as if she were being absorbed into the very fabric of the girl's clothing, into the child herself, momentarily losing all consciousness until she and the girl became one and the person known as Lucy Welbourne no longer existed.

9

A MEMORABLE JOURNEY

THE GIRL HAD BEEN STANDING AT THE WINDOW for some time. It was part of her daily routine, keeping a lonely vigil during the afternoon hours, watching and waiting.

Corrine's beautiful and self-indulgent mother, Lady Arabella Standish, who, having given agonizingly painful birth to a girl instead of the desired male heir to the family fortune, had almost literally turned her back on the girl. She had obdurately refused to subject herself to the distasteful indignity of repeating the process on the off chance that it would produce a son. Consequently, Corrine was the only child of the family.

She was a constant and living reminder of Lady Arabella's past sufferings. True to the adage that children should be seen and not heard—and not necessarily even seen—Corrine was mostly left in the care of Mrs. Monkaster, the Standish's housekeeper, and Madame Granville, her governess. On mercifully infrequent occasions, she was sent up to the north of England to stay with her grandmother, a banishment that Corrine always viewed with more than a little trepidation. She much preferred to remain at the family's residence in Tunbridge Square, an imposing house in London's fashionable district of Belgravia.

And as for her father, it wasn't that Sir Reginald didn't care about his daughter, but he was so far removed from the realities of life in Tunbridge Square that it was inevitable he should take little interest in the mundane trivialities that made up the daily round of Corrine's existence. Nor did it help matters that he was, unfortunately for the child, completely blind to his wife's maternal shortcomings.

Standish was a handsome and highly regarded member of the privileged and pampered upper classes. Besides having amassed his own personal fortune by the time he was thirty, he had married into an extremely wealthy and influential family. It was not surprising therefore that, owing to his remarkable powers of diplomacy, financial acumen, and political perspicacity, he was entrusted with the unofficial position of special envoy to the Foreign Office of His Majesty King Edward VII's government. This prestigious appointment frequently took him all over the world. It was because of this that Standish seldom spent more than a few weeks consecutively at Tunbridge Square; as a result, the girl was virtually a stranger to him.

But, despite his long absences from home, Corrine loved her father dearly. What little affection he showed her was more than her mother could or ever would. She always looked forward with childish anticipation to the rare moments when his presence in the house gave her the welcome opportunity to become re-acquainted with this remote and lofty head of the Standish household.

He, on the other hand, took only a reserved paternal interest in the timid little sprite who crept now and then into his study to watch him at work on some important government papers. She would shyly follow him at a distance from room to room. He had little time to spare for her, and apart from a few words and the occasional pat on the head, he seldom found it desirable or even necessary to unbend enough to get to know the child that he had sired.

But things had changed abruptly at the beginning of that long, sultry summer. Arabella Standish, already weakened by a persistent respiratory infection and against her doctor's advice, went out riding in the rain at her brother's estate in Northumberland and succumbed to a fatal bout of pneumonia.

This unforeseen tragedy turned Sir Reginald's world upside down, forcing him to acknowledge the fact that his obligations to Corrine involved much more than he had ever before realized.

This was brought home to him in a somewhat alarming fashion when, just a few weeks after his wife's funeral, duty to Sovereign and Country required him to leave England once again.

His young daughter became distraught at the idea of being abandoned by her one remaining parent. The cheerless house, empty now save for the staff who remained to minister to the wants and needs of this unhappy child, was no longer a home.

Somewhat surprisingly, her devotion and helpless dependence quickly penetrated the stern and aloof exterior of this outwardly austere and unapproachable man. It touched his heart so deeply that he finally succumbed to her pleading and agreed to take this lonely child with him to St. Petersburg.

This last-minute alteration to his plans threw not only his own arrangements into confusion but sent the whole Standish household into a frantic state of panic.

Meanwhile, Sir Reginald's mother-in-law, Corrine's formidable grandmother, the dowager Duchess of Ravensbridge, protested vigorously against what she considered to be a most foolhardy action on his part.

She mistakenly assumed, following the untimely death of her daughter, that her son-in-law, in the absence of any close relations of his own, would relinquish the care of his daughter to her, or at least to her household. She was surprised and affronted, therefore, when he graciously but obdurately declined her generous offer to take Corrine into the bosom of that illustrious branch of the family. This was a move that was viewed with much relief by the child herself, who secretly dreaded the possibility of being sent away to face an extended exile, miles from the only home she had ever known. Sir Reginald had not, however, heard the last of the matter.

"How could you possibly consider taking the child to such a dangerous place so soon after all that trouble?" the Duke of Ravensbridge, Sir Reginald's strait-laced and somewhat pompous brother-in-law, hastily dispatched from the family seat in Northumberland by his irate mother, had remonstrated just two days before their departure for Russia.

"Rubbish!" Sir Reginald, who had never exactly seen eye to eye with his late wife's family, fired back, prepared to defend his decision come what may. "Of course, she'll be safe! Everything's under control there now."

In addition to his newly discovered desire to establish a closer relationship with his young daughter, Sir Reginald had rather perversely welcomed the opportunity to deliberately aggravate his domineering mother-in-law and her overbearing son. He derived a certain amount of pleasure from taking a stand where Corrine was concerned.

"They wouldn't dare harm anyone representing His Majesty's government, even if it is in an unofficial capacity. Besides," he added brightly, "Isadora Duncan was there in January."

This piece of ill-timed lightheartedness acted like a spark to a keg of gunpowder.

"For heaven's sake, Reginald! Do you expect me to go back to mother and tell her everything's alright just because some...some...!" The duke, whose sensibilities had been duly outraged just as his brother-in-law had anticipated, sputtered and puffed as he struggled momentarily to summon up words sufficient to his indignation.

"Some licentious lunatic," he continued, red in the face, "who prances about half...half...naked!" He mopped his forehead with a spotless white handkerchief and carried on, "Just happened to be in Petersburg when dozens of innocent people were being slaughtered without herself suffering any harm! Though goodness knows," he added sanctimoniously, "a few weeks in chokey would make her sit up and think a bit, the brazen hussy!"

"Of course not!" Sir Reginald replied with barely disguised impatience. He had witnessed the 'licentious lunatic' performing in Berlin the previous year and thought her quite a delightful thing who danced exquisitely. "That's not what I meant at all. No, Bradford!" Standish held up his hand decisively to quell any further argument. "I will not countenance any interference on this subject. Corrine is coming with me to St. Petersburg and that's final."

But despite his outward show of confidence, Sir Reginald secretly had his own misgivings about the advisability of taking Corrine with him.

The duke had been referring, of course, to the ill-fated march in St.

Petersburg at the beginning of the year, when 150,000 men, women, and children marched through the snow-covered streets of the city to the Winter Palace to petition the Tsar for social reforms.

The troops, on edge and fearing a direct attack on the palace, panicked and fired indiscriminately into the crowd, reportedly killing a hundred or more people.

Since then, numerous protests, strikes, and walkouts crippled factories across Russia, throwing the country and St. Petersburg and Moscow in particular into economic turmoil. This, of course, caused alarm in certain quarters of England's financial sector. Businessmen who had invested heavily in foreign ventures were scrambling to cut their losses. The whole situation was very unstable.

Then there had been that flap the year before when Russian ships making up the Baltic fleet had accidentally fired on a number of British fishing vessels on the Dogger Bank, mistaking them for Japanese torpedo boats. As a result, the Russian Ambassador in London, Count Benckendorff, had been busily engaged in trying to reestablish an understanding with the English and had succeeded to a certain extent in repairing the fragile *entente*.

Only three months ago, the Russian fleet was practically decimated by the Japanese. This defeat, along with the ongoing civil unrest within Russia, raised serious questions about the wisdom of investing in such a volatile political climate. In light of this uneasy situation, it was decided that Sir Reginald meet with certain people in St. Petersburg and gauge the position of affairs firsthand.

At least Sergei Witte, the Czar's highly influential policy-maker, had been successful in his negotiations with the Japanese and, with the aid of U.S. President Theodore Roosevelt's mediation, the two countries had signed a treaty earlier that month, bringing a halt to hostilities.

But Sir Reginald was aware that the brewing climate of revolt in Russia remained troublesome. *Well, no use crying over spilt milk*, he thought morosely. He would see what he could do to allay the fears of those more skittish investors, but it didn't look good—not by a long chalk.

And now he was obliged to take his daughter with him. *Confound it!* His heart softened as he thought of the child who had become so dear to him. *It's not her fault, poor little thing.*

But it was a deuced awkward situation! And what about the governess, Madame Granville? Was she up to the job? he wondered. She was no spring chicken, but she had seemed capable enough. Thank goodness he could at least rely on Desmond Adderleigh, his stalwart and briskly efficient young secretary who would be traveling with them.

He wondered how Corrine viewed this proposed trip. She was obviously too young to appreciate the events that had necessitated her father's visit to Russia, but he was confident that she was old enough to benefit from what he hoped would be an educational experience.

Sir Reginald's assumption proved correct, for the young girl would show great interest in all that she saw and heard. He would, for many years to come, be surprised by just how much she remembered of their first journey together.

Corrine had been deliriously happy at the thought of setting out on such an important and exciting journey. Madame Granville had quite a hard time subduing Corrine's natural exuberance, fearing that Sir Reginald would have cause to regret his decision to take them if she could not to some extent curb the girl's wild enthusiasm.

But she need not have worried on that score for Corrine, sensing, remarkably for one of such tender years, that she had reached a critical milestone in her young life, was determined not to do anything to jeopardize the new and highly prized status to which she had been raised. She willingly complied with Madame Granville's wishes with amiable docility.

Nevertheless, Madame had a tight hold of the girl's hand when, amid the tumultuous sounds of steam engines, whistles, and slamming doors, they first boarded the Club Train at London's Victoria Station, the first step on their long journey to St. Petersburg.

Sir Reginald's secretary, Desmond Adderleigh, had handed their tickets and passports to the conductor, who, dressed in the chocolate brown livery of *La Compagnie Internationale,* was standing to attention on the platform. This efficient and deeply deferential railway official escorted them to their reserved coupe, with Sir Reginald and his secretary traveling, as was to be expected, in a separate compartment. Having first offered the gentlemen champagne and other refreshments, which Sir Reginald declined, he hurried away to attend to the comfort of the ladies.

The train puffed energetically through the lush countryside of Kent on its way to Dover without incident, where the party disembarked and transferred to the packet ship, *Queen,* that was waiting at the quayside.

The passage across the English Channel was, as was often the case, exceedingly rough. It took over three miserable hours to cover the twenty-two miles from Dover to the French coastal town of Calais. All had become rather queasy as the vessel ploughed its way valiantly through the waves.

Once at Calais, Adderleigh shepherded them to the Maritime Station where they met the connecting train that would take them to the next stop en route to their final destination.

Even the corridors of this luxuriously ornate mode of transportation were carpeted in deep pile. The accommodations were so spacious that only ten people were conveyed in each coach. In this manner they proceeded to the Gare de Lyon in Paris.

From there they traveled to Berlin, where Sir Reginald, taking advantage of the opportunity, remained with his retinue for two days, attending to pressing business matters before moving on.

They left Berlin at nine o'clock sharp on a gloomy Thursday morning. Corrine and Madame Granville settled back into the lavish accommodations of their private lounge on the Nord Express *train de luxe.* Sir Reginald and his secretary once again occupied a separate compartment, as they had much work to get through during the journey and did not want to be disturbed.

The train, pulled by the powerful *Atlantic* locomotive, which customarily left for St. Petersburg twice a week, was well-equipped for such a long journey. Among its amenities, it boasted a restaurant car that served up a menu comparable to any of the finest eating establishments in Europe, served by waiters dressed in eighteenth-century uniforms. Corrine was fascinated by these elaborately garbed flunkies, who performed their tasks with considerable panache—uncovering succulent dishes with a flourish and pouring wine with a steady hand despite the movement of the train.

Additionally, each car had a servant whose duty it was to brush the clothes, polish the boots, and generally cater to the needs of the passengers. The young German man assigned to them was not only fluent in English but also in several other languages and displayed a calm competence and respectful demeanor.

This multi-talented servant of The International Train Company was also expected to act as barber and occasionally nurse. It could not be denied that he performed his duties with a verve that was most commendable. He always appeared immaculately attired and amiable, despite enjoying little sleep in a hammock slung in cramped conditions.

In contrast, the appointments of the paying passenger's sleeping carriages were as elegant and comfortable as those found in any high-class hotel, with linen of the finest quality always kept scrupulously clean.

It was nearing midnight when they came to a halt at a small border town, and here, during a two-hour stopover, they were obliged to surrender their passports to a policeman stationed outside the railroad car. Following this, they, along with all the other passengers, were directed to a large hall where their portable baggage was placed on long tables for inspection.

As it was already mid-September, Madame Granville had considered it advisable to bring a substantial wardrobe for herself and her young charge. They had therefore been obliged to travel with a considerable amount of luggage, which was subjected to intense scrutiny by the customs officials.

Everything proceeded without mishap, with the grim, blue-jawed administrator glaring at them over the suitcases and trunks. Once the bags had been marked with a white chalk cross, they were grudgingly returned to their owners with a card of passage which, in turn, was exchanged for the passports surrendered earlier.

These formalities concluded, they were now, with the aid of several porters dressed in baggy trousers, fur caps, and high boots, transferred from German to Russian carriages. After this tedious delay, it was with a feeling of relief that Madame Granville retired with Corrine to their new sleeping quarters.

There had been a decided tension in the air ever since their arrival at the Russian border town. Madame Granville did not feel completely at ease until they had pulled out of the station and were mercifully on their way, finally falling asleep, after much tossing and turning, to the train's hypnotic sway and the mesmerizing sound of the wheels clickety-clacking over the remaining five hundred and sixty miles of track.

As they slept, the train rushed on past a rambling landscape of birch trees, marshes, and occasional villages interspersed with wide swathes of isolated moorland occasionally broken by dark pinewoods, all of which were swallowed up by the night.

When dawn broke, it revealed a vastly different landscape, consisting mostly of corn fields. After a brief stopover in Kovno and later Pskov, they arrived on Friday afternoon at the Warsaw Station in St. Petersburg, where a private carriage awaited to drive them to the Cosmopolitan Hotel.

10

A Chance Encounter

They had been staying at the old Cosmopolitan for some time now, and Corrine was becoming restless, confined as she so often was to the hotel with only Madame Granville for company. The others were far too busy with important matters to spend much time with her.

The Cosmopolitan, with its ornate baroque façade, was famous for its impeccable service and well-appointed suites. People of nobility, the arts, and the financial sector found the rooms exceptionally elegant and clean—a far cry from many of the hostelries in the city where bedbugs and other vermin were not unknown.

Despite the availability of a passenger elevator at the hotel, young Corrine always derived considerable pleasure from descending by way of the magnificent staircase. She imagined herself as some royal personage making a grand entrance at a ball, her long hair gathered back with a big bow that matched the green and blue checkered material of her frock. Her small hand, projecting from the deep cuff of her sleeve, slid gracefully over the smooth, polished surface of the balustrade as she made her way to the grand foyer with Madame Granville at her side.

Sometimes Madame would take her into the reading room, where elderly, grey-haired, and elegantly mustachioed gentlemen lounged in deep armchairs, reading with keen interest foreign newspapers carefully censured with strategically placed blocks of ink. Fine ladies dressed in fashionable costumes sat at conveniently placed writing tables, diligently penning letters to friends and relatives.

Her father spent his days meeting with important people at the British Embassy, housed within the solemn, red walls of the Soltikoff Palace, or visiting Russian dignitaries in somber government offices. Meanwhile, Corrine and her governess sometimes passed the hours looking in the stores of the Gostiny Dvor arcade on Nevsky Prospekt.

This large shopping district, like the great bazaars of the East, offered such exotic wares as furs, porcelain, pearls, and embroidered slippers. It was a place where people from every walk of life made their way among the stalls and emporiums while children peered longingly through the windows of the toy shop famous for its tin soldiers. Ladies examined with a discerning eye, yards of ribbon and lace, beautifully designed shawls, or exquisite gold and silver enamel work.

Many of the facades on the stores of the Nevsky Prospekt were painted with pictures of the goods inside, and everywhere seemed to be permeated with the odor of cabbage soup.

They visited the English shop, where Madame purchased smelling salts, Pears soap, and a bottle of her favorite lavender perfume. Corrine also enjoyed wandering through the bustling Sennoi market behind the arcade, where items of a more practical nature were bought and sold.

Here, the townsfolk hurried to stock up on firewood in anticipation of the coming winter months, and fishermen with weather-beaten faces sold herring and dried codfish caught in the Arctic. Street hawkers and artisans, knife grinders, shoemakers, and the like, dressed in white aprons, peaked caps, and homespun coats, noisily plied their wares.

Everywhere you looked, there were people in uniform, from schoolchildren, cab drivers, and city officials to the military band accompanying the changing of the guard at the Winter Palace, the silver spurs on the servicemen's boots jingling softly as they marched smartly along.

A severe-looking policeman in a long, black fur-trimmed overcoat might be seen standing on a street corner talking to a dashing Hussar dressed in white and gold. Swaggering officers from a Rifle Brigade, wearing dark green, fur-trimmed coats, boldly eyed any passing lady as they made their way back to their quarters. Occasionally heads would turn as one of the palace carriages with its lackeys, recognizable in their bright red liveries with capes trimmed in gold braid and black eagles, drove sedately by.

Here in the bustling streets of the city, as the wind wafted an unmistakable odor of sea air and horse manure, beggars waited hopefully for hand-outs at church entrances, while the nobility drove past, seemingly oblivious to the plight of the common people.

One day, while Corrine and Madame Granville were walking near Saint Isaac's Cathedral with its majestic gilded dome and colossal monolithic columns of red granite, they came upon a group of people gathered around a man of impressive height and build with a straggling beard, unkempt hair, and piercing blue eyes. He was dressed in the habit of a monk or holy man and appeared to be in the act of bestowing his blessings on them. These devoted followers, some kneeling on the cold, hard pavement, clustered fervently around him, kissing his grimy hands and touching his dirty garments as though they were imbued with some mystical power. The whispered name of Grigori Rasputin spread like rustling leaves from person to person.

Sometimes, Corrine and Madame watched from the pink granite quays as barges and boats sailed up and down the steely waters of the swiftly flowing River Neva, the commercial lifeblood of the capital. On several occasions, despite the cool autumn weather, they strolled through Petrovsky Park, past open-air theaters where plays, comedies, and light opera were regularly performed, or watched rosy-cheeked children as they ran laughing and shouting after the old man who sold balloons.

There had been one very special Wednesday evening when Sir Reginald put aside his diplomatic duties and took Corrine to the Mariinsky Theater to see a ballet performance of *The Sleeping Beauty*.

Corrine, who had never before attended such an event, was enchanted from the moment she set foot inside the lavish white and gold auditorium, with its blue curtains and chair covers and deep blue pile carpets.

She gazed down from their private box at an audience made up primarily of the social and political elite. Ladies dressed in jewel-covered gowns and men in illustrious uniforms or evening dress gathered there twice a week to pay homage to the graceful and agile movements of such brilliant performers as Pavlova, Nijinsky, and Karsavina.

There was a heady smell of scent and Russian cigarettes. The noisy chatter of the theatergoers continued unabated until the conductor strode out and took his place on the rostrum, raising his baton to summon the orchestra to attention before launching into the music of the overture.

Despite this outwardly festive and lighthearted atmosphere, however, Standish was keenly aware that simmering below the surface was an underlying and uneasy mood of unrest.

Someone at the Embassy had related the story to him of how, during a performance of the opera *A Life for the Tsar* at the opening of the season, when the line "I lay down my life for the Tsar and for Russia" was sung, it was greeted by boos from parts of the auditorium. Since then, several secret agents had been sent to each of the Imperial Theaters to mingle with the audience during subsequent performances to identify and rout out these troublesome dissenters.

But Corrine was unaware of all this. She saw only the ballerina in her pale pink and gold-spangled costume. The young girl thought she was the most beautiful princess imaginable and twirled about the hotel suite for days imitating the dancer's flowing movements.

Corinne and her governess usually took their meals in the hotel restaurant, but that afternoon they enjoyed an early repast in their room. Soon after, Madame Granville fell asleep, gently snoring as the book she had been reading slipped from her hand onto the floor.

Corrine felt a chill run through her thin frame as she strained to catch a glimpse of the people alighting from their carriages down below on the Nevsky Prospekt. *Would her father never come back?*

She was becoming bored, and Madame Granville was rather poor company. Her governess always dozed off, sitting there in the great armchair in the late afternoons, leaving her young charge to sketch or look out of the window at the perpetual stream of life that bubbled around the doors of the great Cosmopolitan Hotel.

Corrine had read some of the books that she'd brought with her to St Petersburg. She had even persuaded Desmond Adderleigh, her father's kind-hearted young secretary, to read excerpts from one of his own books, James Barrie's recently published work, *The Little White Bird*. Corrine had particularly delighted in the adventures of Peter Pan, the baby who had escaped his nursery and flown to Kensington Gardens.

Only a few months before, she would have given anything to have flown away from her home, just like the little boy who never grew up. How she longed to live with the fairies and birds in Kensington Gardens, but now, thanks to her father, she had found her wings and flown further than she had ever imagined possible.

No longer was she haunted by the dreams that had so often disturbed her sleep. In these dreams she would find herself soaring high above the streets of London, swooping and dipping among the clouds like a bird. But, as in many such dreams, whenever she tried to show anyone else what she could do, her feet would always refuse to leave the ground, and so no one ever believed her. They had no idea of what remarkable and breathtaking feats she was capable. When she awoke, it had always been to a feeling of sadness and frustration.

The child continued to gaze from the upper window of the Cosmopolitan as three men dressed in long chesterfield overcoats and high-crown derby hats emerged from a vehicle rather like a Hackney carriage pulled by two glossy black horses.

As the horses snorted restlessly through steaming nostrils, impatiently tossing their heads and stamping their hooves against the paving, one of the passengers remained behind to haggle with the driver. This person was a stubble-chinned individual dressed in a thickly padded blue coat, a flat beaver hat decorated with a copper buckle and upturned brim, and a broad leather apron covering his legs. The negotiations, expedited by a brisk and chilly wind that whipped about the group, were brought to a satisfactory conclusion. The man handed over the agreed fare, after which the carriage clattered away over the cobblestones.

Several minutes passed before a lighter, more elegant carriage, pulled by a smartly trotting bay horse, drew up. A man quickly stepped out, and

Corrine, upon seeing the tall, distinguished figure dressed in a dark Vicuna evening coat with its high military collar and short cape, initially thought it was her father. However, she was disappointed to see, as he turned towards the building and removed his high silk hat, that it was not him. She sighed heavily.

The glass of the window felt cold to her touch, despite its double layer. The light outside was fading rapidly, and she reluctantly relinquished her vigil, dejectedly turning away from her vantage point.

Corrine crept past the sleeping governess and returned to the sketchbook that she had abandoned earlier, the pages of which were covered in drawings of various animals. The child picked up a pencil that lay on the table and desultorily resumed her sketching.

She could hear voices coming from the suite next door. It sounded as though a party were in progress, for the conversation was noisy, and occasionally she heard the clinking of glasses. Someone had even been playing a piano earlier. Women were laughing, and more than once she heard a man, louder than the others, burst into explosive guffaws.

Corrine had vague recollections of the parties that her parents had given at their house in Belgravia—glittering, lavish affairs that she'd glimpsed only briefly from her perch on the landing two floors up. Spellbound, she had watched the ladies in their gorgeous evening gowns, the refracted light of the chandeliers seeming to compete with the brilliance of the diamonds, rubies, and other precious stones that graced necks, ears, and wrists as they moved from room to room. Those rooms that had become silent now, for the most part, since her mother's death.

And as though imitating that silence, the voices next door suddenly ceased, and everything became quiet. Corrine sat holding her breath, listening for even the minutest sound. Had they all gone home? She felt a pang of disappointment, for despite being separated from these unseen guests by the intervening wall, they were, in some respects, company for her.

Then, just as she had become convinced that everyone had left, someone began to sing—a man's voice, deep and rich, unpolished and unaccompanied.

The words, obviously Russian, were unintelligible to her, but they were the sweetest sounds she had ever heard. She sat enthralled as the song wound its way around her heart.

When it ended, there was a momentary, almost reverent hush, and then enthusiastic applause broke out, and the lively conversation resumed once more.

Corrine heard a door open and close as more people arrived to swell the number of partygoers. She wondered, as she continued to sketch the picture of a little Pekingese dog, just who these people were who seemed to be having such a jolly time.

Corrine was so wrapped in her own thoughts that she was taken somewhat by surprise by the sound of voices just outside their apartment, and thinking for a moment that her father had returned, she wondered briefly if she should rouse Madame to save her from any embarrassment. Something held her back, however, and after listening for a minute or so, she recognized the voice of the man with the booming laugh. He was talking to someone in the hallway. Corrine felt an impulsive urge to connect a face to the voice, to see what this man looked like.

Stealing a furtive glance at Madame, she moved quietly across the room. Putting her hand carefully on the doorknob, she turned it cautiously so that the door opened just enough to afford her a tantalizingly narrow view of the hallway outside.

Two men were standing just a few feet away, deep in conversation. Between them stood a large, sleek, and silky dog. Corrine thought it was a Borzoi, a breed of hunting dog, but she wasn't sure.

Did they allow dogs in the Cosmopolitan? She didn't think so. Her father had refused to allow her to bring her own dear Peke, Nanki-Poo, with her to St. Petersburg. It had been a considerable wrench for Corrine, leaving the little animal to the mercy of Mrs. Monkaster, so far away at the house in Tunbridge Square.

The two men chatting on the other side of the door were of comparable age—not more than twenty-two or three—but there the similarity ended. The one, of medium height, slim, and with delicately effeminate features undisguised by a thin black moustache, was listening attentively to the other, a tall, broad-shouldered giant of a man who was standing with his back to Corrine.

They were conversing rapidly in their native language. The shorter man smiled and nodded as his companion, who had dropped his tone to an almost conspiratorial whisper, appeared to reach the punch line of what seemed to be some kind of joke. They both exploded with laughter, the thin man tittering in falsetto fashion.

The other, with an almost indecent heartiness, shook with mirth and clapped his companion on the shoulder, almost knocking him to the ground. Although their words were gibberish to her, Corrine laughed in spite of herself; the big man's humor was infectious.

She looked on in fascination as they continued to talk, the tall man gesticulating expansively with a large hand that held a long, smoldering cigarette. His companion, reaching inside his coat pocket, extracted what appeared to be several banknotes, and handed them over, putting his finger to his lips, indicating some secrecy in the transaction. Then Corrine heard a woman's strident voice summoning the two men back to the party, and she watched with dismay as they turned their attention towards the suite at the other end of the corridor.

The curious child had still not seen the big man's face, and as they moved out of sight, she risked opening the door a little wider. Putting her head out, she watched as the two companions sauntered slowly away, the dog following close at their heels.

She watched dispiritedly as they turned out of sight but brightened almost immediately when she realized that the door through which they had entered remained open. She could still hear the sound of their voices. Taking one last look over her shoulder at Madame Granville, who thankfully appeared to remain in a deep sleep, Corrine boldly slid through the narrow opening and crept down the hallway. The thick carpet deadened the sound of her black patent leather shoes as she tiptoed towards the inviting lure of merry chatter.

She had only taken a few daring steps when something shiny caught her attention. Stooping down, she discerned an ornate golden ring lying half-hidden amidst the pattern of the carpet. Corrine wondered if one of the men had dropped it and reached out to retrieve the prize. Clutching the ring, which still retained the warmth of its owner's hand, she continued along the corridor.

She wasn't exactly sure what she was going to do when she got there, but the question was merely academic, for just as she was within a few feet of her goal, a booming voice rang out close by—and suddenly the big man stepped into the hallway right in front of her.

Corrine's heart leaped into her throat. She backed away, intending to flee to the safety of her own suite, but in her haste, the startled girl tripped helplessly over her own feet, sprawling awkwardly on her back.

The giant towered over her, looking first with amazement and then with a slightly amused expression as he reached down to grasp her wrist and effortlessly pulled Corinne to her feet. He continued to hold on to her, and Corinne, terrified and feeling like a thief that had been caught red-handed, opened her fist to reveal the ring resting on her small, damp palm.

He laughed and clapped his hand to his heart with relief. He evidently assumed that she had been on her way to return this trinket that he'd so carelessly lost; he took it from her, pouring a torrent of unintelligible words of gratitude over the bemused child.

He slid the ring onto his finger, moving it up and down to indicate its loose fit, and continued a constant stream of unfathomable verbiage as the girl watched him wide-eyed and awe-struck.

The young man, whom she had seen earlier with this jovial giant, wondering what all the commotion was about, joined them. His smile, now transformed into something of a sneer, gave his gaunt face a rather unpleasant, rodent-like quality. Standing at his side, Corrine saw the dog that also seemed to be grinning at her, baring its long sharp teeth in an alarming fashion.

Several of the partygoers, including a rather austere man with a long beard and monocle, had come out into the hallway. They looked on with amusement as the blonde colossus went on talking excitedly, indicating the ring and patting Corrine's head with unintentionally painful heartiness. A woman dressed in beaded turquoise velvet with a low, square-cut décolletage and brightly painted lips laughed animatedly, cooling herself periodically with a lace-covered fan. They were all talking at once now, jabbering on so quickly that the girl could only stand and look about her, her mind in a whirl.

Then, forcing its way through this babel, came the voice of Madame Granville, shrill, panicky, calling Corrine's name as she dashed out into the hallway. Momentarily arrested by the sight of her young charge amid this crowd of strangers, she could only stand and stare in horrified silence. Then, recovering her wits, she ran forward and upon reaching the little group, pulled the girl roughly by the arm from where she had been standing next to the big man and thrust the child behind her as if defending her from a pack of ravening wolves.

In the heat of the moment, the irate governess's command of the English language deserted her and she let fly her full arsenal of admonishments in an expressive torrent of Gallic indignation. Some of it was aimed at Corrine, but the majority was directed at the dumbfounded party and, in particular, the figure who seemed to be their ringleader. He, however, appeared fully cognizant of her meaning, as his reply, rendered in fluent French, took Madame aback, stopping her tirade in mid-stream.

Corrine felt her governess's hold on her loosen. She watched with amazement as this normally stalwart custodian appeared bathed in confusion. *Was she blushing?* Corrine thought she was. *What had he said to her?* Something about beauty, anger, Madame's dark eyes, and her heart. The woman was positively simpering now.

Corrine tried to interpret the words that passed between them—her knowledge of the French language thanks to Madame Granville's earlier tuition was tolerably good for a child of her age, but she could only grasp the occasional word. It was all spoken so rapidly. Something about the ring…"*Merci, merci.*"

Suddenly, the conversation was over. Madame was taking Corrine back to their suite, and the Russians had returned, laughing merrily, to theirs.

The girl knew without a doubt that she was in trouble. There could be no other possible outcome following such a foolhardy escapade. Corrine fully expected to bear the brunt of Madame's anger once the door closed behind them, but the woman was strangely uncommunicative when they reached the privacy of their apartment.

The wary child watched in bemused silence as her governess fluttered about the room, stopping to gaze at her reflection in the huge mirror that hung over the marble fireplace, patting her hair, tweaking a stray curl into place, and a ghost of a smile turning the corners of her thin lips. When she finally spoke, it was with almost wheedling persuasiveness, not at all the tone of voice that Corrine had anticipated.

"Please, *mon cher*, I beg you do not mention to your father what happened just now. We should not worry him. He is a busy man and should not be bothered by such insignificant details." Madame Granville shrugged and gestured helplessly. Corrine looked at her quizzically, but there seemed nothing left for the governess to say.

Somewhat surprised by this unexpected reprieve, Corrine breathed a sigh of relief. The child knew she had disobeyed a direct order from her father.

"Under no circumstances are you to leave this suite without Madame," he had told her emphatically when they had first arrived in St. Petersburg.

But she was also astute enough to realize that her father would likely hold Madame Granville in large part to blame for what had happened. Had her errant governess not been asleep, Corrine's daring foray out into the hallway would have been impossible. She didn't want to get Madame into trouble, however, for she felt an affection for the woman and hadn't the heart or the inclination to tell tales. After all, no harm was done. They would both remain silent, and her father would not be any the wiser.

"No, Madame. I won't say anything," the child assured her.

"*Bon! Bon!*" Madame Granville nodded, then sensing it was time to take a firmer line, she continued, not uncharitably, "Now *mon petit fleur*, it is getting late, and you should be in bed."

And, with both parties feeling that they had gotten off lightly, the governess led the girl into the adjoining bedroom.

Later, as Corrine lay in bed waiting for sleep to come, she thought about the jolly people in the suite next door and wished with all her might that she could have joined them.

Corrine had been captivated by all that she'd seen since her arrival in St.

Petersburg. It seemed to her like a place in a fairy tale—a city of golden-domed cathedrals and palaces, statues, and spires. Corrine eagerly absorbed all these sights and sounds, but never had she felt as happy as when she listened that evening to the voice that sang so beautifully or been more in awe of any sight than that of the massive figure who bent to lift her to her feet with such ease and gentle kindness.

She was just beginning to drift off when suddenly she was drawn back from the brink of sleep by the sound of her father's voice and that of Madame.

"*Très bon, Monsieur.*" The woman seemed to be assuring him that everything was alright.

Corrine knew that her father visited their suite every night before retiring to enquire about her health and well-being from Madame, but she guessed that he would not come in to say goodnight. The hour was very late, and he probably wouldn't want to disturb her. But she needed to reassure herself that he was there, so leaving the comfort of her warm bed, she pattered across the wide expanse of her room to open the door and peer out.

He was sitting in the great armchair by the dying fire, looking very tired, his white bow tie undone, the collar of his stiff white evening shirt open at the neck. He held a glass of whisky in one hand, and with the other, he massaged his left temple while he gazed down at his highly polished black shoes. Then, leaning back with a sigh against the high, plush back of the chair, he closed his eyes.

She tip-toed cautiously into the room and approached where he sat, her small, bare feet leaving momentary imprints on the polished wood floor. She would like to have run, jumped into his lap, and hugged him as she had seen other children do with their parents. Instead, she approached him shyly, and when he finally noticed that she was there, he gave a weary smile and said, not unkindly, "You should be in bed, young lady."

"I just wanted to say goodnight, Papa." She touched his hand as if to reassure herself that he was not merely an illusion.

"Very well. Goodnight, my dear." He reached for her hand and kissed it, his moustache tickling her fingers. It was a strange gesture from sire to child, more suited to the drawing-room etiquette of ladies and gentlemen, but Sir Reginald was not yet wholly comfortable with his rediscovered role of fatherhood and did not always know quite what was expected of him or how to act.

"Oh, I almost forgot," he exclaimed, attempting to cover his embarrassment as he released her hand. Reaching into his pocket and producing a small velvet bag, he gave it to the child.

Corrine was overwhelmed. This was the first gift that her father had ever personally given to her, and her eyes shone with excitement as she loosened the delicate silken cord that held the bag closed. Carefully shaking the contents into her palm, she gave a little squeal of joy upon discovering a small white mouse made of carved chalcedony, with a golden tail and ears, its eyes two cabochon rubies.

Standish had seen it quite by chance when he'd visited the celebrated Fabergé establishment with its huge granite pillars on Morskaya Street. He'd gone there to purchase the grey enameled cigarette case with gold borders chased with leaves that he had admired so much on an earlier visit. The thought of buying the mouse for his daughter had not occurred to him until later, while sitting in the blue and gold chair of the hairdresser's salon nearby. Having emerged from there refreshed and invigorated, he returned to Fabergé's with an unaccountable feeling of delighted anticipation at the idea of giving the child such an extravagant and unexpected gift and made the additional purchase.

"Papa! It's beautiful!" The young girl could not contain herself and threw her arms impulsively around her father's neck, kissing his cheek over and over again.

Just then, Madame came bustling in and, realizing with horror that Corrine was standing there, the unfortunate woman felt a hot wave of apprehension flood over her. *Was the child about to break her promise?* She ran forward, apologizing profusely for the young girl's intrusion upon her employer's reverie. She had just put her hand on Corrine's shoulder, preparing to propel her back to her room, when Madame Granville froze in her tracks.

"Papa." Corrine tugged at her father's sleeve to gain his attention once more. "Who are the people in the next room?"

Madame's heart skipped a beat, and for the moment she stood motionless and silent.

Sir Reginald looked at the child curiously.

"Why do you ask?" he asked cautiously.

"Oh, I just wondered," Corrine said innocently, unaware of the upheaval she was causing in Madame's inwardly trembling bosom.

"I heard them this evening," the child went on unconcerned.

Standish looked at Madame questioningly.

"They were rather noisy, Monsieur. A party, I believe," she explained hurriedly.

"That doesn't surprise me," Sir Reginald responded with evident distaste.

"But who were they Papa?" the child persisted.

Standish seemed hesitant to respond to her question, but presently, feeling that it would be wiser to give some kind of answer, he deferred to the child's curiosity.

"A man named Mr. Samuel Solomons is staying here at the hotel. He is a great patron of the arts and holds open house for all those people of note who happen to be in town."

"I heard one of them singing," Corrine volunteered. "He had the most beautiful voice, Papa; very deep but gentle and soft, like an angel. And there was a man with a big dog."

A look of concern passed over her father's face like a shadow.

"Oh? And how did you come to see this man?"

"An error, Monsieur," Madame interposed rapidly. "He came to the wrong room. I answered the door and directed him down the hallway—a young man with a wolfhound. The child must have seen him through the door. Right, Cherie?"

"Yes, Madame. I saw him through the door," Corrine readily agreed.

The explanation, however, did little to ease Sir Reginald's mind—quite the reverse, in fact.

That man! Here! he ruminated darkly. *Was there no escaping his odious presence?*

11

An Unpleasant Scene

Sir Reginald's mind returned to the time of their arrival in St. Petersburg. He had been almost immediately invited to stay for the weekend at the country home of a certain high-ranking official named Piotr Smolensky. Although he was reluctant to leave his daughter and Madame Granville alone at the Cosmopolitan, he nevertheless felt it advantageous to accept.

Despite allowing Corrine to accompany him on this trip to Russia, Standish promised himself that he would in no way allow her presence to interfere with the obligations of his position. He had been at some pains to explain to Madame Granville that her responsibilities would be onerous, that his time would necessarily be taken up largely by his work, and that accountability for his daughter's welfare rested squarely on her shoulders. She seemed a strong, capable woman, willing to accept the charge that he laid upon her. He felt confident in leaving her in charge.

And so, aware that his prospective host not only had the ear of some of the most important members of the business sector but was also an influential member of the Romanov court, he accepted Smolensky's invitation with a clear conscience, committed to putting every moment of his time to good use in the service of his country. Thinking that this would be a work visit, he was surprised to find the villa, situated out on the islands of the Neva River, filled to capacity with a strange assortment of guests.

Besides the entrepreneur, Samuel Solomons, and one or two government officials whom he recognized immediately, he also found the place inhabited by a number of theatricals—singers, actors and musicians—three dissolute young men who he knew to be members of the Russian aristocracy, as well as several women, some of whom were of dubious moral character but extremely good looks.

These latter he viewed, rather hypocritically, with a certain amount of moral rectitude. He had, after all, not been averse to the occasional dalliance with such of their ilk in the past, when he was still a young man and before his marriage. He knew from heady experience, though somewhat to his shame, the enticing blandishments with which these women performed their services.

The gathering was a lively, noisy affair. Rather than being able to discuss important matters of state in a quiet and confidential atmosphere, as he had hoped, Sir Reginald found himself constantly forced to share the attention of his host with other members of the house party.

He wondered if Smolensky had deliberately arranged these inopportune circumstances in order to avoid the necessity of 'talking shop.' It was possible, of course, but why then had he invited him unless the wily statesman had thought it expedient to curry favor with his English counterpart by lavishing him with such extravagant hospitality?

Standish didn't altogether approve of Smolensky's choice of weekend guests. Although he was no prude himself, he disliked the oftentimes crude and boisterous behavior displayed by those of his fellow guests, who apparently did not feel bound by the constraints of propriety and social decorum. He could not, however, find fault with his host's hospitality. Indeed, nothing had been left wanting in Smolensky's effort to entertain his guests.

Sir Reginald had passed much of his time strolling about the grounds of the villa stopping occasionally to watch a game of croquet or tennis and talking to some of the older guests, politicians, and businessmen who had managed to escape the ties of home life for a carefree weekend in the country.

The evenings were spent listening to the brilliant piano playing of an up-and-coming young English composer named Neville Wyndham, and a giant of a man, Nikolai Dvorkin, held them spellbound as he sang and recited poetry.

Smolensky had also invited a Romani band to perform for them. These picturesque characters, with their copper-colored skin and ebony hair, made a lively addition to the gathering. The men, wearing brightly colored Russian blouses, long-sleeved black caftans embroidered in gold, baggy trousers over high-topped boots, and wide-brimmed hats, played wild and strangely haunting melodies. The women, outfitted in gaudy, gathered skirts, and shawls, with flashing sequined necklaces and heavy gold or silver bracelets, sang and danced with uninhibited exuberance.

The house guests played cards until late into the night, winning and losing large sums of money and consuming vast amounts of caviar and vodka until they were bleary-eyed and perilously unsteady on their feet. Some stumbled off to their rooms accompanied by the women, Dvorkin's arms invariably about the waists of two of the more beautiful and alluring ones, while Sir Reginald retired weary and alone to his bed.

Among this eclectic company, Standish was rather intrigued and yet at the same time repelled by one young man in particular, Count Vladimir Bronowski, who seemed to shun the company of the women but made a great display of fawning over the genial blonde singer.

Sir Reginald observed the young dandy sitting with his arm about the other man's shoulders as, taking advantage of an abnormally warm day, they gathered at an impromptu picnic lunch hastily set up outside in the gardens under a brightly colored awning beneath the trees.

The foppish gestures of this sycophantic dilettante sickened Standish. It wasn't so much that he disapproved of this nobleman's sexual proclivities. Some of his closest friends, decent and honorable men in the diplomatic service, were so inclined, but an underlying trait of cruelty along with his arrogance and condescension seemed to fuel Standish's aversion to the man.

He watched as, with one hand, Bronowski playfully ruffled his companion's hair while, with the other, he carelessly threw scraps of food from the table to two large Borzoi dogs.

These hungry animals snapped up the proffered morsels, looking expectantly at their master as he sought amongst the plates and dishes for the choicest cuts of meat with which to feed them.

They were hunting dogs, lean and swift. They required a strong hand on the leash when the count had taken them to chase after wolves on the hunting preserves of the Grand Duke Nicholas's estate of Perchina. There, long lines of hunters mounted on ponies, each man carrying a whip and dagger and holding in his hand a leash of three of these magnificent animals, would, at the signal note from a hunting horn, bound forward, Bronowski leading his companions.

Looking at this seemingly dissolute young aristocrat, who appeared so deceptively languid in this present company, Standish found it difficult to reconcile that fearless and audacious huntsman with the vapid nobleman that now lolled before him.

He watched as the two hunters, receiving no further largess from the count, roamed restlessly around the tables. Although these dogs were docile enough with the count, he had quickly discouraged anyone else from touching them, for they were not of a friendly nature where others were concerned, as Standish had soon discovered when he'd come across them, drowsing on a rug, soon after his arrival at the villa. He had backed away as the beasts, suddenly awakened by this unwelcome intruder, rose and advanced silently towards him, their lips curled back menacingly to reveal long, sharp teeth. Fortunately for Standish, the count had appeared at that moment to restrain them.

Sir Reginald, shaken by the encounter, protested vigorously. "I say, Bronowski! Those animals of yours are dashed dangerous! You should keep them on a leash, man!"

"Not at all, my dear Standish," the count replied haughtily in perfect English. "They're as gentle as lambs as long as they're not disturbed. You must have annoyed them."

Standish knew it was pointless to argue, and he hadn't wanted to create a scene. If the brutes were as gentle as Bronowski claimed, why had he warned everyone not to touch them? Had he not, in everyone's hearing, cautioned Madame Le Mont to keep her pet dog by her side at all times lest it be taken for sport and eaten?

In the distance, the sound of someone playing a concertina on one of the barges going upriver could be heard, and the rhythmic thud of a racquet hitting a ball came from across the lawn as some of the party remained behind on the tennis court to finish their game.

Madame Le Mont's Pekinese, very like his daughter's own dog that he had always thought of as hardly a dog at all—a fussy, nervous little beast—was contentedly nestled in her lap. But as the woman picked at the food before her, the Peke's attention was suddenly drawn to a bird that had flown down to peck at some crumbs dropped nearby. The animal, wriggling out of his mistress's grasp, jumped down onto the grass and playfully chased after it, its little legs working gamely as it half-waddled, half-ran across the lawn.

Immediately, the two Borzois sighted the movement and with lightning speed fell upon the unfortunate Pekinese, tearing it to shreds before the horrified gaze of the guests. Madame Le Mont screamed and fainted; many of those sitting at the table looked away, nauseated, but Bronowski merely sat and laughed.

"Call the brutes off for heaven's sake!" Standish urged him, jumping to his feet, but Bronowski, ignoring the plea, continued his conversation with Dvorkin, who was not paying any attention.

The company was powerless to act and could only wait for the command that failed to come; there was only one man who possessed the ability to control the beasts. Finally, Bronowski, tears of mirth running down his face, snapped out an order, and the dogs ran back obediently to his side, leaving what remained of the Pekinese—which was precious little—to be cleaned up later by the servants.

Smolensky's guests had understandably lost their appetites after witnessing such an unpleasant scene. The majority of them got up and wandered away, as two of the men helped Madame Le Mont to her feet, escorting her back to the house.

The only people who remained at the table, surrounded by upturned chairs and hastily discarded napkins, were Bronowski, Dvorkin, and Sir Reginald.

The count, unconcerned by the preceding debacle, poured another glass of champagne for his compatriot and then, after replenishing his own glass and draining it at a single gulp, wiped his mouth daintily with a napkin. He said to Sir Reginald, "Well, why do you look so disapproving, my dear Sir Reginald? My babies are natural hunters. I warned the stupid woman not to let go of that idiotic toy of hers, but what can one do? Nicky, darling!" He turned to the man sitting beside him, laying a limp hand on his friend's brawny forearm. "You don't blame me, do you?" Bronowski looked at him beseechingly with fluttering eyelashes, and Dvorkin, somewhat the worse for an overindulgence of vodka and champagne, stood up rather unsteadily, belched loudly, and said, "Not a bit, dear boy. Come, let us join the ladies."

This suggestion was not to the count's liking, however, and he pouted. "I'd rather stay here with you and finish the champagne, my dear."

"Just as you like," Dvorkin replied. "But you must make do with Sir Reginald's company, for I feel the need for some sport between the sheets after all that unpleasantness, unless, of course..." he added, gesturing towards Sir Reginald, "you too had the same thing in mind, my dear Standish."

Sir Reginald arose and replied with hauteur, "It is not six months since I buried my dear wife, Monsieur Dvorkin."

The singer shrugged, as much as to say, what does that matter, but merely muttered, "Just as you like. I'll see you later, Vladimir."

Bronowski nodded. "Very well. If you must, you must, I suppose." Then, turning his attention to Standish, he continued, "Never mind. Sir Reginald will keep me company, won't you?" He reached across the table for the other man's glass. "More champagne, my dear?"

"No thank you," Standish declined frostily. "I've lost my taste for it, somehow. If you'll excuse me." He walked purposefully around to Bronowski's side of the table to head back to the house, and as he did so, the borzois that were lying at Bronowski's feet, sprang up, snarling, their bloodlust evidently unabated.

"Gently, my babies," the count rebuked them. "You've had enough sport for one day. Let the nice gentleman pass."

"I'm obliged to you," Standish thanked him austerely and strode away.

The remainder of the weekend had been, despite sporadic efforts to dispel the mood, dismal, and Sir Reginald had returned to the Cosmopolitan with a feeling of disappointment and dissatisfaction.

* * *

Sir Reginald shook his head, as if to dispel the memories. *Count Vladimir Bronowski!* He was incensed that the insufferable man had been here tonight, right outside his door. He shuddered involuntarily and looked at the governess.

"Madame, I think it's just as well that we are departing for Moscow tomorrow. Have everything ready to go in the morning. The carriage will be here at eleven o'clock to take us to the station.

She nodded, relieved that the moment of disclosure had apparently passed. But she wasn't to be let off the hook quite yet.

"But who was he? The man with the beautiful voice?" Corrine persisted with blind, childish stubbornness. She stood there in her cotton nightgown, a determined expression on her face.

"It must have been Nikolai Dvorkin."

* * *

Lucy heard the man pronounce the name and, in the same moment, felt as though her body was being torn in two—as if an enormous hand was pulling her heart from within her. She saw the girl, the man, Madame Granville, all grouped around the dying embers of the fire. She felt herself being pulled back, but she didn't want to leave. She reached out, trying to cling to the child that she had once been, but it was useless.

She called aloud.

But no one in the past could hear her.

Slowly, the scene in the suite at the Cosmopolitan began to dissolve before her eyes, until there was nothing but darkness. She sat crying until she heard a voice calling her name, quietly at first, then more insistently. Realizing that it was a call back to life, she opened her eyes.

Frakes was kneeling beside her chair, looking up at her with concern.

"Lucy? Are you alright?"

"Yes…yes. I think so." She felt exhausted and, putting her hands to her face, discovered that her cheeks were wet with tears.

"Take your time, my dear." Frakes patted her arm reassuringly. "Just sit there and I'll get you another cup of tea." His remedy for everything. "There's still some in the pot." He got up and shuffled over to the table, feeling the tea pot under its green knitted cozy. "It's still quite warm," he told her cheerfully.

"But surely…How long have I been gone?" Lucy felt confused and disoriented.

"Frakes chortled. "You've been away for about fifteen minutes."

"But that's impossible…several hours at least!" Lucy exclaimed.

"No. I assure you." He pointed to the clock on the mantelpiece and the candle that hardly seemed to have burned down at all.

"Well, my dear, I take it we were successful?" Frakes rubbed his hands together and looked at her expectantly.

"Yes, at least…partly." Lucy told him what had happened. She remembered it all so clearly—not like a dream, elusive and hard to recall, but a solid recollection, something that had really happened, everything vivid and unclouded, every word that had been spoken, the sound of the voices imprinted on her memory.

"But there has to be more, Jasper." She used his Christian name unthinkingly as though a new bond had been established between them.

"What I felt—feel—for Nikolai Dvorkin was far more than just a childish curiosity."

"Of course, my dear. But one can't expect everything to happen at once," Frakes sympathized. "Next week, perhaps—"

"Next week!" Lucy exclaimed, appalled at the thought of postponing any further contact until then. "Jasper, I can't wait that long! Can't we try it again tonight?"

"Good heavens no!" Frakes was aghast at the suggestion. "It wouldn't be safe."

"But how can I wait for a whole week? Besides, I have to go back home in a few days. Please, can't we try it sooner?" Lucy pleaded.

Frakes shook his head emphatically. "I couldn't possibly take the responsibility. You don't understand—"

"I'm willing to risk it. I'll pay you double what we agreed."

The old man removed his glasses, passing his hand in front of his eyes, up over his forehead, and back across his thinning hair in a paroxysm of anxiety and indecision.

"Come on, Jasper! It'll be alright." Lucy grasped his arm and shook it, letting go almost immediately, afraid that she'd gone too far.

Finally, he capitulated. "All right. Come back tomorrow afternoon. We'll try again then."

Frakes knew he was taking a chance, but the woman was so insistent. He felt powerless to refuse. *And anyway, what did it matter now?* So maybe he hadn't used this stuff on anyone other than himself. He wasn't going to tell her that, was he? She was a perfect subject and he was reasonably confident that she wouldn't suffer any ill effects, although he had strictly limited his own use of the potent mixture to once or twice a week. *After all, what was the worst that could happen? It might knock her out for a bit, but where was the harm in that?*

Besides, the promise of further and possibly frequent payments was proving to be too much of a temptation. Moreover, he was curious to see where this experiment would lead her.

For he too had been present there in the hallway of the Cosmopolitan in St. Petersburg; he had seen the child and had been part of the tableaux that had formed outside the suite where she'd fallen.

As Lucy took her leave, she thought about how slight and insignificant Frakes looked, how deceptively bland and uninteresting. *Who would guess that this little man had the power to transform one's world beyond all imagining? He was a magician! A genius!*

She turned with a feeling of exhilaration and walked lightheartedly down to the gate as she heard Frakes close the door behind her. Nothing could stop her now from finding out the truth about her past and the connection that she was certain existed between Nikolai Dvorkin and herself.

And then she staggered. Everything seemed to swim before her eyes, and, barely managing to reach the sidewalk without collapsing, she leaned against the brick wall that separated the small front garden from the pavement in order to prevent herself from falling down.

What had been in that potion he'd given her? What a fool she'd been to drink it. But he'd seemed to know what he was doing. The results had been remarkable, to say the least; and she really had felt alright until now. The dizziness persisted. She felt a sudden surge of nausea and her heart was racing.

Was she going to die out here on the street? The horror of what might happen, of the risk she had taken, made her break out in a feverish perspiration as she tried desperately to focus on her surroundings.

Traffic had thinned considerably by this time and there were few people about, a circumstance about which Lucy was both pleased and sorry. Further along the road, a couple were making their way into The Bishop's Miter; a woman, pushing a pram on the opposite side of the street, looked briefly in her direction but continued on her way; a cyclist pedaled rapidly by and, turning right at the next corner, disappeared from view.

Lucy, rejecting outright the idea of returning to Frakes's apartment for help, thought she could make out a taxi coming towards her. Stumbling to the curb, she held out her hand to flag it down. She feared that he hadn't seen her, but the driver, spotting her at the last moment, screeched to a halt a few feet beyond where she was swaying and backed his cab to draw level with her.

"'Ello, luv," he addressed her in a thick cockney accent through the open window.

"Bit the worse for wear, are yer, darlin?" He chuckled chirpily, assuming that she'd just come out of the pub.

Reaching back, he threw open the rear door invitingly.

"'Op in, dearie."

Lucy lurched forward and almost fell into the back seat.

"Cor blimey, you 'aint 'arf in a state, and no mistake. Where to, luv?"

She gave him Jackie's address in Chelsea.

"Right-O. We'll soon get yer back 'ome, duck. Just don't throw up back there, alright."

Once she was sitting down, Lucy began to feel better. By the time they had reached their destination, the cabbie, who had looked uneasily back at her through the rear-view mirror for the entire journey, was surprised to see that she'd almost fully recovered.

Astonished by her remarkable restoration to sobriety, he thanked her heartily for the generous tip as Lucy recklessly handed him several notes from her purse. Accepting her assurance that she was quite alright, he drove away, leaving her standing clear-headed but somewhat weak-kneed on the pavement outside the Shellaby's house.

* * *

Once again, Jackie was waiting anxiously for Lucy's return. When she saw her friend's flushed face and slow and unsteady gait, she couldn't help herself. "Oh, Luce! I knew this was a mistake. What on earth happened? I told Lionel we should have gone with you."

She led her friend into the living room and helped her to the sofa. She rearranged the pillows and pulled off Lucy's shoes while sending Lionel, who had cautiously put his head around the door to see if there was anything he could do, to pour a stiff brandy.

"You look all in."

"No, I'm alright, really." Lucy closed her eyes, nevertheless.

"Can you tell us what happened?" Jackie, who was bursting to hear Lucy's account of the afternoon's events, took the glass from her husband and handed it to Lucy.

"It was incredible. I don't know if I really thought he could do it, but he did," Lucy told them. "It was so real! I could have sworn I was there with him."

"Dvorkin?"

"Yes! I saw him, Jackie! He was there! I was only a child, and he reached out his hand to me."

Lucy told her friends everything that had happened, though she was careful to omit any mention of the drug that Frakes had given her.

"That's fantastic, Lucy!" Jackie was feeling self-congratulatory in the face of Lionel's earlier skepticism but was honest enough to confess, "Oh, I know I told you I thought he could do it, but really, to tell you the truth, I was more than a little doubtful. But how do you feel now? You didn't look too good when you came in."

"I did feel sick at first, when it was all over and I was leaving Jasper's place," Lucy admitted. "The fresh air really seemed to knock me for a loop. But the nausea passed quick enough. I just feel very tired now." She smiled and Jackie was glad to see that she had regained some of her normal color.

"At least you found out what you wanted to know. You won't need to put yourself through all that again," Jackie said, sounding relieved.

"But I'm certain there's much more," Lucy said, finishing the brandy in her glass. "That's why I'm going back to Jasper's tomorrow."

"Like hell you are!" Jackie protested. "Oh, Lucy, for goodness' sake, don't risk it again. You don't know what could happen. Lionel, tell her she mustn't go back," she pleaded.

Lionel looked helplessly from one to the other.

"It'll be alright, honestly," Lucy reassured her friends. "I'll know what to expect next time. I was in too much of a hurry, didn't wait long enough to get readjusted. I have to go back. There's no other way."

By the end of the evening the Shellabys had reconciled themselves to Lucy's plan. Little did they realize that the die had already been cast and Lucy's fate sealed long ago.

12
DANCING WITH THE DEVIL

THE FOLLOWING AFTERNOON, Lucy returned to the flat. Jasper, unaware that she'd almost collapsed after leaving him the previous afternoon and seeing that she appeared none the worse for her earlier experience, welcomed her with a feeling of relief. Lucy, for her part, was determined that he should remain ignorant of the fact for fear he wouldn't continue with the experiment.

The house, despite the mild day outside, was cold and quiet. Frakes's room appeared just as she'd left it, the curtains drawn and the lamp lit. This time, however, Lucy was more confident as she took her place in the armchair by the little table.

The process of the previous afternoon was repeated, and once again she found herself enveloped in a silent, black void. When she was at last able to make out her surroundings, however, it came as no surprise to find that she was no longer in Frakes's flat.

* * *

The artificially induced dimness of the room had now given way to the natural darkness of a night sky filled with stars. Lucy drew a deep breath. The air was warm and laden with the heady perfume of night-scented flowers and newly cut grass. The scene stretching out before her was lit by the blazing headlights from a line of cars that extended the length of a far-reaching *allée* lined with overarching plane trees.

Standing at a pair of open lodge gates framed by a weathered stone archway ornamented with *fleurs-de-lys* and topped by crouching lions wearing a mantle of green lichen, Lucy watched as a procession of sporty Bugattis, sedate De Lages, and square-cut Voisins made their way slowly past her. German Mercedes, English Bentleys and Daimlers, Italian Fiats, and American Duesenbergs, their wheels crunching crisply over the gravel, proceeded majestically along the driveway.

She jumped instinctively aside as a horn blasted impatiently behind her; but as she stepped back, she realized that, as on her previous journey into the past, she was invisible to those around her. This time, however, she was relieved to find that movement seemed to be considerably easier.

The chauffeur of a gently purring Silver Ghost Rolls-Royce opened his window to make enquiries of the uniformed driver of a Lancia passing in the opposite direction. Lucy could hear him speaking rapidly in French and caught sight of a shadowy figure in the back seat leaning forward and touching him on the shoulder. The car proceeded on its way, and Lucy resolved to follow, walking quickly along the grass verge unseen.

As she made her way up the cathedral-like nave formed by the trees, her attention was drawn to the building that loomed ahead of her. The massive structure, a magnificent sixteenth-century chateau, was a masterpiece of French architecture—an amalgam of additions and restorations to the original building that had been instituted over the years, yet the whole appeared surprisingly harmonious.

Before this bold stone façade, the driveway spilled out into a large circular forecourt, the perimeter of which was embellished with classical statuary and carefully clipped topiary. The center was dominated by an elaborate marble fountain, the water cascading into an enormous shell-like basin adorned with frolicking bronze mermaids and dolphins.

Lights shone out from the mullioned windows, welcoming the guests who, stepping from their limousines, were now ascending the sweeping stone stairway that led to the porticoed entrance. Here, women, resplendent in glittering evening gowns, escorted by debonair and elegantly attired gentlemen, were greeted by uniformed footmen.

Lucy crossed the drive and stopped beside the fountain, watching unobserved as the Rolls Royce, taking its turn in line, drew up at the foot of the stairway. The driver leaped out to run around and open the doors, and three young women emerged in a flurry of sequins and silks.

She watched as they made their way up the steps. The skyline of the chateau—a crenellated silhouette of turrets, buttresses, and chimney pots atop steep, blue slate roofs standing boldly out against the night sky— towered above them, but the women did not appear overawed by the grandeur of their surroundings. They chatted gaily amongst themselves as though thoroughly accustomed to living life on such a grand scale, and, catching up to an older couple who had arrived just before them, they all paused for a moment to exchange pleasantries. The man turned back to place his hand momentarily on the shoulder of the woman at the center of the trio, and laughing, they continued up the steps.

Lucy, too, felt that she belonged there. Her place was with those three women, she was certain. If only she could reach them. Once again, she found herself maddeningly frustrated by an inability to move; in fact, the scene seemed to pull away from her, putting more and more distance between her and the three young guests as they reached the top step. Lucy desperately wanted to call out to them to wait, but she knew they would not be able to hear her.

Then unexpectedly, just as she was beginning to feel herself being pulled unwillingly back into the present, she was suddenly propelled forwards as though shot from a catapult. Passing wraith-like through everything in her path, across the forecourt, and up the steps toward the retreating figure, the wind rushed past her. Everything but the person before her becoming a blur until, when she thought the two of them must collide, she was flung the final few feet to merge with the person she had once been.

The past came alive once again.

* * *

Corrine Standish mounted the imposing flight of stone steps that led to the chateau with mixed feelings. She had heard her father often speak of the place and the remarkable woman who lived there, and she was curious to see for herself both the person and the famous estate that was her home.

Her invitation had come about as a result of her visit to Paris with Lord and Lady Lockstone, the first time that Corrine had traveled to the French capital without her father. It seemed unnatural to her that he was not now by her side.

* * *

The relationship that she had until so recently enjoyed with her father had undergone a remarkable change since her mother's death. They had become, over the years, a good deal closer as a result of their shared loss. Corrine had accompanied her father on almost all of his trips abroad, and she had seen much of the world as a result.

Even during the darkest days of the Great War, she refused to remove herself to the comparative safety of her uncle's estate in Northumberland. Instead, she stayed in London with her father, or waited anxiously at Tunbridge Square for his return from visits to Rumania, Spain, and Portugal, countries imminently in danger of becoming embroiled in the conflicts of an ever-increasing battlefield. He was loathe to admit that he had done little to discourage her, for he'd come to rely on the presence of his daughter to lighten the burden of his onerous responsibilities and be the one constant companion to fill the lonely void left by his bereavement.

Life, after the conclusion of the war to end all wars, when everyone had breathed a collective sigh of relief, had returned to something like normalcy at Tunbridge Square. Corrine had undertaken to write an account of her father's experiences, and for the next four years she had divided her time between this endeavor and a constant round of social engagements, charity work, and foreign travel.

They had just returned from a visit to America, a pleasant stay marked by generous hospitality, despite the restrictions of prohibition, and a genuine feeling of goodwill, that had lulled her into rather a false sense of stability, when Corrine was once again reminded of the seriousness and sensitivity of her father's position.

One morning, as they breakfasted, he looked cautiously over the stiff white pages of *The Times* at his daughter and, after some hesitation, remarked casually, "It looks as though I shall have to be away again for a while, my dear."

This statement gave Corrine no special cause for concern, for she assumed that she would, as always, be going with him. She and Desmond Adderleigh had become accustomed to these spur-of-the-moment excursions and thought nothing of leaving at such short notice.

"Really dear? Where are we going this time?" she asked with interest, putting down her cup and looking inquiringly at her father.

"Not we, I'm afraid, Cora. Not this time."

"Oh." Corrine's expression turned to one of surprise and disappointment.

"I know. It's a nuisance, kitten. I'm very sorry, but there it is." Sir Reginald's tone was regretful but became more resolute as he continued, "I have no choice in the matter, Cora," then almost immediately softened, as though fearing he had upset her. "I...well...It's a bit of a tricky situation. Can't explain. Rather hush-hush."

"Even for me?" Corrine asked playfully, although she was already sensing an exclusion that seemed to fall like a curtain between them.

"Ridiculous, I know. We've never had any secrets, you and I, but you must trust me, my dear. This really is a most important and extremely delicate matter."

"You'll take Desmond, though." Corrine felt a momentary pang of jealousy, which turned into an unaccountable uneasiness when her father replied.

"No. Desmond won't be going with me this time. He has pressing business to take care of on my behalf here in London." He recognized the look of apprehension in his daughter's eyes.

"Don't worry, my dear. This will be over in no time, you'll see."

"But where? Where are you going? Can't you at least tell me that, dear?"

Corrine could practically count on the fingers of one hand the number of times he had left her behind at Tunbridge Square since that first journey to St. Petersburg. She thought for a moment, with a curious sense of foreboding, that he was about to refuse to tell her, but he capitulated grudgingly, as if afraid she might follow him like a suspicious wife on the trail of a philandering husband.

"Well, I suppose it could do no harm to tell you. I know you'll keep this in the strictest confidence. I'm going to Darmstadt. Just a hop, skip, and a jump really. I'll be back before you know it."

"I see." Corrine pictured the broad German streets as she remembered them, shaded by avenues of chestnut trees and delightful little white houses with their picturesque gardens full of sweet-smelling lilacs, syringa, and lime trees, and the surrounding countryside with its meadows burgeoning with bright cornflowers, buttercups, and poppies.

Despite this idyllic image, however, she guessed that there was a distinct element of danger involved in this latest assignment— French troops had only recently secured their occupation of the Rhineland by seizing bridgeheads in the region. She embraced her father upon his departure with all the energy and passion of her young heart, reluctant to relinquish her hold on him until he had gently disengaged himself, and with an encouraging smile, took his leave, passing through the front door and out into the dank, early morning mist and his waiting car.

With each day that marked his absence, Corrine became uncomfortably aware of an increasing presentiment of impending disaster, a feeling so strong that she became convinced, despite reassurances from Desmond Adderleigh, that she would never see her father again. There was no one else to whom she could turn for information, for she was uncertain as to which of her father's many acquaintances were privy to his whereabouts. Even Lord Lockstone, Sir Reginald's closest friend and Corrine's godfather, seemed unaware of, or at least unwilling to discuss her father's business abroad.

Her mood of gloomy pessimism continued unabated until, with an awful inevitability, her worst fears were realized. Lockstone arrived at the house late one evening to break the terrible news that his old friend had met with a fatal accident.

According to John Lockstone's account of events as they had been related to him, Sir Reginald was killed whilst hunting near Darmstadt. The shooting party had gone in search of wild boar in the beech woods, where violets and lilies of the valley carpeted the place upon which he had fallen, and his companions, try as they might, had been unable to revive him.

"A stray bullet, most tragic." Lockstone told her, but Corrine could tell by his manner that he was uneasy with his own explanation.

Of one thing, she at least was positive; it was no accident.

Corrine wanted to go out immediately to Darmstadt.

"It wouldn't do any good, Cora. Far better to wait here. Everything will be taken care of, you can be certain," Lord Lockstone assured her.

It was only too obvious to Corrine, once she had time to reflect, that her father's life, governed by the strictures of diplomacy, meant his death would be shrouded by the same cloak of tact and secrecy. Far more convenient, she thought bitterly, for the government to pass off his untimely demise as the result of a tragic accident than to cause an unwanted international incident in a world still in a fragile state of recovery by casting such words as murder or assassination about.

And so, she was at last prevailed upon to remain at home to await events as they unfolded. She refused, however, the Lockstone's invitation to go to Pendlehurst, their country residence in Cambridgeshire, but insisted on remaining at the house in Tunbridge Square. She did accept, albeit unwillingly, Lady Lavinia Lockstone's offer to stay with her until after the funeral. Following the funeral, Lord and Lady Lockstone took it upon themselves to watch over their goddaughter from a discreet distance, for Corrine Standish had been left an extremely wealthy young woman.

For several months after her father's death, she lived in seclusion at the house in London, receiving few visitors and seldom venturing outside. Much of the house was closed up, and many of the servants, including her own personal maid, were dismissed, for Corrine seemed determined to hold everyone at arm's length. Desmond Adderleigh had remained long enough to put her father's affairs in order, but eventually he too was relieved of his duties, for there seemed to be no further need for his services.

The days of traveling to exotic destinations were over. Corrine could not imagine visiting places such as Rome, Madrid, or St. Petersburg without her father, and she settled into a mind-numbing routine surrounded by mementos and memories of happier times.

But the Lockstones, finding this cloistered existence unnatural in one so young and once so vibrant, felt obliged to persist in their efforts to persuade Corrine to leave London, at least for a few months, and join them on an extended visit to Paris. It would do her good, they said, to leave the mausoleum-like atmosphere of the great house in Belgravia and meet new people. They would see to it that she wouldn't be bored, promising her a pleasant and refreshing interlude that would restore her spirits and bring the roses back into her pale cheeks.

Finally, early in September, she allowed herself to be persuaded to join them, and the party left immediately for the continent before she could change her mind.

The Lockstone's two daughters, Florence and her younger sister, Maude, were delightful girls of about Corrine's age who, despite their affluent and socially prominent background, had lived surprisingly sheltered lives. As far as they were concerned, Corrine made a welcome addition to their little gathering, which might otherwise have seemed rather dull despite their colorful surroundings. They listened with avid interest to the stories that she related about the places and people she'd seen and the various adventures that she'd enjoyed as her father's companion.

It seemed to do her good to share these memories, bringing about a measure of acceptance of her father's death by talking of him in this manner.

She had seen so much of life at only twenty-five. How lucky she was, Maude said, to have done so much in such a short space of time.

"You will find life rather dreary in comparison, I'm afraid, staying here with us in France," Florence had told her regretfully.

"Not a bit of it." Corrine did her best to reassure her friend. "Most of my visits to Paris occurred when I was a child. In those days, Madame Granville kept a very tight rein on me, and I saw very little of the city. My outings were confined to educational trips to the Louvre and the *Bibliothèque Nationale*. Very nice, no doubt, but I was too young then to appreciate art and culture. I just wanted excitement and adventure."

"Well, we'll do our best to see that you get plenty of both while you're here." Maude, who, unlike her older sister, longed for such things herself, and had been looking forward to Corrine's visit with hopeful anticipation, suspected that her presence would greatly increase their chances of seeing a little more of life in the City of Light.

And things had certainly not been dull. In an unstinting effort to bring her back into the whirl of social life, Corrine was taken to dinners, parties, plays, and concerts, introduced to countless people, and shown all the sights that Paris had to offer.

She certainly was a pleasure to take about, John Lockstone thought proudly. All those years of accompanying her father on his diplomatic ventures had stood her in good stead. She was charming, witty, and gracious, and, thanks to Sir Reginald's foresight, intelligent and accomplished; yet she had remained remarkably unspoiled by her life of privilege.

When it had become apparent that she was destined to live the semi-nomadic life of a diplomat's daughter, her father had gently and generously eased Madame Granville into retirement and hired a tutor and personal maid who had traveled everywhere with them. Corrine had been carefully groomed, from childhood onward, to be a credit to the name of Standish—and she had not disappointed.

She made friends easily with both men and women, young and old, and knew how to have fun without stepping over the boundaries of propriety. Her considerable inheritance allowed her to stay abreast of the current fashions. She took considerable delight in dressing in the haute couture for which Paris was so famous, the style of the early 1920's suiting her tall, slender figure perfectly.

There had never been a special beau in her life, although dozens of hopeful young men had courted her, drawn either to her elegant good looks and pleasant disposition, or, more often than not, to her considerable fortune. She had become adept at distinguishing the genuine article from the cunning fortune hunter; it was something of a game to her, and she had never lost her heart or her good sense in matters of romance.

* * *

"They say Nikolai Dvorkin will be here tonight," Florence confided to Corrine as they followed Lord and Lady Lockstone up the steps of the Chateau.

"I heard mother telling Mrs. Montgomery the other day that the countess managed to persuade him to sing for her while he's here in Paris for the opera season, which is really quite a feather in her cap."

The memory of her meeting with Dvorkin in the Cosmopolitan hotel in St. Petersburg had remained with Corrine, comfortably tucked away with so many other reminiscences of her days spent traveling the world with her father. It had not resurfaced with any significance until two years ago in London, when she had gone with Richard Adderleigh, the nephew of her father's secretary, to the Royal Albert Hall to hear Dvorkin in concert.

"Yes, Uncle Desmond told us that you'd run into him in St Petersburg. He's quite a character, I understand," he'd told her cheerfully.

Hearing Dvorkin's voice once again stirred up the memory of that first encounter, and from then on, she made it a point to look for any mention of him in the many newspapers and magazines that came to the house in Tunbridge Square.

There was definitely no shortage of material for the press to write about, and not all of it was necessarily complimentary. Dvorkin was a notorious philanderer, despite his marriage to a beautiful Polish wife, Eugenia, and he was said to be extremely temperamental, his moods changing as quickly as the weather. He seemed to have an unhappy knack of saying the wrong thing at the wrong time and had often offended people in high places, but it appeared that most were willing to forgive or at least overlook his sins. "How could you not?" they asked. There was no denying that the man was a genius, and when he wanted, he could be the most charming, irresistibly good-natured person imaginable.

"They say he's an awful rake," Maude asserted with obvious relish, joining in the conversation. "Which may be true, of course, but he is certainly a most attractive man, even if he is a little long in the tooth. And he is undoubtedly a wonderful singer," she added as an afterthought, gently patting her recently bobbed hair.

"Yes, I've heard all about his tantrums and escapades." Corrine agreed.

She didn't mention the incident in St. Petersburg. For now, at least, she wanted to keep it to herself. *Did he remember it?* she wondered. *Probably not.* And those people who had stood beside Dvorkin, looking down at her as she scrambled to recover some vestige of dignity as she lay there on the floor of the corridor in the Cosmopolitan, surely had dismissed the incident from their minds long ago.

Corrine and the two Lockstone girls were ushered by the attendant footmen, dressed in satin knee-breeches and powdered wigs, into the spectacularly sumptuous foyer of the Chateau, a large, circular grand salon under a high dome. Here, new arrivals lingered long enough to be greeted by their hostess before moving on to other rooms and finally to the grand ballroom, from which the sounds of music floated above the conversational hubbub.

As they drew nearer to where their hostess was waiting to receive her guests, Corrine was surprised to realize how wrong her preconceived notion of the chatelaine of this grand castle had been. She'd expected a somewhat larger-than-life figure, flamboyant and rather overbearing. Instead, the woman dressed in black, lace-covered satin who held out her hand to Lord Lockstone in greeting proved to be a petite, elderly, white-haired lady whose voice could scarcely be heard above the noisy gathering. Despite her age, however, her eyes twinkled as she stood, stooping slightly yet seemingly tirelessly, speaking a few words of welcome to each newcomer in turn.

When Corrine approached and Lord Lockstone introduced her, the old lady turned her head a little to one side in a rather bird-like fashion and looked up at her. Smiling kindly, she took Corinne's hand and said, "My dear Miss Standish, I am so pleased to meet you, at last. Your father and I were great friends, and I was so very sorry to hear of his death. I hope that while you are here you will feel, as your father did, that you are at home."

Corrine was deeply touched by these few simple words. She knew, from the stories her father had told her, that after the death of the countess's German husband Rudolph, she had lived alone for many years with the restless spirits that were said to wander through the halls and corridors of the chateau. And yet, frail as she was, she seemed quite comfortable within these imposing stone walls, each in their own way preserving the mellow beauty of the past.

The Lockstone group moved on through an adjoining room whose walls of carved fruitwood paneling and painted ceilings contained furniture adorned with silken upholstery, satinwood inlay, and ormolu fittings to a wide gallery lined with priceless Flemish tapestries and artwork. The blue and white checkered, marble-paved walkway was thronged with partygoers.

Florence and Maude looked about curious to see who else was there. Corrine thought she recognized several of the guests as her eyes swept the milling crowd around her. Suddenly, Maude Lockstone grasped her arm and pointed to the far end of the gallery, where a short flight of stairs led up to the doors of the ballroom.

"Look! There he is!"

"Who?"

"Dvorkin! Over there!"

Corrine's gaze traveled quickly to where Maude had indicated and her heart seemed to skip a beat as she saw the tall figure of the famous singer. He was standing with one foot on the lower step, his right hand thrust deep into his trouser pocket; his other hand, holding a cigarette, gestured animatedly as he carried on a conversation with the four men who were gathered around him.

Maude, who missed nothing, quickly perceived her friend's interest despite Corrine's effort to hide it and asked, not without a measure of mischief in her voice, "Would you like to meet him? I'm sure Pa would introduce you. He's already made his acquaintance in Monte Carlo and knows him quite well, I believe."

Corrine was about to decline the offer, but Maude had already hurried away. She watched in horror as the girl, catching up to her father, reached up to whisper something in his ear. John Lockstone turned to look back as Florence and Lady Lockstone joined Corrine, who was doing her best to look unconcerned.

"What's this I hear, Cora?" Lockstone brayed heartily as he returned to his family. "Maudie tells me you'd like to meet Nicky Dvorkin. Is that true?

I really wouldn't recommend it, you know."

Lady Lockstone shuddered in agreement and fanned herself, as though the very idea had been enough to make her feel faint.

"I...I don't really—" Corrine struggled to extricate herself from the situation.

"Of course, she does," Maude interjected.

Lockstone lowered his voice to a discreet aside. "Well, it would be against my better judgement, but—"

"Oh please, Pa! Be a sport!"

Maude Lockstone was determined to petition on behalf of her friend. Corrine, who was trying to quell Maude's enthusiasm with little success, found herself acutely embarrassed by her friend's persistence, although her reluctance to put herself forward was tempered, she had to admit, by a desire to meet Dvorkin again—to see him once more, not through the eyes of a child but those of a grown woman.

Still...better not, she thought.

But before she could make her escape, Lockstone had pulled her arm through his, and he began escorting her over to the group of men gathered at the further end of the gallery.

As they walked purposefully across the floor, Corrine took in the familiar features of the singer, his tall figure draped in correct evening dress towering above the others. He had a rather bored and supercilious expression on his face now, aware that he was the center of attention and confident that he was the reason so many people had come to the chateau. In the presence of such blatantly projected superiority, Corrine suddenly felt uncharacteristically nervous and unsure of herself.

Dvorkin drew on his cigarette, and the blue smoke drifted lazily about his head as he listened with wavering interest to his companions as he watched Lord Lockstone approach.

The two Lockstone girls, standing beside their mother, watched with amusement mingled with a certain amount of envy as Corrine was led, rather like a sacrificial virgin—in the mind of Lavinia Lockstone at least—to where Nikolai Dvorkin stood.

"Monsieur Dvorkin," John Lockstone addressed the other man in

French. "How are you? It's good to see you again." He shook hands cordially with the singer.

"May I introduce Mademoiselle Standish, who is staying with my family at present."

Dvorkin turned his liquid green eyes to take in the young woman, dressed charmingly in a gown of soft, snowy-white chiffon covered with delicate crystal bead flowers, his expression one of polite regard.

"Mademoiselle...the pleasure...is entirely mine," he said hesitantly in English, struggling to find the correct words. "I'm afraid my English is not good."

That much was evident, but Corrine, perhaps buoyed by this admission of weakness and recovering her nerve, replied carefully in his native tongue,

"And my Russian even worse, sadly."

Hoping that her limited knowledge of the language, acquired some years ago during an extended stay in Moscow, would be sufficient, she continued, "But I hope between the two of us we can hold a reasonably intelligent conversation."

She held out her hand. He raised it to his lips, gently touching the backs of her fingers with a respectful kiss.

She saw, with a thrill of recognition, the ring that she had returned to him all those years ago. It appeared to fit more snugly now; he had gained some weight since the days in St. Petersburg. But on the whole, the years had been kind to him. He had hardly aged—a few wrinkles at the corners of the sparkling eyes, his complexion still clear, and the sensuous mouth firm, amazingly, despite the excesses of good living that he was reported to enjoy.

"You speak Russian!" he exclaimed, evidently delighted.

"Very little, I'm afraid, but what I lack in Russian I make up for in French," she added, switching easily to that language.

Just then, Lord Lockstone, touching her arm, claimed her attention. "Will you excuse me, my dear. I've just seen someone with whom I really must have a word. May I leave Mademoiselle Standish with you, Nicky, just for one moment?"

"Certainly!" He waved Lockstone away with an imperious gesture and a gleam in his eye, which fortunately that worthy gentleman did not see, and continued in a rather bewildering mixture of Russian, English, and French. Corrine struggled at first to keep up with this confusing hodgepodge of languages but found it easier as the minutes went by and replied in the same manner.

"Please allow me to introduce some friends of mine," Dvorkin said as he turned to the others who were waiting patiently for him to return. "May I introduce Mr. Samuel Solomons." He indicated an elderly man with a grey beard and wire-rimmed spectacles who looked vaguely familiar to Corrine. "And Dimitri Gurvich, who is like a son to me." Dvorkin touched the shoulder of a young man standing next to him, who blushed profusely and greeted her in Russian. "And this is Neville Wyndham, my dearest friend in all the world." The slim, middle-aged man stepped forward and, kissing her hand, said in perfect English, "Miss Standish, I'm delighted to make your acquaintance."

"Neville is one of your fellow countrymen, but I think of him more as one of mine."

"My parents lived in Russia for many years. My father had business that kept him there," Wyndham explained. "But when my grandfather became ill and died, we returned to England. My father inherited the family estate in the Lake District, but my wife and I live much of the time in France now— a little place near Honfleur."

"But we don't let you settle there for too long, do we, Neville?" The big man boomed cheerfully.

"No, it's true. No sooner do we settle down then Nicky sends word to join him in America, Argentina, or some such place, and I must pull up stakes and go wherever I am summoned. Such is his power over us all." He waved his arm around to include his companions, and the men laughed and nodded their agreement.

"Nicky commands, and we obey," Wyndham said good-naturedly.

"Fortunately, we are all able to work no matter where we are in the world. Dimitri paints pictures, and I seem to be able to compose my music wherever I am. Of course, it's rather hard on our wives and sweethearts. I can't speak for the others, but I know my wife, Marina, sometimes wishes that I would stay at home more often."

"Is she in Honfleur now?" Corrine asked with interest.

"No. This time she insisted on accompanying me to Paris. She's here somewhere." He looked about but couldn't immediately locate her.

"Marina is a good woman," Dvorkin expounded, "And she adores to travel and see the world, but like all women, she is never happy unless she can complain about something, and, naturally, I am the one who must be the scapegoat. Oh Neville! Why must we follow this big, ugly peasant around from town to town?" He imitated a querulous feminine voice and the others laughed, but Wyndham protested.

"That's really too bad of you, Nicky! You know Marina loves you like a brother and is normally very understanding, but there are times when the ladies prefer to stay at home, as you are well aware."

"Yes, yes," Dvorkin interrupted impatiently. "But enough of these fellows who will bore you to death if I do not rescue you immediately."

He took Corrine's arm and led her away through the crowded gallery into another room that gave out onto a terrace overlooking the grounds of the chateau.

They stepped across the threshold into the night, and Corrine, who resented being hustled away from the festivities so peremptorily, gave an involuntary gasp of pleasure. Looking over the balustrade at the edge of the terrace, she gazed out across the gardens of the chateau. A series of intricate parterres planted *en broderie*, framed by box hedges, interspersed with myriad tinkling fountains, and intersected by long walks bordered by pleached limes, were all lit with what seemed like a thousand flickering flames, giving the place an almost fairy-tale quality. The sight was breathtaking.

Leaning his elbows against the stone parapet, Dvorkin stared out, apparently unmoved by the scene below.

"So, Miss Standish, you are staying with Lord Lockstone, a splendid fellow and his wife, a very pleasant person, though I fear they are unwilling to let me near their daughters." He laughed at this piece of self-deprecation and, casually flicking a smoldering cigarette stub over the side of the balcony, turned to look at her.

"Your reputation precedes you, unfortunately," she told him.

"Not totally undeserved, alas, but I'm not nearly as bad as they make out."

"Well as to that, I can only go by what I've read in the newspapers, and I don't believe half of what I see there."

"Thank you." He grinned and, reaching into his breast pocket, withdrew a silver cigarette case, offering the contents to Corrine, who shook her head. He took a Balkan Sobranie from the case and cupped his hand to shield the wavering flame from a playful breeze that skipped intermittently about the terrace.

They stood in silence for a moment, looking out over the gardens, but as the seconds turned to minutes, Corrine, who was beginning to wonder if he'd forgotten her existence, remarked casually, "I'm glad to see, Monsieur Dvorkin, that you still have the ring that I returned to you."

She could not resist the temptation to bring to his attention the one thing that they had in common.

He was puzzled and looked down at his hand. "The ring?"

"Yes. In St. Petersburg. You lost it at the Hotel Cosmopolitan. You probably don't remember. I found it in the hallway. I was bringing it back to you when I fell."

He appeared surprised then, turning to grasp both her shoulders so they were standing face-to-face. With a look of disbelief, he exclaimed, "But you are never that child!" He tried to picture her sprawled inelegantly on the carpet but couldn't equate the attractive young woman who was standing before him with the ungainly figure that he remembered seeing tumbled on the floor of the Cosmopolitan.

"Indeed yes," She assured him.

He gazed at her with renewed interest and obvious admiration. "I cannot believe it."

"It's true. I thought I would be in extremely serious trouble when my governess, Madame Granville, found me, but I was determined to see you."

Again, he looked puzzled, and she explained. "I heard you singing that night at the party, through the wall adjoining our apartments. Madame was asleep, and I crept out. That was when I found the ring, but I was so frightened when you came out into the hallway, I fell over."

He laughed, the booming guffaw that she remembered so well from St.

Petersburg.

"Who was the young man who was with you that night? The one with the dog?" Corrine didn't know why she had asked, except that it was an image, however unwelcome, that had always stood out in her memory.

Dvorkin thought for a moment then, recalling the incident, said, "Ah, that was Count Bronowski. He's over there somewhere." He pointed to where several men were standing talking and laughing at the further end of the terrace. Corrine immediately recognized the thin features and effeminate gestures of the count. He hadn't changed much either, over the years, just that much older, as they all were.

Strangely, it was as though he knew they were talking about him, for just at that moment he turned to look in her direction, and the smile fell from his lips as he saw her standing there next to Dvorkin. The impression she had taken away with her from St. Petersburg of this aristocratic aesthete was disturbingly reaffirmed; he was a dangerous man, unwholesome, and vindictive. He scared her. She shook off the unpleasant feeling that seeing him again had given her and turned her attention back to the man standing beside her.

"You are here for the season at the Paris Opera House?" she asked.

"Yes. *Mefistofele,* but only three performances. Do you like the opera?"

"Very much. The Lockstones have a box there and we'll be attending tomorrow evening's performance. I'm looking forward to it immensely."

"Wonderful, wonderful!" he boomed approvingly, then suddenly assumed a look of disappointment.

"Ah, I see our hostess approaching. I must sing for my supper even when I am not performing in the theater. But I hope I may have the pleasure of talking to you again later this evening."

"I hope so too."

"You will come and listen to my humble warbling now, won't you?" he begged, like a wistful child seeking approval.

"I wouldn't miss it for the world," she laughed.

"Good! Is there something that I may sing especially for you, for this?" He lifted his hand indicating the ring.

"You're very kind. Would you sing the folk song? The one that you sang that night in St. Petersburg? I'm not sure of its name, but I adored it."

"I remember. Then it will be my pleasure to sing it for you again this evening." He gave a bow and was immediately led away by the countess's secretary. Corrine, deep in thought, watched him go and was startled when Maude came up behind her and linked arms.

"So how did you find Monsieur Dvorkin? What did he say? Was he charming? You must tell me absolutely *everything* that he said. What did *you* say? What was he *like*?" Maude asked excitedly, not stopping for breath.

Corrine laughed. "Slow down, Maudie. You're making my head spin. He was very nice—quite charming."

"What did you talk about?"

"We talked mostly about St. Petersburg." She related the story of the ring to her companion as they mingled with the other guests, who were making their way slowly to the salon that had been prepared for Dvorkin's performance that evening.

"You sly thing. You never told us that you'd met him before."

"I didn't think he would remember it, and I was only a child at the time. I didn't even know who he was then, and besides, it all happened so quickly."

"How exciting! But do let's hurry. We must get a seat before they're all taken." She practically dragged Corrine along. "Oh, look, there's Mother and Pa and Florence sitting right in front. Come on. They've saved our places."

A pale young man in evening dress, seated at a grand piano on the flower-bedecked dais, flexed his fingers nervously and, shuffling through the sheet music in front of him, glanced occasionally at the door through which Corrine assumed Nikolai Dvorkin would emerge.

It was warm and stuffy in the room with so many people crammed together, and there was an excited buzz as everyone, anticipating the appearance of the great man, gossiped while they too kept one eye on the door.

Then the countess walked out slowly on the arm of her secretary, a distinguished military-looking gentleman, who led her up to the front of the improvised stage and raised his hand for silence.

When the chatter had died down, the old lady began in a voice that many, especially at the back of the room, strained to hear. "Ladies and gentlemen. As you know, this evening is dedicated to a charity that is very close to my heart. So many dear children were made orphans by the Great War and even now desperately cry out for our help."

The audience nodded in sympathetic agreement, aware that the countess had opened her doors to many of these unfortunate victims herself, generously providing temporary shelter for the homeless and food for the hungry. Not a few of those present, especially those who had made a considerable profit from the war, arms manufacturers and the like, felt a fleeting pang of remorse that they had done so little to help. But tonight, they would make up for it, dig deep into their pockets, and salve their pricking consciences. The countess had chosen her guests well.

"I am extremely happy to introduce to you someone who feels as I do, and he has graciously agreed to sing for us tonight. I hope you will give a very warm welcome to Monsieur Nikolai Dvorkin."

The room burst into loud applause as Dvorkin strode on cue through the door. Beaming effusively, he slapped his accompanist encouragingly on the back and, throwing his arms wide as if to embrace every member of his audience, gazed out into the crowd. He continued to soak up the applause for a moment or two longer, and then, as he motioned to the man waiting with hands poised over the piano keys, the first notes of the concert rang out.

Corrine listened as Dvorkin proceeded effortlessly from song to song, changing mood and tempo to suit each offering, acknowledging the rapturous applause between each number with a bow and a smile.

When at last it seemed that the program had reached its conclusion, Corrine, who had until then enjoyed every moment of the performance, found herself rather disappointed. He hadn't sung her song. Maybe he hadn't really remembered the occasion as well as she had. It hadn't meant so much to him after all. They were empty words, spoken out of politeness, that had flattered and charmed her, but to him, were just so many meaningless expressions of gratitude. She tried to tell herself that it didn't matter, but the omission hurt her more than she cared to admit.

The countess joined Dvorkin on the dais, as the man who'd escorted her to the stage once again called for silence. But the audience wanted more, especially those Russian expatriates who, like Dvorkin, had escaped the grim realities of a revolution in their own country only to face an uncertain and, in some cases, impoverished future in Paris. For now, they had been transported back to their beloved homeland. They clapped, cheered, and whistled their appreciation. Only when the towering figure beside the old lady held up his arms, did the noise eventually subside, and the countess was able to say, "I would like to thank Monsieur Dvorkin for that wonderful performance and all of you for coming here this evening to support those who are not in a position to help themselves. I—"

She would have continued, but the singer interrupted her unceremoniously. "Just one moment. With your permission I have one more song that I would like to perform for your guests this evening."

The amused tittering that this breach of good manners had evinced changed to renewed cheering, and the accompanist, surprised by this late addition to the repertoire and who had no idea what was expected of him, waited to see with which song this unpredictable performer had decided to conclude his recital. The applause subsided once more, but still, he had not given any indication to the unhappy pianist—the young man sat helplessly, his fingers hovering in uncertain anticipation.

But no music was necessary. Nikolai Dvorkin needed no other sound than the strength and beauty of his own voice as the strains of the old Russian folk song filled the packed room and Corrine's heart. How it brought back nostalgic memories of her father and that first trip they had made together to St. Petersburg, and that night when, waiting for him to return, she had heard this same voice that had held her spellbound as it did now.

When the concert finally came to a close, Dvorkin glanced down at her briefly before he was surrounded by admirers and eventually led off by the countess to be presented to several important personages who were waiting to greet him. Meanwhile, Florence and Maude took Corrine away in search of something to eat.

"Did you see the way he looked at you?" Maude Lockstone asked as they helped themselves hungrily to strawberries and caviar.

"No, I saw no such thing. You're letting your imagination run away with you, Maude." Corrine laughed. In self-defense, Maude repeated the story of Corrine's first meeting with Dvorkin to her sister.

"Maude's right," Florence Lockstone agreed, after digesting the information along with a champagne truffle. "He was looking directly at you while he sang that last song. Oh, Corrine, how romantic!"

"Really, Florence! You are as bad as your sister. Look, there's your mother over there." They took their plates and went to join Lady Lockstone, who'd been abandoned by her husband and was looking for a familiar face in the crush.

The sounds of lively music filtered through to them from the ballroom. Although jazz had already taken hold of the music scene in Paris and the Charleston was beginning to make its presence felt on the dance floors of Europe, the Countess's taste in music was, as was to be expected, more deeply rooted in the past. The orchestra, however, although more in tune with the tempo of the waltz, was prepared to play music more suited to the foxtrot, quickstep, and even the occasional tango. Corrine, who loved to dance, urged her companions to hurry up and join her as she made her way through the crowd of guests who were still eating and drinking.

She did not have to wait long before she was whisked away by a young military officer who twirled her exuberantly around the dance floor to the strains of The Blue Danube. Thereafter, there was a constant stream of partners vying to maneuver her through the ever-increasing number of dancers. Many of them she knew, old friends of her father or young men she had met at embassy balls or other social gatherings. Some were total strangers. A few danced well, most adequately, and some abysmally, but she took everything in stride and coped admirably with the ones that appeared to have two left feet. Occasionally she glimpsed Florence or Maude being led onto the floor, and once she saw Dvorkin, who'd come into the room with Neville Wyndham and one or two others, standing watching the dancers going by as though he were looking for someone.

He had not been there many minutes before he was joined by an extremely attractive woman clad seductively in an orientally-inspired evening gown of clinging, rich lacquer-red, lavishly embroidered with panels of diamante and colored silks. She seemed to be well acquainted with him, for she touched his arm playfully, inclining her head close to his and tapping at his chest in a familiar and flirtatious manner as her sleek black hair, bobbed in the latest fashion, brushed against his cheek.

Corrine could not help noticing that several of the women who stood nearby looked as though they would like to tear this flighty Jezebel apart, and she began to realize just what an effect this charismatic performer had on the many women who so adored him. She could readily imagine these elegant society ladies, all of whom were dressed in stunning gowns created by the Paris fashion houses of Molyneux, Philippe et Gaston, or Lucien Lelong, and immaculately coiffed and perfumed, scratching each other's eyes out in order to gain his attention. She thought that it might be best not to become embroiled in such tempestuous company.

After an hour or more of dancing, she finally found a moment to rest and, thankfully reaching for a glass of champagne from a waiter who was passing, made her way around the outskirts of the room, stopping now and then to exchange a few words with old acquaintances. The musicians had also taken a break, and the dancers were milling about now, talking noisily or hurrying off to replenish their glasses and plates.

A man who seemed to be trying to attract her attention approached her through the crowd. She immediately recognized him as an official from the Italian Embassy—someone she'd met while in Rome—and she was thankful that he would not now have the opportunity of asking her to dance. She remembered that this was one partner who liked to hold his women a little too close for comfort on the dance floor.

"Miss Standish, how nice to see you again," he beamed effusively, then almost immediately assumed a more somber expression. "I thought it was you, and I just had to come over and say how sad I was to hear about your father." He bent and kissed the hand she offered, leaving behind beads of perspiration that had previously been clinging to his upper lip.

Corrine unobtrusively brushed her damp hand against the folds of her skirt. "Thank you, Senior Martinelli. You are very kind."

His air of commiseration promptly receded into the background, his mobile features reverting to an ingratiating grin as he enquired, "Are you staying here long in Paris?"

"For another week or two…possibly," Corrine replied hesitantly, for she was afraid he may seek to further his acquaintance with her.

"I hope I will see a little more of you then." The Italian's eyes lit up with delight. He chattered on as Corrine saw with dismay the members of the orchestra returning to their instruments. She fervently hoped that Senior Martinelli would move on before they resumed playing. This was not to be, however—as the music resumed once more, he seized his opportunity.

"Won't you give me the pleasure of this dance, Miss Standish?"

He took the glass peremptorily from her hand and was about to lead her away when a deep voice behind him said, "I believe Mademoiselle had promised this dance to me."

"Excuse me. I think you are mis—" Martinelli spun around indignantly, ready to contradict this upstart, whoever he might be, but the words died on his lips as he found himself looking at the shirt buttons of a man who was not to be so easily dissuaded. Deeming that discretion was the better part of valor, the Italian diplomat bowed and stepped back, reluctantly relinquishing his prize.

"I'm sorry, Senior Martinelli." Corrine tried to sound apologetic. "I did promise Monsieur Dvorkin, but I hope you will not abandon me altogether. Perhaps I may have that dance with you later on?"

"*Si, Si.* Excuse me." Martinelli beat a hasty retreat, and Dvorkin took her hand.

"I hope you didn't mind."

Corrine laughed and shook her head. "No, far from it. It was most gallant of you to rescue a maiden in distress. Thank you."

He led her onto the floor and guided her through the mass of partygoers who fell back to watch and applaud. As the conductor saw the singer about to take center stage, he quickly directed the orchestra to strike up the waltz from Gounod's *Faust*, just as Dvorkin put his arm around Corrine's slim waist.

Dancing with the devil, she thought lightheadedly as she felt the warmth of his hand against her back. Slipping easily into the rhythm of the music, she began to follow his lead as the dance, whose tempo increased with every turn, sent them whirling about the room.

Corrine, breathless and exhilarated, could have gone on forever. However, the next number was not to Dvorkin's liking, and he escorted her off the floor without bothering to ask if she would care to continue.

Somewhat relieved, she made to return to the Lockstones, but once again, Dvorkin took charge of the situation, securing a bottle of champagne and two glasses and directing her towards a little salon far removed from the inquisitive gaze of the other guests. He closed the door, shutting out the sound of the music.

"You know a lot of people here," he observed as he poured out their drinks.

"Yes, mostly friends of my father." Corrine had not wanted to be corralled in this manner, but the least she could do was be polite.

"He is not here tonight?" he asked as he handed her the glass.

"No, unfortunately not." Although reluctant to discuss personal matters with this man, who was virtually a stranger to her, Corrine thought it only fair to tell him of her father's death. Dvorkin, embarrassed by his *faux pas*, replied, "I'm so sorry. I had no idea."

"Oh, please, don't apologize. You weren't to know. I'm beginning to come to terms with his loss now. Life goes on, after all, but there are times when I miss him most terribly."

"Is that why I saw tears in your eyes when I sang that song?" he asked gently as he moved closer.

"Partly, yes." She found her natural reserve slipping away in his presence. "It reminded me of our visit to St. Petersburg. I hadn't spent much time with him before then, but that trip was the beginning of many happy years together. And also—" Her fingers strayed to a jeweled locket that hung from a gold chain around her neck. "Well, it's not important." She dismissed the thought and said quickly to change the subject, "Do you make your home here in France now?"

"Only for the time being. I am here, there, and everywhere. First Paris, then Milan. Sometimes in London. The life of an artist is not very settled.

My wife and children live in Brussels, so that is where I go when I have not the obligations that keep me away."

"They must miss you most awfully."

"Yes," he admitted without false modesty. "But we have good times when I go home, so everyone is happy."

Yes, everyone is happy, Corrine thought. But what a price Eugenia Dvorkin paid for that happiness, seeing her husband's name constantly blazoned across the newspapers, his picture taken with countless society beauties—scandal and dirty linen hung out for public scrutiny. Did he bother to try explaining any of it away, or was it just an accepted mode of life that the Dvorkin family had come to expect from this colorful character?

Just then, their *tête-à-tête* was interrupted as the door was flung open and several partygoers, including Count Bronowski, burst noisily into the room.

"So here you are!" Bronowski addressed his compatriot in their native language.

Someone standing behind him joined in, saying, "We've been looking for you everywhere."

The count glared at Corrine with open hostility in his grey eyes. "Come on, Nicky! We've organized a game of cards in one of the rooms. Who knows, you may actually win back some of the money that I took off you in Monte Carlo. Stefan is certain his luck has changed—isn't that right, Stefan? Come! Enough of this polite drawing room conversation."

He hadn't realized that Corrine could understand him. He looked at her scornfully, but the expression turned to one of surprise when she replied, "By all means. There is nothing like a game of cards, especially if one is holding the winning hand."

Dvorkin stood up. "Will you forgive me if I go with them? They will let me have no peace until I do."

"Oh, please, do just as you like," Corrine replied as casually as she could.

"I'll stay and keep Mademoiselle Standish company if she'll permit me," Dimitri Gurvich, who had just joined the party, volunteered shyly.

"Excellent! But I will see you again before you leave, won't I?" Dvorkin enquired of Corrine.

"Possibly. I couldn't say, but I've enjoyed our little talk, Monsieur Dvorkin." She smiled and offered him her hand once more. He took it and pressed her fingers to his lips, lingering a little longer than was necessary, then turned away, linked arms with Bronowski, and left the room, laughing in that infectious, booming way that proclaimed his progress through the crowded ballroom.

"Are you quite sure you wouldn't rather be playing cards?" Corrine asked Gurvich as he sat down beside her when the others had departed.

The young boy grinned sheepishly. "They always take advantage of my inexperience, I'm afraid, and besides, I really don't enjoy playing that much. I would much prefer to stay and talk to you, unless, of course, you'd rather dance, but I don't do that very well either," he confessed apologetically.

"No, that's alright. Let's stay here for a while and talk." Corrine smiled at him and he blushed.

She guessed that he was only a year or so younger than herself, and she was somewhat surprised that this bashful young man should be one of Dvorkin's party.

"Do you travel with Monsieur Dvorkin very often?"

"Oh yes. As he himself says, he is like a father to me, and I'm happy to do any service that I can for him."

"And tell me, is Count Bronowski a friend of Monsieur Dvorkin's also?"

The young man tried to appear impartial, but it was easy to see why he had little success at the gaming tables. His face was like an open book, his expression of dislike ill-concealed.

"Count Bronowski has known Nicky for many years, of course. They are very friendly."

"And do you like Count Bronowski?"

"I…we…that is." The young man was tongue-tied, but as Corrine continued to smile at him encouragingly, he felt he could be nothing less than honest with her. "No, I don't particularly care for him."

"No, I thought not," she said. "I've seen him only once before myself, but I must admit I find him rather…unpleasant."

This confession seemed to put Gurvich more at ease.

"He is not a good man," he confided in the charming young woman, who looked at him with such sympathy and interest.

"And yet Monsieur Dvorkin seems to enjoy his company," Corrine observed.

"Unfortunately, yes. But, of course, they are related by marriage. Eugenia is Bronowski's cousin. He was the one who introduced them," Gurvich explained.

"I see. Perhaps that accounts for it—their friendship, I mean." They relapsed into silence for a moment as Corrine seemed to be thinking about something.

"Will you be staying in Paris long?" Gurvich asked, breaking into her reverie.

"Only for a little while longer. I'm beginning to miss my home in London," Corrine confessed.

"I wish I had somewhere like that—somewhere where I felt I really belonged," the young Dimitri said sadly. "I was just a child when both my parents died in a cholera epidemic. I was sent to live with my uncle in Moscow, but I wasn't happy there. He didn't really want me. He had his own life to live, and as soon as I was old enough to leave, I went back to St. Petersburg, where I met Nicky. He was very good to me, and I went everywhere with him, but we never were in one place for very long—nothing permanent, always moving on, even after he married Eugenia."

"Perhaps one day you will find the right girl, marry and settle down somewhere." Corrine endeavored to revive his drooping spirits.

He looked at her and blushed again. "If only I could," he said wistfully.

"Then we must look around," she told him gaily. "But you won't find her by sitting here in this secluded spot with me." Corrine stood up and, pulling Gurvich to his feet, took his arm as she made him take her back to the ballroom. She insisted on introducing him to several young women of her acquaintance, including Florence and Maude Lockstone, who shook hands with him most cordially, while the modest Gurvich turned crimson to the roots of his hair.

Later that night, as many of the guests were taking their leave, Dvorkin sought her out again.

"I'm sorry to have left you for so long, but I have returned, as you see, and I observe you have not been lonely." He was referring to Senior Martinelli, who had seized the opportunity to reclaim his prized and promised dance and who had only just now released Corrine from his sweating grasp.

"No, I haven't been lonely." How arrogant the man was, she thought. Did he think he was the only person worthy of attention in all this glittering array of guests?

He drew deeply on his cigarette and, exhaling a thin stream of smoke between his lips, threw it carelessly down on the blue and white delft tiles of the salon floor. Stepping on the smoldering remains to extinguish its glow, he crushed and ground it moodily with his heel. "How long are you staying in Paris?"

"At least another week or two. My invitation to stay with the Lockstones was for an indefinite period, but I don't want to wear out my welcome, and I am beginning to feel a little homesick, to be honest. And speaking of my godparents, it looks as though they are ready to leave." Corrine motioned towards where the family had gathered, Florence beckoning her.

"I must go." She held out her hand in farewell. "It's been a pleasure to meet you again. Goodbye, Monsieur Dvorkin."

But he was reluctant to let her leave and continued to hold on to her hand with a firm, almost painful grip. "Will I have the opportunity of seeing you again while you are here in France, do you think?"

"I don't know if you will see *me* again, but I will certainly be seeing you, tomorrow night at the opera." She pulled away from him before he could say more, and he watched her as she went quickly, without a backward glance, to join her friends.

As he stood looking after her, Neville Wyndham came up beside him and, following his friend's gaze, saw the little group preparing to leave.

"Have you lost that romantic heart of yours again, my friend?" he asked, slapping his companion's broad back.

"No, Neville. Not lost," Dvorkin replied thoughtfully. "I think I have finally discovered it and find that it is a very fragile thing that could very easily be broken if I am not careful."

As the Lockstone party prepared to leave the chateau, the three girls chattered incessantly. Florence was enthralled by the latest fashions and had made a mental note of all the things she would like to buy. The list was substantial. John Lockstone winced as he thought of the imminent assault on his finances, knowing full well that his wife and youngest daughter would also be requiring a not insubstantial refurbishment of their respective wardrobes. Still, he thought philosophically, one must keep the ladies happy.

Lavinia Lockstone was more interested in the people who had attended the gala event.

"Did you see that Danielle DuPlessis creature?" she twittered as she allowed her husband to assist her with her wrap. "So brazen in her bright red dress! Goodness knows what the men see in her. Marianne Fortescue calls her one of the *Grande Horizontals*. I really can't think why, unless—"

Lord Lockstone coughed loudly to cut off further speculation, and the girls giggled at their mother's naiveté.

Maude could talk of only one thing as they descended the steps towards the waiting cars: Dvorkin and his obvious interest in Corrine.

"You had him completely captivated, Cora. I saw the way he was looking at you as you were dancing together."

"It was only one dance."

"But you were with him for ages. What on earth did you two find to talk about for so long?"

"Maude! Really!" Lady Lockstone was appalled at her daughter's inquisitiveness.

"Oh mother. Aren't you the least bit curious? Did he ask if he could see you again, Cora?"

"He's a married man, Maudie, in case you'd forgotten. And besides, even if he wasn't, his reputation is, to say the least, somewhat tarnished," Corrine rebuked her friend.

"But don't you feel just the tiniest bit attracted to him?" Maude asked as they climbed back into the Silver Ghost.

"It really is no particular honor to receive the attentions of a man who, if one is to believe only half of what the papers say, has wooed and won half the female population of France, not to mention every other country that he's visited. No Maude, I'm afraid you won't be able to rely on me for any further information about Mr. Nikolai Dvorkin."

Corrine said it confidently enough, but at the same time, as she looked back at the dwindling image of the chateau, she experienced a feeling of almost physical pain—a tugging at her heart that she found most disturbing.

13

BEHIND THE SCENES

ONCE AGAIN, LUCY FELT HERSELF BEING TORN from the body that had once been hers. But this time, when she returned to Jasper Frakes's room, it took some time before she could focus on the objects around her, and Jasper's voice seemed to be muffled, as though her ears were plugged with cotton wool.

"Are you alright?" His hand was on her shoulder, shaking her gently.

When things finally began to clear, she said, "Yes, yes, I'm fine." Then, the memory of what had happened came flooding back. "It was incredible!

"Well, I did tell you that you'd be pleased with the results," Frakes told her with an air of self-congratulatory smugness.

"Oh Jasper! You're a miracle worker!" She jumped up and hugged the old man, almost knocking him off his feet. "You will let me come back tomorrow."

He shook his head, but Lucy, thinking that she'd discovered his weakness, wheedled persuasively, "I've got the money."

"Oh, it's not that. It's just...well...I don't know about...so soon. We've already taken a chance. I—"

"I'm feeling fine, Jasper. I'm sure it'll be alright. I can pay you now if you'd like."

"No! no! It's not that, really!" He seemed determined. Lucy was somewhat surprised that the promise of more money hadn't swayed him.

"Maybe there's someone else I could go to," she said truculently. "I'm sure there must be other people who do this kind of thing."

She stole a glance at the old man and saw him waver as he replied, "But they don't have the travel enhancer."

"Perhaps I don't need it." Lucy's obstinacy was beginning to annoy Frakes.

"You'll never see him again!" the old man fired back, losing his temper.

"You don't know that for sure."

"I'm telling you! You'll never see him again!"

"And you'll never see my money again!" Lucy was all the way to the door, her hand just a fraction of an inch from the doorknob.

"Alright! Alright!" Frakes conceded wearily, slumping down into his chair. "I'm too old and tired to argue. But don't say I didn't warn you."

"Oh, thank you, Jasper!" Now that he'd agreed, Lucy felt ashamed that she'd pressed him so unmercifully. She rushed back to him, kneeling on the floor at his feet. "I'm sorry, Jasper. I didn't mean to yell. Everything will be alright—you'll see." But though she spoke to him in a conciliatory fashion for some minutes before leaving, he remained pensive and uncommunicative, refusing even to acknowledge her farewell as she closed the door behind her.

When she arrived back at the house in Chelsea, Jackie sniffed as she helped Lucy off with her jacket.

"Has Jasper been leading you astray with his bad habits?"

"What? Why?"

"I thought I could smell cigarette smoke. I wondered if he might have tempted you to one of his ghastly home-made things, but—" she sniffed again. "On second thought, this has more of a classy odor to it. You weren't smoking, were you?"

"No, honestly. In fact—" She tried to remember if she'd seen Frakes smoking that afternoon. Unless he had lit a cigarette while she was at the Chateau, she was almost positive that he hadn't.

"No. I'm sure he didn't smoke while I was there."

It didn't occur to Lucy to consider it strange that she'd thought of the episode at the chateau as being an actual experience, a real-life encounter with people of solid flesh and blood. But it was peculiar, now that Jackie had mentioned it. She could just detect a very faint trace of smoke on her clothes, or was it in her hair? It must have come from the taxi that she'd ridden in from Jasper's flat. Never mind; she'd be taking a shower before they went out again that evening anyway.

Going with Jackie to The Opera House at Covent Garden had been an annual ritual for longer than Lucy could remember. But this year, she'd been so lost in the obsession that had gripped her so exclusively that she'd forgotten all about it until Jackie had mentioned the tickets for *Mefistofele* that night.

Lucy was particularly thrilled because it was an opera that Dvorkin had so often performed—something to which she'd listened over and over again those past few weeks while working in the room looking out over the garden at Dover Street.

Then suddenly it struck her. Of course! At the chateau, the last thing she'd said to him: "I'll see you at the opera."

Mefistofele! And wasn't that the name of the cat that Jasper had befriended? What a coincidence! Of course, she knew that whoever was singing the part that night would never measure up to Dvorkin's performance. It was always something of a letdown to hear others falling far short of his genius, but still, she could imagine that he was there.

* * *

Despite heavy traffic, they arrived at the opera house with plenty of time to spare. After leaving their coats with the cloakroom attendant, Jackie suggested they have a drink in the bar. While sipping glasses of Chardonnay, the two friends stood looking discreetly around at the other patrons, putting their heads together occasionally to comment on a dress or hairstyle. A young man in a suit fidgeted uncomfortably with his obviously unfamiliar tie and tightly buttoned collar. An elderly woman with a blue rinse and poorly applied make-up, making her look like a ridiculous caricature, was talking loudly to her companion. This companion, a short, stocky man with thinning grey hair, was making a pretense of listening to her but, from time to time, cast surreptitious glances at an attractive young woman in a short skirt standing just behind her.

"Things are definitely not what they used to be." Jackie sighed. "Isn't that awful! I sound just like an old woman, but really! Some of these people make you feel positively overdressed." She nodded towards a female in a green silk dress with a neckline that plunged virtually into non-existence.

Lucy laughed. "I'm sure the men don't mind. Let's face it, we just wish we could still wear things like that." She looked down at her own modestly-cut black dress.

"Look at those shoes," Jackie continued. "My God! If I wore things like that now, I'd be crippled for a month. How do they do it?"

"She'll be sorry later on," Lucy predicted. "I remember when we used to totter about in high heels and skirts so tight we could barely jump on the bus."

"And wore dark glasses all the time, even at night, because we thought it looked cool. I'm sure that's what did my eyesight in," Jackie said regretfully, hoisting her spectacles a little higher on the bridge of her nose.

"Either that or reading books until two in the morning under the bedcovers," Lucy reminded her.

"Possibly. Anyway, don't you ever miss those days when you could get away with wearing clothes like that or doing crazy things and no one caring just because you were young and were expected to behave just a little bit weird?"

"Yes, sometimes," Lucy said thoughtfully.

"Do you think we're having a mid-life crisis, or is it too late for that?" Jackie asked ruminatively.

Lucy, buoyed by her experience of that afternoon and for whom life had suddenly taken on a whole new meaning, said cheerfully, "I prefer to think of it as a re-awakening, something that happens to remind us just how great life can be. We shouldn't look on it as a crisis but a wonderfully enlightening experience."

"Well, I'm glad you can think of being on the wrong side of fifty as a wonderfully enlightening experience," Jackie told her pessimistically.

Just then the warning bell sounded. Finishing their drinks, they filed into their seats along with the rest of the audience. Once everyone was settled, the lights dimmed, and the conductor appeared, acknowledging the polite applause. Raising his baton with a flourish, he launched the orchestra into the overture. As the music gradually built to a crescendo, Lucy imagined how Dvorkin would have been waiting in the wings, giving his costume its final inspection before stepping out onto the stage.

She felt a sudden surge of warmth and a momentary dizziness and wondered if she should have worn something a little more lightweight. These increasingly frequent hot flashes that she'd been experiencing lately could be very inconvenient at times. However, Lucy had been determined to soldier on without resorting to a lot of doubtful medications. As a consequence, she found herself flinging off cardigans and fanning herself frantically during the day, and opening windows wide and casting off all the bedclothes at night.

The sound of the chorus seemed to ebb, and the stage was no longer clearly visible. Although they hadn't been able to secure seats in the most advantageous position, they were near enough to the stage to make the constant use of opera glasses unnecessary. But now, Lucy could barely make out the elaborate scenery.

She hoped she wasn't coming down with the flu or something worse. Her eyes didn't seem to want to focus, and she squeezed them shut in an effort to clear them. In that moment, she missed the entrance of Mefistofele, and suddenly the voice—*his* voice—proclaiming *"Ave Signor,"* forced its way into her consciousness.

It…it couldn't be! And yet she would have recognized that arrogant declaration anywhere. She opened her eyes, and with growing alarm, she was certain now that either they or her fevered imagination were playing serious tricks on her. For surely, that figure, the diabolical face, the cloak insolently flung aside to reveal the semi-nude body, were all those of someone alarmingly familiar to her. It was absurd, and yet she knew without question that the man who was singing on the stage was Nikolai Dvorkin.

* * *

The fiendish creature who now commanded the attention of every single person in the subdued brilliance of the red and dark gold auditorium of the Palais Garnier bore absolutely no resemblance whatsoever to the charming bon-vivant of the night before. He had become so thoroughly immersed in his present role that he was no longer Nikolai Dvorkin playing the part of Mefistofele—he was the very devil himself.

What a superb yet satanic figure he presented as, half naked, he paced about the stage like a fierce yet cunning beast; his voice, so in tune with the demonic character he was portraying, sent chills through Corrine's body as she watched spellbound.

As he stepped from the stage into the wings, she felt a zephyr of cool air on her back. She realized that someone had crossed the raised, copper-edged threshold and entered through the polished-wood door into their box, silently slipping between the interior velvet curtains and approaching Lord Lockstone's chair.

The man, of medium height and wiry build, was not in evening dress but was smartly turned-out nevertheless. As he drew near, he placed a well-manicured hand on Lord Lockstone's shoulder. Lockstone, somewhat startled, turned to the man, who bent to address him in hushed tones so as not to disturb the others. Lockstone nodded in assent, and the man, having delivered his message, went away.

Corrine wondered what had passed between them and hoped that he had not brought bad news. She'd become accustomed in the past to ill-omened messengers who had on so many occasions pitilessly interrupted such pleasant evenings with her father. They often called him away from parties, plays, or concerts at a moment's notice to intervene in some crisis or other, placate an agitated ambassador, or soothe the ruffled sensibilities of a demanding member of some foreign legation.

But Lockstone didn't appear concerned by the intrusion. Her fears allayed, Corrine's attention was again drawn to the story unfolding on the stage.

During the entre-act, they all made their way to the lounge, where Lord

Lockstone had ordered champagne for everyone in the party. Lady Lockstone chatted enthusiastically about the character who had so easily dominated the first part of the performance.

"Wasn't he marvelous?" Maude gushed. "I don't think I've ever enjoyed an opera so much before. What a physique the man has!"

Her mother, overhearing this remark, looked rather shocked by her youngest daughter's indelicate observations. She wondered if Corrine Standish hadn't been something of a bad influence on her daughters these past few weeks.

"And a spectacular voice," added Florence, who, out of loyalty to her fiancé back home in England and respect for her mother's finer feelings, preferred not to dwell on the stunningly sensual attributes of the great singer that the daringly immodest costume had more than adequately displayed.

When Lord Lockstone returned, followed by the sommelier skillfully balancing a tray laden with glasses and a magnum of champagne, he announced to everyone assembled at the table, "We've been cordially invited to go backstage after the performance. That was Nikolai Dvorkin's man who came to the box during the first act."

Florence gasped with pleasure and Maude clapped her hands. Her mother gave her a reproving glance but couldn't hide her own delight at receiving such an invitation. They all began talking at once.

Lord Lockstone smiled and bent down to whisper confidentially to Corrine, "I have a feeling that we are indebted to you for this singular honor."

"But—why?"

"Oh, just a mild observation, that's all." He smiled at her, but then his face took on a more serious aspect. "Be careful, my dear."

She knew he was concerned for her safety and well-being, but Corrine couldn't help feeling a twinge of resentment. Did he think she would be so easily bowled over by this flamboyant Casanova? Fortunately, just when the moment promised to develop into an awkward situation, the tension was broken by the arrival of Neville Wyndham, Dimitri Gurvich, and Count Bronowski. Corrine introduced them.

"How are you, Miss Standish?" Wyndham enquired.

"Very well, thank you."

"And how are you enjoying our friend's performance?"

"Superb! He has the character down to a fine art."

"Yes. Nicky is very adept at playing both the devil and the angel, on stage and off," Bronowski observed. "One is never quite sure with whom one will be confronted at any given moment."

They all laughed politely, and general conversation resumed until the bell summoned them back to their seats.

After the performance, Dvorkin's man came to escort the Lockstones' party backstage, as promised. They followed him closely along the circular promenade paved with Venetian mosaics. They passed busts of famous composers, mounted atop marble plinths, who gazed stonily down at them. Their path led through salons and corridors with gilded walls, lit by rows of *torchères,* which seemed to come alive with the stunningly executed motifs of mythology, history, flora, and fauna.

At the foot of a flight of white marble steps, they passed through a plain wooden doorway, leaving behind the glittering domain beyond the footlights and stepping into the noisy, crowded passageways of a completely different world, squeezing past workers busily engaged in dismantling scenery and little groups of supernumeraries and chorus members standing about gossiping or helping each other with their costumes.

On they went, past wooden carriages waiting to lift performers up toward the stage, under catwalks and over trap doors, between a forest of wooden rostrums and battens, across sub-stages and through a labyrinth of ropes, counterweights, and winches, until at last they reached their destination.

Samuel Solomons, Dimitri Gurvich, and Neville Wyndham were already in the dressing room when they entered. The three friends watched with some amusement as Dvorkin made a great show of welcoming the newcomers, heartily shaking hands with John Lockstone and exuberantly kissing the hands of Lady Lockstone and her daughters, leaving traces of stage make-up on their white kid gloves.

He had fully expected to see Corrine with them; his disappointment was evident when she failed to follow them into the dressing room. "I thought Mademoiselle Standish was with you this evening," he remarked peevishly.

"She is…at least she was with us a moment ago," Lockstone observed with a note of concern. "She must have been delayed along the way. Perhaps you would be kind enough to send your man back to look for her."

Dvorkin perfunctorily seated his guests, his initial enthusiasm deflated like a punctured balloon until, looking back over his shoulder, he saw Corrine framed in the doorway. His mood changed instantly to one of boyish charm and joie de vivre as, hurrying forward and kissing her outstretched hand, he brought her into the room. "I was afraid you had not come," he said as he led her in.

"I'm sorry," Corrine, who had been fascinated by the magical world behind the scenes, laughed. "I stopped to speak to one of the chorus members and lost my way." Wyndham rose to offer her his seat.

"No, thank you all the same, Mr. Wyndham," Corrine told him, as Arturo, Dvorkin's manservant, hurried forward with drinks for the assembled guests. "I'd much rather stand." While the others chatted, she wandered about the room looking at the pictures that decorated the walls.

There were several hastily yet skillfully drawn sketches of Dvorkin in various costumes, mostly those of the character he was currently portraying, but some showing him in previous roles and one in everyday clothes. Corrine thought how marvelously his tall, expressive form lent itself to such informal works of art. She noticed too that most of the pictures had been executed by the talented hand of Dimitri Gurvich, his sprawling initials appearing in the lower right-hand corner of the portraits.

The others were still talking, and Corrine, turning back to observe the little party, was struck by how animated everyone had become. They all seemed so much more alive in Dvorkin's presence.

"Would you be kind enough to sign my program, Monsieur Dvorkin?" Maude finally had plucked up the courage to ask him.

"And mine also?" Lady Lockstone handed Maude her program, and the young girl advanced hesitatingly over to where Dvorkin stood. He held out his hand to receive them, the red silk dressing gown draped carelessly about his body falling open to reveal the imposing musculature of his broad chest and well-shaped legs barely covered by the material of his costume.

"Of course. It would be my pleasure." He took the programs and, finding a pen on the dressing table, signed the cover page of each with a flourish.

Emboldened by his obvious good humor, Maude remarked, "Your make-up is most convincing, Monsieur Dvorkin. I'm quite trembling with fear."

"Thank you, Mademoiselle Lockstone," the big man replied with a laugh. "I take that as a compliment." He handed the programs back to Maude, giving her a radiant smile. Then, turning to Corrine, he asked, "Would you like me to autograph your program also?"

Corrine remained where she was and held out her program, forcing Dvorkin to cross the room to where she stood. The others were talking with Solomons, Neville Wyndham, and Dimitri Gurvich, their attention momentarily diverted. As Dvorkin returned the signed program to Corrine, their hands touched inadvertently, and he said in a lowered voice, "And do I make you tremble, Mademoiselle Standish?"

"If I tremble at the touch of your hand, Monsieur Dvorkin, it is not from fear."

Almost as soon as the words left her lips, she regretted them. Why on earth had she said such a provocative thing? Was it really this easy for him to be so irresistible? It was as though, like some magician, he cast a spell on those around him. He really was the devil!

She withdrew her hand quickly and turned her attention to the miscellaneous paraphernalia spread out on top of the singer's dressing table: bouquets of flowers, letters and telegrams, make-up and hairpieces, and, presiding over all, a photograph of a most attractive woman surrounded by four children whose ages ranged from only a few months to possibly seven or eight years. The sight of such happy and innocent faces made Corrine feel all the more guilty for the thoughts that had flitted briefly through her mind.

Naturally encouraged by the words that she had let slip, Dvorkin followed her, and seeing that she was looking at the picture, he picked it up and said with pride and affection, "My wife Eugenia and our children."

"She's very beautiful," Corrine told him.

"Yes. This is the most recent picture I have of her. She sent it to me only last week. The children are growing so quickly."

Just then, the door opened and Count Bronowski entered the room.

"Ah, Vladimir! Here you are at last." Dvorkin advanced to shake the newcomer's hand, then went off in search of further refreshments, leaving Corrine still holding the picture.

Bronowski looked around and, noticing Corrine, casually made his way over to her side.

"Miss Standish," he addressed her offhandedly with a nod of the head. She acknowledged his greeting with equal indifference, "Count Bronowski."

"I see you are admiring the picture of my cousin Eugenia. She is a handsome woman, is she not?"

"Yes. I was telling Monsieur Dvorkin I thought her extremely beautiful."

"She is indeed. She was very young when Nicky married her. He was head over heels in love from the moment they first met at my father's house in St. Petersburg."

"He must be sorry to leave her behind when he travels abroad," Corrine remarked.

"Yes," Bronowski agreed, then added, "but as you see, he always leaves her with a little something to remember him by." He snickered, and, disgusted by the man's coarse inference, Corrine put down the photo and walked away, leaving Bronowski smiling contentedly.

Meanwhile, Dvorkin, who appeared to be in no hurry to divest himself of costume and make-up, possibly because of the effect it seemed to be having on the ladies, sat down and began to tell a story with much gusto about an innkeeper and his daughters. Suddenly, a knock sounded at the door and Arturo went to answer it. He came back and whispered something to Dvorkin, who jumped up.

"Of course, yes!" he exclaimed. "I had forgotten. I'm sorry, please excuse me. A suit that I ordered yesterday has arrived." Then, after appearing to hesitate for a moment, he said, "Wyndham, my dear fellow. Can you possibly pay the man for me? I thought they would deliver it to the hotel, and I have no cash here."

The Englishman seemed happy to oblige and went away to complete the transaction, while Dvorkin returned to his guests and continued with the story.

After an hour or so, Lord Lockstone, feeling that the conversation was becoming less and less suitable for mixed company, stood up to take his leave, and the ladies followed. Corrine, who was the last to exit the room, brushed past Dvorkin, who had conveniently stationed himself in the doorway.

He caught hold of her arm. "When will I see you again?" he whispered urgently.

Corrine, who was momentarily taken aback by the directness of his question, said the first thing that came into her head. "Well, unless you happen to be near the *Rue de Tournon* tomorrow morning, I couldn't say. But it's a small world, Monsieur Dvorkin. Who knows, we may meet again someday."

How stupid! she thought, annoyed with herself. She hadn't been able to bring herself to say, *Never!* It was too final. But she felt confident nevertheless that there would be little chance of him parading up and down the streets of Saint Germaine on the slim chance that he might see her there. He surely had much more important things to do.

Maude came back to the dressing room at that moment in search of her friend, and seeing Dvorkin still holding on to Corrine's arm, she said brightly, "Come on, slow coach. You keep getting left behind. Goodnight again, Monsieur Dvorkin."

Maude hurried away. Corrine was about to follow when Dvorkin grasped at her ungloved hand, kissing it and pressing it passionately to his cheek. She pulled away from him, affronted and confused, and yet experiencing that same familiar tug at her heart.

* * *

Lucy felt someone touch her arm and realized that Jackie was saying something to her.

"Luce, are you alright?"

"Yes, yes, absolutely!" The house lights were on and people seemed to be leaving their seats.

"I asked you if you wanted to come out for a stretch, but you were miles away."

"Oh, I'm sorry, yes. I could do with another drink, actually." Lucy seemed in a bit of a daze. Jackie took hold of her arm.

"Right. Let's go then. The line will probably be a mile long at the bar."

Some minutes later, while they were standing with their glasses, Jackie remarked, "Not bad so far? The opera, I mean."

"No," Lucy agreed. "Quite good, actually."

"Is that a bruise on your hand?" Jackie asked curiously.

"What?"

"That mark, on the back of your hand. You didn't hit it on something, did you?"

Lucy looked down and touched the dark stain on her skin, smearing the greasy mark with her fingertip.

"No. It's nothing. I must have rubbed against something," she said dismissively, as once again she felt the imprint of Dvorkin's kiss upon her hand.

* * *

The next evening, as Lucy made her way to Battersea, she wondered if she should tell Jasper about the episode she had experienced at the opera house. Was it normal to fall into these hypnotic states at any time without even trying and without the benefit of the drug? If so, things could become very awkward, to say the least. And the stain on her hand? That certainly wasn't normal.

She rang the bell and waited. No one came. She pressed the bell again. After a minute or so, just as she was about to give up and go away, the door was pulled open. A slovenly man with a stubbled chin and uncombed hair, wearing jeans and a grubby grey-white T-shirt stretched over a bulging beer belly, stood looking at her.

"Yes?"

"I'm here to see Mr. Frakes."

"Oh, yes? Well, you'd better come in then. Number three at the back." He pointed down the hallway.

"Yes, thanks. I've been here before."

He followed her a short distance and stopped at his own door, watching her as she continued on to Jasper's flat. She knocked on the door and was rather surprised when there was no answer. She knocked again, with a little more force this time, but there still was no reply. She turned and realized that the man was watching her from his doorway.

"Do you know if Mr. Frakes is home? He was expecting me."

"The old coot's as deaf as a post." He came out into the hallway again and slouched down to where Lucy was standing. She knew that Jasper's eyesight was bad, but she was fairly sure that there had been nothing wrong with his hearing. The man thumped on the door and bellowed, "Frakes! You've got a visitor. Get up, you lazy sod!"

When there was still no answer, he shrugged. "The silly old bugger must have forgot you were coming. He's probably down the pub."

He turned and went back to his flat, this time closing the door behind him. Lucy was by turns angry and apprehensive. She wondered if Jasper was alright and put her ear to the door, but she could hear nothing. Jackie had said that he was unreliable, that was true, but still. Maybe he was at the pub.

She went back out into the street and walked down to The Bishops Miter. The interior was smoky and crowded. Someone was playing a piano that was badly out of tune, but no more so than the customers who were singing to its accompaniment.

She looked around, hoping to find Jasper there among the regulars, but there was no sign of him. She went up to the bar and ordered a small glass of sherry. She wasn't used to being in places like this on her own, and she felt rather self-conscious as she took her drink over to an empty table and sat down. She noticed that some of the patrons were watching her, summing her up, probably wondering if she were meeting someone. She waited in the public bar for thirty minutes, hoping that Frakes would come in, determined not to stay longer but stretching the deadline to an hour when he didn't show up. She ordered a second drink and watched the door for another fifteen minutes, starting up hopefully each time someone came in and subsiding in disappointment as she realized that none of them was Frakes.

Inevitably, a man who had obviously had rather too much to drink approached Corrine's table and, breathing whiskey fumes in her face, confidently leaned down to ask her if he could buy her another round. This final indignity was the last straw, and getting up, Lucy left The Miter and returned to Chelsea.

"Well, I did tell you," Jackie began when Lucy explained what had happened.

"Yes, I know," Lucy cut her off. "But there may be a reasonable explanation."

"We'll give him a jingle in the morning if you like, just to make sure he's alright," Jackie suggested.

"Yes, I think we should. I must admit, I am rather worried about him." Lucy remembered anxiously how Frakes had appeared when she'd left him the day before.

* * *

The next day, Lucy dialed Frakes's number and waited apprehensively until someone picked up the phone at the other end.

"Hello, Jasper?"

"Yes."

"It's me, Lucy Welbourne. Are you alright?"

"Yes, why?"

"I came over last night. You weren't there. Did you forget that I was coming?"

"Oh, my dear Lucy! Oh...I'm...sorry. I...yes. It slipped my mind completely. I really am very sorry. One of the curses of old age, I'm afraid. I went to the cinema. I hope you weren't inconvenienced too much."

He couldn't bring himself to tell her that he'd been there at the flat all along. At least, he had been there, but far, far away too; he had stayed in the past much longer than he'd intended and missed his visitor.

"No, that's alright," Lucy told him, feeling rather annoyed by his admission but willing to excuse Frakes's absentmindedness in view of his age. "I stopped in at The Bishop's Miter for a drink, then went back to Chelsea."

"Would you like to come over this evening, instead?" he asked hopefully.

"Yes, alright." She remembered then that she'd planned to go out for dinner with the Shellabys, but she was sure they'd understand.

"Yes, right...well, I'll see you this evening then. Seven o'clock shall we say?"

Having made the assignation, Lucy, much relieved at finding Jasper in better spirits, went to look for Jackie to excuse herself from their dinner plans.

"How long are you going to go on with this experiment, Luce?" Jackie, a little put out by this sudden change of plans, couldn't help feeling that Lucy's continued visits to Jasper Frakes's flat were becoming obsessional, and she felt responsible.

"I don't know. As long as I can, I suppose. It all seems so real."

"But it's not, is it. Not real in the sense that anything actually happens."

"Oh, but it does," Lucy contradicted. "I wish you could see what I see. It's like getting a second chance at life. And I have to know what happens next."

"But what if you're disappointed, Luce? You've read the books. You know he never left his wife. What if it turns out that this Corrine was just a casual fling like all the others? Ever since we found out her name, I've been scouring every single thing written about or by him. You would think that if she played a major role in his life, there would be some mention of her, but do you ever remember seeing her name in any of the biographies? Did he ever refer to her in his writings? No. I just don't want you to be hurt, that's all."

"Isn't it just possible that no one ever found out about Corrine Standish? The press was far less intrusive back then, and I feel certain he would never have mentioned her in public."

"But even so..."

"I know. It sounds ridiculous, but even if it only turns out to be a one-night stand, I have to go through with it. I must know."

Jackie shook her head. "I have a bad feeling about all this, Luce."

But Lucy, like Jasper Frakes, was already hooked, and nothing anyone could say would change her mind. The stage had been set and the show was about to go on.

14

HOPE FOR THE FUTURE

"JASPER, IS IT POSSIBLE TO GO INTO one of these hypnotic trances without actually going through the usual process? I mean taking the drug and everything, you know?"

He looked rather alarmed. "Why?" he asked warily. "Has it happened to you?"

Lucy was disconcerted by his sudden concern and quickly brushed the question aside.

"No, no. I just wondered, that's all." She wouldn't tell him now. She was afraid he might call everything off. She couldn't risk that.

But he'd already sensed that something was wrong. "No, I've never had such a thing happen before," he said slowly. Realizing that it was probably pointless to say but still feeling the need to stress caution, he added, "But don't you think we should wait for a while? Maybe give it a week or two before we try again." He was reluctant to turn her away; he couldn't stand another argument, but there was no sense in killing the goose that was so readily laying the golden eggs.

"No!"

Frakes was stunned but not surprised by the vehemence in that single word.

"No," she repeated more calmly. "I don't want to wait. I told you before. Let's not go through all this again. I'll pay you double the amount to go on with it today—now. How can you refuse, Jasper?" Lucy placed herself in front of him, arresting his movement, grasping his frail arms in the old grey cardigan, and looking into the watery blue eyes behind the thick, scratched lenses of his glasses.

"You know, don't you? You know what it's like to become part of the past. That's why you had to quit the job at the shop, why you couldn't answer the door when I came here last night." She'd guessed the truth; she could see the silent admission in his eyes.

He nodded, bowing his head. Lucy released him.

"You're right, of course." He couldn't deny it. It was a relief, in a way, to admit to the truth. "I can't imagine any other way of living now. It's an addiction, oh not…not the drug itself, that's safe enough, but…the need to revisit one's past, the bad as well as the good times. I've been doing it for so many years now." He gave a cynical smile. "I find the past is so much more palatable than the present."

"Yes, I know what you mean. I'm beginning to feel the same way myself."

"But do I have the right to draw you into the same kind of dependency?" the old man fretted.

"I'm free to choose, Jasper. No one's holding a gun to my head. Come on, we're in this together now, for better or worse. Don't let's argue anymore. You must know I'd give you everything I have to be with him again. And if I die tomorrow—well, it wouldn't be such a terrible thing."

* * *

As she sat waiting for the drug to take effect, she thought back to what Jackie had said earlier in the day. *What if she was right?* If that night at the opera had been the last time that Corrine Standish had seen Dvorkin, it might have all come to an end right there—before it had ever really begun. Had Corrine been so determined to remain aloof from the allure of Dvorkin's magnetic personality that she'd deliberately avoided any further contact with him? Lucy was about to find out.

* * *

It was early in the morning when Corrine, accompanied by Florence and Maude Lockstone, set out from the hotel near St. Michael's English Church on the *Rue du Faubourg-St-Honore*. They were driven in the Lockstone's Silver Ghost, crossing the *Pont de la Concorde* towards the tree-canopied boulevards and narrow cobblestone streets of Saint Germaine.

The girls left the car near the *Palais du Luxembourg*, and as they strolled along, an enticing aroma of freshly brewed coffee and warm croissants wafted up to meet them from the quaint cafes nestled among the art galleries and book shops lining the sidewalks.

Already the street bustled with activity: a shopkeeper, unlocking and throwing open his doors, called a cheery "Bonjour" to the little waiter in his crisp white apron, industriously sweeping under the tables on the pavement outside the corner bistro, who in turn passed on the greeting to the local gendarme returning from his beat, who gave a brief but courteous salute in reply.

The conversation that morning between the three girls had centered largely on the proceedings of the evening before. They continued in this vein, recalling with pleasure every word, nuance, and gesture that had impressed and intrigued them as they joined the ever-increasing throng of pedestrians making their way up and down the boulevards of Paris.

Florence had just finished relating to the others the conversation that she'd had with Neville Wyndham when Maude said excitedly, "Look! Isn't that him? Nikolai Dvorkin, coming towards us?"

"My Goodness! Yes, I believe it is." Florence patted her hair and smoothed her skirt, while Corrine's heart sank as the immaculately dressed figure in a white linen suit came up to meet them.

"Good morning, Mademoiselles!" Dvorkin raised his hat and bowed theatrically.

"What a charming surprise to meet you here." The note of astonishment in his voice did not deceive Corrine, but Florence acknowledged his greeting, and he turned to fall into step beside them.

"You do not object if I join you?" Although it was put in the form of a question, it was obviously more a statement of fact, for he seemed determined to escort them no matter what.

"Of course not. Really, we'd be delighted!" Maude exclaimed enthusiastically. Encouraged, he took her arm and put it through his own, causing her impressionable young heart to flutter.

"I'm surprised to see you out and about this early in the morning," Corrine observed, mentally kicking herself for ever letting slip the fact that they could be found there.

"Oh, I don't need much sleep, and there are too many beautiful things to see in Paris." Dvorkin ignored the jibe and squeezed Maude's arm meaningfully.

"Where do we go first?" he asked her.

"Florence wants to buy perfume. I intend to purchase lingerie, and Corrine is looking for a book shop," Maude eagerly volunteered their itinerary, much to Corrine's dismay.

Dvorkin listened with polite interest, and Corrine, who could have cheerfully strangled her friend right there on the pavement, came to a sudden halt and addressed him.

"Really, Monsieur Dvorkin, I hardly feel that our little shopping expedition can be of any interest to you." She hoped he would find their plans too frivolous or tedious to want to accompany them. "Please feel free to pursue other more worthwhile activities if you prefer."

"On the contrary." he replied. "I am fascinated. And please, call me Nicky. All my friends do."

They again fell into step, with Corrine walking in silence as Maude and her sister kept up an animated conversation with Dvorkin until they reached the *parfumerie*.

He opened the door, allowing the three girls to pass ahead of him into the shop, as the tinkling bell announced their arrival.

The girl behind the counter looked up as they entered, and Corrine thought she perceived an unmistakable expression of recognition in the eyes of the pert young shop assistant as she caught sight of the man who accompanied them.

After several minutes of intense discussion on the merits of various perfumes, Maude applied a dab of *L'Heure Bleue* and held out her wrist to Dvorkin for his approval. "What do you think of this one, Nicky?"

He inhaled the perfume, which smelled strongly of a heady mixture of jasmine, rose, and vanilla, and replied, "Heavenly, Mademoiselle Maude! It's perfect for you."

"Or should I get the Chanel Number Five. It's all the fashion just now. I really can't decide."

She hurried away to consult with Florence, who was looking wistfully at a flacon of Guerlain's *Mitsouko*. Dvorkin casually sauntered over to where Corrine was examining a gleaming array of delicately fashioned bottles displayed to their best advantage on the counter.

"And which one do you favor, Mademoiselle Standish?"

Corrine did not reply but selected a bottle and dabbed a little of the fragrance on the inside of her wrist.

Dvorkin drew closer and lowered his voice. "I am told by many women that the perfume should be placed here, between the breasts. Is that correct?" He put his finger out towards the pink silk of her dress—she quickly stepped back, startled by his blatant boldness.

"Yes, you're well informed," she said, quickly recovering her equanimity.

Undaunted, he continued, as though nothing had happened. Picking up a large black flacon, he removed the gold-topped stopper and sniffed at the contents. "Mm, very nice. My Sin," he read the label with a little smile. Holding out the bottle to Corrine, he added, "And what is your sin, Mademoiselle Standish?"

She took it from him and, sampling the fragrance, said, "I don't know that I have one, or at least not one worth mentioning."

"Then maybe you would permit me buy the perfume for you, and you would possess one."

Corrine looked at him with contempt. "Why, Monsieur Dvorkin, you've quite mistaken your calling. You should have been a shopkeeper." She handed the bottle back to him and walked away, but moments later, when his attention was momentarily diverted by the two Lockstone sisters, she asked the assistant to include a small bottle of My Sin with her other purchases.

Stung by Corrine's comment yet determined to pursue her, Dvorkin brushed aside the insult and kept up a cheerful banter with the Lockstone girls as they walked along the busy boulevard until, a little further on, they came to a shop selling women's intimate apparel. Maude, despite Florence's attempts to dissuade her, insisted on entering with the others in tow.

Under normal circumstances, Florence, who had rather old-fashioned ideas regarding what was appropriate behavior, would not have dreamt of entering such an establishment in the company of a man. She blushed bright crimson, while Corrine, who was not easily shocked but who nevertheless felt ill at ease in Dvorkin's presence in any case, tried to assume an insouciant air of indifference as they were confronted by items of dainty and decidedly feminine underwear.

Dvorkin stood and watched with amused interest, taking a perverse pleasure in embarrassing the two young women. Meanwhile, Maude, carried away by her new-found daring and oblivious to their discomfort, did nothing to help the situation. She gayly asked his advice on the suitability of silk versus satin for pajamas, while the singer fingered the filmy garments with a practiced air. Finally, once Maude made her purchases, they left with a sigh of relief.

Dvorkin was humming a merry tune as they walked in the sunshine through the district of St. Germaine when suddenly he took off his hat and waved it energetically in the direction of two men who were walking in the opposite direction on the other side of the street.

Neville Wyndham and Dimitri Gurvich crossed over at his bidding and greeted them in an ebullient manner.

"Bonjour, Mademoiselles," Neville beamed at them. "We are just on our way to *Pierre's* for lunch. Won't you join us, ladies?"

Maude, who had fairly got the bit between her teeth, answered quickly, "Yes, we'd love to," and Corrine, thinking that there was at least safety in numbers, offered no objection.

When they arrived at *Pierre's,* they found the outdoor seating area already crowded. But Dvorkin, with the advantage of height, spotted a table that had just been vacated, and they made their way over to it.

Neville Wyndham pulled back a chair and held it for Florence, and Maude, hoping that Dvorkin would do the same for her, was disappointed when Gurvich performed the duty instead. Dvorkin, meanwhile, was endeavoring to catch the eye of a waiter who was serving the people at the next table, and Dimitri eagerly hastened to assist Corrine, who was standing looking about her at the other diners. As he was about to pull the chair back from the table, Dvorkin, realizing what was happening, stepped between them, brusquely shouldering the young man aside.

"Please, let me help you, my dear Miss Standish."

Corrine took her place, and as Dvorkin guided the seat forward towards the table, he leaned down, his face close to her hair. It happened in an instant, and she thought she might have been mistaken, but Corrine could have sworn he'd whispered, "You are adorable."

Before she could react, however, he'd seated himself at the opposite side of the table between the two sisters, all smiles, beckoning to the waiter who hurried up to take their order.

Corrine could not help noticing the whispers and glances of the people at the surrounding tables as they looked over to where she sat, several of them pointing furtively in her direction. *Thank God!* She at least was unknown to them, even if they recognized her male companions. But too many more chance meetings like this, and they would soon begin to wonder just who she was.

"So how do you like Paris, Miss Standish?" Wyndham, who was sitting to her right, asked, finally gaining her attention.

"I adore it. It's so full of life; hope for the future."

"You've been here before, of course."

"Yes, many times before the war, but I don't think I fully appreciated the true vitality of the place until now."

She looked across the table at Dvorkin who was watching her intently and she quickly turned back to her neighbor.

"Did you hear what happened to poor Chagall last week?" Dvorkin boomed, taking command of the conversation as he usually did. They all shook their heads.

"He went back to his *La Ruche* studio to retrieve some of his paintings that he'd left there before the war, and they were all gone. Can you believe that? All that work, gone!" He laughed unsympathetically, but Gurvich, who could sympathize with his brother artist, was horrified.

"Tragic! How can you be so heartless, Nicky? Think of it. What a loss!"

"Oh, of course, I went to his hotel to see if there was anything I could do, but…" Dvorkin added, shrugging expressively. Then, changing the subject he turned to Florence. "Did you see the premier of Stravinsky's new ballet *Les Noces* in June? No? Ah, my dear Miss Lockstone, you missed a treat. Gerald and Sara Murphy hosted a superb dinner in celebration afterward on the barge down by the Pont de la Concorde. They insisted that I attend, and it was too good an opportunity to pass up. Naturally, Diaghilev was there, and Picasso too."

The others appeared entertained by this anecdote, and Dimitri was about to make an observation when Dvorkin interrupted, pointing to a girl on the other side of the street. "Look, Dima! Isn't that the little tart from *Le Chabanais*? The one who turned up at Roscoff's party the other night?"

Dimitri, reluctant to claim an association with anyone from that famous Parisian brothel in front of their present company, assumed an air of innocence, but Dvorkin would not let the matter rest. "I'm sure it is. Most agreeable, but of course she can't hold a candle to that plump coquette, Mimi; wouldn't you agree, Dima?"

Gurvich blustered and quickly turned the conversation to a safer topic, although he would have been much relieved to know that the Lockstone sisters were quite unaware of *Le Chabanias'* reputation. Corrine, on the other hand, knew exactly what went on at such places.

After lunch, the two friends accompanied Dvorkin and the girls to a nearby bookstore. Once inside, Dvorkin grasped Neville's arm urgently.

"For God's sake, keep these two chattering magpies busy for a moment will you," he whispered, indicating Florence and Maude, and hurried off leaving Wyndham to point out titles and discuss plots and sub-plots with the two sisters.

Dimitri was about to follow, but Dvorkin waved him back, and the young man, suddenly realizing what his friend had in mind, reddened and returned to the others.

Corrine had wandered through to the back of the shop and was turning over a pile of torn and dusty books that had obviously been set aside for repair. She picked up a copy of *Crime and Punishment* and was leafing through the pages when Dvorkin joined her.

"Do you like Dostoevsky's work?" he asked, leaning over her shoulder to see what she was reading.

"No." She put the book down abruptly. "It's too grim. Everything you Russians write is so depressing." The remark was unworthy of her, Corrine knew, but it was meant merely as a rebuff.

Dvorkin wasn't to be put off so easily, though. "But it's well written; you must admit that," he persisted doggedly.

"Yes, but it leaves one feeling as though life is hardly worth living."

"For many in Russia, it hardly is," Dvorkin said coldly.

"True—I was there and saw the poverty as well as the luxury," Corrine was quick to remind him. "But when I read, I want to be entertained, not made to feel guilty about people's hardships." Again, she felt embarrassed by her own words but couldn't resist the urge to argue every point with him.

"Well, what about your Dickens?" Dvorkin countered. "He made the same kind of social commentary, didn't he?"

"But he did inject a subtle humor into his stories."

"Yes. It makes poverty, disease, and death much more palatable." He sounded bitter. Corrine instantly regretted her words.

Dvorkin's own past was shrouded in mystery. It had pleased him for people to think that he'd sprung from humble beginnings, but it had also been rumored that, in fact, his background was one of wealth and privilege. Only he knew the truth, and since no one, friend or family, rich or poor, had come forward to confirm or dispute his antecedents, his roots remained an enigma.

"I'm sorry. I didn't mean to sound unfeeling."

"Oh, you have nothing for which to be sorry." He leaned closer. "I could forgive you anything."

"But you misunderstand me," Corrine bristled. "I don't want to be forgiven for having an opinion."

She walked away, hoping that he would take the hint and leave her alone, but he followed and, catching up to her by a display of poetry books, took a volume down from the shelf and examined it with feigned interest.

"You are right, Corrine. I do misunderstand you. One minute you seem to be welcoming me with open arms, and the next you trample on my good intentions."

She smiled in spite of herself. "I have no desire to trample on anything. But as to welcoming you, I don't know what you mean by that."

"Oh, come now. You are not such an innocent." He laughed sardonically.

For Corrine, this was the last straw. "I may not be innocent, Monsieur Dvorkin, but I do have certain moral standards, something that you seem to be sadly lacking." She pushed the book that she'd been holding back onto the shelf and returned to where Maude and Florence Lockstone were discussing the works of Arthur Conan Doyle with Neville Wyndham.

"I think it's time we were getting back." Corrine looked pointedly at her watch.

The men protested, but Dvorkin, who had come up to join them, mumbled tersely, "Let them go."

Florence, looking from Dvorkin to Corrine, sensed the note of discord between the two. "I think Corrine is right. We should get back. My fiancé is arriving from London this evening."

"Yes. We're dining at *Adrian's*," Maude added unnecessarily, glancing at Dvorkin and wondering if he would make use of this generously proffered intelligence. Would he go there? He was so charming, so handsome. If only she could have the same kind of effect on him that Corrine seemed to command. She couldn't help noticing how he had looked at her friend ever since that night at the chateau. But Maude had also taken note of Corrine's cool demeanor towards him that morning. Was she only playing hard-to-get? Well, all was fair in love and war, and if she could steal the prize away, she would. Surely, he wouldn't waste his time on a woman who showed so little interest in his advances when there was someone so close at hand who was more than willing to give him anything he wanted.

She blushed at the wanton thoughts that this imposing figure had inspired in her—she, who until now, had given only modest kisses to the young men who'd escorted her, with her parents' permission, to various social functions and events.

"At least allow us to accompany you back to Faubourg St-Honore," Dimitri offered solicitously.

"Thank you, but it really isn't necessary," Corrine refused the offer. "We'll take a taxi back."

Outside, the sun had disappeared behind a blanket of dark grey clouds, and the pavement was becoming spotted with raindrops as Dimitri hailed a passing cab. Goodbyes were said, but Dvorkin remained sulkily aloof from the group, making a point of ogling two young girls as they walked past, giggling. Not until the last moment did he turn his attention to the departing car, waving a brief farewell to its passengers.

Damn the man! Corrine thought as they drove away. Why did she always feel this terrible, wrenching sensation whenever they parted?

* * *

The next morning at the house in Chelsea, the phone rang, and Jackie, swallowing a mouthful of toast, went to answer it. When she returned, she told Lucy, "Sorry, last-minute crisis. I've got to go to Wimbledon to look at a collection of first editions. The people want a decision today. They've got several prospective buyers, but they wanted to give me first refusal, so I really should go and see if the things are genuine. You could come with me if you like."

"No that's alright." Lucy already had other plans. "I'll amuse myself."

"If you're sure. It won't take long. I'll be back by mid-afternoon, most likely."

"Go ahead. Really, I'll be alright."

Lucy had already toyed with the idea of looking for Corrine's house in Belgravia; this seemed like the ideal opportunity.

She'd already located Tunbridge Square on Lionel's map of London, but when she eventually arrived there later that morning, Lucy realized with dismay that she had no idea which of these elegant residences had belonged to the Standish family.

She had supposed she would recognize it, that she'd retained enough of Corrine's memory to lead her directly to her old home. She was disappointed when, looking about, hoping to see something familiar, nothing suggested itself.

Lucy disconsolately followed the ornamental iron railings surrounding the little garden in the center of the square and found the gate slightly ajar. She gave it the merest touch, and it swung open with ease, as though inviting her to enter.

Stepping gingerly inside the enclosure, meant only for the use of the residents in the surrounding houses, she fastened the gate carefully, hoping that no one would discover her intrusion, and, sinking down on a bench beneath a magnificently crowned London Plane tree, she became lost in thought.

She wondered whether Corrine Standish had played here in this secluded oasis, under the watchful eye of Madame Granville. Although the house itself had not struck any chord of remembrance, she felt strangely at home in this miniature park, with its neatly kept flower beds filled with sweet-smelling roses and the lifelike bronze statue of a fawn that stood perpetually grazing on the little patch of lawn.

Lucy could imagine the young girl walking sedately along the pathways or dabbling her fingers meditatively in the little fountain at the heart of the garden. Corrine had been a lonely child, quiet and shy, not given to running and skipping about as other youngsters might, but placidly passing the hours under the strict and subduing influence of her governesses.

It was as though Lucy could see her, at various stages of her life, growing before her very eyes. First, toddling on unsteady legs as she took her first steps in the garden; then playing with a small, yapping dog, throwing a stick for it to run after; next, a demure adolescent pacing contemplatively in the dappled play of sun and shade beneath the twisted branches of the plane tree, reading a book. In one moment, a child, and in the next, a young woman.

And then came the day when John Lockstone arrived at the house to tell Corrine that her father was dead. Lucy could tell immediately, for she experienced a feeling of such deep sorrow that she wanted to cry out. She watched, fascinated, as Corrine came hurrying down the steps of the mansion and ran across the street to the garden. She saw her drop to her knees beside the fawn and fling her arms about its rigid neck as though seeking solace from an old and trusted friend.

After some minutes passed, Lord Lockstone followed her, and Lucy felt strangely comforted as she watched him help Corrine to her feet, offering consolation and a clean white handkerchief with which to dry her tears.

"Oh, Daddy! I do miss you so much," Lucy heard herself saying, although whether grieving for her own father or Corrine's, she couldn't tell.

Somewhere a car horn sounded, and Lucy, startled by the sudden noise, was roused from her reverie, the figures quickly fading.

Once again, she realized with alarm, these shadows from the past had come unbidden—so real, so lifelike. This time, however, as Jasper had suggested, she'd merely been a spectator, a silent witness to the events that had unfolded so many years ago.

Lucy was beginning to feel hungry. Looking down at her watch, she saw that it was already midday and time for lunch. But she was disinclined to return Chelsea just yet. Standing up stiffly, she left the garden in search of a suitable place where she could get something to eat.

She hadn't walked far before she came to a likely-looking restaurant. Glancing first at the menu posted in the window, she stepped inside.

They were busy with the usual lunch-time crowd, and Lucy listened to the clacking of dishes and conversation as she waited to be seated by the hostess, who eventually led her past tables filled with diners to a booth situated near the doors to the kitchen.

Better than nothing, Lucy thought philosophically, as the hostess dropped the menu on the table in front of her with a weary smile. "Enjoy your meal," the woman uttered the well-worn phrase unconvincingly before hurrying away.

Some time passed, and Lucy began to wonder if they'd forgotten about her when the waitress finally arrived to take her order.

Not surprisingly, the delay seemed interminable before she returned.

Beginning to feel rather drowsy, Lucy was on the verge of nodding off, when her order was put down unceremoniously in front of her with an apologetic, "Sorry for the wait, dear. We've been rushed off our feet today."

Lucy smiled sympathetically as the beleaguered server hurried away. Picking up a soup spoon, she was about to dip into the steaming bowl of minestrone, when all the lights went out, the sound of people talking and knives and forks clattering on plates fading into silence.

It lasted for only the briefest of moments; then, the talking and clinking glasses resumed, and the lights came back on.

* * *

Adrian's was an older establishment, much patronized by English visitors to Paris. While the 'bright young things' sought entertainment in the clubs and cabarets of Montmarte, thrilling to the dynamic performances of singers such as the young Josephine Baker, many of the Lockstones' generation took pleasure in dining to the strains of Rubinstein's *Melody in F*. This piece was played by a resident quartet consisting of two aging female violinists, a drooping-mustachioed cellist, and a portly piano player, their evening repertoire in the manner of salon music of the *fin de siècle*.

Corrine had taken extra care with her toilette that evening, dressing in stunning Nile-green satin strewn with coral beads and had, at the last moment, put a little of the My Sin in the delicate hollow of her throat.

The evening proceeded with polite conversation, accompanied by succulent appetizers. The waiters had just cleared away the remnants of an excellent cheese soufflé when everyone's attention was suddenly diverted by a commotion caused by the entrance of a large party consisting of several attractive young women accompanied by as many boisterous gentlemen in evening dress.

Even before they'd all been seated at their table, Corrine recognized the booming voice that dominated the newcomers' conversation. Feeling a mix of anger and embarrassment and seeing Lord Lockstone looking at her enquiringly, she tried hard to assume an air of sublime indifference, as though this latest arrival was not of the slightest significance or interest.

Nikolai Dvorkin was calling noisily for vodka and caviar while the others chattered and laughed.

"I say, who is that awful lout?" Arthur Walmsley, Florence Lockstone's fiancé, who was seated next to Corrine, asked, surprised that the other diners seemed prepared to tolerate this boorish behavior.

"I…I've no idea," Corrine lied and was immediately unwittingly betrayed by Florence, who, seated on the other side of Walmsley, leaned forward to address her, "There's Dvorkin again."

"Oh yes, so it is." Corrine's reply was nonchalant.

"Would you believe it, Arthur? This is the second time today that we've run into him." Florence related briefly their encounter earlier in the day, carefully omitting any mention of the lingerie shop.

Walmsley was about to make another remark, but Corrine was saved any further comment by the waiter, who, busily serving the second course of roasted breast of duck with *gratin dauphinois* and *foie gras* sauce, had insinuated himself between them.

Maude, who was seated to Corrine's left, however, nudged her and nodded towards the adjacent table.

"Look who's here."

Corrine ignored her.

Was this mere coincidence that their paths had crossed once again, or had he deliberately sought her out? Surely, she'd made it abundantly clear this morning that his attentions were unwelcome. No, it must have been sheer chance that had directed his footsteps here tonight.

The newcomers had finally settled down to the business of ordering. Even Dvorkin's voice subsided as he scrutinized the menu, but as the evening progressed, the conversation at his table became more animated.

Since Dvorkin's arrival at Adrian's, Corrine had been determined not to look in his direction and had, for the most part, been successful. But now she could no longer resist the temptation to steal a glance at the neighboring table. He must have already been watching her, though, for, much to Corrine's chagrin, their eyes met. She wanted to look away but couldn't. It was as though she'd been turned to stone, and she watched mesmerized as, eyeing her meaningfully, he put his arm around the pretty mademoiselle seated next to him. As his vivacious young neighbor turned her face toward him, he kissed her full on the lips, his left hand sliding up from her waist, over the velvet, peach-tinted material of her dress to her breast.

The gesture lasted only a moment despite encountering merely token resistance, and he released the young woman with a laugh. He looked defiantly back at Corrine, and seeing that she was still observing him, he raised his glass to her, a mocking smile broadening his sensual mouth.

How abominably crass and vulgar the man was! Did he really think she cared about his crude antics?

The dessert, a vanilla pannacotta with warm raspberries in a delicate pastry case, arrived accompanied by a late-harvested Muscat, and for several minutes, the company devoted themselves entirely to the enjoyment of this delicious culmination to their meal.

Corrine, who now felt that another morsel would choke her, made an effort to finish this last confection, when a voice said, "Is there anything wrong with the soup? Would you like me to get you another one?"

* * *

Lucy blinked and put down the spoon.

"I…no, that's fine. I'm sorry. I'm not as hungry as I thought. Could you just bring me a cup of coffee and the check please?"

"Well, I don't know." The harassed waitress sounded doubtful. "I've already put the order in."

"That's alright," Lucy assured her. "I'll pay for it."

The waitress relented. "Alright dear. No problem." She hurried away to get the coffee, wondering if she could expect a tip.

* * *

"That's a nice perfume you're wearing. What is it?" Jackie asked when Lucy arrived back at the house later that afternoon.

"My Sin," Lucy said without thinking, then realized that it was the name of the fragrance she'd purchased in St. Germaine. She remembered how Dvorkin had reached his hand toward her breast as they stood so close in the *parfumerie*. What an agony of indecision—a turmoil of confused and tortured thoughts had consumed her just then. She knew that he wanted her, and she'd longed to give in to him, but visions of his wife and their children arose like an invisible barrier between them. After all was said and done, did she really want to be just another member of his harem, a passing fancy to be forgotten as soon as he moved on to his next engagement?

The scent conjured up an intense image of that evening at Adrian's too—so real, so clear, but of course it hadn't been, and yet how could the perfume, that tantalizing mixture of lily of the valley, lilac, and jonquil, have permeated her skin?

Again, Lucy had to remind herself that these things hadn't actually happened, at least not to her, but the memory was so vivid that it was difficult to separate fact from fantasy.

More importantly, however, was the growing problem of those increasingly frequent shifts in time. How would they affect her daily life in the future? Would she suddenly find herself, at work or in a store, succumbing to one of the now familiar trance-like states? Lucy was beginning to wonder if, after all, Jasper hadn't been right about the effects of the drug and his insistence that they use it only sparingly. She couldn't decide whether to tell the old man about these lapses or not, and when she went to bed that night, she still hadn't made up her mind what to do.

Of one thing she was sure, though: fate, as it had in the past, would decide her actions. Life would go on for Lucy as it had for Corrine, the two becoming inextricably linked by the man who dominated their every move.

15

FORGIVE AND FORGET

FLORENCE LOCKSTONE STOOD GAZING speculatively at the painting entitled *The Death of Sardanapalus*, the work by Eugene Delacroix that had inspired Neville Wyndham to write an opera for Nikolai Dvorkin.

"Oh dear," Florence sighed heavily. Was Corrine doing the right thing? She was very much concerned about her friend and had doubted the wisdom of her father's usually sound advice.

"Miss Standish is not with you today?" The voice, echoing deeply in the cavernous and empty gallery of the Louvre, made Florence jump.

"Monsieur Dvorkin, you startled me. No, I'm afraid not. She left Paris this morning."

"To go where?" Dvorkin seemed surprised and rather put out.

"I'm not sure." Florence, who was not used to subterfuge, wasn't very convincing. "She had some business to attend to. I—"

"Ah, no doubt she has gone back to London then," the big man surmised.

"I couldn't say." Florence wished he would leave before she could unwittingly be drawn into betraying her friend's confidence.

"Will she be coming back soon?" he persisted.

"No, it's not likely."

She looked around for an avenue of escape, but he continued, "I myself am only here for a week or so longer; then I will be taking a holiday, a trip home to Brussels, to see my wife and children."

"I'm sure they must be looking forward to seeing you again," Florence remarked politely, and was relieved to catch sight of her family strolling through from an adjoining gallery at the further end of the room.

"Yes, I'm hoping—"

"Well, if you'll excuse me, I really must get back to my party. They'll be wondering what's happened to me." Florence smiled, and Dvorkin inclined his head in farewell.

He turned and watched her walk away towards a group of people standing at the far end of the gallery. He recognized them all: Lady Lockstone, her youngest daughter Maude, and the man who had been with them at Adrian's, probably Florence Lockstone's fiancé. But no Corrine, he thought bitterly.

Ever since he had first set eyes on her at the chateau, he'd wanted her, longed to hold her in his arms, and not just to dance around the floor as they had done that night, although that had been delightful. Despite a life of romantic attachments and, some would say, downright debauchery, his sexual appetite was not yet jaded. He'd been blessed with enduring good looks and a certain charm that women seemed to find irresistible, and they threw themselves at his feet. How could any red-blooded man resist the temptation?

Of course, being a celebrity was an additional attraction, but it could also be a curse at times. For he couldn't make a move without it being reported in the papers, and it had tugged at his conscience on more than one occasion to think that his wife would read of his exploits and know that he was still up to his old tricks.

She was an amazing woman who had forgiven him time and time again for his infidelities and who'd finally come to accept, with stoical fortitude, the fact that he was incapable of being true to one woman alone. She refused to divorce him, however. Apart from the fact that her religion would not allow her to sever the bonds of matrimony, she couldn't give him up, for she was certain that he still loved her, and, of course, there were the children. He loved them dearly and tried to be a good father, even if he wasn't always an ideal husband. He knew he didn't see them as often as he ought. He'd quickly discouraged any idea that the family might travel with him when he was on tour, knowing that their proximity would necessarily curtail any amorous adventures in which he might feel inclined to indulge.

He sent them presents when he remembered, and when he was with them in Brussels, he did his best to make up for his many deficiencies. Well, he thought resignedly, he would make love to Eugenia like a dutiful husband; after all, it wasn't so very irksome, for she was still a most desirable woman. But it would be very difficult to shake the image of Corrine from his mind, even in the embrace of someone as beautiful as his wife, and he sighed because, for once, he was at a loss. Should he pursue his inclinations and continue to court this young woman, or was she really so impervious to his overtures? He suspected that she may already have a lover. Her hand often strayed to the golden locket at her throat, and he cursed this unknown rival who seemed to command her affections and loyalty. But surely if that were the only thing keeping her from giving in to him, he could, with all his knowledge and experience of the fair sex, overcome such a minor obstacle.

Yes, he thought there might yet have been a chance, for although she'd seemed so cool towards him ever since their walk along the boulevards of St. Germaine, he thought he had detected that familiar spark of desire when he'd kissed her hand at the chateau. Hadn't she said herself just the other night that he made her tremble, and not from fear either? If only there hadn't been that unfortunate incident at his hotel yesterday. Why couldn't she just forgive and forget?

And now she'd gone—stepped out of his life with no word of farewell. Nothing. How could he have been so mistaken? *Damn her!* He wouldn't waste any more time daydreaming about her. There were plenty more pebbles on the beach. *I could have anyone I want!*

But he wanted her, and she'd turned her back on him. He couldn't forgive that blow to his ego or forget her. This unprecedented predicament was giving him a headache.

Was it really likely that Florence Lockstone didn't know where Corrine had gone? he wondered. *No, it was not possible. They must know where she is!* He would find out somehow.

He walked slowly after the Lockstone party, keeping a discreet distance between them, and he remained unnoticed until an opportunity presented itself some minutes later when Maude Lockstone became separated from the others as she lingered to look at *The Poet's Inspiration*. He joined her.

"How nice to see you again, Mademoiselle Maude. You are looking as beautiful as ever."

"You shouldn't flatter me so, Monsieur Dvorkin." Maude, who had seen him approaching and had deliberately remained behind in the hopes that he would engage her in conversation, replied coyly, fluttering her eyelashes in what she hoped was a becoming manner.

"But it is true," he protested. "You are the most radiant creature around. More beautiful even than the Mona Lisa here in the Louvre. I have not seen anyone in Paris who can compare with you."

"Oh, come now, Monsieur Dvorkin…Nicky. I've seen the way you look at Corrine. Don't tell me you don't think she's beautiful."

"Oh, her. She is nothing. Anyway, I understand that Mademoiselle Standish has left Paris already. Where is it that she has gone? Back to London?" He tried to sound nonchalant.

"Oh, I don't think I can say…that is…I don't really know." Her lie was as unconvincing as Florence's had been, but Dvorkin was confident that he could coax the truth from her, that this particular flower would open.

"Ah well, it does not matter. But on a topic of more importance, tell me, is there a chance that you might come out to dinner with me this evening?"

"Oh, I don't think that's possible." She hadn't expected him to be quite so direct and became flustered, but seeing his look of disappointment and not wishing to let the opportunity slip away, she hurried on, "But I might be able to manage lunch tomorrow if you're free."

"That would be delightful. Shall I call for you at—one o'clock—shall we say?" He'd already guessed the answer, but he wanted her to make the suggestion.

"Oh no, no. I think I'd better meet you somewhere." After all that fuss with Corrine, Maude was certain that her father would be furious if he knew of this secret meeting.

"Of course. How stupid of me." Dvorkin apologized. "We must be discreet, must we not? Do you know a little hotel on the *Rue St-Lazare* near the Opera called *La Belle Lola?*"

"I believe so, yes."

"Then shall we meet there?"

"Alright. Yes, I'll be there at one. I must go now, before they come back for me."

"Until tomorrow, then." Dvorkin kissed her hand. "I long for the moment."

Maude hurried away, her heart beating wildly at the thought of the coming tryst.

* * *

It was on the following night that Corrine Standish threw open the windows of her bedroom in a villa several miles from Paris and looked down at the moonlit courtyard below.

She'd made her escape from the city and the man who had inspired so many conflicting emotions within her. Ever since that night at the chateau, Dvorkin had seemed like one of the dozens of roses that he'd sent her, romantic yet capable of inflicting wounds that were deep enough to draw blood. How apropos that he should have showered her with this particular floral tribute on that last night in Paris, as if to say, *Here I am, one of the most miraculous creations of nature. Accept me, but beware. I will cause you great pain.*

Well, she didn't choose to be hurt, and she was thankful that she hadn't given in to him. But had it, after all, been rather a storm in a teacup? Looking back, from the safety of this sanctuary in Cerisiers, she wondered why she had fled the city. Had it really been such a necessary expedient? Was she so insecure in her feelings for this man that she couldn't trust herself to stay near him—that given enough time, he would eventually overcome her defenses? Well, it didn't matter now. Out of sight, out of mind. He would soon forget about her, and she would be free to return to London.

Her first instinct, when she'd realized that things were getting out of hand in Paris, had been to fly to the safety of the house in Belgravia. But realizing that it would be too easy for Dvorkin to trace her there if he was really determined to see her again, she had decided against it.

She had all but resolved on her course of action when John Lockstone found her alone and deep in thought after dinner one night.

Guessing that something was amiss and having a reasonably good idea as to the source of the problem, he approached her and, hoping to bring the matter out into the open, hazarded, "Something's troubling you, my dear. I wish you'd tell me what it is. Perhaps I can help."

When Corrine didn't reply immediately, he couldn't help giving voice to his suspicions.

"It's that scoundrel, Dvorkin, isn't it?"

Corrine looked up in surprise. "Is it that obvious?"

"I'm afraid so, my dear." Lockstone was already blaming himself for introducing her to the incorrigible Russian star— admittedly, in all innocence— merely to gratify his daughter's whim. Why did he give in so easily to these silly girls? He should have known better!

"The blackguard deserves a horsewhipping if he's as much as laid a finger on you!" he rumbled threateningly.

"No, no!" Corrine was startled by his anger. "It's not as bad as that, truly, but he is persistent, and it's becoming rather a nuisance. I don't want to sound melodramatic, but I'm afraid if I go back to London, he is quite capable of following. He seems very determined. I did think of maybe taking a trip to Italy."

"It's outrageous!" Lockstone interjected hotly. "The man's a menace! Mark my words: if he's not careful, one of these days someone's going to take matters into their own hands. He leaves a trail of irate husbands and outraged fathers wherever he goes, but he has the devil's own luck and always manages to talk his way out of any serious trouble. He should be locked up for his own and everyone else's good!"

He stopped short when he saw with dismay Corrine put her hand to her face, her eyes suddenly filling with tears.

"Well, well. That's as maybe," he said more gently. "I didn't mean to

210

upset you, Cora. It's certainly not your fault. But really, there's no need for you to travel so far afield, my dear. I think I may have the solution to your problem if you're agreeable. My sister Agnes—you remember her—owns some property, a charming little villa just outside Cerisiers. She's traveling in America just now, so she won't be there for at least a month or two. The family has made use of the place from time to time, and I'm sure she wouldn't object to your staying there for a week or so until all this how-de-do blows over. She keeps a permanent staff, a housekeeper and so on. I'll send word to expect you, shall I?" Then, struck by a sudden idea, he added brightly, "Florence and Maude can go with you."

Corrine didn't want to hurt his feelings, but she felt she must speak her mind.

"Would you think it terrible of me if I begged you to allow me to go there alone? I love Florence and Maude like sisters, of course—that goes without saying—and at any other time I'd welcome their company, but these past few weeks have been so hectic. I really need some time to myself. Your suggestion that I come and stay here with you all was most generous. I've enjoyed my visit to Paris enormously, and it has helped me to get over father's loss, believe me. But it's all becoming a little overwhelming, and with everything that's happened recently—well—I'm sure they'll understand."

Corrine remembered with affection his reply and felt rather guilty for causing him such concern on her behalf.

"Well, if you're sure, of course, my dear. I quite understand. We've overtaxed you with all these social functions and so forth—done with the best of intentions, naturally—but we've been rather thoughtless, I'm afraid. I know you'll be in good hands in Cerisiers, and a week or two in the country will do you the world of good. I'll hire a car to drive you down there, then all you have to do is send word when you're ready to go home. You won't have to worry about a thing."

And John Lockstone had been as good as his word. The following evening, he'd told her that everything was arranged, and, bidding everyone a fond farewell, Corrine left for the villages and vineyards of Burgundy.

The only people who knew of her whereabouts were the Lockstone family, and under strict orders from Lord Lockstone, they were duly sworn to secrecy.

Corrine felt confident, therefore, that her temporary exile would be uneventful. Thus far, she had enjoyed the blissful tranquility afforded her by this unexpected stay among the half-timbered houses of the quaint village nestled among the rolling countryside of the Sens Valley.

Her time there had, for the most part, been spent alone. The only people living at the villa besides herself were Alain and Elise Roulot, the husband and wife who served as housekeeper/cook and handyman, but their presence was discreet and unobtrusive. Corrine was grateful for the opportunity to recover an equilibrium that the brief but disastrous brush with Nikolai Dvorkin had almost shattered.

It was a relief too, she had to admit, to get away from Paris and the sometimes-wearying company of Florence and Maude. The Lockstones had been extremely good to her, and she was grateful for their concern, but since the death of her father, she'd been accustomed to moving at her own pace, pleasing herself wherever she went and with whom. The unintentionally oppressive and overbearing solicitude of her godparents and their daughters had, at times, irritated her.

Here she passed the days as the fancy took her, sometimes cycling into the village on a rusty old bike borrowed from Alain Roulot. She'd ride past the church of St. John the Baptist with its imposing square tower on her way to watch some of the older inhabitants playing *boules* or stop to buy gingerbread at the patisserie.

She would sit for hours at the villa, in the shade of an old cherry tree, in a courtyard whose sunbaked walls were clothed in wisteria and climbing roses, reading or sketching, or wandering childlike through the surrounding fields, chasing butterflies and picking wildflowers. This was a freedom unlike anything she'd ever known.

Occasionally she would find Alain in the kitchen garden, his sleeves rolled up above his roughened elbows as he worked about among the chards and cabbages, and he would stop to offer up, with modest gardener's pride, a dusky aubergine or vine-ripened tomato for her approval.

Sometimes she stood in the kitchen watching Elise Roulot as the woman bustled about preparing the most succulent meals for her enjoyment. Nothing was too good for the goddaughter of Milord Lockstone—*boeuf a la Bourguignonne* made with the meat of creamy-white Charolais cattle, and *poulet de Bresse,* chickens fed solely on brown wheat, white cornmeal, and milk. These dishes were invariably accompanied by some of the finest wines of the region, such as the delicately flavored red or white *Cote de Beaune* or fruity *Pouilly-Fuisse,* and delicious cheeses such as *Bleu de Bresse* and *Meursault.*

The combination of this excellent food, fresh air, and exercise generally ensured Corrine a good night's sleep. However, on this particular night she remained wakeful.

The air was warm and filled with the fragrance of the basil, tarragon, thyme, and rosemary that grew in large terra cotta pots in the courtyard below.

From time to time, a light breeze blew the draperies at the window, and they rustled as the material fluttered, light as gossamer, within the bedroom.

She turned back into the room and slipped once more between the cool, crisp sheets that smelled of lavender, reminding her suddenly of Madame Granville, and sank blissfully into the down-filled mattress, her eyes closing wearily.

But it was no use. Now, whether because of the association made with Madame Granville or some other reason, she could not stop her thoughts from wandering back to that moment in St. Petersburg when, as a little girl, she had felt her heart racing at the sight of the handsome Russian singer.

Yet things were so much different now, and she couldn't regret her decision to repulse his advances. A clandestine affair with this demanding and egotistical personality could only have ended in sorrow and disappointment, she was sure—besides, she had no desire to be cast in the unenviable role of 'the other woman.'

She tried to empty her mind of the emotional chaff that clung so tenaciously, focusing instead on the mundane happenings of the day. She was just drifting off to sleep when a sound roused her, and she was once again wide awake. She listened, straining to catch any noise that was unfamiliar, but everything was silent. Deciding that it must have been an animal on some nocturnal venture, she dismissed it from her thoughts.

But now Corrine found it impossible to sleep, and after a few minutes of restless tossing and turning, she lit the lamp by her bedside.

Ever since her childhood, she often resorted to the soporific effects afforded by late-night reading. Now, unwilling to resort to the artificial aid of sleeping pills as so many among her acquaintances did, she reluctantly left the comfort of her bed to run and retrieve the book she'd left on the table downstairs.

Finding it, she picked it up, running her fingers lightly over the cover. Opening it, she looked at the inscription written in a large, flowing hand on the first page.

"To Corrine, with deepest affection. Nikolai Dvorkin."

He'd sent it to the hotel on the night of the dinner at Adrian's—the same book of poems that she'd picked up at the shop in St. Germaine. He must have returned there that afternoon and purchased it. Every instinct told her that she should refuse this token, which she took to be an apology for his boorish behavior, and that she should send it back. But something had stopped her. And she'd paid the price, for her misguided acceptance of this gift had opened the floodgates to a torrent of unwanted attempts by the singer to see her again.

The next day, he had called at the Lockstone's hotel, fully expecting to receive Corrine's grateful thanks, and was angered when she refused to see him. He stormed off and proceeded to drown his sorrows in vodka, indulging himself in a drinking binge that lasted until well into the afternoon, resulting in a late arrival and disastrously subpar performance that night at the Opera House.

Neville Wyndham, who had guessed the reason for his friend's condition, advised caution, counseling Dvorkin not to make a nuisance of himself in that quarter as Lord Lockstone had important connections in the city and could, if angered, make trouble for him.

Dvorkin, with his usual perversity, ignored the warning and continued to cherish the hope that, despite all rebuffs, he would win over the lady of his dreams.

The following morning, having read a scathingly adverse critique of his performance in one of the Paris newspapers and listening with uncharacteristic meekness to the admonitions of his long-suffering manager, Dvorkin settled down to write a letter that he had delivered to the hotel on Rue du Faubourg Saint-Honoré later that morning.

When Corrine received it, instead of just tearing it up unread, she opened it and was appalled to see the contents.

My Dear Miss Standish,

I am puzzled to know why you have been avoiding me these past two days. I had hoped that in accepting my gift, you had expressed a desire to continue our friendship, but apparently, I was mistaken. Had I known, I would not have wasted my money. However, it is of no consequence. I can only say that I wish you joy of it and hope that it will serve as a constant reminder that you treated me very shabbily.

Nikolai Dvorkin.

Corrine was furious, but she kept the matter to herself, causing the others to wonder what had put her in such a foul mood.

Later that day, still fuming from the insolence of his letter, she went out alone and made her way to Dvorkin's hotel. When the concierge called his room to tell him he had a visitor by the name of Mademoiselle Standish waiting for him in the lobby, he asked that she be sent up to his suite. Corrine accepted the invitation with alacrity, anxious to give him a thorough roasting and determined to put him completely in his place.

When Arturo opened the door, Corrine walked smartly in, prepared to launch immediately into her attack. But Dvorkin was nowhere to be seen.

"He'll be with you shortly, Mademoiselle Standish. Monsieur asked me to see that you are made comfortable. Would you care for a drink?"

"No, thank you."

This delay not only deflated her mood but also gave Corrine time to realize that she'd forgotten to bring the book with her. She'd meant to throw it back at him, but in her haste to get the confrontation over, she left it in her room. Well, never mind. It could go in the rubbish bin for all she cared.

Just then, a door opened, and Dvorkin entered. He was elegantly dressed and appeared calm but aloof.

"Well, Miss Standish, to what do I owe the pleasure of this visit?"

"It's no pleasure for me, I can assure Monsieur Dvorkin. I received your letter this morning and I can only say that, as one might have expected, they were not the words of a gentleman. I have merely come to tell you to your face that I have absolutely no interest in you as a friend or, for that matter, any other capacity. I want nothing more to do with you. Do you understand?"

"But you are here."

"Only to be certain that you are under no misapprehension about my feelings on this matter. I hope that I have made it abundantly clear to you that I find your attentions loathsome, that I am appalled at your persistence, and fervently hope that from now on you will please leave me in peace."

"Then go away and be damned!" His eyes were flaming with anger as he grabbed a nearby statuette and smashed it on the floor at her feet. Corrine did not flinch.

"Goodbye Monsieur Dvorkin."

She turned to leave, and as she walked through the door, she heard him call out, "Wait! I'm sorry, Corrine. I didn't mean what I said. I love you, and I cannot let you go. Please, let me explain how I feel."

She had failed. She'd been unable to convince him, to make him understand. Frustrated and in tears, she fled from the scene, leaving him to stare after her and Arturo to literally and figuratively pick up the pieces.

Her anger spent, she returned to the hotel, having decided that she must get away, but the book still remained in her possession. That night, much to her chagrin, Dvorkin had sent her dozens upon dozens of red and white roses, but it was too late. The wheels had already been set in motion for her escape.

* * *

She returned to her room with the book and, settling back against the pillows, was turning the pages in order to pick up where she'd left off when she again heard a furtive rustling outside her window. In the next second, she was astounded by the sound of a familiar voice, soft and clear, singing in soulful tones the refrain that she had first heard so many years before in St. Petersburg.

She leapt up and flinging on the peignoir that she'd left draped carelessly over the chair at the foot of the bed, hurried over to the window. In the courtyard below stood the figure of Nikolai Dvorkin.

Her first instinct was to interrupt this impromptu serenade and send him packing, but she couldn't bring herself to put an end to that well-remembered song sung so exquisitely. She allowed him to continue, fully intending to give him his marching orders at the conclusion. When it was finished, however, she could only watch bemused as he bowed low, sweeping the ground with the white fedora clasped in his hand.

She quickly pulled herself together. Thank goodness there was no one else there to witness this charade. The Roulots slept in their quarters over the old stables at the further side of the house. There was little chance that they would awaken from their slumbers at this late hour, for they always slept soundly, or so Elise had told her once during one of their kitchen *tête-à-têtes*.

"Corrine," he called softly up to her. "Please say you forgive me. I know I acted hastily…no…unthinkingly in Paris. I frightened you. That's why you ran away isn't it? I'm sorry. Can't we still be friends? You left and I had so much more to say to you. Won't you come down?"

It seemed churlish not to accept such a gallant apology, and since it was evident that he intended to hold his ground and fearing that he would cause a scene unless she relented, she pulled the robe more closely around her and went downstairs to open the door.

He stood penitently, hat in hand like an overgrown child, his blonde hair highlighted by the silver moonlight, his body throwing a giant shadow across the patio.

She beckoned him to come inside, but he remained motionless, and she felt a moment's regret that she'd come down. Leaving the security of the doorway and stepping out onto the paving of the courtyard, she walked slowly out towards him.

Reaching his side, Corrine looked at Dvorkin with a mixture of defiance and forgiveness. He took her hand, meekly kissing her fingers, though his eyes greedily devoured this charming vision that had appeared before him. Despite the nightgown and robe that she wore, the filmy material left little to the imagination, and it was all that he could do to resist the temptation to take her in his arms and crush her in his embrace there and then. But he was determined to fight off the impulse and behave as he supposed a gentleman was expected to, and though it tested his willpower almost beyond endurance, he reigned in the natural urge to take what he most desired. Releasing her hand, he stepped back a little in order to put himself at a safe distance from the delightful warmth and delicate fragrance of her body.

"You're forgiven," Corrine said softly. "At least for your behavior in Paris, but really you shouldn't have come here." It was meant as a rebuke, but it carried little conviction.

"You won't send me away so soon?"

"I must! Really Nicky! Surely you must realize you are putting me in a most compromising position by coming here like this."

His expression became sulky, and his lips were set like those of a petulant schoolboy, his eyes glittering fiercely with an underlying anger that was fed in part by an irrational jealousy of the unknown.

"Is he so very dear to you, that man who holds your heart in such a tight grip that you are not free to give it to anyone else?" he demanded, beginning to lose patience, his good intentions rapidly dissolving there in the moonlight. He pointed menacingly at the locket that hung around her white throat, then clenched his huge hand possessively in front of her face—she did not flinch.

"Yes," she answered truthfully. "He is everything to me. I believe I love him more than anyone or anything else in the world."

Smarting with the knowledge that he'd been so mistaken in his assessment of her feelings for him and that he'd come all this way only to be humiliated and rejected, his temper flared. His hand shot out towards her. Corrine, thinking that he was going to hit her, pulled back quickly, but not quickly enough. He did not strike, however, but grasped the locket and wrenched it away, leaving an angry red mark where the gold chain had bitten into her flesh.

"At least let me see this miserable dog, this worthless wretch who is my rival!"

He threw his hat aside and Corrine stood stunned as she watched him force his thumbnail into the golden heart, tearing the two halves apart at the hinge.

Now, however, it was his turn to be dumbfounded, for when he glared down at the picture inside, it was as though he were looking into a mirror. His likeness smiled up at him as though laughing at the incredible irony of the situation.

Too late, Corrine's hand had reached up to protect her secret, her shaking fingers still at her throat.

"I…please…return it. You have no rival," she admitted, and, mortified that she'd been discovered, she held out her hand.

But he did not return the shattered trinket. Instead, he slipped it into his jacket pocket, and with a groan of passion that could no longer be restrained, took her in his arms. She clung to him, and his mouth sought the soft, delicious tenderness of her lips. She was lost; drowning in the ecstasy of his kisses, all her resolve and self-righteous principles flew like paper petals in the wind.

No longer able to think rationally, she allowed him to lift her effortlessly off her feet. Turning towards the open door, her head pressed against his shoulder, he carried her upstairs to the bedroom.

16

THE HONFLEUR SUITE

"COME BACK TO PARIS!" It wasn't a question or a suggestion, but a command.

They were together in the big feather bed at the villa in Cerisieres, and, ever eager for more caresses even after a night filled with passionate lovemaking, the morning found them still entwined, rediscovering the pleasures of the preceding hours.

"No, I can't," Corinne whispered, half afraid, half regretful.

"You can! You must! I want you there with me!" Dvorkin was insistent.

She studied his face, her fingers gently tracing the determined line of his jaw.

"You know there's nothing I would love more than to be with you, but you must see how impossible it would be."

"But why? There is nothing I wouldn't do for you, Corrine. When there is such a love, anything is possible. Come back to Paris," he urged, his strong yet gentle hands stroking her breasts, the thrill of his touch giving added persuasion to his words.

"I wish it were that simple, but—" She was silenced from any further argument by an ardent kiss.

Later, when they were dressing, he resumed his entreaties.

"I give my last concert in Paris on Saturday." He looked at her speculatively beneath his blond eyelashes, trying to gauge her mood. "I have a three-week break before my next engagement—the longest of the year, thank God! I need the rest, but listen, the first week I go to Brussels to see Eugenia and the children."

Corrine felt a stab of resentment at the mention of his wife's name but kept silent, allowing him to continue.

"The two weeks after that, I plan to go and visit Neville and his wife in Honfleur. You must go and stay with them while I'm away. They can easily stop and pick you up here, and then I will join you all in Honfleur."

"But I can't just propose myself as a guest. They haven't invited me, and you can't possibly expect Neville to drive all the way out here to collect me."

"He will! Neville is my greatest friend. He will do anything for me," Dvorkin declared confidently. "When I get back to Paris, I'll go and see him, tell him that you must go with them to Honfleur."

"And what if he refuses?"

"He won't. Neville and I are like brothers. He will do this for me. And you will be waiting for me at Honfleur." He held her close and buried his face in her hair. "You will, won't you?"

Corrine, unable to summon up the power to resist him, capitulated. "Yes, of course. You know I will."

Just then, she was startled to hear someone knocking on the bedroom door and a voice calling urgently, "Lucy!"

* * *

Light was already forcing its way through the curtains; Lucy sat up in bed with a start. As she rubbed her eyes and tried to focus, the door opened and Jackie's tousled head appeared.

"Sorry Luce, we overslept. It's eight o'clock."

Lucy jumped out of bed and began pulling on her clothes. She'd planned on catching the early train back to Swannington, stopping briefly at the house on Dover Street, before going on to her job at Vanguards.

"I've put the coffee on. Would you like Lionel to take you back home, save you taking the train?"

"No, there's no need, honestly. I'll call the office and let them know I'll be in this afternoon. It's no problem really."

Lucy, who was completely disoriented, was only just beginning to realize that she was indeed there at the Shellaby's and not at the villa in Cerisiers. Luckily, she'd already packed her bag the night before, and it only remained for her to throw a few items into the suitcase and hurry downstairs, where Jackie and Lionel were scurrying about making a hasty breakfast of toast and cereal.

"Sorry Luce," Lionel told her. "Are you sure you don't want me to take you back to Birchford? Really, it's no trouble."

"No, honestly Lionel. If you can just run me down to the station, that'll be fine."

She wanted to be alone, to have time to think about what had happened last night. Once she was safely aboard the train for Swannington, she would have the luxury of being able to devote herself entirely to remembering that night at Cerisiers.

* * *

The house on Dover Street seemed cold and quiet when Lucy returned, the rooms impersonal and vaguely unfamiliar, her presence merely transitory, as though a visitor in someone else's home. She wandered through the rooms as if reacquainting herself with their layout, finishing up in the studio, where the painting of the house in Honfleur lay propped against the easel. That was where she belonged now, she told herself, as she looked more closely at the canvas.

Going back downstairs to the kitchen, she found several messages waiting for her on the answering machine. The first voice was her daughter, Robin, the words tumbling out, half cheerful, half apologetic.

"Hi mum! Just calling to let you know that I won't be able to make it over there this weekend for your birthday after all. Sorry! Dianne sprang it on me last night. She managed to get tickets for that show in Milan, so we're flying out on Friday night. Couldn't pass it up, could I? Hope you don't mind. But we can do something when I get back next week, promise.

Anyway, I'll talk to you later. Love you. Bye."

There was a click and silence. Lucy was bemused. Was it really her birthday, already? The months had slipped by almost unnoticed, and now that the present had become so mixed up with the past, she hardly knew what day it was. This time last year, if she'd received such a message from Robin, she would have been bitterly disappointed. As it was, it left the weekend free to go to Honfleur, or rather Jasper's flat, she corrected herself, but of course, it amounted to the same thing. She would have to call Jasper and set things up.

The next voice was Jackie Shellaby's. "Hey Luce! Just wanted to let you know that in the rush this morning you left your reading glasses here on the little bedside table, but I'm sure you've got spares. And also, the book. I didn't know you were into poetry. It's a beautiful edition, Luce. Where did you get it? Don't worry. I'll take great care of it till you get down again, or do you want me to send it back to you? Give me a call. Bye."

Again, a click and silence. *Book? What book?* Lucy couldn't remember. *Had she taken a book with her to Jackie's?* No, she was sure she hadn't. It would merely have been 'taking coals to Newcastle,' for there was a wealth of reading material at the house in Chelsea—Jackie had almost as many books in her home as she had at the shop.

She tried to think back to last night. She got back from Jasper's rather later than she'd expected and felt guilty, it being the last night of her visit to the Shellaby's. But Jackie and Lionel had been so enormously understanding. Lucy felt she owed them a debt of gratitude that she could never repay. If it hadn't been for Jackie's introduction to Jasper, she would never have met Nicky.

Nicky! The book! Of course! She'd been reading something in bed—not at Jackie's but at Cerisiers, just before Nicky's arrival. But how on earth had the book found its way to the house in Chelsea? Had the smell of his cigarettes and the perfume from the little shop in Paris, as well as the appearance of the book been mere coincidences, or was something happening that Jasper hadn't anticipated?

The old man might well have been concerned had he known of these unexpected occurrences and the ease with which Lucy had slipped into those hypnotic states without his assistance. Indeed, Lucy herself had wondered if another visit and further payment would be necessary given the circumstances, but try as she might, during the days after her return from London, the ability to step back into the past eluded her. By Thursday evening, she had to admit that she still needed Jasper and the travel enhancer.

It came as no surprise to the old man when her call came to hear that she simply must come to see him at the weekend.

Lucy kept this and all subsequent visits to Jasper to herself, fearing that her friends would again try to discourage her from pursuing her search for the truth about Corrine Standish and Dvorkin, thereby giving herself entirely into the hands of the person who had proved himself to be the one indispensable link between Lucy and her former life.

* * *

As Dvorkin had anticipated, the Wyndhams drove without complaint to Cerisiers to collect Corrine.

"Good heavens, Neville, this really is traveling in grand style!" Corrine exclaimed as she surveyed the gleaming Maybach in which they'd motored from Paris.

"Yes, thanks to Nicky, of course," Neville explained enthusiastically, giving the hood an affectionate pat.

"The countess generously put this magnificent machine at his disposal while he's staying in France, and Nicky kindly lent it to us while he's away. We got the little beauty all the way up to sixty-eight on the way here, didn't we, Dima?"

Neville looked for corroboration, and Dimitri Gurvich, who'd traveled from Paris with the Wyndhams, agreed as he jumped out of the car like an eager young puppy to help put Corrine's suitcases in with the rest of the luggage. When they were safely stowed away, he held the door open for her to enter. As she brushed past him, he caught a tantalizing whiff of My Sin and felt the softness of her skin as his hand briefly came in contact with her arm.

Marina was sitting in the back seat and Corrine slid in beside her. The two women exchanged greetings and Neville took his place behind the wheel while Dimitri climbed into the passenger's seat.

"Neville, do be careful." Marina, her voice holding just the smallest hint of some indefinable accent, leaned forward and tapped her husband's shoulder as he revved the engine in the manner of a race-car driver preparing for a quick start.

"He really is the most awful driver," she told Corrine with a sigh. "He's like a little boy with a new toy. I just hope we can return the car to the comtesse in one piece."

Sitting back and resigning herself to her fate, Marina turned her full attention to Corrine. "Well, my dear, it's so nice to meet you at last. Neville has told me very little about you, only that you are beautiful and intelligent and most agreeable."

"Your husband is too kind."

"Oh, I do not doubt him; the beauty I can see for myself. As to the rest, I hope we will get to know each other very well while we are in Honfleur."

"It was extremely good of you to come all this way to fetch me. I feel I'm being an awful nuisance."

"Oh, it's no bother. Neville knew how much it meant to Nicky. But will your uncle not wonder what has become of you?"

"I sent a wire telling him that some friends were stopping by to take me with them to Nice and that I would see him when I got back to London."

"Ah. And does he not mind?"

"Contrary to what you may have been told, I wasn't a prisoner in Cerisiers."

"But you didn't want your uncle to know that you were spending time with Nicky."

"No, I thought it best not to—well—not to worry him."

"Yes, I understand." Marina smiled knowingly and patted her hand. "Have you been to Honfleur before?"

"Briefly, before the war. We didn't really have much time to relax and enjoy the scenery." Corrine remembered those whirlwind visits to the

225

Continent with her father, hurrying from one city to another, while she was entertained by the wives of politicians and ambassadors as their husbands plied their trade at one diplomatic meeting after another.

"You'll love Villa Cheminon," Marina told Corrine as Neville inexpertly guided the Maybach along the winding country roads. "I've told Neville we should try to buy the place and live there permanently, but he refuses to break with England completely."

Neville shook his head. "I know," he admitted. "Marina's right. I can't explain it, but I feel like a part of me belongs in the Lake District, even though we rarely spend time in England these days. Marina thinks it's gloomy and dull, but it can be beautiful too. I've done some of my best work there."

"Then you should hold on to it, Neville," Corrine advised wholeheartedly. "I feel the same way about the house in London. Realistically it's far too big for me. Most of it is closed up now, but it's the most tangible thing I have left to remind me of my family. My father called it his safe haven. We spent so much time traveling around the world, seeing wonderful places, beautiful sights, and meeting the most interesting people, but he was always happy to get back home."

"Ah! A place to call one's own." Dimitri, who'd remained silent throughout much of the journey, sighed wistfully. "A place to put down roots and raise a family. You are a lucky man, Neville. You can drop anchor and know you have reached home. Nicky never seems to want to stay in one place for very long."

"But that's the life of an artist, Dima," Marina told the young man, patting him sympathetically on the shoulder. "You should know that by now. At least Neville isn't forced to travel about. He does, of course, because he enjoys it, but I'm lucky that I can keep him with me for months at a time, unlike poor Eugenia who only sees Nicky no more than two or three times in a year."

She realized, too late, her faux pas. "Oh, my dear! I'm so sorry! That was thoughtless of me." She put her hand on Corrine's and gave it a little squeeze. "I didn't mean to offend you. Please forgive me."

Corrine, certain that Marina's apology was genuine and sensible of the awkward situation into which Dvorkin's impetuosity had thrust his friends, replied, "Of course. I know this must put you in a very difficult position, having a foot in both camps, as it were. It's very good of you to befriend me like this. I've asked myself a thousand times if I'm doing the right thing. If only I could be sure."

"Nonsense!" Neville told her, glancing back over his shoulder and narrowly missing a car approaching from the opposite direction. "We're only too happy to have you stay with us."

"I meant about Nicky and me," Corrine whispered to Marina, not wishing to distract Neville from his driving any further than was absolutely necessary. Despite being a sophisticated young woman, Corrine had found herself in unknown territory as far as her passion for Dvorkin was concerned, and she suddenly felt very vulnerable and naive.

"I know, my dear," Marina reassured her. "Don't worry. You'll see, everything will be alright."

The sun was already beginning to set as they motored down a road, banked by apple orchards, that ran a few miles outside the 17th-century harbor town of Honfleur. Villa Cheminon lay nestled among the trees, its pink brick facade peeking coyly between festoons of cascading ivy. A curving, double stairway led up to the entrance of the three-story building, the balconies of which were draped in the same clinging vines.

The interior of the house, with its ornate oak woodwork, appeared cozy and welcoming, and Corrine was enchanted with the bedroom that had been chosen for her by Marina. She was given a tour of the rest of the house by Neville while Marina saw to the domestic arrangements. Dimitri trailed along behind them as, completing a circuit of all the rooms, Neville led them outside to view the surrounding grounds in the rapidly fading light.

After dining sumptuously on roast duck with an apple-jelly sauce enriched with Calvados followed by pears steeped in Benedictine, they had no inclination to do anything other than relax. They sat around drinking cocktails while Neville played the piano.

"That was beautiful, Neville." Corrine, who was already beginning to feel sleepy, put down her glass and applauded appreciatively.

"Thank you, my dear," Neville replied modestly. "I wrote it after I'd proposed to Marina and she accepted. I was so ecstatic, I had to pour my feelings into music, and that was the result."

"How romantic! How does it feel to be the inspiration for such a brilliant piece, Marina?"

"Neville is passionate about his music. That is something that we share: a passion for each other and his music."

"Are you working on anything now, Neville?" Corrine asked.

"Yes, it's almost finished. I began it last year when we were here. I think I shall call it *The Honfleur Suite*. Perhaps by the time we leave next month it'll be done."

"Well, Cheminon is certainly an inspiration in itself," Corrine said, kicking her shoes off and tucking her slim legs beneath her as she made herself comfortable on the sofa. "How did you come to discover it?"

"Actually, Cheminon belongs to an English friend of mine, Derek Foxworth," Neville explained. "He used to stay here with his wife every summer, but now that they're older and rather infirm, they are no longer able to travel such distances. Rather than relinquish the property altogether, they rent it out. I suspect that Daphne still hopes to persuade Derek to live out their days here, but he doesn't seem to want to leave England."

"I can imagine it would be difficult to part with such a gem," Corrine agreed.

Dimitri, who'd been sitting quietly most of the evening looking wistfully at Corrine, suddenly felt compelled to speak.

"No gem could compare with the beauty of two ladies such as yourselves." He stood up and bowed to his hostess and Corrine.

"Why, darling Dimitri! How gallant!" Marina, amused by the young man's old-fashioned chivalry, thanked him as she fitted a cigarette into a long, black, silver-tipped holder.

"You are a real gentleman, Dimitri," Corrine added kindly, recognizing in the flowery tribute the inescapable influence of his mentor. With no companions of his own age with whom he could interact, he had adopted the mannerisms and speech of his elders. The imitative gestures and words seemed anachronistic and incongruous.

"But it's true!" he insisted, suspecting that she was making fun of him, and, flustered by his own boldness, sank back down into his chair.

"Dima is trying his wings," Neville told his wife, laughing. "One day he'll find a ladylove of his very own and fly to new and undreamed-of heights."

"Stop embarrassing the boy!" Marina scolded her husband. "Play something lively to put us all in a light-hearted mood."

Neville proceeded to pound out an impromptu mazurka, and Marina, pulling Dimitri to his feet, danced gaily around the furniture in time to the rhythm of the music, pulling the boy with her as she went.

* * *

The next morning, after breakfast, Marina and Corrine strolled down to the stream that ran through a copse of trees at the northern boundary of the property. The conversation naturally turned to Dvorkin.

"I know people will think very badly of me; I did try to avoid becoming involved, but it was as though he—" Corrine corrected herself. "No. It's wrong of me to blame Nicky."

"Once Nicky makes up his mind about something, it's very hard to dissuade him," Marina told her. "When you left Paris, he was desolate. We knew he wouldn't rest until he brought you back. And it's easy to see why. These things happen, and love isn't something that can be ordered up like an entree in a restaurant or dismissed like a waiter with a wave of the hand. When it comes, as it has for you and Nicky, there's nothing one can do about it."

"But Eugenia…the children. I never wanted to hurt anyone."

"And you won't," Marina assured her. "If you're discreet, as I know you will be, everything will be alright."

"But it's so deceitful." Corrine, who had always been so honest and open with everyone, sounded unconvinced.

"You really must learn to accept the hand that life has dealt you, Corrine. If this is truly what you want and Nicky is happy, then don't be afraid to enjoy the kind of passionate relationship that most people seldom know. Life's too short to sacrifice our dreams for some misplaced sense of propriety."

"It's true. I couldn't leave him now, however high a price my conscience has to pay. But it sounds—well, I don't mean to pry, almost as if you were speaking from experience."

"Oh yes," Marina admitted, bending down to pick a wildflower growing beside the path. "I stole Neville from another woman, but that woman was his mother. She didn't approve of me; she did everything she could to keep us separated. It tore him apart, poor boy, to see her so upset by his refusal to part with me, but I hung on to my little bit of happiness, and in the end, I won the battle. Eventually she came to accept me as a daughter-in-law, and I was sorry, when she passed away, that we hadn't become friends sooner."

"Well, I hardly think that Eugenia would come to accept me if she knew."

"No, but don't forget, she has everything that she wants. She's married to Nicky, has his children, is well provided for, and, despite what you may think, is quite happy with the way things are as long as nothing happens to change the status quo. She doesn't stay with him out of love, at least not the kind of love that you have for him, but she'll never let him go."

"No, I don't suppose she will."

"Then don't, for the love of heaven, worry about something you cannot change." And with those final words of advice, Marina linked arms with Corrine and led her back to the house.

* * *

The first week at Villa Cheminon passed pleasantly enough, but for Corrine, the days went by at an agonizingly slow pace. She tried not to think about Nicky in Brussels with Eugenia, but it was impossible to dismiss him from her thoughts completely. Every so often, she would experience a moment of anguish mingled with jealousy at the notion that he was probably enjoying this precious time away from the rigors of the theater and the constant and often intrusive adulation of his many admirers, with his family. She quickly put these misgivings aside whenever she felt them, knowing that this was something to which she would have to become accustomed if she was ever to sustain such a fragile relationship.

But now the day had finally arrived when Nicky was expected to return to Cheminon and all the doubts and fears that had crowded Corrine's thoughts were completely forgotten. All she could think about was that he would soon be there in her arms. The moment she heard the car driving through the gates, she ran out onto the balcony outside her bedroom and looked down onto the driveway, where Neville, who had driven to Paris to meet the singer and his man Arturo, had pulled up in the driveway.

Dvorkin's imposing frame finally appeared as he climbed out of the Maybach, stretching his arms high above his head in an effort to ease the tension in his aching muscles. He had already thrown off his jacket, and his white shirt gleamed in the sunlight. Corrine watched as Dimitri ran out to greet him and saw the two embrace and converse animatedly as they disappeared from view.

Her first impulse was to run downstairs, but on second thought, she decided it would be better to give the two friends some time alone. She forced herself to wait as she watched Arturo carrying his employer's suitcases inside. It wasn't long however before the bedroom door burst open and Dvorkin came quickly across the room to take her in his arms.

* * *

Dvorkin had only been at the house in Honfleur for two days before his pent-up energy and restless spirit caused him to look elsewhere for new diversions. Thinking only of his own amusement, he took Dimitri to visit friends in Deauville, leaving Corrine at Cheminon with the others.

He hadn't told her of his plans, and it was left to Neville to explain his abrupt departure when she came down to breakfast that morning.

"Don't worry. He'll be back tomorrow," Wyndham said apologetically, knowing full well that his words would provide little consolation for the young woman who had waited so longingly for her lover to return from Belgium. "You know how impulsive he can be."

"Well, I must find something to pass the time then," she answered, summoning up a smile.

"Why don't we drive into Honfleur, just the two of us?" Wyndham suggested. "Marina has a sore throat and has decided to stay in bed today."

Corrine gratefully accepted, and when breakfast was finished, they departed.

* * *

The boats slapped gently against the water, the rigging of the masts jangling periodically as the gaily painted, little vessels rocked lazily on their moorings. The harbor was dominated by multi-storied grey and brown houses with their slate roofs and half-timbered facades.

They made their way past women who were selling flowers and produce from their stalls in the cobbled square of Place Sainte Catherine. Neville then led Corrine down a labyrinth of narrow passageways and uneven steps to Quai Sainte Catherine where they sat outside one of the many cafes overlooking the harbor.

Neville watched his companion as they drank their coffee, and feeling that small talk would be unwelcome, he ventured to say what was uppermost on his mind. "May I be brutally frank, my dear?"

"Of course, Neville." Corrine put down her cup and delicately applied a pastry fork to the generous slice of apple tart that was on her plate. "I hope we'll never be anything less than honest with each other, since we are friends." She tasted the deliciously warm pastry with its tangy fruit filling and waited for Neville to speak, looking at him with bright and trusting eyes. She had guessed the subject of his conversation and feared what he might say, but she valued his good opinion and wise counsel and was willing to listen to his advice even if she wasn't prepared to follow it.

"Nicky loves you, more than I thought he was ever capable of loving anyone, even Eugenia, which at the moment you may find hard to believe. But Nicky is...who he is. He can't help himself. I'm sure you're well aware of his weakness for a pretty face, and even though his heart is completely yours, that's no guarantee that he won't look elsewhere for...well, you know what I mean."

"I know, Neville, and it's sweet of you to concern yourself, but I'm walking into this affair with my eyes wide open. I realize that Nicky will never change, and maybe that's just as well. I love him for what he is now, not what I or anyone else would like him to be. I don't want him to ever feel as though he's trapped in this relationship."

"Believe me, Corrine, he would never knowingly do anything to hurt you. He can't bear to cause anyone grief; that's why he'll do everything he can to keep Eugenia from finding out about you. I can't imagine what kind of bribe Bronowski is demanding of him for his silence. He is loyal to his cousin only up to a certain point and when it suits him, but I'm sure if there's anything to be gained by keeping a secret, he will not scruple to do so. She understands that Nicky will have his fling every once in a while, and like you, she accepts it; but if she knew that he shared something more with you than just a casual flirtation, it would wound her deeply. I hate to take sides in this matter. Eugenia is a good woman, but Nicky is my dearest friend, and I know that he is happier now than he has been for a long time."

"I'll do everything that I can to make this work, Neville, but I know it won't always be easy."

"Good girl!" Wyndham seemed relieved, and Corrine too felt easier in her mind as the bells of the Clocher Ste-Catherine began to peel, reminding them that it was time to return to Villa Cheminon.

* * *

As Wyndham had predicted, Dvorkin and his young protégée returned the next day, just in time for lunch, and Corrine, remembering Neville's words, was relieved to find the warmth of her lover's affection in no way diminished.

Later that afternoon, Neville suggested that they all go for a walk, an idea that was welcomed by everyone except Dimitri, who had suddenly developed an upset stomach.

Neville and his wife, who was feeling better after a day's rest, followed

Nicky and Corrine along the path that wound through the trees. They laughed as Nicky helped the two women across the stream, balancing precariously on two large stepping stones. They emerged from the trees on the other side, into the fields beyond, and Neville, holding back for a moment to remove a stone from his shoe, watched as his friend walked on with Corrine by his side.

They were holding hands, and every once in a while, Nicky would lean close to Corrine and whisper in her ear. They were so totally wrapped up in each other. Neville had never seen his friend so at peace with himself and the world.

Marina observed them too and, standing beside her husband, put her arm around his waist.

"He's so happy. If only he'd been free to marry," she said wistfully.

"Yes," Neville sighed. "It does my heart good to see them together, but one can't help wondering how it will all end."

Oblivious to everything else, Nicky pulled Corrine close to him and kissed her. Not wishing to intrude on this idyllic scene, the Wyndhams turned back towards the stream, leaving the two lovers in their own little paradise.

The tall grass waved like flames in the warm, gentle breeze, and the mellow fragrance of autumn, along with the sound of twittering birds and humming bees, filled the air. Dvorkin, who was lying on his back, chewing thoughtfully on a blade of grass, pointed skyward. "Listen," he said, enthralled. "Do you hear that, Corrine? What wonderful music!"

Corrine looked up and smiled. She found it somehow endearing that the man who had entertained kings and emperors with his own powerful voice was capable of being charmed by the song of a lark. The bird flew away, its departure reminding them that it was time to return to the house.

As they walked back, they stopped for a moment before crossing the stream. Nicky pointed to a heron standing impassively on the bank, waiting, watching the water with an unblinking black and yellow eye as a large fish swam lazily unaware of its presence. Smiling at the sight, Corrine was reminded by the heron's long legs and large body of a charcoal drawing of Nicky that she had seen in Dimitri's sketchbook.

How long would it wait there? she wondered. Its patience seemed inexhaustible. A frog croaked fretfully from the opposite bank, and, alert despite its stony immobility, the heron moved its head imperceptibly in its direction, the black tufts on the nape of its neck raising slightly.

A spider, extending its spindly legs in cautious exploration, crawled tentatively across Corrine's shoe. The heron, no longer interested in the inhabitants of the stream, began preening itself, pushing its long beak amongst the grey feathers, rearranging and smoothing them, apparently indifferent to the constant movement of nature just inches away from its large splayed feet.

A dragonfly darted by, its wings shimmering in the dappled sunlight. It hovered momentarily in front of the heron and flew on. The fish, circling above the stony bed in the deepest part of the little inlet in search of a tasty morsel, breached the glassy surface of the stream and fell back into its depths with a watery plop.

The heron remained unimpressed. The spider scuttled on its way unimpeded, having paused unnoticed on the toe of the peach-colored shoe.

Suddenly the heron's head shot out on its long white neck, and cleaving the water, it speared a small green frog, pausing a moment with the hapless creature in its beak before swallowing it whole.

Dvorkin picked up a pebble and threw it into the water—the heron, startled by the movement, let out a cry, and spreading its huge wings, flew away through an opening in the trees.

The spell was broken. The magic of the moment was gone.

"Does it all end here in Honfleur?" Corrine asked, watching the heron disappear in the distance.

"End? No. This is only the beginning. I want to love you, Corrine, forever, if you'll let me. But are you willing to live the kind of life that our love imposes on us? To be apart for weeks on end; to keep secret our strongest, deepest feelings for each other. Can you learn to ignore the things they say and write about me, knowing that some of it, at least, may be true? For I cannot hide from you the fact that there may be times when, lonely and far away from your tender caresses, I may be tempted to seek refuge in someone else's arms."

Although Neville had warned her of his friend's amorous proclivities, the words stung her. She grudgingly gave Dvorkin credit for his honesty, however. Had he told Eugenia the same thing when he married her, she wondered?

"I leave for America the day after tomorrow," he said suddenly. Corrine was stunned. Until that moment, he'd kept silent about his plans, and she had avoided asking him, knowing—and fearing—that they would not include her. "What will you do, little bird, while we are half a world apart?" He looked searchingly into her eyes.

"I'll go back to London. There's plenty to keep me busy." Corrine tried to sound cheerful. I may even learn to drive. Who's going with you?"

"Dimitri and Vladimir, I think. Neville and Marina are going back to England for a while.

"And where will you go after that?"

"I will come home to you in London. You will be there, yes?"

"Of course. Will you write to me while you're away?"

"When I can."

She turned to leave, not wanting him to see the disappointment in her eyes, but Dvorkin grasped her wrist and pulled her to him.

"Corrine, will you stay true to me while I'm away?"

How typical of the man! To admit in one breath his inability to remain faithful and, in the next, demand her own fidelity—was he so supremely confident of his hold on her?

When they returned to the house, the doors to the living room were closed and they could hear the muffled tones of someone playing the piano.

"Neville is putting the final touches to his latest masterpiece," Dvorkin said as they stood listening.

"Perhaps we should leave him in peace then." Corrine started to climb the stairs to their room.

"Go ahead. I'll be there soon. I want to talk to Neville."

When she walked into their bedroom, Arturo was there packing suitcases, and Corrine felt a pang of regret at the sight of this reminder that their time at Honfleur was drawing to a close. The days had flown by so quickly, and she knew only too well how slowly the coming months would drag until Dvorkin's return in December.

He had still not come up to dress for dinner for some time. Wondering what could be keeping him, she descended the stairs to look for him. The doors to the living room were still closed, but she could hear the sound of voices coming from within. She turned the handle, peeking in so as not to disturb the conversation. Dvorkin was standing by the piano with a glass in his hand. Neville was seated at the keys, looking closely at a music score, a pencil tucked behind his ear. They hadn't noticed her.

Dvorkin continued to speak. "Love is like an eternal song, Neville. It flies on and on through the ages, sung by one person, then another. The melody often changes, but the underlying theme remains the same no matter who sings it." He turned to see Corrine come into the room, and holding out his hand to her, he said, "And here is the little bird who sings my eternal song." He drew her to his side and put his arm possessively around her waist.

"How lucky I am, Neville, to have found my precious little bird. I will never let her fly away. Never!"

* * *

Corrine had been determined not to shed any tears at his departure.

"Goodbye, Corrine. Never forget that I love you," he had told her as she held him close.

"Oh Nicky, I'll miss you so terribly. Hurry back to me. I love you so much."

He kissed her one last time and left her standing in the middle of the bedroom. She wanted to run after him, hold him, and keep him there with her just a moment or two longer, but she knew it would be pointless. Instead, she wandered out onto the balcony, and looking down, she saw Dimitri gazing up at her, waving his hand.

Arturo took his place at the wheel, and Dvorkin gave Neville Wyndham a final hug. Just as he was about to climb into the car, he turned and looked up at Corrine. He kissed his hands, and with a final wave, disappeared into the car.

How quiet the house seemed now, with the big man gone. Only the Wyndhams and Corrine remained at Villa Cheminon. All three were traveling back to England together, Neville and Marina to their home in the Lake District and Corrine to wait in London.

17
CELEBRATIONS AND RESOLUTIONS

WHEN CORRINE RETURNED TO THE HOUSE in Tunbridge Square, it seemed gloomy and cold after the pleasant months spent in France. She telegraphed ahead to give the household time to prepare for her arrival, and they did their best to have everything ready. Mrs. Monkaster, who probably would have already retired from her position as housekeeper had it not been for the death of Sir Reginald, refused to leave Corrine to cope with the task of hiring someone to replace her. She had bustled about, supervising the management of the re-awakening establishment.

The skeleton staff, who had until now merely been taking care of themselves and each other and who were becoming rather bored, sprang to the task of preparing for their employer's return with renewed enthusiasm.

They hoped that Corrine would return from her trip to the Continent in happier spirits, but such was unfortunately not the case. Everyone naturally supposed that her continued despondency was due solely to the loss of her father, unaware of the attachment she had formed to the Russian singer and her dejection at his leaving so soon for America.

Corrine, who looked forward to hearing from Dvorkin almost from the day of his departure, seized upon the letters that arrived every day in the hopes that she would recognize his florid handwriting. However, it wasn't until several weeks after he had left for New York that she received word from him, and then only a brief note to say that they had all arrived safely and that everything was going reasonably well. It was a small crumb of comfort and left her hungry for something more substantial. But she didn't hear from him again for quite some time, causing many sleepless nights during the intervening weeks and, much to the cook's chagrin, an untold number of meals left untasted.

Finally, when it had been agreed that Mrs. Monkaster should try to persuade her mistress to see the family's doctor, Corrine received an envelope heavy with numerous pages of sprawling script that brought balm to her aching heart and a sparkle to her eyes.

My darling Corrine,

Will you ever forgive me for not writing to you sooner? As usual, I have not had a minute to myself on this trip, and only now that we have arrived in Chicago am I able to finally sit down and put pen to paper.

Everything went splendidly in New York, although the audiences were somewhat difficult to please, but they soon came around, though most of them couldn't understand a word. How I miss, even now after all these years in exile, being able to perform before my own countrymen in my own homeland. But I will never be able to return there, alas.

Dimitri has been as miserable as a man who has 'lost a pound and found a sixpence,' as you would say, ever since we left Honfleur. I can't think why as I have done my best to amuse him, although I have naturally been extremely busy myself. It is quite depressing to see him moping around.

Life is very jolly here, but extremely fast paced, everyone rushing around in constant turmoil and thinking only of making money. It will be good to get back to London and relax for a while. As for prohibition, I can only say thank God that I do not have to live here permanently.

Gambling too is frowned upon in many of the towns, but, nevertheless, Vladimir has found no shortage of gentlemen who are willing to take a risk, and he has consequently had every opportunity of padding his pockets.

As for me, it is nothing but work, work, work! Rehearsals begin tomorrow, and I hear that several of the performances are already sold out, so that is good. Ariadne Beauforte arrived yesterday and started throwing her considerable weight around. She doesn't like this, and she won't have that, but I tell her one must work around these things sometimes.

Corrine laughed at this. When had Nicky ever 'worked around' anything? Things were done his way, or not at all. He was quite capable of refusing to perform and had done so on more than one occasion when things had not been to his liking.

And now my darling, how are you? Are you lonely without me? I hope so. How I miss you, my little bird. Those beautiful moments in Honfleur still haunt my dreams and I long to hold you in my arms again. When I come back to London, we will spend every minute together. I will not let you out of my sight. Nothing and no one will keep me from your side. Do you remember how we made love in the grass in the meadow by the stream? That's how it will be when I come home, my darling, I promise you. Please, please stay true to me.

I will always be your own, adoring, Nicky.

Corrine, anxious not to break the tenuous thread of this correspondence, replied immediately:

My dearest love,

I haven't the words to tell you how much I miss you. I held your letter close to my heart this morning and tried to imagine you were here with me. Every night I feel like poor Rusalka singing to the moon, 'Shine on him, wherever he may be and tell him of the one who awaits him here.' I never thought I could be so utterly miserable, but I get through the days knowing that in the not-too-distant future I will be in your arms once more. I don't mean to crush you beneath a mountain of sentimentality, but you are all the world to me. Please hurry back as soon as you can.

Yours forever,
Corrine.

Now that she had finally heard from him, her depression quickly fell away, and, and, deciding that the time would pass more easily if she would only put the best possible face on things, she threw herself into a whirlwind of activity.

She began by ordering new draperies for several of the rooms, discarding the dark, heavy fabrics for lighter, brighter materials, instantly giving the place an airier, cheerful appearance. The simple addition of more vases, filled with extravagant, sweet-smelling flowers spread about the rooms, also gave a much-needed touch of color.

Next, she enlisted the services of a piano tuner who came one morning to overhaul the instrument that had once been one of her mother's most treasured possessions. The former mistress of the house had played with a delicate touch, and Corrine could remember her father, during his rare sojourns at Tunbridge Square, sitting and listening to his wife as she ran her hands skillfully over the keys. Corrine had learned to play on this same piano, although she had never reached her mother's proficiency. Still, she had played for her father when they'd been alone together at the house. Now she was determined to polish her skills so that when Nicky returned, she would not be ashamed to play for him.

On top of all this, Corrine caused much consternation below stairs when she announced one day that she was about to embark on a series of driving lessons. This horrified Mrs. Monkaster and Edwards the butler but greatly impressed the younger members of the staff, Agnes the parlor maid and Tompkins, a young man who had recently been hired to help the aging Edwards with some of his more strenuous duties.

Then, one day, amid all the hustle and bustle of life at Tunbridge Square, came a not altogether surprising visit from John Lockstone. He had, ever since Corrine's departure from Paris, been uneasy in his mind about his goddaughter. When she'd confided to him the reason for her hurried exodus from the city, he'd applauded her decision to remove herself from a situation that was becoming fraught with problems. But when he heard some time later through a friend that she'd gone to Honfleur with Neville Wyndham and his wife, he suspected that Dvorkin had managed to persuade her against her better judgement to join him there.

Although he had made several attempts to see her since her return from France, he'd been unsuccessful. Corrine was always either out or indisposed.

When Edwards announced his arrival that morning, Corrine, who had, while still in Honfleur, looked forward to this inevitable encounter with grave misgivings, received her godfather with calm self-assurance, now that she was in her own home and in control of her life once more. She was quite prepared to be absolutely honest and open about her love for Dvorkin, at least with this man who had, in many respects, taken the place of her father. She did not intend to be lectured, however, and was fully determined to stand firm in defense of her feelings.

Their meeting began cordially enough. He enquired after her health, admired the alterations that had already been put into effect at the house, applauded the progress she'd made with her music lessons, and listened, with some trepidation, to an account of her first attempts at driving an automobile.

It was inevitable, however, that the conversation would take a more personal turn, which it did when Sir John enquired after Dvorkin.

It had often puzzled Corrine how Dvorkin had discovered her whereabouts in Cerisieres. She'd never asked him. She could scarcely credit that John Lockstone would have divulged her secret plans or that any other member of his family would give away her hiding place. But there was, as far as she could tell, no one else on whom to lay the blame, and she couldn't help but suspect that one of them must have, however inadvertently, let slip the location of her secluded hideaway. Although things had worked out well in the end, Corrine could not help feeling, in a sense, betrayed.

John Lockstone had been pondering the same question. He knew himself to be innocent of any indiscretion. The last thing he would have done was to point Dvorkin in Corrine's direction. He was well aware that his own wife could be a trifle muddle-headed at times, but both she and the girls would surely never go against his wishes in such a matter, for he'd ordered them on no account to give out any news of Corrine to Dvorkin or his associates. Even so, he felt obliged to question them and was satisfied only when they vehemently denied any complicity. Lockstone was left, therefore, with only one possible conclusion: that Corrine herself must have contacted Dvorkin.

With both Corrine and Lockstone harboring false suspicions, the introduction of this topic into the conversation was bound to produce the spark that would set such a dangerously volatile situation ablaze.

"Um...have you heard anything from Dvorkin lately?" Lockstone asked casually.

"Yes, I had a letter from him last week. Why?"

"Ah. No reason. I just wondered. I had a feeling he might try to get in touch with you. You didn't reply, of course."

"Yes, as a matter of fact, I did."

"Look, Corrine, I could say that it's none of my business but—"

"And you'd be right," she cut him off abruptly, determined not to let him launch into any kind of lecture. "I made it quite clear when I left Paris that I wanted my whereabouts kept strictly between ourselves. Nothing would have happened if someone hadn't told him where I was. You were the only ones who knew." Lockstone tried to interpose, but Corrine wasn't about to give him the opportunity to defend himself. "Be that as it may, I cannot honestly say that I regret what happened."

"But I most certainly do," Lockstone, much put out, finally managed to say. "You are making a grave mistake if you think that anything good can come of a relationship with that man. Your father would have been appalled to think that you'd thrown yourself at someone who has such a reprehensible reputation."

"I didn't throw myself at him. If you remember rightly, you were the one who introduced us."

"Something that I now deeply regret."

"Nor did you refuse his invitation to join him backstage at the Opera House, even though you suspected that the only reason he had for wanting you there was to meet me again. And then to give my hiding place away when I made it clear that I wanted nothing more to do with him. It really is the absolute limit to blame me for the consequences. As far as I'm concerned, you've forfeited any right to interfere in my personal matters. What I do from now on is my own affair."

Corrine turned and walked out of the room leaving, Lockstone confounded and speechless. Angry and upset at being unjustly accused and thinking that women were the very devil to understand, he left the house ruffled and hurt. What had been intended as a conciliatory call had developed into a fiery confrontation, and he was damned if he would shoulder the blame for what had happened. *Well, she'd regret it. The silly young thing was headed for disaster. That man would take advantage of her and break her heart.* He wanted to wash his hands of the whole business but was uncomfortably aware of the possible consequences and, despite his injured feelings, felt the responsibility for her well-being, placed on him by his old friend Sir Reginald Standish, weighing heavily upon his shoulders.

* * *

Christmas was rapidly approaching, and with it the return of Nikolai Dvorkin from America. Once again, as in years past, the Standish household was exhorted to give of its best and they all set to with a will. The staff had not been told who their distinguished visitor was to be, but they knew instinctively that whoever it was must be of great importance. They speculated amongst themselves as they sat down to dinner below-stairs.

"Miss Corrine bought several new dresses last week," Agnes supplied. "And a bottle of My Sin."

"Whoever it is," said Mrs. Pughsley, the cook, "he likes his grub. Miss Corrine gave me a list as long as your arm and made a point of ordering the best caviar."

Edwards, who did not usually indulge in below-stairs gossip, found himself caught up in the excitement. "She asked me to make sure we had plenty of Vodka in the house."

"Ooh, that sounds like he might be one of those Russian blokes," Florrie, the kitchen maid, surmised with unwitting accuracy.

"We had some Russian gentlemen staying at the house back when Sir Reginald was alive," Edwards recalled. "Rather offhand they were; very serious and not easy to please, I can tell you," he added, dampening the spirits of the rest of the staff seated around the large table in the kitchen.

"Of course, he's not the only one that's staying." Mrs. Monkaster felt obliged to add her contribution to the conversation. "Miss Corrine informed me there's to be a whole houseful. Agnes and me have been told to get four of the bedrooms ready, and I understand there's to be a big do on Christmas Day."

"That's right. Dinner for ten, I was told." Mrs. Pughsley nodded sagely.

Jimmy Tompkins, who'd remained silent until now, dropped a decided bombshell. "Well, I know who at least four of them are," he declared proudly.

"Oh, Clever Dick. And who might they be?" The cook asked skeptically, feeling that whatever this cocky youngster knew wasn't worth tuppence.

"Lord and Lady Lockstone, that's who, and their two daughters," Tompkins supplied with a self-satisfied smirk.

"And just how do you come to know that?" Edwards enquired rather indignantly, wondering why the boot-boy had been privy to information of which he was unaware.

"I just happened to be out in the area the morning that Miss Maude and Miss Florence Lockstone came to visit. Miss Corrine walked them out to their car when they left, and I heard her saying how she looked forward to seeing them all on Christmas Day."

"Maybe you should spend more time getting on with your work instead of standing around earwigging," Edwards admonished the unrepentant lad, causing Florrie to titter behind her hand.

"Well, the boy did learn something at least," Mrs. Monkaster said defensively.

"That's as maybe. But we can't have the staff listening in on conversations above-stairs."

"Blimey, Mr. Edwards, you can't tell me you haven't heard some juicy bits of gossip up there over the years." Jimmy Tompkins scoffed openly, drawing a swift response from the housekeeper in the form of a clipped ear.

"That'll be enough of that." Mrs. Monkaster glared at him, swiftly changing her allegiance in favor of the butler.

"Well, that's only four of them, anyway," Agnes observed. "We still don't know who the others are."

"Nor are we likely to until the time comes," Edwards told them as he rose from the table, feeling that there had been enough conjecture for one day. The others followed his example.

* * *

Corrine had decided to invite the Lockstones for Christmas, partly as an olive branch extended in an earnest desire to heal the unfortunate breach between them but also, somewhat rashly, in order to present Lord Lockstone with something of a *fait accompli*. By bringing Lockstone and Dvorkin together in the more intimate surroundings of the London house, she hoped that her godfather would have a chance to get to know him better and form a more favorable opinion of the man. She deeply regretted the words that led to the falling out with her father's oldest friend. He too had expressed a desire to let bygones be bygones, as Florence had told Corrine during one of several visits that the Lockstone girls had paid to Belgravia in the ensuing weeks.

"Honestly, Corrine. I don't know how things got so out of hand. No one seems to know who told Dvorkin that you were in Cerisieres. It was all very unfortunate," Florence had told her.

"Well, it doesn't matter now," Corrine had replied. "As I told Uncle John, the important thing is that Nicky did come to Cerisieres, and as things have worked out, I couldn't be more pleased that he did."

"Do you think he'll get a divorce?

" It's not likely, but who knows. Anything might happen. But will you do me an enormous favor, Florence? Speak to your father. Tell him I'm sorry if I upset him. I didn't mean to hurt his feelings. I know he's just thinking about what's best for me, and I'm sure he considers that I'm heading for the most awful fall, but there's nothing I can do about it. I just want him to accept the fact that I've made my decision, right or wrong, and I won't hold anyone responsible but myself if things don't work out. I want you all to come to Tunbridge Square for dinner on Christmas Day. Nicky will be here and I'm sure if Uncle John gets to know him better, he'll see things in a different light. It would mean a great deal to me if he would just try to get along with Nicky and the others. I know it's a lot to ask, but do see what you can do."

The message was duly delivered and, much to Corrine's surprise and relief, John Lockstone accepted her invitation on behalf of the family.

* * *

The 20th of December dawned crisp and clear, and Corrine awaited Dvorkin's arrival in London with eager anticipation. Dvorkin and Dimitri Gurvich came directly from the station, and as the car drew up outside the house in Tunbridge Square, Edwards threw open the door. Jimmy Tomkins, temporarily elevated to a position above-stairs, stood, his hair neatly combed and his boots hastily polished on the backs of his trouser legs, ready to carry the visitor's luggage to their rooms. He was prepared to hurry downstairs, as soon as his duties allowed him, to give a report on the new arrivals to the others.

Corrine was hard-pressed to stop herself from throwing her arms around Dvorkin's neck. It wouldn't do to show such familiarity in front of the domestic staff. Instead, she contented herself with the more subdued and traditional greeting of a brief handshake and kiss on both cheeks as she welcomed the two friends to her home.

Dimitri looked rather pale but seemed happy enough. Nicky, who'd thankfully recognized the need for discretion, had followed Corrine's lead in toning down the warmth of his salutations. It wasn't until she visited his room sometime later, when everyone was dressing for dinner, that they were able to finally give vent to their true feelings.

Neville and Marina Wyndham arrived just as they were returning downstairs, and the friends, reunited after several weeks of separation, found plenty to talk about.

That night, after everyone had retired, Corrine tiptoed down the hallway to Dvorkin's room. He'd seemed ill at ease during dinner, and as soon as he opened the door and took her in his arms, she knew he was going to say something unpleasant and unwelcome.

"I must leave tomorrow."

"But I don't understand. I thought you were staying here with the others until after Christmas."

"I'm sorry, Corrine. I must be with my family at Christmastime. It's a tradition I couldn't possibly break. The children expect me and I haven't seen them for so long."

"But why didn't you tell me this before?"

"I thought you would realize. Well, never mind. You will have everyone here to keep you company."

Corrine wanted to shout, *But I don't want everyone! I want you!* but she forced the words back and remained silent.

"I'm sorry my darling. I didn't mean to upset your plans," he said contritely.

"No, no. It's alright." The thought briefly crossed Corrine's mind that he did not want to be at the house when Lord Lockstone arrived and was using his family as an excuse for absenting himself, but she brushed it aside as being unworthy of him. No, he would not be afraid to stand up to John Lockstone.

"It doesn't matter. As you say, there'll be a full house. I'll have plenty to keep me busy." She was almost afraid to ask him, "When will I see you again?"

But he was eager to please her now. "As soon as I can get away. New Year's Eve for certain. May I come back here?"

"Of course. The others are more than welcome to stay until you get back."

"Then we'll have a party and you and I will be together forever."

"Until the next trip at least," Corrine replied, remembering the last time he had vowed to be by her side forever.

"No! The next time I go away, you are coming with me. I was most miserable in America without you. Oh, don't worry, little bird," he reassured her as he saw her look of surprise. "You will travel as a friend of the Wyndhams, which you are, of course. Nothing could be easier or more natural. But let us not talk of parting or what may happen in the future," he urged her as he pulled her closer. "Love me, this moment. This is all that matters now."

* * *

After Dvorkin's departure the following day, Corrine was determined to keep everyone's spirits up, and she almost managed to forget that he was no longer there as they all worked together to trim the Christmas tree that had been installed in the drawing room, filling the air with its fresh, woody scent of pine needles. When the last piece of tinsel had been adjusted and the final ornament hung on the highest bough, Corrine reached up to hand Dimitri the crowning glory: a *papier mâché* fairy with golden hair and gauzy wings, dressed in pink taffeta, that had made its first appearance at Tunbridge Square on the occasion of Corrine's first Christmas. They all cheered as he placed it ceremoniously atop the tree. His smile was radiant as Corrine helped him descend from his shaky perch and rewarded him with an enthusiastic kiss on the cheek for his bravery. Edwards passed around celebratory glasses of champagne, and Neville proposed a toast to the tree, while Dimitri, still in a state of euphoria, gazed adoringly at Corrine over the rim of his glass.

* * *

When the Lockstones arrived at Tunbridge Square accompanied by Florence's fiancé, Arthur Walmsley, on Christmas Day, they found the other guests already assembled. John Lockstone, who, up until that moment, still had grave misgivings about attending Corrine's dinner party, was somewhat surprised but at the same time enormously relieved to find that Dvorkin was not one of those present.

"I'm sure you remember Dimitri Gurvich and Neville Wyndham, and this is his wife Marina," Corrine made the introductions, and Lockstone shook hands with the two men and kissed Marina's hand.

"Monsieur Dvorkin is not here?" Lady Lockstone asked Corinne, sounding rather disappointed, while her husband's attention had been diverted by something Neville was saying.

"No Aunt Lavinia. He's visiting his family in Brussels."

"Oh dear. That is unfortunate. At least, not for them, of course, but for us. I was quite looking forward to meeting him again." Although she knew that her husband strongly disapproved of the man, Lavinia Lockstone, who was rather a romantic at heart, could not help harboring a sneaking admiration for the singer.

It was some time before Maude could draw Corrine aside to speak to her privately.

"What happened? I thought Nicky was going to be here."

"Yes, I thought so too, but he had to leave almost immediately."

"But why?" Maude sounded disappointed.

"Family commitments. It doesn't matter. Everyone else is here. And you're looking well, Maude."

"So, when do you expect to see him again?"

"He hopes to be back in London for the New Year," Corrine explained, mildly irritated by Maude's persistent questioning. "But you know how things are. He'll be off again to Paris soon after that, and who knows where next."

"Are you going with him?"

"I don't know. Possibly."

"Well, I hope we see something of him in January at least."

"Yes. I thought I'd give a little New Year's party here. You're all invited of course."

"What's this?" Florence asked, joining them.

"Corrine is giving a party for New Years. I was saying it's too bad Nicky isn't here."

"Yes. I'm sorry Corrine. Are you terribly disappointed?"

"It couldn't be helped," Corrine shrugged, trying to sound unconcerned. "The children…you know. I can understand."

"Well, of course, I suppose he had to go." Despite the words of regret, Florence had a definite sparkle in her eye.

"Florence is absolutely bursting to tell you her good news," Maude told Corrine, temporarily setting the subject of Dvorkin aside for later discussion.

"What is it?" Corrine was only too happy to talk about something else.

"Arthur and I have finally set a date for the wedding: the fifteenth of June. I was hoping you'd agree to be one of my bridesmaids, Corrine."

"I'd love to! How exciting! Where will you live? Have you got a place yet?"

"Yes. Daddy is giving us the most marvelous wedding present. A house in Hampstead. Arthur and I went to see it last week. You'll love it, Corrine."

"Do you think Nicky will be able to come to the wedding?" Maude asked hopefully.

"I don't know. Possibly, if he has no other commitments, but I couldn't say off hand; besides…well who knows how things will be six months from now."

Later that evening, when the men had finished their after-dinner port and everyone had adjourned to the drawing room to play a hand or two of bridge, Corrine drew Lord Lockstone aside.

"I can't tell you how happy I am that you and Aunt Lavinia accepted my invitation—and relieved too. I know we don't see eye to eye on certain things, but it would be too bad if we let those issues come between us. I hope you've forgiven me for my outburst the last time you were here."

"Forgiven and forgotten, my dear. No need to dredge up the past. But tell me, are you happy?" He looked at her quizzically.

"Yes."

"Even though he's not here? It must have been a bitter disappointment for you."

"I can't deny it. But it was merely a misunderstanding. My fault entirely, I expect."

"You shouldn't be so ready to take the blame for things, Corrine. I promise not to lecture you, especially on Christmas Day, but I hope you will allow me to say just one thing: Don't let him take advantage of you, my dear." He quickly held up his hands. "And that's all. No more advice." They both laughed.

"Thank you, dear Uncle John." Corrine felt tremendously relieved. "I understand from Florence that she and Arthur have named the day and that you have been the absolute soul of generosity as always—a house in Hampstead, no less. Maude will miss her when she moves."

"Mmm." Lord Lockstone appeared thoughtful. "I don't know what's got into Maude just lately. She's been very restless. After you left us in Paris, she seemed to be eager to return home, but once we got back, she was moody and not quite herself. I admit I'm just an old fuddy-duddy when it comes to understanding you girls. I've done my best to keep her amused. Do you have any idea what's wrong with her?"

"I think her reaction is quite natural. She probably finds the prospect of Florence getting married and leaving home rather unsettling. It's understandable. They've been so close all these years. I expect she feels let down to some extent. But she'll get over it; you'll see."

"I hope so. I hate to see her like this—one minute quite fizzy and full of fun, and the next, down in the dumps and perfectly miserable."

"Does she have any admirers, do you know?"

"Young Frederick Benson was taking her about for a while when we first got back to London. He kept hanging about the house looking like a lost dog for weeks on end, but I think Maude must have given him the 'heave-ho' because all of a sudden, he didn't show up again, and when I mentioned him, she brushed the matter aside and changed the subject, so I just assumed it was over."

"Ah."

"Since then, we've seen one or two new faces at the house, but nothing too serious, thank God. One wedding in a year is quite enough for any father to cope with."

"Good heavens, yes."

"So, tell me, my dear, what are your plans now?"

"Well, it's all rather uncertain, as you can imagine. Nicky will be back here for the New Year. I'm giving a small party. I hope you and Aunt Lavinia and the girls will be able to come."

"I'm afraid not. Your aunt and I will be back in the country by then, but Florence and Maude can stay on in town and join us later. I'm sure they'd love to come. And after that, what then?"

"Nicky has an engagement in Monte. I may go out there with him, but nothing's settled. And after that, who knows. I'm trying not to think too far ahead."

"How do you get on with the others?"

"Very well. They're wonderful people. It's an extremely close-knit little group, but they have been very good to me, and I feel as though I've known them all my life."

"That young lad Gurvich, is he related to Dvorkin?"

"No, but Nicky is like a surrogate father to him, and Dima worships him."

"I must say I like that chap Wyndham, very intelligent and quite amusing. His wife's an engaging little thing too."

"Yes, they are very nice people."

"Well, that's as maybe, but I must just say this—" Corrine drew her breath in sharply, but Lord Lockstone continued, "I know! I know! I promised I wouldn't interfere, and I don't mean to, but you know my objections to all this. I can't help saying it. It's wrong and will only end in heartache for you, but whatever happens, I want you to know that, for the sake of your father, I'll be here for you if you should need my help—whatever happens." "Thank you, Uncle John." She put her hand on his arm and squeezed it gently. There may come a time when she would need his steady guidance, but for now, she would trust only in her own fate and hope for the best.

* * *

In the meantime, Christmas and Boxing Day came and went, and Corrine insisted that Dimitri and the others stay at the house until Dvorkin returned for the New Year's Eve party. The Wyndhams accepted her invitation gladly, and Gurvich was more than happy to remain close to Corinne.

When Dvorkin finally arrived at Tunbridge Square, the others had already slipped back into the informal and comfortable way of life that they had come to enjoy in Honfleur.

On New Year's Eve, Florence appeared, accompanied by her fiancé

Arthur Walmsley, and Maude brought an acquaintance whom Corrine had never met before. As they exchanged greetings, Corrine noticed that although the others had merely shaken hands, when Maude approached Dvorkin, she had unexpectedly reached up to kiss his cheek. He seemed taken aback by this unexpected show of affection, his head pulling away from her in an involuntary action that seemed strange to Corrine, but he recovered almost immediately, smiling and talking animatedly in his usual fashion.

At a point in the evening when the hands of the clock were gradually ticking toward midnight, Dvorkin, realizing that his cigarette case was empty, excused himself from the party and went upstairs to his room to replenish his supply. He had just refilled and closed the case with a snap when there was a tentative tapping at the door.

"Come!" he called out.

The door opened and Maude Lockstone appeared on the threshold, the light from the hallway shining on her hair and shoulders. She stepped into the room and quietly closed the door behind her, turning the key in the lock to forestall any interruption. She stood and looked at Dvorkin, who showed no surprise at seeing her there.

"Well, Nicky. Are you sorry to see me here?"

"Sorry? No, why on earth should I be sorry? It's always a pleasure to see you, Mademoiselle Lockstone."

"Mademoiselle Lockstone, is it now?" She sounded put out. "Why so formal?" She cajoled him, adding in seductive tones, "You didn't call me that when we were in bed together in Paris. Or had you forgotten that already?"

He seemed unruffled by her insinuations. "No. I hadn't forgotten. It was a pleasurable experience that we both enjoyed."

"Oh, yes, it was all of that," she said as she walked slowly towards him. "But I don't delude myself into thinking that I was the only thing you wanted that afternoon. You knew I would tell you where Corrine had hidden herself. You used me to get the information that you needed, didn't you?"

"Maybe."

"Well, thank you for that piece of honesty, but you'll never make me believe that you didn't feel something for me."

Dvorkin raised his hands as if to stop her advances. "I don't deny it. I was not thinking of Corrine when I made love to you. But what more did you expect of me? I made no commitments. It was a harmless moment of passion. Do you regret it?"

"No, absolutely not. I only regret telling you where to find Corrine. If I hadn't done that, I might have kept you to myself. But it's not too late, is it? We can still enjoy one another. Corrine need never know."

He watched as she stood before him, slipping the straps from her dress over her smooth, white shoulders, the silky material sliding over her hips and dropping with a soft rustle to the floor, leaving her completely naked.

"I'd do anything for you, you know that." Maude raised her arms and entwined them around his neck. "Did Paris mean nothing to you?" she whispered, pressing her body against his.

Dvorkin, although aroused by her sensuality, replied casually, "A moment's pleasure for both of us," as he disengaged himself from her caresses.

Just then someone turned the doorknob and, finding the door locked, knocked, and a voice asked, "Are you alright, Nicky?" It was Dimitri.

"Yes. Yes, I'm fine. I'll be with you in just a moment, Dima."

Dvorkin continued to look at the girl standing before him, and then, shaking his head, he slipped his cigarette case into his pocket. "I'm sorry. I must go. I confess my weakness for beautiful women, but I love Corrine. Be unfaithful to her under her own roof? There are limits, even to what I would do, Mademoiselle Lockstone." He brushed past her, leaving her humiliated and filled with rage.

"And what would Corrine think if she knew you had made love to me in Paris?" Maude cried defiantly after him.

Dvorkin appeared unperturbed. Looking back over his shoulder, he replied, "You would risk your supposed friendship with her and chance that your family would find out about our little indiscretion?" He smiled. "I don't think so, do you?"

He turned back and, unlocking the door, went out, leaving Maude burning with unrequited desire and fury. Yet despite Dvorkin's declaration of fidelity to Corrine and his mortifying rejection of her, Maude was not at all sure that he would not have succumbed to the temptation had they not been disturbed by Dimitri's untimely arrival. Even now, as angry as she was with him, she still longed for him, and as the chimes of midnight rang out, Maude confidently made her New Year's resolutions.

18

EN GARDE

LUCY HAD RARELY LIED TO JACKIE; she stretched or manipulated the truth occasionally, maybe, but certainly never with any malicious intent. But after Corrine's meeting with Dvorkin in Cerisiers, she had become secretive and, fearful that her actions would be reported to her family, had decided that whatever else happened would be kept strictly between Jasper Frakes and herself. So, when Jackie next contacted her, Lucy lied and said that her friend had been right; the relationship between Corrine and Dvorkin had been nothing but a brief encounter, and the lead that had seemed so promising had reached a dead end.

Jackie wasn't so sure but didn't press the matter. Lucy's visits to the house in Chelsea dwindled until finally Lucy said diffidently, "Well, I promise not to bother you both so much from now on. I'm over my little obsession. It was fun while it lasted, but I really think it's time I got back to a normal life."

Later she wrote to Jackie, thanking her and Lionel once again for their help and understanding.

"I feel rather embarrassed now, remembering all the things I said. You must have thought me terribly stupid," she told her friend. Jackie reassured her that their concern had been only for her welfare and happiness. They had certainly parted on the best of terms, Lionel taking them out to dinner on their last night together, and Jackie giving Lucy the gift of a book that she'd recently acquired at auction, a collection of prints by various Irish painters that had been part of the estate of a wealthy landowner from Dublin.

"Don't leave it too long before you visit us again," Jackie had told her as she and Lionel had seen Lucy off at the station.

After that, Lucy kept her visits to Frakes's flat strictly to herself. Even those had become sporadic, as the trance-like episodes that occurred while she was going about her daily activities at home became more and more frequent. This should have been a warning signal to her that things were not as they should be, but she merely looked on such interludes as a blessing.

Now, she sat in the house on Dover Street looking at the book that Jackie had given her on that last visit. Idly turning the pages, Lucy glanced at the paintings. Hamilton, Burke, Yeats, and Orpen were all well represented, and Walter Osborne's *On Suffolk Sands* held Lucy's attention momentarily. Turning the page, she gave an involuntary shudder. A dog, sleek and white, sat gazing into the distance—the title of the picture, *A Borzoi by a Chair*, the artist, St. George Hare.

Where had she seen such an animal before? Suddenly, she experienced a feeling of terror—something from her past, a memory that had been, for so long, hidden away. It was the merest glimpse—a face, a place—but then it was gone. Lucy stared at the picture, trying to recall what had happened, but her mind had, once again, closed its doors and shut out the incident.

Then she recalled something that had occurred more recently. *Yes, of course!* It was at the Cosmopolitan Hotel. Bronowski's dog had looked very similar. Strange, Lucy recalled; she had felt no fear then. But of course, it wasn't she who had been so close that she could have reached out and touched that soft, white hair. It was Corrine who had peeped through the door and seen Bronowski and Dvorkin talking in the hallway, the dog standing by Bronowski's side. The more she looked at the picture, the more she wondered if something had happened to Corrine; something that concerned the dog. She began to feel dizzy, and the picture seemed to grow dim before her eyes as once again she slipped back into the past.

* * *

It was just after dawn when Dimitri Gurvich rang the bell of the apartment in Paris that Corrine had taken for the summer months. It wasn't unusual for Dvorkin to come calling at odd hours or for him to send someone to fetch her, so she was not alarmed by this early arrival. She ushered the young man into the living room, rubbing the sleep from her eyes.

"I'm sorry to wake you, Corrine, but Nicky asked me to come and get you."

"Is everything alright, Dima?" As always, her first thought was for Dvorkin. Was he ill or, more likely, drunk? Passed out somewhere or in some kind of trouble? She was never quite sure what to expect.

"Yes, of course, Corrine, but you know how it is. Nicky pays no attention to time and thinks that no one else does either, unfortunately."

Corrine laughed lightly and shook her head. *How like the man!* "I'm sorry Dima."

"Why?"

"Because he sends you out to fetch me when I'm sure you would probably rather be sleeping."

"No." Gurvich blushed and looked down at his shoes. "It's no trouble, really. I'm always happy to see you, Corrine."

"Where is he?"

"At the fencing salon."

"At this hour?"

"Yes. He was not happy with his performance at the opera last night and was very restless when we returned to the hotel"

"Let me guess. He had one or two drinks?"

"Yes, but not to excess," Gurvich assured her hurriedly. "He slept poorly, then this morning he decided to dash off to the salon and sent me here to fetch you."

Dvorkin often went to the salon to sharpen his fencing skills when he was in Paris. He had on more than one occasion offered to take Corrine there to show off his prowess with a blade, but until now she had never taken him up on the offer. She suspected that he used this particular outlet to give vent to his nervous energy and artistic frustrations and pitied the poor unfortunate who found himself on the receiving end of such alleviation.

When they arrived at the salon, it was deserted, save for Dvorkin, who was already dressed in fencing whites, and another man similarly attired, who was standing talking to him at the farther end of the floor.

Gurvich walked beside Corrine, their footsteps echoing eerily as they made their way into the great hall. Dvorkin heard them and turned, lifting his hand to acknowledge their presence.

"That's Charles Deshayes, Nicky's fencing master." Dimitri told Corrine. "He has won many championships but is seldom willing to teach anyone else his skills. He's Bronowski's latest amour. That was how Nicky came to be introduced to him. And speak of the devil!" Dimitri looked behind him and lowered his voice to a whisper. "Here he is, now." He gestured slightly with his head towards the doorway from which they had emerged just a few minutes before, and Corrine saw Count Bronowski in full fencing costume, leaning casually against the wall, three deep-chested borzoi hounds standing vigilantly by his side.

"*Bonjour*, Vladimir," Deshayes called out to him. "I was not expecting you here today, *mon ami*, but *Mon Dieu*! Why did you bring those creatures with you?" Deshays exclaimed.

"They won't be in the way," Bronowski assured him. "Will you, my dears?" He whispered a command to the three glossy-coated animals, and they immediately sat, watching their master attentively as he walked away.

He strode across the floor of the great hall, ignoring Corrine and Dimitri and reaching the two men. He put his arm around Deshayes' waist, kissing him on both cheeks.

"Charles, don't nag me today, my dear. I couldn't stand it. Nicky, how are you?" He turned and reached up to peck at the big man's cheek.

"I am quite well, Vladimir," Dvorkin assured him.

"Yes, I hear you have discovered the fountain of youth." He turned to look at Corrine meaningfully. "I must say you are looking very well on it."

"Since you are here, perhaps you would care to give Nicky a match?"

Deshayes suggested. "I am more than willing to yield the floor to you."

"Certainly, if he wishes it," Bronowski agreed. "Would you care to take me on, Nicky? I can promise you a good workout."

He tittered at the double entendre and winked at Deshayes, who blew a kiss to his amour and walked away, leaving the two men facing one another.

"By all means," Dvorkin replied. "We'll see who can outlast the other."

"Mm. It sounds delightful." Bronowski smiled broadly as he saluted Dvorkin and walked away to take up his position on the floor.

When Corrine realized what was happening, she looked apprehensively at Dimitri. "Who will have the better of this, do you think?"

"Bronowski, unfortunately—although Nicky will give him a good run for his money. But Bronowski is an accomplished fencer, second only to Deshayes in skill and agility. I'm afraid it will put Nicky in a bad mood. He hates to lose at anything, and in front of you...well—"

"Perhaps he will try that much harder. We must hope for the best."

The two opponents stood face-to-face at either end of the *piste*, their masks held under their left arms like ghostly heads, tucked against the hip. Each combatant took up his stand and saluted the other with his foil, bringing the blade slowly up in front of his face and then swishing it smartly downward. They then repeated the action, this time directing their salutes towards Deshayes, who was serving as the referee of the match. They put on their masks and Deshayes called out, "*En garde!*" Both men assumed the opening stance, and Corrine saw with alarm the three borzois stand up, alert and poised to leap forward at a single command. Again, Deshayes called out, "Are you ready?" and the reply came, "Ready."

The match went back and forth with lightning speed, the two opponents advancing and retreating on the *piste*, their weapons tapping and clicking one against the other. As the match progressed, the men became more determined, their lunges accompanied by loud exclamations, each thrust and parry evincing fighting words uttered through the mesh of their masks that only they could hear.

At first, it looked as though Dvorkin might have the upper hand, with his long reach keeping Bronowski successfully at bay. But his opponent's speed and agility were more than a match for the singer, whose unhealthy lifestyle eventually betrayed him.

Bronowski scored the winning hit.

They stood facing each other as they had begun, each taking off his mask. Nicky revealed a face ruddy with exertion and thunderous in mood. Bronowski presented the face of a man who had just taken a stroll in the park, with a smile on his thin lips beneath his glistening moustache and a malicious gleam in his eye. They saluted each other and stepped forward to shake hands.

"Well played," Bronowski said lightly. "But perhaps you are a little out of practice," he added. "Maybe more time spent thrusting with this," he said, tapping the blade of his foil against that of Dvorkin's, then raising it slightly, "instead of this." He made to press the tip of the foil against his opponent's groin, but Dvorkin stepped back, the redness drained from his face, leaving it white with rage. He said nothing, however, and stood silently as Bronowski turned his back on him and walked away, whistling to the dogs who darted forward, falling into step with him as he made his way back across the floor to where Dimitri and Corrine were standing. When he was a few steps away from them, he stopped, and feigning surprise at seeing them there, he said, "Oh, Dimitri, dear boy, I didn't realize you were here. And Miss Standish. How delightful." She nodded to him, and he continued, "But really, Miss Standish, you should allow Nicky to get a little more rest. The poor boy looks absolutely exhausted. Perhaps Dimitri here could take his place in your bed sometimes. Or maybe he already does?"

"You cad!" Gurvich was beside himself and sprang toward Bronowski, heedless of the dogs that were snarling menacingly. Corrine tried to pull him back.

"Dimitri, no!"

Instantly, Bronowski gave a command, and the dogs leapt, not at Gurvich but at Corrine, knocking her to the ground. As Bronowski grappled with his young adversary, the wolfhounds, their jaws snapping, were upon Corrine in a flash. One sank its teeth into her ankle, another gripped at the hand that she had thrown up to protect her face. She screamed out frantically, "Nicky! Help me, Nicky!" The third dog had penetrated the flimsy fabric of her blouse at her shoulder with its long teeth, blood already staining the material.

It all happened so quickly, but when Dvorkin and Deshayes realized what was happening, they sprinted down the length of the hall, Deshayes to separate the two men who were rolling on the floor locked in combat, and Dvorkin desperately swiping at the dogs with his foil. Dvorkin delivered a stinging sideways blow to the one at her ankle, and letting out a terrible yelp, it released its grip, one of its legs shattered by the blow. The second, momentarily diverted by this unexpected attack, let go of her hand to bare its long yellow teeth at Dvorkin, who landed a blow on its back, which sent it howling to the ground. Wrenching the tip from the end of the fencing foil, he lunged at the third beast that had moments before been gnawing Corrine's shoulder but was now looking for a deadlier hold on her throat as she tried to push it away with her uninjured hand. The foil found its mark, piercing the animal's body to the heart. The dog collapsed in a pool of blood.

Bronowski fought to free himself from Deshayes' grasp, and screaming, he prostrated himself over the body of the dead hound.

"My babies! You've killed them, you monster!"

"Damn your creatures! Look what they've done to Corrine!" Dimitri cried as he dashed forward to help Dvorkin lift Corrine, who had fainted.

* * *

Lucy stared at the book on her lap, the page coming slowly back into focus. Her heart was beating rapidly and she felt an incredibly sharp pain in her shoulder and ankle. The experience, as always, had seemed so real. She automatically looked down, fully expecting to find bite marks in her flesh, but there was nothing there— just the pain and the memory of what had happened.

So that explained her fear! But could one's phobias reach so far back into the past?

Again, Rose Cooper's words came back to her. "He will harm you if he can." Was that the reason her palm had been so difficult to read, why Rose had faltered as she tried to decipher the lines that spoke of Lucy's past and future, the two so closely interwoven? Was it possible that she had seen Bronowski's sinister form lurking in the shadows? And if he were indeed the one, would he succeed in his attempt to destroy her, or had she already succumbed in the person of Corrine, back there in Paris, London, or even Honfleur?

There was only one person who could tell her that, and she was probably miles away. Rose Cooper would know, but how to find her? It was a million-to-one shot, the chance that she might be close by in Birchford, but if she were, Lucy knew exactly where to find her.

* * *

Lucy took the bus to the outskirts of town and alighted at the crossroads by a pub called The Rising Sun. She then walked east along Miller's Way and up the hill towards the old farmhouse. After she had gone about a mile, she struck out around the perimeter of a cornfield and, reaching the far side, passed over the railway lines and across a field on the other side, cautiously eyeing a herd of cows that stood impassively, swishing their tails and chewing meditatively as they watched her hurry by. Climbing over a wooden stile in the hedgerow, she came out into a narrow lane, and following this for another quarter of a mile or so, she arrived at an opening in the fence where muddy tire tracks, freshly made, revealed the presence of several ramshackle motor homes pulled into a field. The smoke from a campfire drifted up amid a few stunted trees nearby, and the sound of children's voices shouting and laughing could be heard as they ran back and forth.

The Romani had returned to Gill's Farm, the one place in the area where they had always been assured of a welcome; the landowner, himself the youngest son of an itinerant knife-grinder who had finally settled in Birchford and who had eventually made his fortune in scrap metal, had never turned anyone away. But how different everything looked today.

Gone was the picturesque scene of the brightly colored caravans that Lucy remembered seeing as a young child. They had long been replaced by motor homes, some of which were comparatively luxurious, but most were dilapidated and down-at-heel.

Lucy had no idea if Rose was there. She could be anywhere in the country. These footloose nomads traveled the length and breadth of Great Britain, never staying in one place for very long. Still, Lucy guessed that if her friend was anywhere in the area, this would most likely be the place to find her.

An elderly woman was shaking out a rug on the steps of her caravan.

"Good morning," Lucy greeted her cheerfully, but there was no reply. The woman merely looked at her with idle curiosity. Lucy continued undaunted.

"Is Rose Arnold traveling with you, by any chance?"

The woman shrugged and turned away, going back inside the caravan. Lucy wasn't surprised by this taciturnity. These people, especially members of the older generation, were naturally suspicious of anyone who was not of their kind. She remembered how Rose had been when the two of them were at Gordon Street together.

She was walking towards the next caravan when she was suddenly arrested by the sight of a large dog standing on guard outside the door. The animal, having spotted Lucy almost simultaneously, began to bark—a loud deep noise that resonated around the campsite.

Lucy froze. Again, that feeling of terror. A vivid scene thrust itself into her mind's eye, dragged unwillingly back from her memory. A field, but not here. Somewhere in Birchford. She was a child. A familiar face looking down at her. But that had been long after the incident with Bronowski. Something that had happened to Lucy, not Corinne. It was becoming increasingly difficult to separate the two lives.

Suddenly, the caravans began to fade and she felt her body slipping into the past. She was lying in a field; the smell of a dog was strong. A feeling of terror mixed with helplessness took over her body. She caught a glimpse of her legs protruding from beneath her pleated, plaid skirt.

This wasn't Corrine's body; it was her own.

She was back in Birchford, a little girl who had just been swinging in the park.

Lucy struggled to move, but she was paralyzed. A tall man reached his fingers down, pulling up her skirt, sliding his hand along her inner thigh. She tried to scream, escape—but her body refused to comply. The man continued to inch his hand upward, exploring her with his fingers, as though she were a treasure he had found.

Lucy opened her mouth to scream again—this time her voice worked and she let out a blood-curdling cry.

"Missus, Missus! He won't hurt you missus. He's tied up. Look!"

Lucy looked around and saw the park in Birchford had been replaced by the farm and caravans. A young boy, six or seven years of age, with a dirty face and beaming smile kneeled beside her.

"Missus, it's okay. You're okay."

"What happened?"

"Here let me help you up, missus," the boy replied, gently guiding her to her feet. "One minute you were looking at the dog, the next you fainted. Or, at least, I think you did. Your eyes were wide open like you'd just seen a ghost!"

"I think I did," Lucy replied, dusting the dirt off her skirt. She was shaken up and confused, but the gravity of what just happened hadn't quite settled in.

Lucy tried to focus on the reason for her visit, pushing the unwelcome flashback from her thoughts. But this time, she knew the memory would be hers forever; there was no longer a void from that fateful day in the park.

"Do you know a lady called Rose?"

"I've got an Auntie Rose," the boy informed her helpfully. "But are you sure you are okay, missus?"

"I'm fine, thank you," Lucy replied calmly, her tone the opposite of what one would expect from someone who experienced—or, more accurately, re-experienced—what she just had. "Is her last name Arnold?"

"I dunno."

"Is she traveling with you?"

"Yeh."

"Could I see her, do you think? Is she here now?"

"Dunno. Might be."

"Where am I likely to find her?"

"Here." The boy pointed a grubby finger at the caravan.

"Thank you. You've been a big help. Do you think you could knock on the door for me?"

The lad, unafraid of the dog, climbed the step and knocked on the caravan door. There was no answer and he knocked again. After a few seconds, the door opened slowly, and a figure appeared. Lucy could barely recognize the woman who stood before her. Her hair had turned grey, one of her front teeth was missing, and her eyes were no longer sparkling with the health and vitality of someone used to an outdoor life. In fact, the flesh around one of them was puffed and blackened, as though she had received a nasty blow.

"Rose?"

The woman peered at her cautiously.

"Yeah," she admitted reluctantly. And then she recognized the other woman. "Lucy? Is that you?"

"Rose, what happened to you?" Lucy was horrified. It was obvious that more than time had wrought these changes in her old friend.

Rose leaned forward and appeared to be scanning the campsite, looking for something or someone. When she was satisfied that it was safe, she beckoned Lucy inside.

"I can't talk long, love. He'll be back soon."

"But Rose, who did this? Was it Cliff?" Lucy reached her hand towards Rose's face, but the woman pulled away, covering the bruises with her own hand.

"No, not Cliff. He never would have done anything like that. No, he passed away a long time ago—the year after I came to your house. I knew it was coming, of course. It was cancer that got him. After that, I was alone for a while—then I met Denny.

"And he did this?"

"It's nothing. He don't mean to hurt me, my Denny," she explained wearily. "It's just he gets angry sometimes, you know," she said, turning away and sitting down on the edge of a narrow bed that had not yet been made. She motioned to Lucy to sit down in the only seat available, an old folding lawn chair.

"Can I do anything?" Lucy asked helplessly, knowing from past experience that Rose would refuse any offer of assistance.

"No. That's alright love. Don't worry about me. But you, Lucy? Why did you come? How did you know I was here?"

"I took a chance. I knew this was the place where your family was camped when—" Lucy stopped, not wanting to bring up the past, but Rose didn't seem to mind.

"When Dad killed that bobby. Yeah, fancy you remembering after all these years. We stayed up at the house with old Mr. Gill. He were very good to us—took care of me and Auntie Sarah when dad was locked up."

"I remember you telling me that you married a roustabout from the fair. I'm so sorry about Cliff. And then you married Denny?"

"Well, no. Not exactly. We're just living together," Rose admitted.

"But why do you stay with him, Rose? If he does things like this to you, why do you put up with it?"

"He's a good man, really," the woman replied, not very convincingly.

Lucy couldn't suppress a note of exasperation. "But you're afraid of him! You're afraid now! Is it because I'm here?"

"He don't like strangers coming round. We had the people from child welfare come poking round the other day and I can guess who sent them."

"But you don't have any children, you told me."

"No, but the others do. They came, asking questions about the kids in the camp. Trying to pin trouble on us any way they can. The woman who came, Denny told her to clear off. I was afraid she'd report it, bring the police here. We didn't want no trouble. After old Mr. Gill passed away last year, his son took over the place. He kept coming to the camp, hanging around. Denny saw him. He wouldn't let me go outside and they had a row. I couldn't really hear what they were saying, but it had something to do with the kids. Of course, Den says it's my fault, that's why he gave me this," she pointed to her eye.

"Look, why don't you come and stay with me, Rose?" Lucy offered. "Just you. Leave Denny. Get away before it's too late, before he does something worse to you."

"Nah. I'll be alright. You're forgetting Luce, I know what my future is gonna be. I don't worry too much about it." She gave Lucy a piercing look. "You know how it is. I told you the truth, didn't I? That day when I came to your house—I saw what you had in store. Was I right?"

"Yes. You told me someone would leave my life, and you were right. My husband left me for another woman. You told me I would travel far, and I have gone further than I ever imagined anyone could possibly go."

Rose nodded sagely, her brow furrowed. "And something else, right?"

"Yes, the man who wished me harm."

"Did he come?"

"Yes. I think he did. I think he came into my life long before I met you, but you knew it wasn't a simple matter, didn't you?"

"It wasn't easy to see. I couldn't tell exactly—so many conflicting lines."

"That's why I've come to see you, Rose. I want you to look again. I want you to tell me if he'll come back. Has the danger passed, or do I still need to fear this man? I know who he is. I know the things he's capable of. Should I still be on my guard?" Lucy held her hand out to Rose, confident that her old school friend could tell her what she needed to know, but Rose was hesitant, unwilling to commit to any further predictions. Lucy, however, would not be denied and continued to hold out her hand, looking steadfastly into Rose's eyes.

Rose finally relented and drew Lucy's palm towards her, all the while looking at her face. "I can see already that you've been through much. I see things in your face that tell me you have found true love and deep sorrow. I see the fear too." She looked down at Lucy's palm and continued to gaze at it, disentangling the skeins of Lucy's life, separating each thread until finally she could see everything clearly. She nodded. "I see him there. Just like I saw him in Appleby. But I can't tell—"

Just then the door flew open and slammed back against something with a terrific bang. Both women jumped. Lucy had been sitting with her back to the door, but she saw the terror in Rose's eyes and knew that Denny had come back—standing there, glaring down at them.

"Who's this?" he demanded in a surly voice. "Someone from the borough?"

"No, Denny, a friend. This is Lucy."

Lucy stood up and turned around. The man who stood before her was tall and lean, his long, dark, greasy hair greying at the temples, pulled back into a ponytail. His face, brown and weather-beaten, was stubbled and grimy; the nose thin and hawk-like; and the cruel mouth stretched in a grimace, showing uneven and nicotine-stained teeth. Lucy hesitated a moment, then held out her hand, but the man made no move and continued to look at her suspiciously.

"What do you want?"

"I told you, Denny, she's a friend of mine." Rose had gotten up from the bed and moved closer to Lucy, but whether to protect her or be protected by her, Lucy couldn't tell.

"Shut up. I'm not asking you." The man lifted a finger and pointed it menacingly at Rose, then turned his attention back to Lucy. "What are you doing here, then?"

"I came to see Rose. We were at school together." Lucy tried to keep the indignation that she felt from her voice.

"Did you ask her to come here?" He looked once again to the cowering woman.

"No Denny, honest. I didn't know she was coming."

"If my being here is a problem, I can leave and come back another time," Lucy said placatingly, desperately hoping that she had not brought more trouble on the long-suffering woman who stood by her side.

"Yes, Lucy. You'd better leave," Rose agreed hastily, pawing nervously at the other woman's arm.

"Don't bother coming back. We won't be here," the man told Lucy bluntly.

Rose moved forward as if to see Lucy out.

"Stay where you are," the man ordered her.

"Take care, Lucy," Rose said as Lucy reached the door. Lucy turned back to see the man take a step towards her friend and raise his arm.

"He'll strike again," Rose called after her.

The man kicked the door shut as Lucy went down the steps and she heard a soft thud and nothing more.

Later she wondered about Rose's last words. Lucy thought at first that she had been referring to the beating that she was sure was coming as soon as Lucy left. But then Lucy remembered the tone that her friend had used. It was more of a warning than a statement of fact. She had been trying to tell Lucy something, something that she had seen in that brief moment when she had looked at her friend's hand. She was sure of it now. Rose had been trying to warn her that Bronowski was not yet finished with her.

19

REVELATIONS

SEVERAL DAYS LATER, Corrine had returned from the hospital to the Paris apartment. Nicky was sitting next to her on the bed when Neville arrived in a highly agitated state with the latest edition of the local newspaper. Nicky took him into the outer room so as not to disturb Corrine, who had just fallen asleep.

"I can't believe this!" Neville exclaimed incredulously, waving the paper under Dvorkin's nose.

"What now?"

"It's Bronowski! He's telling anyone who will listen that you killed his dogs out of sheer spite for losing to him the other day at the salon. It's outrageous! You'll have to say something!"

"No! It's impossible. I can't do that without dragging Corrine's name into it."

"But damn it, Nicky, they could have killed her, and Bronowski didn't even try to stop them!"

"How could he? He was too busy fighting with Dima."

"Oh, so now it's Dimitri's fault?" Neville flung out.

"No, I didn't say that, but Vladimir couldn't get to them."

"He could have called them off."

"We don't know that. What does Deshayes say? He was the only other person there who saw what happened."

"Of course he's on Bronowski's side. What would you expect? He's evidently been told what to say."

"Well, there's nothing we can do. It's just one more falsehood that those rags are using to boost their sales. Everyone knows I have a vile temper, so no one will be surprised to read that I am capable of killing three defenseless animals."

"You would have done better to run Bronowski through."

"Calm yourself, Neville. After all, I hear Vladimir suffered a broken nose and a black eye. Dima made him pay for his insolence." Dvorkin laughed.

"But how can you compare that to what those brutes did to Corrine? How can you take it all so lightly?"

"Because I must. Thank God, she will recover. She lost a good deal of blood, but miraculously, no serious damage was done. She doesn't want a big fuss made. It was an accident, pure and simple."

Neville made to argue, but Dvorkin held up his hand to silence him.

"No, Neville. My mind is made up. Whatever they say in the papers, I won't pursue it. Better they think I killed those creatures out of spite than defending my mistress. I'll settle up with Vladimir and pay him for his loss. I know those animals were worth a great deal of money, but it can't be helped."

Neville shook his head. "Really, Nicky. Sometimes I just don't understand you."

Dvorkin put his arm around his friend. "Put your mind at ease, Neville. This will all blow over, as everything always does."

* * *

The following week, they returned to Honfleur, and Corrine discovered that she was pregnant.

"Oh ho! My little bird!" Dvorkin was elated by her news and putting both hands on her waist, hoisted her off her feet, then immediately recalling her condition, put her down and led her to a chair. "You must rest! But when? When will the baby be here?" Dvorkin spoke as though the child were about to arrive at any moment by train.

Corrine laughed at his happiness because it pleased her, but also from relief. She hadn't been sure how he would react to her news. "Not for several months. February, the doctor says. But you mustn't fuss, Nicky."

"Of course I must fuss!" The big man pulled her to her feet again and enfolded her in his arms. "This is our child, Corrine. Yours and mine. You must go back to London, where you will get the best care, see the greatest doctors, immediately."

"I'd rather stay here in Honfleur, at least for a few more weeks," Corrine told him. She saw that he was about to become argumentative. "I will go back to England, I promise, but not until Christmas."

"Very well then, if you insist," Dvorkin capitulated. "But I must tell the others."

* * *

As Dimitri Gurvich descended the staircase, he could hear Nicky's voice, and as he reached the bottom step, he could see the big man standing with Neville Wyndham and heard him exclaim with pleasure, "But this is wonderful news, my dear friend! My heartiest congratulations!"

"Thank you, Neville. I wanted you to be the first to know. I can't tell you how happy I am."

"When is the baby due?"

"Not for another six months yet."

"May I tell Marina? She'll be so delighted."

"Yes, by all means; but no one else just yet, dear friend."

At these words, Dimitri realized that he had accidentally overheard a conversation that had been unintended for his ears. Not wanting to be discovered, he slipped silently past the library door and out into the garden. Walking slowly down the driveway, he turned the words over in his mind. *Was Eugenia pregnant again? But how was that possible?* The baby was due in six months, and Nicky hadn't been back to Brussels in ages. Three months ago, they had all been in Paris: Nicky, Neville, Maria, Corrine, and himself.

And then the truth hit him. *Of course!* How stupid of him not to have realized. It was Corrine. It must be her. He turned aside and, striking out across the lawns, made his way past the tennis courts towards the stream, his brain in a turmoil.

As he walked, his thoughts seethed. Anger at Nicky and outrage on behalf of Corrine, mixed with feelings of self-pity, tumbled confusingly about in his earnest young mind.

Then suddenly, he stopped in his tracks. He had spotted Corrine a little way ahead, standing by the stream. She hadn't noticed him, and as he approached her unseen, he hoped against hope that he had been mistaken.

She was looking out over the water at a kingfisher as it darted from a nearby branch, her hands dreamily stroking the soft, shantung material of the dress that covered her belly as if caressing the life that she now carried within her. Dimitri was certain now, and his heart sank. The expression on her face was one of pure and utter contentment.

"It's true, then." He hadn't meant to startle her, but she had been so deep in thought, and he had been unable to restrain the bitter words that betrayed his own shattered hopes and dreams.

Corrine turned quickly to face him.

"Dimitri! You made me jump." She saw the anguish in his eyes and guessed that he knew her secret.

"Nicky told you?"

"No. I overheard him telling Neville up at the house." He stepped closer to her. "I...I don't know what to say."

"Congratulations, I think, is the usual term one uses on such occasions." Corrine tried to relieve the tension that was so palpable between them, but she could see that her words were having little effect. She took his hand and held it to her cheek. "Please be happy for us, Dimitri."

"I am...that is..." He was momentarily lost for words, then stumbled on, "But this means, surely, that he will have to marry you now."

"Marry me? No, dear Dimitri. You know there can be no question of marriage."

"But he must—the baby."

"And what about Eugenia, or had you forgotten that he has a wife already?"

"Of course not, although he seems to forget, when it suits him. But the child must have a name."

"The baby will have a name. He or she will be a Standish." She put her arm around the young man's shoulders. "Don't look so shocked, dear. I have no cause for regret. Of course, the fewer people that know about it the better. It's obviously not something he wants Eugenia to hear about or read of in the press, which is why, for now, only Neville, Marina, and you must know."

"But where will you go? How will you explain away the child to your friends and family?"

"I only told Nicky about it this morning, so we haven't had a chance to plan anything yet, but everything will be alright."

"But you can't do this, Corrine!" Dimitri cried, beside himself with frustration at her inability to see things in proper perspective.

"Corrine, I…Marry me. I implore you! I don't mind about the baby. I'll love it like my own because it's yours and Nicky's. You can't go on facing the future alone. Not now. I love you, Corrine. You must have guessed. I'd do anything for you. I know I'm just a child, compared to Nicky, but I've got money. I can take care of you, and the baby will not be forced to bear the stigma of illegitimacy. It won't seem so strange to anyone. Forgive me, but there are rumors already that we are lovers. We are seen in each other's company so often, and Nicky does nothing to discourage the stories because it suits his purpose. And I don't mind." He added hastily, "Even if I didn't love you to distraction, which I do, most assuredly, I would gladly shield Nicky from any scandal. Don't you see? This is the answer to everyone's problems. I don't expect you to love me. I don't ask it of you. I'll make no demands or put any constraints on you. I'm willing to go on playing second fiddle to Nicky if that's what you want, Corrine—only do, do marry me, darling." He moved closer to clasp her in his arms, but she stepped back aghast.

"No! It's impossible, Dima!" His declaration of love had taken her by surprise. In all the time they had been together, she had been so wrapped up in her love for Dvorkin that Dimitri's feelings for her had gone completely unnoticed. "Please, let's not talk about it any further. When you've taken time to think about it, you'll see that it just wouldn't work. Come on, let's walk back to the house."

As they returned through the garden, Dvorkin came walking down to meet them. Corrine waved to him, but Dimitri, still tormented by this new revelation, turned aside in order to avoid meeting him and went up to the house by means of the path that led around to the kitchen door.

"What's wrong with our young friend?" Dvorkin asked.

"He overheard you telling Neville about the baby."

"Oh. That is unfortunate, but why should that cause him such distress?"

"I don't know." He obviously hadn't noticed, and she couldn't tell him how Dimitri felt about her. She guessed that if she did, Dvorkin would probably react either with anger or, worse yet, ridicule. She could not bear for him to make fun of Dimitri.

They found Neville and Marina in the drawing room, and Corrine received Marina's congratulatory hugs and good wishes with pleasure.

"Neville suggested that you might like to stay here in Honfleur for the confinement," Marina said. "He thinks the lease can be extended and will make all the necessary arrangements if you are both agreeable."

"It's a generous offer, Neville," Corrine answered before Dvorkin could speak. "But I've been thinking; I will need to get away before too long. It's no good waiting until my condition becomes obvious. And I need to be somewhere where there's no chance of anyone recognizing me. It would be too easy to run into someone I know here. Look how we came across those friends of my uncle's last week."

"In that case, my dear Corrine, I have the perfect place," Wyndham proposed. "Why don't you come and stay at our house in the Lake District. We can arrange to have the necessary domestic staff installed, and Doctor McIntosh, I'm sure, would be only too willing to take care of you. I know we can rely on his discretion." He looked to his wife, who nodded her approval. "What do you say, Corrine?"

"It sounds ideal, Neville!" Dvorkin exclaimed.

"Then it's agreed, my friends!" Neville said, raising the glass of wine that Marina had poured to celebrate their plans. "Ah, Dima! Come in and have a drink with us." Neville beckoned to the young man who stood in the doorway. "This is a happy day for us. Corrine and Nicky are going to be proud parents, and they have agreed to travel with us to Penhampton to stay until after the baby is born. Isn't that wonderful?"

"Yes, most assuredly." The reply was less than enthusiastic, but he entered the room and accepted the glass that Marina proffered. "Congratulations." He toasted the happy pair and forced an unwilling smile to his lips.

"But of course, you will come with us too, won't you, Dima?" Neville felt the young man's unease. Was it disapproval or jealousy? Wyndham was aware of Gurvich's attachment to Corrine and pitied him.

"Of course, he will!" Dvorkin was adamant. It was unthinkable that his young protégé would wish to be anywhere but with them at such a time. He was part of their family.

"Yes! Naturally!" Dimitri acquiesced with as much enthusiasm as he could muster and Corrine linked her arm through his, squeezing it encouragingly.

"I wouldn't dream of going without you," she told him.

To Dimitri, the words seemed to mock his misery, but, as much as he wanted to run away and try to forget his love for her, he knew he could never desert her. He must stay by her side and pick up the pieces when things finally fell apart, as he knew they would.

"Then that's settled! We'll celebrate Christmas at Evershed House."

* * *

"I'm going to the Lake District for Christmas," Lucy told her daughter on the phone as Robin listened incredulously at the other end.

"Are you sure that's wise? The roads may be a mess and you're not used to driving. What on earth made you want to go there for the holidays?"

"I thought I'd try something different this year. I'll be going up a week or so earlier, so hopefully I'll get in ahead of any bad weather."

"But you won't know anyone there. You'll be alone. Surely that won't be much fun for you, or are you going with someone?" Robin suddenly realized that her mother may have been planning a romantic get-away.

"No. Nothing like that," Lucy laughed.

"Well, if you're sure." Robin sounded doubtful and was feeling decidedly puzzled as she hung up the phone, wondering what on earth had prompted her mother to decide to go up to the Lake District on her own for Christmas.

20

CONVERGENCE

THE PLANS THAT LUCY HAD MADE for the Christmas holiday had been, like so many other things that year, on the spur of the moment.

When she realized that Corrine was pregnant and would be in England for Christmas, she felt an inexplicable longing to be near her. It wasn't enough to share her experiences through those strange manifestations, such as had occurred in London or, more frequently now, in Birchford. The truth was that she was feeling, more and more, a reluctance to return to the present; she felt that if she could somehow stay connected to Corrine, she would be able to cast off her life as Lucy and remain in the past with Dvorkin.

She had not, at first, been too hopeful that Evershed House would still be in existence, or, even if it were, that she would be able to gain access to it. But after spending some time on the internet at the library, she discovered to her profound relief that not only had it survived the years, but it had been converted into a bed and breakfast establishment. Her luck held when she called the telephone number listed and was told that, due to a last-minute cancellation, there was still one room available for the week leading up to Christmas.

The weather had remained, if not sunny, at least mercifully dry that December. Lucy set out for the Lake District in the car she had rented for the occasion, with cautious optimism. She'd been unable to obtain the car model with which she was most familiar. The one they had given her was much larger, and she wondered how difficult it would be to maneuver and park; she had never really mastered the art of parallel parking. But apart from these minor considerations, she felt confident that she would manage.

She wasn't quite sure what to expect when she got there, but she was hopeful that everything would fall into place once she arrived at Evershed House.

* * *

Corrine had arrived at Evershed House, a mile or so outside the village of Penhampton, with Dvorkin, Neville and Marina Wyndham, and Dimitri Gurvich in mid-October. The countryside was painted with autumnal colors, and, on the odd occasion when the sun put in a brief appearance, the bracken-covered hills seemed bathed in a warm, golden glow.

Dvorkin had only stayed a short while, his professional engagements calling him away from the dank and blustery solitude of the fells and returning him to the demands of a busy calendar of performances and appearances in Paris and Milan.

As was his habit, he had planned to spend Christmas with his wife and family, who were traveling to England to be with him, but had promised to return to Cumbria for the New Year. Corrine made no objection, realizing that he would not deviate from this annual commitment no matter what her condition.

* * *

Lucy decided to stop for a meal in Appleby before making her way to Evershed House. Her curiosity about the town was in part due to a recollection that Rose had mentioned about going to the horse fair there, and for that reason, Lucy felt drawn to the place. Of course, things would have looked a lot different there in early June, but still, she could imagine Rose and Cliff happily making their way through the busy streets along with all the hundreds of other travelers on their way to this popular annual event. But that was in earlier times, when Rose had been content to go on the road with her husband. She had been there this year with that man,

Denny, and things had not been so idyllic, Lucy was sure.

The pub, The Rising Lark, where Lucy decided to stop for lunch, was fairly busy, and the meal she ordered took quite a while to arrive. The bar was becoming crowded; several people had come in after she'd been seated, and Lucy looked around with interest while waiting to be served.

After she'd eaten, Lucy collected her coat and purse and, making sure she'd left nothing behind, went out into a day that had not improved much with the hours. It now looked as though there could possibly be snow in the air. Lucy hurriedly made her way back to where she'd parked the car and set off for Evershed House, hoping she would get there before the weather deteriorated still further.

Although she had some difficulty finding the place, she eventually arrived there just as daylight was starting to fade and a few snowflakes were beginning to settle on the ground. Almost immediately, she felt a pang of disappointment, though not with the appearance of the house, which was pleasant enough. The disappointment lay in the fact that she had felt no sense of having been there before, such as she had experienced with the picture of the villa in Honfleur. Could she have sent herself on a fool's errand? Perhaps Corrine had never actually arrived in Cumbria. Maybe she'd decided to stay in Honfleur, or gone to London instead. Since the episode in Honfleur when Corrine had told the others of her pregnancy, Lucy had had no further visions of the past and, unable for some reason to contact Jasper Frakes, was rather unsettled by the realization that she had no idea what had happened next.

Parking the car in a rather cramped area next to the bed and breakfast was something Lucy had dreaded, but after several attempts, she finally managed to squeeze in between two other vehicles and fervently hoped that no one from the house had witnessed her overly-cautious maneuvers.

As she followed the path up to the entrance of Evershed House, her feet left well-defined tracks in the ever-increasing layer of snow that had formed, and she was glad that she'd worn her warm winter coat as the air felt chill after the warmth of the car.

Inside, she was greeted by a young woman who produced a visitor's book for Lucy to sign, as well as the usual papers involved in credit card transactions.

After exchanging a few pleasantries, Lucy picked up her suitcase, which felt as though she'd packed enough clothes for a month instead of a week, and followed the woman up the flight of stairs that led to the bedrooms.

"Are you the owner of Evershed House?" Lucy asked as she stopped outside the room to which she had been assigned.

"No. My parents, Bob and Mary Brooks, are the ones who own the B & B. I just help out here till I go back to Uni after the winter break," the girl volunteered. "I'm Justine, by the way. Justine Brooks." She held out her hand. The handshake was brief but friendly.

"Pleased to meet you, Justine,"

"Same here. Hope you enjoy your stay. Let me know if there's anything you need. Breakfast is from 6 a.m. to 10 a.m. We'll be serving a special dinner on Christmas day for our guests; otherwise, most people go to the pub in the village for their meals. Of course, if the weather gets too bad, we won't let you starve." The young woman laughed. "We can always whip up some soup and sandwiches if we get snowed in."

"Great," Lucy responded thankfully, not relishing the idea of driving into the village on snow-covered roads. "I'm sure I'll love it here. Oh, by the way, before you go, perhaps you can tell me something."

"If I can."

"Who owned Evershed House before your parents took it over? It wasn't a family by the name of Wyndham by any chance, was it?"

The girl appeared to give the matter some thought. "Mm...no. I don't think so. I believe their name was Matthews. They bought the place just before the war, but he was killed. Shot down over France. Mrs. Matthews tried to keep the place going but had to sell in the end. That's when my parents came to live here."

"Oh." Lucy sounded disappointed. "So, the name Wyndham isn't familiar to you at all, then?"

"No. Sorry. I can ask Mum and Dad, but I don't ever remember hearing them mention the name."

"Well, thanks anyway."

That night, as Lucy lay in bed, she felt more and more as though she was on a wild goose chase. Nothing about the house felt even remotely familiar, and try as she might, she could not summon up any kind of vision of Corrine. The past seemed as dead to her as if she had never met Jasper Frakes or fallen in love with Nicolai Dvorkin.

* * *

When Corrine returned from a short walk along the lane, the woman, who was employed to cook and clean for the household, presented her with a note sealed in a rather grubby envelope.

"The boy brought it up with the groceries, Ma'am. Told me he was supposed to give it directly to you, but since you weren't here and he had to get back, I said I'd be sure to hand it to you as soon as you came in."

"Thank you, Bessie." Corrine frowned when she saw that the envelope was addressed to her in Dvorkin's handwriting.

"You're welcome, ma'am." The woman gave a slight bob and added, "Mrs. Wyndham's in the drawing room, and Mr. Dimitri is in his room writing letters."

"Alright, Bessie. Will you tell Mrs. Wyndham I'll be down directly?"

"Yes, Ma'am."

Corrine took the letter to her room and, opening it, saw that it was indeed from Dvorkin. The message was succinct yet cryptic.

My darling, Meet me at The Rising Lark in Appleby on the evening of the 19th. I must see you! Tell no one you are coming, I beg you! Nicky.

Corrine gave a murmur of exasperation. *Really! This was too bad of him! Why hadn't he just come to the house? And the 19th!* That was today, and already the daylight was starting to fade. If she took the car, she might get there before it was dark, but would he still be there? The letter must have been delayed. And why the secrecy? Had he got into some fresh scrape that he didn't want the others to know about? She paced the room in agitation. How to explain her absence? What could she possibly tell them?

She dropped the note into the drawer of her nightstand, and putting her coat back on and snatching up her handbag, she ran downstairs.

Marina looked up from a book as Corrine entered the drawing room and seemed surprised that her friend was still dressed in outdoor attire.

"Hello! I thought Bessie said you had already come back."

"Yes, I had, but she gave me late word that some relatives of mine are staying in Appleby and they've asked me over to dine with them. I'll take a room in town overnight so as not to be driving back late. Will you tell Dimitri and Neville when he comes in? I'm sorry. I must dash! I'll be back tomorrow," she called over her shoulder.

"Be careful, Corrine!" Marina cautioned her. "The weather seems to be taking a turn for the worse. Are you sure you don't want Dimitri to drive you?" But Corrine had already gone.

When Dimitri came down for dinner, he found Marina and Neville in the dining room.

"I thought I heard Corrine come in earlier. Is she not eating with us?"

"She went out again."

"Out? Where did she go?"

"She took the car and has driven over to Appleby. Some relations are staying there. She'll be back tomorrow," Neville informed him.

"But I don't understand." Dimitri sounded puzzled. "No one apart from us was supposed to know that she is here. How did these people find out?"

"I don't know. It did seem rather strange, and Corrine appeared rather flustered," Marina said anxiously.

"She shouldn't be driving around in her condition!" Dimitri put his hand to his brow as, perplexed, he drew aside the curtain and peered out of the window. "It's starting to snow again."

"I asked her if she wanted you to go with her, but she seemed in a hurry to leave. Don't worry, Dima. I'm sure she'll be alright. She said she would take a room in town tonight and return tomorrow."

"Yes, yes. It's just…the weather. The roads can be so treacherous."

"Well, there's nothing we can do about it now," Marina told him philosophically.

"No, I suppose not." Gurvich sounded resigned but spent the rest of the evening worrying and torturing himself with all kinds of imagined dire scenarios.

* * *

Rather to Lucy's dismay, she slept soundly that night. She'd intended to stay awake as long as possible in the hopes that she would get some sense of Corrine having been there, but sleep had overtaken her. In the morning, she went downstairs to breakfast without having experienced any of the usual symptoms associated with her visits to the past.

Although it was no longer snowing, the grey clouds seemed to presage further flurries, but Lucy thought perhaps the fresh air would clear her head, so after going back to her room to put on her coat, boots, and gloves, she emerged into the morning stillness. Opening the driver's side window, she drove down the lane towards the village of Penhampton, passing one or two hearty souls who had braved the elements in order to get their daily exercise. She stopped in at the little post office that doubled as a newsagent's and bought a chocolate bar and a local newspaper, a precursor to enquiring whether the lady behind the counter was familiar with the name of Wyndham.

"Wyndham, you say? No dear, I'm sorry. Is it someone who lives here in the village? Working in the post office, I know most of the names, but I don't recognize that one."

"No. This would have been some time ago. Before the war. They lived at Evershed House."

"Well, that was a bit before my time. Wyndham…" She repeated the name and gazed up at the ceiling, but it did nothing to jog her memory. She shook her head. "Sorry dear. Have you tried asking the Brooks'? They might know."

"Yes, but they don't remember the name. I suppose people come and go. It was rather a long time ago. Well, thanks anyway."

Lucy collected her purchases and, dropping a few coins into a container left hopefully on the counter in aid of the RSPCA, she left the shop. Lucy kept looking around her as she walked down the main street that ran through the village, as if waiting for something to strike a chord of remembrance, but she may as well have been on the moon for all the good it did.

It was too early for lunch, so she crossed the road to a quaint little teashop and ordered tea and a scone with raspberry jam. She always felt rather self-conscious when eating in a restaurant on her own, so she unfolded the newspaper and immersed herself in the headlines, sipping tea and nibbling on the scone that crumbled apart onto the rose-patterned plate.

The paper had evidently just been published and was dated December 19th, today's date. *DEADLINE ARRIVES WITH NO SETTLEMENT IN LOCAL DISPUTE OVER RIGHT OF WAY*, Lucy read. It was difficult to get interested in something that didn't concern her, but she finished reading the article and turned the paper over to peruse the back page. She had already deduced that it would be pointless to ask the waitress if she had ever heard of the Wyndhams. She was much too young and had a heavy Irish accent.

So, what now? Had this whole idea been a waste of time? She was beginning to doubt that Corrine had ever been here. Might she not have been better off staying in her own home or even visiting Jasper Frakes? She could have taken him a little Christmas gift and spent some time looking around the shops. Even though Jackie and Lionel were away, she still could have found plenty to do in London. Why on earth had she decided to drive all the way up here? And in winter, too!

She left the teashop and continued to walk to the further end of the village. Among the few buildings that stood like sentinels between the edge of the village and the fells was a country church, its stone walls worn and weathered by the winds that always seemed to be blowing down from the hills and across the commons. The church, St. Anselm's, was set atop a gentle slope. She walked along the path between lichen-covered gravestones to the ancient, wooden door. She expected it to be locked. The churches at home weren't left unattended these days. Too many robberies and, worse still, vandalism. But here they were apparently not subject to such desecrations—the door opened, the clank of the latch echoing hollowly through the old building.

Lucy stepped inside, pleased to find some temporary shelter from the biting cold. The interior was illuminated only by the sparse light that filtered through the large stained-glass windows. As she made her way down the aisle, rather like a bride who had forgotten to invite anyone else to the wedding, she peered about her, trying to distinguish the vague shapes of the octagonal stone font, the carved wooden pulpit, and the stone pillars that flanked either side of the naive.

She slid into a pew and kneeling down, closed her eyes and murmured a prayer remembered from her youth. Lucy had never considered herself a religious person. Her marriage to Lawrence had taken place at the local registry office. Still, there lingered a few of the old observances, a respect for something that, if not exactly sacred to her, commanded a certain automatic response. After a few minutes, she sat down and waited. Surely something would come to her here—some recollection of Corrine's visit. It was so quiet and secluded—nothing to distract or detain her in the present.

But if Lucy thought she was alone there, she was wrong. She was suddenly startled when a door, presumably to the vestry, was opened, and an elderly man dressed in clerical attire stepped out.

Lucy got quickly to her feet, making her presence known, feeling that her entrance had been somewhat furtive and her reason for being there not something of which the vicar would approve.

He did not seem surprised by her presence, however, and raising his hand, as if offering some kind of blessing, he wished her a good morning.

"Hello. I'm sorry. I didn't realize anyone was in here," Lucy said guiltily, as though she'd been caught pilfering from the donation box.

"No need to apologize, my dear. We receive few visitors here at this time of year, except of course for Christmas, so we are especially happy to welcome you."

Lucy wondered if he was speaking on behalf of God and decided that he probably was.

"Thank you."

"Are you staying in the village?"

"Yes, at Evershed House. Just for the week." She wondered if the name would invoke some response, but he appeared not to recognize it.

"Well, I hope you get to see something of the countryside while you're here, although this probably isn't the best time to go walking about. Have you been to Penhampton before?"

"No. This is my first visit. I wonder: could I ask you something?" Lucy had stepped back into the aisle and was standing facing the elderly cleric.

"Of course, although whether I'll have the answer..." He smiled and held out his hand, indicating that they should take a walk back through the church while they talked.

"Have you been in the parish long?" Lucy enquired.

"I arrived just after the end of the war."

"That would be about the time when Mr. and Mrs. Brooks took over Evershed House. Did you know the lady who lived there before them? Mrs. Matthews, I think her name was."

"No, I'm afraid not."

"In that case, you probably won't recognize the name of Wyndham either." Lucy didn't sound too hopeful.

"Oh, but of course! Neville Wyndham! I believe he and his wife lived here in the village at one time. He died in France just after the war but had requested that he be buried here in Penhampton. It was my first funeral service in the parish. A very quiet ceremony. His wife had predeceased him, and they had no family. Only a few people attended—a Russian gentleman, if I remember rightly, with a lady and a young girl." He appeared to be trying to conjure up the scene. "Yes, that's it."

"Was she Russian, too?"

"No, she was definitely English."

Lucy felt her heart soar. Could it have been Corrine? And a daughter? She tried to contain her excitement.

"I don't suppose you remember their names by any chance?"

"No. I'm sorry. It was all rather a long time ago now," the grey-haired cleric apologized.

"Of course."

"But I can show you where Mr. Wyndham is buried, if you'd care to see."

"Oh, yes please!"

"Just let me get my coat and I'll be happy to show you." He left Lucy waiting by the font, then, rejoining her, they went outside.

"Most unusual—two visitors in one day," he said, pointing to the far side of the churchyard. A man and a dog were stopped near one of the gravestones. "We don't get many visitors here, other than the regular parishioners, I mean."

Lucy shuddered. "Well at least it's on a leash."

"Oh, the dog? Yes. I suppose that is a good thing."

Lucy's eyes weren't what they used to be, but from a distance the dog did bear a striking resemblance to the one Bronowski had owned and the same one—

Her thoughts were interrupted when the cleric said, "It's just over here, near the oak tree."

Lucy stole one more glance at the man and the dog, then followed the vicar until they came to two weathered gravestones side by side. Lucy looked down at the now familiar names and felt inexpressibly sad.

"Well, thank you very much for your time," she said gratefully.

"I hope I've been of some help."

"Yes, yes indeed."

Lucy looked for the man and his dog, but they were nowhere to be seen, and she turned to walk back down the path. She stopped at the gate and called back, "Thank you," her words scattering on the wind that carried fresh snowflakes.

* * *

The vicar had certainly given her something to think about. She ruminated on this new-found piece of knowledge over lunch at the local pub. The news that Corrine might have been here for Neville Wyndham's funeral gave her hope that she may yet learn what had happened at Evershed House all those years ago.

Lucy was more determined than ever to follow Corrine's story to its conclusion. Finishing off the last of her lunch, she left the pub and returned to Evershed House.

The establishment appeared deserted as she made her way back to her room. There was no one to greet her at the front desk, and she passed no one on the stairs or in the upstairs hallway. The silence felt eerie, and Lucy began to experience a familiar muffled sensation as though she was no longer in the present but looking in on something happening in the past. The feeling left her as suddenly as it had come, however. She heard the door click as she closed it behind her, and she sat down on the bed with a deep sigh. Perhaps she should try lying down. If nothing else, she might take a brief nap. But then what? What if she stayed here all week and nothing happened?

She tried to calm her thoughts. Although the curtains were drawn apart, the room seemed dark and rather depressing. What on earth would she do with herself all evening? She didn't feel like going out again for dinner and she had forgotten to pack a book to read. Of all the stupid things! If she were to be honest with herself, Lucy had given little thought to this trip beyond finding out what had happened to Corrine. She had certainly not envisioned sitting hour upon hour on her own in a room, waiting for something to occur.

The effects of Jasper Frakes's travel enhancer must have worn off. It was crazy of her to think they would last forever. She wished he were here with her and then wished she were in the shabby flat in London. The thought occurred to her that perhaps the travel enhancer hadn't completely worn off, but rather was working its magic differently—there was the flashback to the event in the park in Birchford which had seemed so real, as if she had reentered her childhood body. But she quickly pushed the thought out of her head. She would revisit what happened to her on another day. She needed to solve one mystery at a time.

And so she passed the time, berating herself for her foolishness and wondering desperately what was happening to Corrine, until the daylight began to fade, and, unable to bear being cooped up any longer with nothing to do, she jumped up and began to pace the floor. *Maybe I should just abandon the whole idea and go back home.* She would tell Mrs. Brooks that she had to return home on urgent business. No need to refund any money. Lucy would swallow the loss.

She'd hardly had time to unpack except for a few toiletries and her night clothes, but she checked to make sure she'd left nothing lying around and opened the drawer of the bedside table.

She gasped, unable to believe her eyes. Inside lay an envelope addressed to Corrine. It had been opened as if in a hurry. Lucy pulled out the enclosed note, reading it with difficulty in the gathering gloom.

19th December! That is today's date! Corrine must have gone to Appleby then. She would not have ignored Dvorkin's summons. And to think, she'd been in the Rising Lark the day before and not felt any sense of recognition! How could she not have known? Well, she would go there now—she'd drive to Appleby and have dinner at the Rising Lark.

Lucy hurriedly changed her clothes and touched up her makeup. *At last! Here is a reason to stay! Now something would surely happen!*

Putting on her heavy winter coat, boots, and gloves, she gathered her handbag and went down to the front desk. Justine Brooks was on the phone but held it away from her ear as Lucy called, "Just driving over to Appleby for dinner."

"Okay, but be careful! The snow's picking up and the roads may be slick. See you later!" Justine called after Lucy, but she'd already gone with a cheerful wave of her hand.

* * *

Corrine knew the way to Appleby fairly well by now. Even in the dark, she felt confident that she could manage the drive into town quite easily, but she hadn't reckoned on the weather being so bad. It had certainly deteriorated quickly since she'd left Evershed House. The snowflakes seemed to form a lacy curtain as the car made its way along the winding lane towards Penhampton. As she drove through the village, there were few people in sight, the lights from the cottages appearing like small, bright spots on either side of the road.

She was through the village now and onto the road between Penhampton and Appleby. It was almost dark and the lights from the car reflected dimly on the road ahead, the wheels crunching over the fluffy white snow, leaving dirty tracks in their wake. Still, Corrine was not uneasy. She'd driven in this kind of weather before in London, and surely this could not be that much different.

As she made her way, she pondered on the reason for Dvorkin's strange request. What had happened to bring him up here to Cumbria, and in such secrecy too? She couldn't begin to guess, although she suspected he was in some kind of trouble. Down the hill now, and then that sharp bend in the road. Corrine could picture it in her mind's eye. The lane to Ravenswick met the road just at that point. She coasted down the hill, feeling the wheels of the car begin to slide very slightly on the snowy surface of the road.

* * *

Lucy was fairly sure of her way back to Appleby. She'd made a mental note of certain landmarks on her way to Evershed House the previous day. She looked out for these now as she followed the lane to Penhampton. Now the village came into sight—Christmas lights twinkling in one or two of the shop windows. She drove on past the church, where Neville and Marina Wyndham's final resting place now lay covered in snow. Not far to go before she reached the main road to Appleby, just over the narrow stone bridge, which hardly afforded room for two cars to pass each other, and down the hill to where the road met the lane to Ravenswick.

* * *

Corrine slowed as she rounded the curve at the bottom of the hill when, all of a sudden, a car, black and without lights, shot out from the lane right in front of her. She braked hard, but her car was unresponsive, the tires merely sliding as the vehicle went sideways for several yards, hit the grass verge, and plunged down a rocky embankment to land on its side in a half-frozen stream. The other car had stopped. The driver, opening the door and climbing out, walked back to the embankment and looked down to where Corrine lay, half in the car, half in the stream, blood from her head mingling with the freezing water.

* * *

Lucy barely had time to react after she rounded the curve at the bottom of the hill as a vehicle, black and without lights, came screeching out of the lane from Ravenswick. She tried to right the car as it veered off the road, but conditions were too bad for the tires to gain any kind of purchase on the slippery surface. The car shot across the grass verge and down a steep incline, finally coming to a halt on the frozen surface of a boulder-strewn stream.

The other driver had stopped and, leaving their car, was moving quickly across the road, a large dog walking beside him. They made their way down to where Lucy sprawled, stunned and bleeding.

A hand reached down to feel for a pulse, one that could hardly be detected.

Lucy's eyes fluttered open.

At first, she thought she saw Bronowski leaning over her, his cold grey eyes searching her face for signs of life, but then she realized it couldn't possibly be him; she was in the present.

The man with the dog reached toward her; she could see something long and shiny in his hands.

Lucy felt a sudden, sharp pain in her chest.

She closed her eyes in shock, and when she opened them, the dog was gone and now a man hovered over her—a man who looked frighteningly familiar. "It can't possibly be—" she whispered, feeling her heart and breath slow.

"Corrine! My little bird. I've come to take you home."

AUTHOR BIO

Sue Farwick combines her lifelong fascination with the murder mystery and supernatural genres in her novels. Born and raised in England and now residing in the USA, she is an avid genealogist and gardener. In addition to her fiction writing, she writes about her experiences as an amateur photographer and regularly writes for her blog *The Nature of Things* under the name 'Mac's Girl.'

Visit Tribuspress.com/Sue-Farwick or scan the QR code below for more about Sue Farwick and her publications, and to connect with her.

Scan for More About Sue Farwick

MORE FROM TRIBUS PRESS

FROM SUE FARWICK

SMOKE: BOOK II IN *THE CONNECTIONS SERIES* (2025)

> Sue Farwick returns with the captivating follow-up to *The Eternal Song* (Book II in *The Connections Series*). Dive into the enigmatic world of Marianne, Lucy Welbourne's flatmate in *The Eternal Song*, for a story of mystery, peril, and intrigue.

FROM CHRISTOPHER AND SIMONE CARROLL IN CHILDREN'S BOOKS

WINNIE-THE-POOH AND THE HONEY JAR MISHAP (AVAILABLE NOW)

> Join Winnie-the-Pooh and his friends on an enchanting adventure through the Hundred Acre Wood. This whimsical tale, written and illustrated by a father and his 5-year-old daughter, pays homage to the 1926 classic by A. A. Milne and E. H. Shepard. It marks the opening book in *The A. A. Milne and E. H. Shepard Legacy Series*, proudly presented by Tribus Press.
>
> As Pooh and Christopher Robin set off for a picnic with their dear friends, Pooh's tummy begins to rumble. They decide to make what should have been a quick stop at Pooh's house for a yummy snack. However, Pooh's curiosity and independence lead him into a very sticky and comical misadventure. Along

the way, Pooh learns valuable lessons about friendship, listening, and asking for help.

NINA THE SLOTH GOES TO PARIS (2024) & NINA THE SLOTH GETS LOST (2025)

The father-daughter duo is back with the first two books in their new series, *Nina the Sloth*. Meet Nina and her Hoatzin bird friend, Squawk, as they go on epic adventures.

WINNIE-THE-POOH LOSES HIS HEAD (Coming Soon)

Pooh seems to have "lost his head" when he becomes obsessed with his new phone. Join Pooh and his friends as they try and solve this very modern dilemma. Join the father-daughter duo for their second book in the *A. A. Milne and E. H. Shepard Legacy Series*.

Scan to Connect with Tribus Press
or visit Tribuspress.com for More Books